py 226

D1158281

Flight of the Raven

Center Point
Large Print

Also by Morgan L. Busse and available from
Center Point Large Print:

Mark of the Raven

**This Large Print Book carries the
Seal of Approval of N.A.V.H.**

THE RAVENWOOD SAGA

BOOK TWO

Flight of the Raven

MORGAN L. BUSSE

CENTER POINT LARGE PRINT
THORNDIKE, MAINE

This Center Point Large Print edition
is published in the year 2019 by arrangement with
Bethany House Publishers, a division of
Baker Publishing Group.

The text of this Large Print edition is unabridged.
In other aspects, this book may vary
from the original edition.
Printed in the United States of America
on permanent paper.
Set in 16-point Times New Roman type.

ISBN: 978-1-64358-227-6

Library of Congress Cataloging-in-Publication Data

Names: Busse, Morgan L., author.
Title: Flight of the raven / Morgan L. Busse.
Description: Center Point Large Print edition. | Thorndike, Maine :
    Center Point Large Print, 2019. | Series: The Ravenwood saga ;
    book 2
Identifiers: LCCN 2019012502 | ISBN 9781643582276 (hardcover :
    alk. paper)
Subjects: LCSH: Large type books.
Classification: LCC PS3602.U84496 F55 2019b | DDC 813/.6—dc23
LC record available at https://lccn.loc.gov/2019012502

To Kaitlyn.
May you always follow the Light.

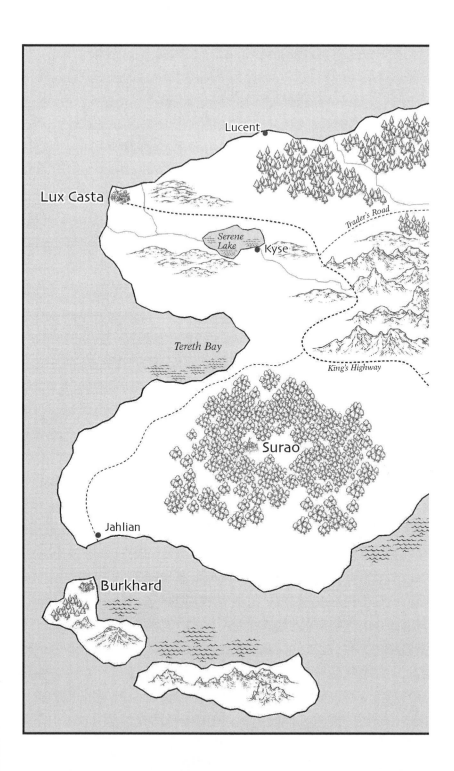

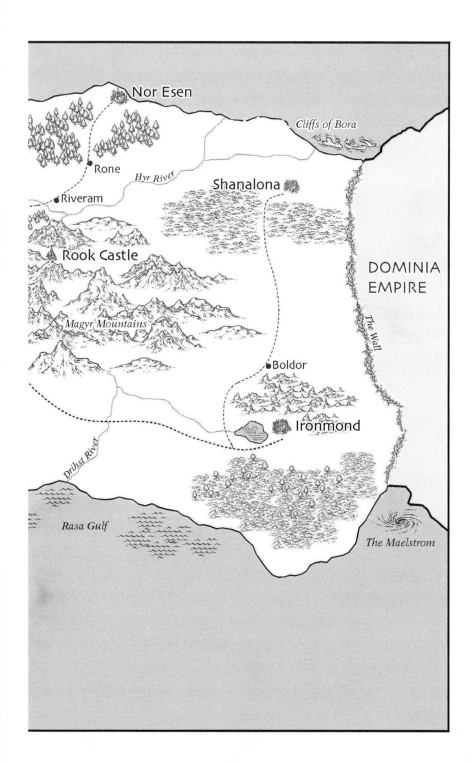

Character List

HOUSE RAVENWOOD
House of Dreamers

Grand Lady Ragna
Caiaphas (consort)
Amara
Opheliana

HOUSE MARIS
House of Waters

Grand Lord Damien
Grand Lady Selene Ravenwood
Grand Lord Remfrey (deceased)
Serawyn (deceased)
Quinn (deceased)

HOUSE FRIERE
House of Fire and Earth

Grand Lord Ivulf
Raoul

HOUSE VIVEK
House of Wisdom

Grand Lord Rune (brother) (deceased)
Grand Lady Runa (sister) (deceased)
Renlar

HOUSE RAFEL
House of Healing

Grand Lord Haruk
Ayaka

HOUSE LUCERAS
House of Light

Grand Lord Warin
Leo
Tyrn
Elric
Adalyn

HOUSE MEREK
House of Courage

Grand Lady Bryren
Reidin (consort)
Grand Lord Malrin (deceased)

Flight of the Raven

1

D^{ark.}
 So dark.

Selene shivered and pulled her cloak and hood closer around her shoulders. Her clothes were still damp from crossing the Hyr River, and the cold wind did not help. The trees that lined Trader's Road appeared like bony fingers reaching up toward the darkening sky. Twilight slipped across the road, blending the forest edge with the dirt path. Up above, streaks of red split the sky, as if some large animal had torn open the heavens.

Brittle leaves crunched beneath her boots as she followed the guards, Sten and Karl. Karl was a few inches taller than Sten, and younger by at least ten years. His hair curled along the edge of his cloak, and his hand hovered near the hilt of his sword. Sten was round and muscular, with greying hair and a neck as thick as a man's hand. He pointed at something, and Karl answered in a low, gruff voice.

Cohen, the monk, walked quietly beside her, his presence warm and friendly. He was as tall as he was skinny, with straw-colored hair that stuck out around his face. And behind her . . .

Her stomach lurched and her fingers curled

around the edge of her cloak. Lord Damien followed a couple of feet behind, his steps firm. No, not lord. Not to her anymore.

Damien. Her husband.

Selene kept her eyes ahead, but every part of her could sense him. The moment the monk had finished the rites and the flame had jumped between their hands, she *knew* him. Most of it she had already discovered during her dreamwalks, but having that knowledge imparted into her innermost mind and soul, rather than seeing it as memories, were two completely different things. And just as much as she now knew him, he knew her as well. He knew who she really was. He knew what she could do.

He knew her gift.

She could still see the shock on his face the moment her dreamwalking gift was revealed to him. Yet he was still able to turn away and maintain enough mental capacity to raise the river barrier in time to save them.

Selene lifted her hand and brushed her cheek. That power. To raise water. It was amazing. And terrifying. And if he hadn't chosen to bond with her minutes before . . .

Her hand slid down and rested on her throat. She would have drowned alongside those men.

Instead, Damien had chosen to save her. In a permanent way.

A wave of dizziness hit her, darkening her

14

vision for a moment. Mere days ago she was heir to House Ravenwood's secret and training to be a dreamkiller, only now to be crossing a whole new country on her way to a new home and new life.

A dead branch caught her foot, and Selene stumbled forward. A hand caught her by the forearm while something gripped her cloak and pulled her back.

"Are you all right?" Cohen asked beside her.

"Careful there," Damien said behind her.

"I'm fine. I didn't see the branch." She didn't want to explain how her thoughts and emotions were a jumbled mess, making it hard to concentrate. That, and she was tired. So very tired.

Damien kept his hand on her back—a light touch, but every part of her was focused on that spot between her shoulder blades, right where his hand was.

Right where her mark was.

"We should be close to Riveram. Then we can all rest for the night." He removed his hand, but Selene could still feel the imprint of it. Would she ever get used to him? She was not a woman who touched people or liked to be touched herself. The only person she ever truly let past her physical barrier was Ophie—

Her heart clenched and she missed a step, but no one seemed to notice this time. She held a fist

15

to her chest to ease the pain inside as she pictured her youngest sister. Her sweet smile. Her dark curly hair. The way her eyes communicated what she was thinking in a way she could not say with her mouth.

Would she ever see her little sister again?

"Ophie," she whispered as moisture collected along her lower eyelids. She blinked before the tears could collect and roll down her cheeks. She would not waste this opportunity that fortune, chance, or perhaps even the Light himself had given her. She would not leave her sisters behind—even Amara. She had an opportunity now to find a way to free them from the Raven-wood legacy.

"I wish we had our horses," Karl grumbled up ahead, so quietly that Selene barely heard his words.

"Stop your bellyaching. Would you rather have a horse or your life?" Sten replied, just as quietly.

"Do you really believe she did this to rescue us? Or was it to find a way to the Northern Shores and then finish her job?"

"Do you not understand what Lord Damien did back there?"

Karl grunted out what sounded like a no.

"By marrying her, Lord Damien ensured that Lady Selene can never take his life."

Selene sucked in a breath. He did? How much did she not understand about the marriage rites?

Sten continued. "Cohen bound them together. She can never harm him in that way. She cannot kill him."

She frowned. Was that why Damien proposed a marriage alliance? To save himself? It also explained why her Ravenwood ancestors took consorts from lesser houses: not only to protect their secrets, but to make sure the men who knew those secrets could not turn around and kill them. It seemed that in return they could never kill their husbands either.

The guards did not seem to realize she could hear their conversation, something for which she was thankful, as they had provided her with information. But what they didn't seem to understand was that she had no plans to fulfill her mission. In fact, if Damien was truly the threat from the north her mother feared, then all the better if he lived.

But it did make her wonder. What was the true reason Damien chose to bond with her? To save her . . . or to save himself?

Just when it seemed it would be too dark to go on, a faint light appeared in the distance up ahead on the road.

"Riveram. Finally," Sten said, his voice sounding fatigued.

"Looks like it," Karl replied.

"Thank the Light," Cohen said beside Selene.

17

Selene didn't say a word. Instead, she focused on twinkling light. Every part of her body was past exhaustion, and the only thing making her move was the thought that if she didn't, someone would have to carry her. And that wasn't going to happen.

The light ahead brightened as night fell. A sliver of a moon hung in the sky, partially obscured by the trees. Selene focused on the light and the road before her, unwilling to trip on another branch or rock. More lights appeared as log homes took shape in the distance.

"Do they have an inn?" Cohen glanced at the men behind him.

"I don't think so," Taegis replied. "Riveram is small compared to most of the villages along Trader's Road. We'll see if someone is willing to give us a room for the night, or perhaps there is a barn we can sleep in."

A barn? Selene sighed. Well, at least it was out in the open. Much more preferable than the cramped tunnel where they had spent the last day and a half.

"Oh." Cohen sounded crestfallen. "What about food?"

"I'm sure we will find a meal. The people of Riveram are generous."

Her stomach rumbled loudly in response. Selene placed a hand along her middle and bit her lip. Did they hear that? A chuckle behind her, sounding vaguely like Damien, answered her question.

Sten looked back at the same time. "Sounds like I'm not the only one who's hungry."

Selene gave him a small smile, one he probably could barely see in the dark. At least he wasn't as suspicious as Karl.

Twenty minutes later, they reached the edge of Riveram. Taegis was right. The village was small. As far as she could tell, there were only a handful of wood homes with thatched roofs. Yellow light from candles shown through small, square windows, providing the only light in the village. Around the homes, slender logs were stacked and tied together with twine and propped up by posts, creating fences around gardens or pens for livestock. A hint of smoke filled the air, and a subtle hum of voices emerged from the cabins.

"It's been a long time since I was in Riveram, but likely not much has changed," Taegis said as he came forward. Damien joined Selene on the left. "If it's the same as it was before, then the place to ask for hospitality is the house on the right. I can't remember the man's name, but he acts as the village's leader."

Taegis approached the door while the rest of the party stood ten feet away, just outside the light from the house. Taegis knocked. Seconds later, an older man answered. He was bald on top, save for a few strands of hair pulled over his head, and a scruffy beard covered the lower half of his face. His clothes were faded and patched but in good repair. In his hand, he held a knife.

He glanced at Taegis, then squinted into the darkness at the rest of them. "Travelers? We haven't had any travelers to Riveram in weeks. What brings you folks here and at this time of night?"

"We're returning to Nor Esen from Rook Castle," Taegis said, his own hand hovering near the sword at his side.

"Rook Castle? You mean from Ravenwood lands?"

"Yes. In my company is Grand Lord Maris himself. We seek shelter and food—"

"Grand Lord Maris?" The man's eyes widened as he looked past Taegis and toward the group ahead.

Damien stepped forward. "Yes. My companions and I have been traveling without rest and seek shelter and food from your village. You will be compensated for your generosity."

"My lord." The knife clattered to the floor as the old man knelt down in the doorway. "My apologies at such a welcome. There's been talk of highwaymen along Trader's Road."

Damien bent over and placed a hand on the man's shoulder. "No apologies necessary."

"I'm afraid we do not have many luxuries

here," the older man continued, still staring at the ground. "We are a simple people. But what we have is yours."

"Thank you," Damien replied. "Food and a place to sleep are all we ask. And perhaps if there is a stable where we can obtain horses for our travels back to Nor Esen. I'm afraid we were unable to bring ours back from Rook Castle."

The man looked up, puzzled, but he did not ask. "We can provide what you require."

Damien took a step back. "Please rise. And if I may, what is your name?"

The man slowly stood, awe across his face. "Tarren, sir. Jorgen Tarren."

"Jorgen Tarren, House Maris thanks you."

Jorgen smiled. "Please wait inside my home while I find a place for you and your companions to stay the night. I do not have enough for a hot meal, but I do have cold ham, bread, and ale. Please help yourselves." Jorgen stepped back and motioned for them to enter.

Taegis entered first, followed by Sten, while Damien waited by the door. Selene glanced at Jorgen, amazed at the exchange between him and Damien. Mother would have never treated a commoner in such a way. She would have issued firm demands and expected them to be fulfilled.

But Damien had treated the man as an equal.

Taegis checked the cabin, then came back to the door and ushered the rest inside. As Selene crossed the threshold, Jorgen glanced at her with one eyebrow raised. "I did not realize you had a woman in your group. Will your . . . uh, companion need any special accommodations?"

Damien glanced at Selene.

Dart'an! She should have kept her hood up. A lone woman traveling with a band of men was not considered proper, no matter the party. How would Damien explain her presence?

Damien waved toward Selene. "Jorgen Tarren, let me present to you my new wife, Lady Selene."

So he was going to go with the truth. She both respected him for that and at the same time wasn't ready for the world to know. She had hardly had time to accept that reality herself.

Jorgen's eyes grew bigger. "My-my lady," he stuttered. "I-I didn't know. . . ."

"It was very recent," Selene said, hoping to put the man at ease. If nothing else, she could still speak like a lady.

"Then I shall be sure to place you both together."

Selene opened her mouth to answer, then stalled, her own eyes growing wide. *Both . . . together?*

Before she could say anything, Jorgen bowed to Damien and left. Selene stared at the doorway, a cold sweat breaking out over her body.

Cohen stepped inside and closed the door behind him. There was hardly any room within the cabin. A small hearth stood across from her with a cheery fire burning brightly. A sleeping mat lay on the dirt floor, with a chest at one end. To her right was a narrow table with a candle on top and two chairs. And in the back by the larder, a pot, a pan, and a few cooking utensils hung from the ceiling. Overall, it reminded her of the small home of Petur, the gardener at Rook Castle.

"The man was kind enough to offer us food from his own larder," Taegis said as he headed toward the back.

Selene stepped aside and stood by the fire as Damien, Taegis, and Sten gathered around the larder and pulled items from the cupboard. Cohen came and stood beside her. Taegis placed a platter topped with ham on the table. Sten followed with a loaf of brown bread and knife. Damien found a wooden pitcher and two tankards.

At the sight of food, Selene heard her stomach growl again, and a dizzy spell washed over her. She had never eaten cold ham, but at the moment, she felt like she could eat anything.

Taegis began to slice the meat while Sten broke off pieces of bread. Damien took a step back and closed his eyes. His lips moved but no words came from his mouth. Karl moved forward and poured pale liquid from the pitcher into the two waiting tankards.

Selene watched Damien from the corner of her eye. What was he doing? A moment later, his eyes opened, and he held out his hand as Karl handed him a tankard.

Instead of taking a drink, he looked over at Selene and held the tankard out to her. "You first."

She took the wooden cup and held it up to her lips, her eyes never leaving his. The scent of sweet yeastiness filled her nose, and she took a drink. The ale was tepid and tangy, warming her as it flowed down her throat. She took another drink as she realized how thirsty she was. After draining half of the mug, she handed it back. "Thank you."

"You're welcome." Damien took the tankard and finished it off with one long gulp.

"Here," Sten said as he handed her a chunk of bread.

Selene tore off a piece and hardly chewed before she swallowed and broke off another piece. Bread had never tasted so wonderful. Sten handed her a thick slice of ham. The salty and smoky-flavored pork brought a groan to her lips. After living off of hard biscuits and dried meat the last two days, this simple fare was a feast.

The men began to chat and laugh as they enjoyed food and drink. Selene listened as she finished off her own meal. The dim light, pleasant company, and full belly brought fatigue crashing down on her. What she wouldn't give for her bed back home in Rook Castle.

Her spirits dimmed and she looked around. She wasn't home anymore. She could never go home. This was her life now. Her eye caught Damien's just as the door opened and Jorgen walked in.

"One of the families here in Riveram has a loft that two of you can share. Another family has offered their stable. Lord Maris, I would like to offer you and your wife my own home for the night."

"And where will you sleep?" Damien asked.

"In my stable. It's clean and dry, but small."

Selene almost expected Damien to protest. It seemed to be his nature to serve everyone else. Instead, he bowed his head. "Thank you, Jorgen."

The older man made his way through the crowded cabin and opened the chest next to his sleeping mat. He pulled out a faded quilt and cloak, then stood. "Here," he said, extending the blanket to Damien. "It's not much, but it should cover the both of you."

Selene's heart leapt into her throat. She wasn't completely ignorant of all that a marriage entailed, but her parents did not share a bedchamber—not to mention a bed. And it was her understanding that was the usual way for every Great House. Was House Maris different? Did Damien expect her to sleep beside him?

Her stomach clenched even harder at the thought, and her hastily eaten dinner threatened to come back up.

"The rest of you may come with me, and I will show you where you will be staying for the night." Jorgen bowed to Damien. "Grand Lord Maris, good night." He glanced at Selene and continued his bow. "My lady."

Selene tried to nod but found herself frozen in place.

Taegis came up to Damien's side as the other men exited the cabin. "I will be sleeping outside Jorgen's cabin," he said quietly. "We might be in our own lands now, but I will feel better once we reach Northwind Castle. Especially with this talk of highwaymen."

"Thank you, Taegis. I would join you, but I think it would be an offense to Jorgen's hospitality and generosity."

"I agree. Good night, Lord Damien."

"Good night, Taegis."

Taegis turned and caught sight of Selene. He bowed his head. "Good night, my lady."

"Good night." Her voice cracked halfway through her words. She swallowed, but her mouth was dry.

Taegis left, closing the wooden door behind him. Silence descended upon the cabin, only broken by the soft crackle of the fire.

2

I know what you're thinking, and I want to put you at ease. You'll have the sleeping mat, and I'll sleep over here by the table."

Selene turned.

The orange glow from the fire lit up Damien's face. Stubble graced his jaw and twin pinpoints of light shone from within his dark blue eyes. "I felt it was best to let Jorgen know why you are traveling with us. It is better for people to know the truth than to speculate. You are a lady, and I will not let your reputation be tarnished in any way. But"—he raised a hand and rubbed the back of his neck—"this . . . marriage bonding . . . is new. Neither of us was expecting it. I think it is best to figure this out before . . ." He coughed and looked away.

"I agree," Selene said hurriedly. "There is a blanket on the mat. I'll use that and you can use the quilt."

"Good idea."

Damien set about laying the quilt along the dirt floor while Selene put the last bit of ham and bread back into the larder. The air was tense and silent inside the cabin. She hated it, yet did not want to break it either. And Damien had yet to ask her about her gift. Her stomach twisted as she shut the cupboard door. That was a long explanation best left to a later time. She hoped Damien thought the same.

Selene headed over to the sleeping mat and removed her cloak. She still wore the same black tunic and leggings she had worn for her mission. Between two full days and nights of travel, not to mention slogging through a river, her clothing was beginning to smell ripe.

She sighed and placed the cloak down, folded, beside the mat. Nothing could be done about it. Besides, she was sure she wasn't the only one who smelled. She removed her boots, then knelt down and undid the leather cord that held her hair in a braid and began to comb through her hair with her fingers, undoing the knots that had developed.

"I'm sorry we don't have a brush," Damien said behind her.

Her fingers froze, and she whipped her head around. He was watching her?

"After we leave tomorrow, it will be three days before we reach the town of Rone. Rone is a large center of commerce for the Northern Shores. We will be able to procure more supplies, as well as some personal items, such as a brush, or even clothing, if you wish."

"That would be nice." And she meant it. She never considered herself a lady who could not live without the luxuries of life, but right now she missed even the simple things.

"Good night . . . Selene."

Her breath caught in her throat at his use of her first name. "Good night," she said quickly and turned back around. She couldn't say his name. And she couldn't call him Lord Damien.

Selene finished rebraiding her hair, then crawled beneath the blanket, which smelled of hay, and curled up on her side with her back toward Damien. Slowly her muscles began to relax. No matter how agitated she felt, her body was too tired to care. Sleep. That's all she wanted right now. To close her eyes, forget about the world and her new way of life, and rest.

Darkness. A grey haze. Filled with howling wolves. The fog slipped away, revealing burning trees. Then the screaming began. Renata stood next to a burning wagon, her hands held out, her eyes wide. "Please, my lady, save me—"

Selene woke with a start and sat up. She breathed heavily as she looked around. Where was she? Her hand reached out and brushed the edge of the sleeping mat. The last of the burning coals smoldered in the hearth. A figure slept beside it.

Damien.

She let out her breath and slumped forward. It was just a dream. A really bad dream. She lay back down and curled up on her other side. Damien continued to sleep on, apparently unfazed by her sudden awakening. Good. The last thing she wanted now was for him to wake up to every little noise she made. Her experience during her reconnaissance missions was that he was a heavy sleeper.

Selene yawned and snuggled down deep beneath the blanket. Sleep pulled her back under.

A woman wailed beside a burning pyre, beating her chest with her fists as embers shot into the night sky. Fire turned into a dark cabin where a small girl stood crying in the corner, her face gaunt with hunger. The cabin and girl disappeared. Trees as tall as the castle walls surrounded her, and on the path between them lay a red-haired man, his throat ripped open—

Her eyes flew open, her heart racing inside her chest. Selene rolled onto her back and stared up at the thatch ceiling. Faint light from a nearby window indicated morning was quickly approaching.

She recognized the dead man from her dream. Hagatha's father. And she could remember the other dreams, all of them from servants at Rook Castle. But why was she dreaming about them now? She'd never relived anyone else's dreamscape before.

Damien shifted.

Selene quickly rolled onto her side and squeezed her eyes shut. Maybe she could find a little more rest before she had to wake up for the day.

But sleep never came. Only image after image of previous dreamscapes. She curled into a tighter ball, her body so tired she never wanted to leave the sleeping mat. But her mind would not let her drift off.

She heard Damien move as the first rays of light entered the window and shone across the far wall. Too late. Day was already here. A day that would be filled with more traveling.

She pressed her lips together and swallowed hard. Then, drawing on all of her strength, she opened her eyes and sat up. Her body felt heavy and slow, and her eyes were dry and scratchy.

"Sleep well?" a tenor voice asked.

She gripped the blanket between her fingers and stared down. "I'm afraid I don't sleep well in new places." Maybe that's what was causing the nightmares.

"My brother was the same way."

Selene looked over at Damien. He was kneeling down beside the hearth, folding the quilt he had slept on. "Your brother?"

"Yes." He glanced over. "Quinn hated traveling and could never sleep anywhere but in his own bed." He chuckled and stood, but Selene didn't miss the way his eyes shifted and lost their spark.

She vaguely remembered seeing three caskets sent out to sea in Damien's memories and hearing her father speak of another son of House Maris. "My father told me of your loss."

He sighed. "It was almost two years ago. I wish I'd had more time with him."

Selene didn't know what more to say. Her family wasn't close, not as close as Damien's seemed to have been. She couldn't even imagine that kind of closeness. When her grandmother died years ago, she barely reacted. Perhaps she would miss her father if he passed away, and she would cry over Ophie, maybe even Amara, if they passed. She wasn't sure how she would feel if her mother died. And she certainly would not be still grieving two years later.

She frowned as she pulled the blanket back over the sleeping mat. What kind of love had knit House Maris together?

Damien's voice interrupted her thoughts. "We will be heading out soon. Let me know if you need anything before we start back on the road."

Selene glanced over at him and nodded.

Damien left and the cabin grew silent. Selene made sure everything was put away and straightened up. Jorgen had been kind enough to let them use his home; she wanted to make sure they left it tidy. Then she walked over to one of the small windows and looked out. She spotted Damien, Taegis, and Sten standing in the middle of a small group of villagers near the community well. Thatched homes surrounded the village square.

She studied Damien. He appeared confident

and strong as he spoke to those around him. The villagers smiled and laughed. They loved him. She could see it on their faces and hear it in the tone of their voices.

Selene slipped away from the window, picked up her black cloak, and pulled it over her shoulders. There had been a time when her own people loved her. Petur doted on her when she would play in the castle gardens as a little girl. The servant girls would smile when she walked by. Then she started dreamwalking and learned of their darkest secrets. Secrets she buried within her own frozen heart. Then they all whispered that she was the Lady of Ice.

She clenched her hand and held it over her chest. Did her heart even exist anymore? The chilling numbness had become such a part of her that she was afraid it was all that was left.

She pulled her hood over her head and opened the door. Not wanting to attract attention, she made her way along the outskirts of the village to where she'd spotted Karl and Cohen standing on the other side. Only a few people noticed her, but she kept her head low, allowing her hood to hide her features. She caught Damien's last words of thanks as she reached the men.

"Lord Damien is a lot like his father," Cohen said quietly, a smile on his face. His light-colored hair stuck out around his head like stalks of hay.

Karl nodded, his arms folded across his chest.

His dark, curly hair was damp, and there were circles beneath his eyes. "Yes, he is. And well respected too, just like Lord Remfrey was." His eyes slid over to Selene. "House Maris has always been respected." There was a hint of malice in his words.

Selene ignored the surly guard. But on the inside, she felt the shaft of his words burrow deep. She did not belong. A chilling numbness spread over her, stealing away the verbal barb until she felt nothing at all. This was where she was safe. Where nothing could touch her heart.

Cohen turned his attention toward her. "Good morning, Lady Selene."

"Good morning." Her voice came across as crisp and cool.

Cohen frowned and studied her until Damien and Taegis walked over.

"I was able to secure six horses," Taegis said with a smile. "That means we should be able to make it to Rone in half the time."

"That's great news," Cohen said.

"I agree. Thank you, Taegis," Damien said.

"I also was able to obtain enough supplies to see us to Rone. If we start now, we should be there by early evening tomorrow."

Damien nodded as he rubbed his chin. "And after that, almost a week to reach Nor Esen."

"As long as we don't run into any trouble," Sten replied.

"Or bad weather," Karl said ominously.

Selene remained silent, watching the exchange between the men. There was a tightness in her chest. Rone. Nor Esen. These were unfamiliar places to her. While the men were excited to reach home, those names only reminded her that she had left her home, land, and all she knew behind.

But I am alive. That, at least, is worth it.

3

Amara stood in the back of the audience chamber of Rook Castle, the cowl of her cloak pulled over her head, hiding her face from those present. Captain Stanton and his men knelt before the obsidian throne, heads bowed, waiting for her mother to speak. Sunlight poured in along the high windows, but the light brought neither warmth nor comfort.

Lady Ragna placed her hand on one of the stone ravens that flanked the throne and gazed out over the men. Her hair was pulled over her shoulder and her gown followed her curves. She raised her dark eyes and spoke. "House Maris has taken my daughter and fled. Lady Selene must be brought back at all costs."

Captain Stanton glanced up. "And what if the water-wall has been raised between our lands?"

"See if there is a weakness or a place where you can cross. They are over two days ahead. If you can cross, you can reach them before Lord Maris makes his way back to Nor Esen."

"And what do we do if we catch up to Lord Maris?"

She narrowed her eyes. "Whatever you must to get Lady Selene back."

"Anything?"

"He has broken faith with our house and our people."

Captain Stanton bowed in acknowledgment. "And if we can't cross?"

"Then set up a patrol along the entire Hyr River. Lord Damien is young and inexperienced. He can't keep the wall up forever. The moment it comes down, send a message by raven."

Captain Stanton pressed a fist to his chest and stood. His men stood with him. "Yes, my lady." He shouted out a command, and the men turned around and started for the double doors in the back. Amara stepped deeper into the shadows and watched from beneath the hood of her cloak as the men departed.

When the last man left and the doors closed, Amara turned to approach her mother when another man appeared from the left side of the throne. She paused beside one of the stone columns, just out of sight, and frowned. What man had the privilege to approach her mother unannounced and unbidden?

"You don't really believe Lord Maris took Lady Selene, do you?" the man asked, dark humor in his voice.

"No. It is she who led Lord Maris away from the castle through the underground tunnels. And she will pay for that."

Amara's body stilled. Selene betrayed their house? She blinked, hardly believing what her mother had said. Selene? The heir of Ravenwood? The one destined to bring their house to greatness?

Her mother continued to speak to the stranger, but Amara could not hear their words above the pounding of her own heart. What had possessed her sister to do such a thing? Not that she loved Selene, but never did she think her sister was capable of such duplicity—and to leave with House Maris of all families? What was Selene thinking?

To betray their mother . . .

A burning hope sprang up within her heart. Amara lifted her hand and stared down at her palm. With Selene gone, this could be her chance. Her gifting would arrive any day now, and when it did, she could become what her sister had thrown away.

"Amara, come here."

Amara dropped her hand, her mother's harsh voice quenching the heated hope inside. She stepped around the column. The man beside her mother was short, broad in the shoulders, and dressed in a dark robe with a cord around his waist, similar to the ones the disciples of the Dark Lady wore. His face was clean-shaven, and his eyes were as dark as his robes. She didn't recognize him, but then again, she never paid much attention to those who worshiped the Dark Lady.

He glanced over at Amara and sneered.

A rush of heat spread across her body. It was as though he had appraised her and found her wanting. She curled her hands into fists and clenched her jaw. The man didn't know her, nor did she know him. So what right did he have to look down upon her?

Lady Ragna turned back toward the man. "This is my second daughter, Amara."

"Can she walk yet?"

Walk? Did he mean dreamwalk? Amara curled her lip as she made her way toward the throne. Whoever he was, he knew about their family gift.

"No, but she will soon."

"Is she as powerful as the first one?"

Lady Ragna glanced at Amara. "She could be." But there was doubt in her mother's voice.

Amara steeled her jaw.

The man continued to study her. "That could be an issue."

"We haven't failed you yet."

"What do you call the faithless actions of Lady Selene?"

"A gross miscalculation."

"Commander Orion is counting on you—both you and Lord Friere. See that you don't disappoint him. We have a renegade team scouting the lands. Last I heard, they were near the Hyr River border. Perhaps, if we are fortunate, they are still in the lands of House Maris and can take care of this little problem for us, since your men seem ill-equipped to do so."

A dark look came over Lady Ragna's face, a look Amara was only too familiar with. The man—whoever he was—was treading on thin ice with her mother.

"Now, I must report back to my master." The man bowed, almost mockingly, then turned and left through the side door.

Amara crossed her arms and watched him go. Her mother watched him as well, eyes blazing.

After he left, silence fell across the chamber. Amara waited until her mother turned back toward her. She wanted to ask who he was and why he had mentioned Commander Orion. There was only one man with that name. The head of the Dominia imperial forces.

Her mother continued to stand there as if made of stone, like one of the ravens carved into the throne. Amara waited, barely breathing, giving her mother time to gain her composure and thoughts instead of lashing out.

"It is time to meet with the other houses." Her mother's words and movement were abrupt, as if she had just emerged from a trance. "Come, Amara."

Amara waited for her mother to descend from the platform, then followed slightly behind her.

"You will tell no one what you heard. I will explain later."

"Yes, Mother."

"And you will let me know the moment you feel your gifting coming on, do you hear? We have much work ahead of us. The absence of your sister has made our work even more difficult than before."

Amara raised one eyebrow. Even now Mother couldn't seem to say what really happened: Selene had betrayed them and run away.

They left the audience chamber and made their way through Rook Castle toward the meeting room. "You will not say anything to the other houses. You will not speak to them. You are simply here to represent House Ravenwood and to show your support during this crisis."

"Yes, Mother." She was curious as to how her mother was going to explain Selene and House Maris's absence, and the death of Lord Rune and Lady Runa Vivek. Rumors were already spreading that an agent of the empire had infiltrated their castle, but Amara had other suspicions, ones she had harbored about her family for a long time, that House Ravenwood was in the business of death.

The two guards stationed at the door bowed to Lady Ragna and Amara as they entered the circular room. Already the other houses were gathered, sitting somberly around the table, hands folded and eyes cast downward. The silver chandelier threw candlelight across the table, while morning light filtered through the narrow windows beyond the columns.

Upon entering, Amara stole to the right and took her place next to the wall, just inside the shadows that lined the room. There were other guards present from each of the houses, no doubt for the protection of their lords and ladies. She ignored them and watched the table.

Lord Ivulf Friere was the first to acknowledge her mother's presence. Then the others looked up as she came to stand beside her chair. Amara studied the other houses. She knew them by name only, having spent most of her time with Lord Raoul Friere during his stay here.

Lady Bryren of House Merek had a scowl on her face and her arms were crossed, which only made her look even more fierce than usual. Her copper hair surrounded her face in an array of small braids and wild pieces, and her leather garb was a mix of blacks, browns, and the occasional colored skin.

Lord Haruk Rafel appeared ancient, his emerald eyes sunken and the lines around his face more pronounced. He hid his hands in the folds of his green robes as he waited for Lady Ragna to speak.

Lord Leo Luceras had no expression on his face. Amara took a moment to peruse the young lord's physique, enjoying the firm, muscular lines and golden hair. He would have made an

42

excellent match, and she wouldn't have minded being lady of such a prestigious house, but after watching him for the last fortnight, she was sure his heart belonged to Lady Ayaka Rafel. The only question was if her father, Lord Haruk, knew.

The three remaining chairs were conspicuously empty, and everyone's eyes seemed to be avoiding them.

Lady Ragna glanced around the room a second time before she began. "Fellow grand lords and ladies. We have all been shaken by the events of the last few days. Murder and betrayal of the highest degree have been committed. I assure you my men are doing everything they can to discover what exactly has happened and to catch those involved—"

"What do you know?" Lady Bryren asked, interrupting Lady Ragna.

Lady Ragna set her gaze on Lady Bryren, who stared back with the same intensity. Amara couldn't help but admire the wyvern lady in that moment for not being intimidated by her mother. Very few could look Lady Ragna in the eye and not flinch.

"Lord Rune and Lady Runa were found dead in their beds," her mother said smoothly. "And Lord Maris is missing, along with my own daughter, Lady Selene. We believe the empire has something to do with—"

"By what evidence?" Lady Bryren asked.

"Pardon me?"

"What evidence do you have that it was the empire?"

"Come now, Lady Bryren, you must have realized that a meeting such as this assembly would have attracted assassins from the empire."

"But you said the empire was not a threat."

"Our assembly *made* us a threat. I see this as a warning from the Dominia Empire to leave things as they are."

"Or it's their announcement that they plan to take out our houses one by one. That leads me to the next question. How would an assassin or assassins enter Rook Castle? How easy was it for the empire to enter this place?" Lady Bryren uncrossed her arms and leaned forward. "Or was it the empire at all?"

Lady Ragna narrowed her eyes. "What are you implying?"

"That there could be more going on than we know. I think the empire is here, now, amongst us."

"That would support my assassins theory," Lady Ragna said.

"Or the empire has allies in these lands."

Lord Ivulf spoke up, his voice rumbling. "Lady Bryren, are you saying that there are traitors here in this room?"

Lord Haruk looked up. "That is a grave accusation, Lady Bryren."

All heads turned toward Lord Haruk in surprise.

Amara took it to mean the lord of the House of Healing rarely spoke. He seemed more attuned to listening and waiting.

"Yes, it is. But we must consider all possibilities."

"Yes, we should," Lady Ragna said. "And with House Maris gone, I can't help but wonder what Lord Damien's part is in all of this."

"Are you saying House Maris is a traitor? I find that hard to believe," Lady Bryren scoffed. "Perhaps he is dead as well and we haven't found his body yet."

"That is a possibility. But if he left, leaving in the middle of the night is suspicious."

"Maybe he had a good reason. Like running for his life."

Lady Ragna arched an eyebrow. "Or escaping before he was caught."

Amara listened as the conversation between the lords and ladies became more heated. What a fractious group. The assembly was to bring unity, but it seemed to be doing the opposite. Was that Mother's intention? Amara narrowed her eyes as the stranger's words rang in her ears. *"Commander Orion is counting on you."*

Amara stared at her mother as angry voices echoed across the chamber, everything falling into place. Yes, the empire was behind the assassinations. Yes, there was a traitor in their midst.

It was their house.

And her mother was pulling all the strings.

But who killed Lord Rune and Lady Runa Vivek? Her mother or Selene? Was that why Selene ran? So she wouldn't be caught? But Mother would have covered for her, much how she was covering their house now and diverting suspicions elsewhere. And what about House Maris? What part did they play in this? She couldn't imagine Lord Damien was in league with her mother. Perhaps he found out and Mother threatened him, so he ran? But he didn't seem like the kind to run. Lord Damien wasn't her type, but Amara had admired his strength of character.

No, there was something else in play.

Amara watched with morbid fascination as the room erupted into shouts and accusations. Yes, her mother was like a black widow, tugging at the strands of a web she had woven around the Assembly of the Great Houses. Every time Lady Bryren brought up a point, her mother or Lord Ivulf would counter.

Amara leaned against the wall. She would have to be careful. In some ways, she was a naïve fly who, if she wasn't wary, could get caught in the middle along with everyone else.

Better to watch and wait. The answers would come. And if she played this right—showed she could be trusted, unlike Selene, and grew into her own gifting—she could become the very person she longed to be: heir of House Ravenwood.

That's all she cared about.

4

S elene guided her horse behind Taegis and
Karl as they left the small village of Riveram.
Cohen followed nearby, alongside Damien, with
Sten bringing up the rear. Wispy clouds spread
across the sky overhead, and a cool breeze blew
between the colorful autumn trees that lined
Trader's Road. Insects chirruped within the
forest, and here and there a bird would let out
a song. The air smelled sweet and earthy, so
different than the cool mountain scent she was
used to.

The restful stillness of the forest did nothing to
help her stay awake. With each passing moment,
Selene's eyelids grew heavier and heavier. Her
body longed to sleep like someone parched
longed for water.

They stopped midday to rest and eat the bread
and cheese the people of Riveram had provided.
Selene had just closed her eyes when Taegis
announced it was time to go. So back on her
horse she went, her tired body now sore from
riding.

They rode all afternoon, the scenery never
changing. Selene held her cloak close to her body
as evening brought a cold wind with it. The sky
darkened above. She watched Taegis, waiting

for him to announce it was time to stop, while calculating how soon she could call it a night and fall asleep.

When it became too dark to see, Taegis held up his hand. "We'll camp here for the night." He pointed toward a small break in the trees to the right.

Selene slid off her horse before anyone could assist her. Every heartbeat was heavy inside her chest, and her body ached. But she couldn't rest, not yet. She would not be idle while the men took care of the horses and set up camp.

A half hour later, a fire was burning in the middle of the clearing, the horses were munching on the grass along the perimeter, and Sten was passing around dried meat and small brown loaves of bread.

Selene chewed on the meat and watched the fire from a distant log, while the men sat around the fire and ate. She looked up. Only stars shone on the night of this new moon. Tomorrow the disciples of the Dark Lady would meet in the sanctuary, as they did the morning of every new moon.

Selene placed her bread aside and pulled her cloak close to her body. Thanks to Damien's water barrier, her mother could not follow her here to the Northern Shores. But the Dark Lady surely could.

"Not hungry?"

Selene glanced over to find Damien watching her.

"I'm more tired than hungry." She picked up the bread and held it out. "Here. Perhaps someone else has need of it."

He took it, a concerned look on his face, and walked toward the supplies. A moment later, he returned with a woolen blanket in hand and held it out to her. "Feel free to go to sleep whenever you like."

The way he looked at her, and his thoughtful gesture, touched something inside of her. "Thank you."

After he went back to the fire, Selene rolled the blanket out, lay down on top, and pulled half of it over her. Her whole body sighed with relief and before she knew it, she was fast asleep.

Images sped across her mind: a spilled jug of water and a flying fist; a wracking cough from the bed in a corner; staring down at gnarled, lonely hands. And a dark figure, like a shadow, hovering in the background of each dream.

Selene turned toward the figure, but it disappeared in a gust of smoke, only to appear again in the corner of her eye. Always there, waiting. Watching her.

The dream changed. Selene stood on a high cliff within the Magyr Mountains. The sun was setting, a deep ball of red across the mountain horizon. Bitter cold wind sliced through her clothing. She looked down. Her toes were lined up with the stony edge, and past the rim, hundreds of feet below, were jagged rocks and pine trees. Everything inside of her urged her to take that one last step.

Take it. Take it and end the heartache inside. . . .

Selene gasped and her eyes flew open. It took her a moment to realize she was no longer in the dreamscape. She stared up at the sky and clutched the wool blanket between her fingers. The cool night air froze her face as her heart thrummed inside her chest. Nearby, the fire had burned down to coals. Four figures lay around the campsite, and a fifth—Karl, perhaps—sat in the shadows, watching.

More nightmares. Dreamscapes she had visited while training, the fears and secrets of the servants of Rook Castle. But now there was a shadow in the background, a figure draped in black, watching her.

Why? Her face scrunched up, and she pressed her lips together. Was the Dark Lady punishing her for forsaking House Ravenwood?

But I left for the sake of our house. The cycle of hatred and murder needs to be broken. We can't keep going on like this.

Selene squeezed her eyes shut. Apart from her rapidly beating heart, her chest felt hollow. Beneath her eyelids, her eyes burned with tears. *I just want to sleep. Just one night of peace.*

But no peace came.

Every time she started to drift off, the dreams and the shadow returned. The wolves from Hagatha's memories and the fire from Petur's. Each dream she had ever entered.

A half hour later, she rolled onto her side. The hard ground made her hip ache, so she rolled onto her other side. A rock jabbed into her thigh and the cold air seeped down her neck.

A couple of feet away, the man closest to her breathed softly in slumber. Damien.

He lay on his side, his back to her, with his arm tucked under his head. Selene stared at his back and listened to him breathe. There was something calming about his presence.

Her eyes slowly closed. She breathed in the earthy scent of the forest, smelling hints of pine and smoke. A horse neighed, and one of the other men began to snore.

She snuggled down again, finding the right spot on the ground where there were no rocks, and let out a long breath. She slowly drifted off. . . .

And woke up with a start as an image of Renata's captor stood at the edge of her mind.

No, no, no!

Selene rolled onto her back. "Why is this happening?" she whispered. Only the subtle sound of snoring and the soft hoot of an owl answered her. Exhausted, her body finally took over and placed her under.

She felt like she had been asleep for only a few moments before someone was shaking her. She opened her eyes and blinked.

Damien bent over her. "We leave soon."

Her eyes went wide, and she rolled away from his hand.

"Sorry, I didn't mean to startle you."

Selene lifted herself up from the ground and found herself wrapped up in the woolen blanket. "Confound it," she said through gritted teeth as she tried to detangle herself.

"Here, let me help."

Before she could refuse, Damien grabbed the corner of the blanket, freeing her.

She crawled out beneath his arm and stood, face hot. "Thank you," she mumbled, too embarrassed to look at him. She couldn't remember the last time someone had startled her from sleep.

Damien folded the blanket and put it away in one of the saddlebags. Selene massaged the side of her head where her temple throbbed. Her eyes felt even scratchier today. If only she could have slept longer. She had finally fallen into a deep slumber devoid of dreams.

"I'll get you something to eat."

Selene glanced over and nodded. As Damien headed back to the fire, she turned and went into the woods to attend to her own personal needs. It appeared it would be another nice autumn day. Selene yawned and redid her braid. Her hair was in bad need of washing, not to mention the rest of her body and clothes.

She paused and looked down. If there had been any illusion that she was a lady, those thoughts were dashed. Her tunic was stained, and her pants were torn along one calf. And she smelled like something that had been dragged up from a muck-filled pond. Not how most ladies appeared in the days following their wedding.

Selene straightened up and headed back toward the camp. If Damien was expecting a lady like Lady Adalyn, then he was in for disappointment. She might not look the best, or smell the best, but she doubted any other lady had been through what she had.

She came back to the fire. Damien handed her another small loaf of bread, while Cohen and the other men prepared for their journey. She tore off a chunk and chewed slowly as she stood along the perimeter of the camp. She stared off in the distance, her mind wandering when she felt eyes on her. She paused midchew and found Damien staring at her.

Could he see the fatigue on her face? Or did she look as bad as she smelled?

He never said a word. Instead, he went back to packing.

Selene pulled her hood up over her head, her appetite gone.

They finished cleaning and packing in a short

amount of time, and before she knew it, she was back in the saddle and they were on their way. By midday, Selene could barely keep her eyes open. The cool autumn sun peeked out here and there across the trail where there were breaks within the trees. Sten and Karl rode ahead of her, while Cohen, Taegis, and Damien rode behind her.

The mild conversation between the men and the gentle sway of her horse would lull her close to sleep, only for her to start seconds later and sit upright. At this rate, she was going to fall off her horse.

"Is everything all right?"

Selene flinched at the sound of Damien's voice as he rode up beside her. Taegis wasn't too far behind, his focus always on his liege.

"Yes." She glanced at him from under her hood. "I'm just tired."

"You're still not sleeping well?"

"No, but who can on the ground?" She let out a shaky laugh, hoping it would put him off.

Damien studied her thoughtfully. "It's a good thing we'll be arriving in Rone this evening and should be able to find an inn. A bed will be a nice change to sleeping on hard ground."

"Yes, a bed will be very ni—" Her eyes went wide. Would she have to share a bed with Damien? Heat flooded her face. Dart'an!

Karl glanced back, caught the look on her face, and snickered.

Confound it all!

Damien sent a stern look toward Karl, who sobered and turned back around. "We'll be keeping the arrangement we had back in Riveram," he said quietly, so as not to be overheard.

Selene let out a breathy sigh, and her body sagged forward. "I would like that." Eventually she would have to face the reality of her new marriage, but right now all she could handle was today.

As dusk fell across the forest, the trees split, and in the distance, past fields of tall grass, stood the bustling city of Rone. Music, conversation, and laughter drifted over the twelve-foot wall that surrounded the city. Beyond the barrier, narrow two-story homes made of the same stone overlooked the wall, candlelight spilling from the curved windows. A single torch blazed beside the thick wooden door that led into Rone. Up above, the first stars appeared in the night sky.

As they approached the city, the gatekeeper appeared upon the wall above the door and held up a lantern. "Who goes there?" He was an older man, his stringy grey hair shadowed by the hood of his cloak.

"Six weary travelers on our way back from Rook Castle," Taegis said, taking the lead.

"Rook Castle? You've come a long way, strangers."

"Yes. With us is Grand Lord Maris, returning from his trip there."

"Grand Lord Maris?" Like Jorgen from Riveram, the gatekeeper looked over at the other riders. Selene was grateful she had her hood pulled over her head this time.

Damien brought his horse forward. "Yes. We are seeking a place to spend the night. What inn do you recommend?"

"My lord." The gatekeeper bowed, the lantern still in his hand. "The Bored Boar Tavern is the best place for food, drink, and bed. Just follow the first street inside toward the middle of Rone. Tell Mildred I sent you."

"Thank you."

The gatekeeper disappeared behind the wall. Moments later, there was a loud creak, and the door began to shift. When the door was fully open, the gatekeeper appeared again with his lantern and ushered the party into the city. He glanced at Damien as he passed, a smile across his weathered lips.

Selene watched the exchange, once again puzzled. She couldn't recall seeing the mountain people smile when her mother rode into their villages. The gatekeeper's reaction to Damien moved her.

The horses' hooves clicked as they rode across the cobblestone street. Wooden shutters lined the windows that graced the fronts of two-story homes built next to each other with no space in between. Trees devoid of most of their leaves stood on the street corners. The houses disappeared the deeper they rode into Rone, replaced with small shops, smiths, stables, local guildhalls, and a covered market area. At the end of the market stood a large wooden building three times the size of any other nearby, with an array of windows along both floors and candles lit within.

Damien dismounted and gave instructions to Karl before heading over to Selene. He held up a hand and helped her down. The moment her feet hit the ground, she let go and took a step back. She glanced at the faded sign above the door. *The Bored Boar.* Hopefully the inn also had a bath. Or at least some way she could wash up.

Taegis led the way inside, followed by everyone but Karl, who stayed back to see to the horses. Warmth and smoke filled her nostrils as Selene's eyes adjusted to the bright and cheery interior. The inn consisted of one large main room, with a set of stairs over to the right that led up to a second floor overlooking the main room. Wrought-iron chandeliers hung from the wooden beams above, and dripping candles stood on every table, which were filled with a mix of farmers, travelers, and merchants.

Behind the long counter on the left, various animal skins and horns hung as decoration. A short, stout woman stood beneath them, her thick black hair pulled into a dense braid that hung over one shoulder. Her cheeks were rosy, and there was a mischievous glint to her brown eyes.

"Aye!" she hollered over the conversations and laughter around the room. "Travelers! Over here."

Taegis led the party over to the counter.

"Name's Mildred and I run this here establishment. What'll you be needing this evening?"

"The gatekeeper recommended your inn," Taegis said. "We desire food and bed for this evening. And perhaps a bath, if you have the means."

Mildred looked over the party, her eyes lingering on Selene. Selene looked away, but she had a feeling the innkeeper knew she was a woman.

"I have all three," Mildred said, her gaze returning to Taegis. "Might I ask who you all be, and where you're heading?"

"Taegis, guardian for his lordship, Grand Lord Damien Maris. We are returning from our trip to Rook Castle, heading back to Nor Esen."

Her eyes widened. "Grand Lord Maris?"

Voices within the room paused.

"Yes," Damien said, stepping forward. "I do not need any special accommodations. Just rooms for myself and those traveling with me, as well as food and a way to wash from our travels." He reached the counter and leaned forward. "And yes, there is a woman in our company," he said so quietly that Selene barely caught his words. "She is my wife, but she is still adjusting to the title."

Mildred's gaze darted back to Selene. "I see. I have two rooms upstairs that are available. I also have a wooden tub that I will have brought up to the first room. I'm afraid you and your company will have to share."

"I understand." Damien stepped back. "Thank you, Mildred."

She clapped her hands three times and yelled, "Aye! Hobbes! I need the wooden tub brought up to the first room. And get the hot water going."

There was grumbling from the back room.

"Now!"

"I'm coming, I'm coming," a gruff voice yelled back.

"I'll make sure you have soap and some clean linen." Mildred smiled broadly, exposing the gap between her teeth. "In the meantime, take a seat at one of the tables, and food will be brought out."

"Thank you," Damien said again.

As Mildred headed to the back room, the travelers turned and moved toward the largest table set below the balcony. Selene took a seat with her back to the rest of the room, taking care to keep her hood up. A quick perusal of the inn confirmed that, apart from Mildred, she was the only woman in the room.

Damien took a seat beside her, while Taegis and Sten sat across from them, where they could watch the rest of the inn and the front door. Cohen joined Damien on the other side. The men talked quietly amongst themselves, while Selene folded her hands and sat on the bench, her muscles sore and tired, and her clothes feeling like they were caked in dirt and sweat. Minutes later, steaming bowls of venison stew and brown bread arrived, along with Karl, who joined the other guards.

"Water will be ready soon in the first room at the top of the balcony," Mildred said as she placed pewter tankards around the table.

Damien glanced over at Selene. "You should go first."

"Thank you." She had never bathed in anything other than a metal tub or the hot springs back in Rook Castle, and she couldn't imagine sharing the same water with five men. The thought made her wrinkle her nose, and she felt bad for whoever was last.

As Selene took her final bite of stew, Mildred informed them that the bath was ready. Selene stood and stepped away from the bench.

"Follow me," Mildred said, heading for the staircase up to the balcony. Selene ignored the curious glances of the other inn patrons and followed the stout innkeeper. At the top of the stairs, Mildred opened the door and ushered Selene inside.

"My lady." Mildred bowed after she'd shut the door behind her. "I'm afraid I only have tallow soap for your use."

"Tallow is fine. I'm just thankful for a chance to wash."

Selene looked around the room. It was the size of a small sitting room, with four beds lined along the right wall and wooden shutters across the windows. Lit candles were scattered across the small tables between the beds. A handwoven rug sat across the wooden floor, and on the left side, close to the foot of the beds, sat a round wooden tub, steam rising above the water.

Selene took a step forward, then realized Mildred wasn't moving. She looked back. Mildred stood by the door, a curious expression on her face. "This is the first time I've had a consort stay at my inn," she said with a little bit of awe. "Or the grand lord."

"I'm not Lord Damien's consort," Selene said, slightly horrified. Consorts were spouses from lesser houses, whereas she was an equal to Damien. "I'm Lady Selene of Ravenwood."

Or was she? If she was disowned, who did that make her?

"Oh!" Mildred's eyes went so wide Selene could see the whites around the edges. "I had no idea. . . ."

"It was a surprise to all of us." She clamped her lips shut. That was more than she had wanted to share.

"I see." Mildred's mischievous look came back. "I wish I had more to offer, like scented water. Nothing like lavender for a new couple." Mildred clapped her hands. "Well then. Best to use the water while it's still hot. And let me know if you need anythi—"

"Yes," Selene blurted out. "I do need something."

"Yes?"

"Is there a chance you might have a change of clothes? I've been traveling in these garments for days. . . ." Her voice trailed off as she looked down at her black clothing. Not the typical kind of clothes a lady would wear.

She looked up and caught Mildred eyeing her. "You're a bit taller than I am, but I might have something."

"You do?" Selene sighed gratefully. She had never washed clothing before and wasn't quite sure how. With all the servants at Rook Castle, she'd never had to think about it before. "Thank you."

"My pleasure. It's not every day I have the grand lord himself and his wife staying in my inn." She gleefully rubbed her hands together. "What a story this'll make. Now I'll leave you to bathe." Mildred turned and left, leaving Selene alone in the room, with only the candles for light and a tub waiting for her.

After checking that the latch was secure, Selene stripped off her soiled clothes and dumped them near the door, then stepped into the round wooden tub—barely bigger than a rain barrel—careful not to dislodge the wooden plank that lay across one end and held the beige bar of soap.

The moment she sank down, a long sigh escaped her lips. She didn't have much time, not if the men downstairs had to share the water, but she couldn't help taking a moment to savor the water before dunking her head and grabbing the soap.

The soap had very little smell, but it did wash away the grime and dirt from her travels. Selene washed her hair twice, then let it hang over the edge of the tub. Then she leaned over to one side and placed her arms across the edge. Just one more minute, then she would get out.

She laid her head across her arms and closed her eyes. She yawned and before she knew it, she slipped into the darkness.

5

Sten sat back and patted his belly. "Nothing like hot stew and bread when you've been traveling all day."

"I agree," Cohen said, breaking off another piece of the brown bread.

Karl just nodded, his mouth full.

Taegis quietly sipped on the ale next to Damien. Every few seconds, Damien glanced up at the first door along the balcony and wondered what was taking Selene so long.

"How do you think she's doing?" Taegis asked as he placed his tankard down.

"Doing?" Damien said, bringing his mind back to Taegis's question.

"Lady Selene. Her whole life has changed in the last few days, yet she seems to be holding up rather well. Or at least that's how she appears."

Damien studied his empty bowl and tapped the wooden spoon against the side. "I'm not sure. Compared to most women I know, she is strong. I haven't seen her cry once since we left." But he could tell she was exhausted. Was it from the long days of travel or was there something more?

Taegis leaned in closer and spoke quietly. "I saw how you reacted when you bonded with

Lady Selene. I take it you found out more than you bargained for."

"You have no idea." He tapped his bowl again. He hadn't had a chance to talk to Selene about it, and even though he was privileged to the knowledge of her gift via their bond, his men were not. So even if he were to try to broach the subject, her house secrets would probably prevent him from saying anything to others, as it had prevented Selene's father, Caiaphas. When they arrived at Northwind Castle, he would speak to her.

Damien paused his tapping and looked up at the balcony again. "Something's wrong," he muttered. He stood and turned to go to the counter to get Mildred to check on Selene, then realized how odd that would appear since she was his wife and there was no reason why he couldn't do it.

He rubbed the back of his neck and looked one more time at the balcony, then dropped his hand and started for the stairs. Taegis was already on his feet, following.

"You think something is wrong with Lady Selene?" Taegis asked as pairs of eyes turned in their direction.

"I'm not sure, but it's been a while. She should have been out by now. And I feel—" He stopped at the foot of the stairs, on the other side of the wall and away from the looks around the inn. Was it danger? No. "I feel responsibility."

Taegis nodded.

The two men headed up the stairs. At the top, Damien turned toward the first door and knocked. There was no answer. He knocked again, his heart beating faster. Nothing.

"Selene," he said, using her first name as he knocked for a third time. No answer.

He reached for the lever and pressed down on the metal handle. "Wait here," he told Taegis, then entered.

It took a moment for his eyes to adjust to the dim candlelit interior. Then he spotted her, in the middle of the room in a round wooden tub, her head lying unnaturally to the side.

"Selene!" He ran toward the tub. Had she passed out? Was she hurt?

Her head shot up and water splashed over the sides of the tub.

He skidded to a stop just behind the tub as her head twisted around and up toward his.

Her eyes went wide. She wrapped her arms around her legs and hunched forward. "What are you doing in here?" Her long black hair hung in dark strands along her back, blocking any view of her skin.

"You've been in here for over twenty minutes. I knocked three times and called out, but you didn't answer. I thought . . ." He ran a hand through his hair and turned around.

"I-I fell asleep," she said sheepishly.

"Oh." He couldn't get the image of her black hair hanging down her back out of his mind or comprehend the fact that she had nothing on behind him. His heart felt like it was going to explode from his chest, and heat spread across his entire body.

"I'll get out now. I'm sorry for taking so much time." Her voice came out muffled.

"It's all right. I'll leave." He wanted to run for the door but made himself walk instead.

Taegis met him outside. "Is everything all right?"

"Yes," Damien said too quickly.

Taegis quirked an eyebrow at him.

"She fell asleep. In the, uh, bathtub."

"I see."

Mildred stepped off the stairs with clothing hanging over one arm. She glanced at Damien, then at Taegis. "Is her ladyship done?"

"Yes." His heart was slowly returning to its normal rhythm.

"I brought some clothes for her."

Damien stepped to the side. Mildred glanced one more time at him before heading in.

Taegis tugged on the hair below his chin. "I'm going to see if there is a well in town. I'm sure the water has cooled by now, and it's getting late. The other guards and I can use the well to wash up."

Damien stared at the door. "I'll join you. That way Lady Selene has all the time she needs."

After receiving another bar of soap from Hobbes, the men headed out into the brisk night to the well.

"I can't wait to get home," Cohen said through chattering teeth as he splashed water from one of the buckets and washed his upper body as fast as he could.

"Indeed," Karl replied. The stables stood on the other side of the road and a horse neighed, as if to tell the men to keep quiet.

"Wish I could wash my clothes." Sten held up his tunic and wrinkled his nose. "I guess this will have to do." He dumped the shirt in the bucket and took the bar of soap after it. "I'll just hang it to dry in our room tonight."

Karl watched him for a moment. "Good idea."

Damien finished washing up. "I'm heading back. The rest of you take your time. I'll see you in the morning."

He knew Taegis was with him without having to look back. Until he reached Northwind Castle, Taegis would be his shadow, whether he wanted it or not. They walked quietly for a few blocks until the inn came into view.

"I'm assuming you will share a room with Lady Selene," Taegis said.

"I should. Mildred said there were only two rooms and the one with the tub had four beds. Most likely the other room is the same. That leaves everyone with a bed if I room with her.

But . . ." He let out a breath. "It's not something I'm used to."

"That will take time." There was merriment in Taegis's voice.

Damien glanced over at his guardian. There was a small smile on his face, visible by the light shining from the inn's windows.

Damien decided to play back. "And what would you know of it?"

"Nothing, having never been married myself. But I can imagine." His expression sobered a little. "You have a very kind heart, my lord. I have a feeling her ladyship could use that kindness. Permission to speak?"

"You usually give advice anyway. Go on."

Taegis stopped in the middle of the street, a couple of feet from the door. "You were in a tight spot there by the Hyr River. At first, I thought your decision was foolhardy, even though I did not want to see you pained again by hurting someone with your gift. I wished at the time that we had left Lady Selene behind. But now . . ."

"But now?" Damien echoed.

"I think there is something more going on. I'm not quite the follower that your father was of the Old Ways. But there seems to be a touch of destiny on Lady Selene. Perhaps she was meant to come with us . . . which means perhaps the incident at the river was supposed to happen.

Perhaps this union happened for a reason. If nothing else, then for her ladyship."

Damien glanced at the inn as Caiaphas's words came back to him. *"Protect my daughter, no matter what."* Was it possible that Taegis was right? Was there more going on? Did the union happen so Damien would know her gift?

Could Selene be the one to unite the seven Great Houses?

A shiver ran down his spine, wholly unrelated to his damp clothing.

The room was dark when Damien opened the door to the second guest room. It was set up like the first, with four small beds lined up along the right wall, shutters across the windows on the other side of the room, and a table along the left wall. The candlelight from downstairs was the only way he could see inside the room. He thought about searching for another candle, then changed his mind.

"Sten will be guarding your room tonight," Taegis said quietly from the hallway.

Damien nodded, indicating that he had heard.

"Is there anything else you need?"

Damien turned around. "No. Get some rest, Taegis. We still have a long way to go before we reach Nor Esen and Northwind Castle."

"I will, my liege. Good night."

"Good night, Taegis. And leave the door cracked for a moment so I can see."

Taegis bowed, then walked down the corridor.

Damien turned back. A lone figure lay in the third bed from the door. He walked toward the middle of the room. Selene was curled up on her side, her back to the door, her hair unbound and spread out behind her. She appeared to be asleep, evidenced by the even rise and fall of her body.

She looked different tonight. Was it because he had grown used to seeing her dressed in black, with her hair in a long braid? Or because of their encounter earlier?

He shoved the images out of his mind and pulled off his damp tunic, carefully laying it across the first bed so it could dry. Then he made note of how far the second bed was from the door and how narrow the gap was between the beds, then shut the door.

Using his right hand to feel along, Damien made his way to the second bed, pulled back the covers, and sat down. After removing his boots, he lay down on his side, with his back to Selene, and let out a long breath.

In some ways, he was glad Selene was already asleep. The moments they were alone together were awkward at best. He knew her, and yet he didn't. The marriage bond had opened his eyes to her gift, yet he didn't know what she thought of it or how Ravenwood had hidden it all these years or why. Would Selene even want to talk about it?

He didn't even know what her favorite color was, or what her childhood was like, or what she thought of her family, things he knew about Lady Adalyn and Lady Bryren.

Damien closed his eyes. He would protect Selene. He had sworn to, both to her father and through his vows. But could he learn to love the stranger in the bed next to his?

6

Selene listened as Damien opened the door and light spilled into the room. She heard the exchange between Taegis and Damien, then the rustling of cloth before the door was shut, sending the room back into darkness. Boots clapped softly across the wooden floor, then Damien crawled into the bed next to hers and let out a long sigh.

She wondered at the sound, while keeping her own body still. It wasn't the first time they had shared a room. But whether it was because of fatigue or the newness of it all, she hadn't truly noticed his presence until now. Or was it because he had startled her awake during her bath?

She clenched her hand next to her chest, her body flooding with heat again at the memory. Luckily she had washed her hair and left it down, covering her. What if she had been facing the other way? Or pulled her hair up? She swallowed and clenched her hand tighter.

She shouldn't have fallen asleep in the first place. Her vigilance was waning the farther she drew from Rook Castle. She never would have been caught unaware back home.

She closed her eyes. Hopefully she could fall asleep as easily as she had in the tub. Those few moments of slumber had been bliss, even if they had been cut off rather abruptly and in an embarrassing manner.

But sleep never came. Damien breathed evenly close by, constantly reminding her that she was no longer alone. And when the darkness did come, vivid images from past dreamscapes filled her mind, causing her heart to race and for her to wake. And that dark figure was watching. Always watching.

Time dragged. As she lay on her side, staring at the shadowy area where his back was, her body was almost ready to pass out from fatigue, but her mind would not allow it. Part of her wanted to sit up and scream, another part wanted to curl up and cry. She couldn't function without sleep. If only there was a way to diminish the images trapped inside her head. Someplace safe for her mind—

Her heart stopped and her middle tightened as she listened to Damien breathe. There was one place full of peace and light, one place that might give her a reprieve from previous nightmares. Those dreams could not follow her there.

Inside Damien's dreamscape.

Her mouth went dry, and her heart began to beat again, so loud she could hear it inside her ears. She hadn't dreamwalked since the night she'd chosen to let Damien live, and the memory of his luminous soul had faded in her mind as she was thrust into this new life.

But now it all came back, and with it the craving hunger inside of her to have it.

She clutched the covers beneath her chin. She could almost see the outline of his body from the dim light streaming in from beneath the shutter. The gap between their beds was only about a foot. If she slid to the edge of her own bed and reached out, she might be able to touch—

Damien moved, kicking the covers away from his upper body, and faced her.

Selene froze, waiting to see if he had awakened. Minutes ticked by, but Damien didn't move again. She let out her breath and her body relaxed. He was now closer to the edge of his bed, and she was fairly sure his hand was hanging over the side. That meant all she had to do was lean a little closer. . . .

One touch, and she would be able to sleep. Just one touch . . .

She pulled her hand out from beneath the blanket and reached over. The moment her hand made contact with his skin, she lightly moved her fingers, feeling along the lines of his knuckles. Then she wrapped her fingers around the narrow part of his wrist.

Within a breath, she was yanked into his dreamscape. Selene changed into her raven form, a feeling of euphoria expanding inside her chest. With a joyous caw, she flew up into the light blue sky, the familiar beach of white sand, gentle waves, and rolling grass meeting her gaze.

She breathed in deeply and spread her wings, feeling the air buffet her body. After a moment, she dove toward the sand, bringing herself up at the last moment. If she could laugh in her bird form, she would. Instead, she dove and twisted through the air. The feeling of freedom was almost overwhelming.

After a few minutes, she soared upward until she hovered thirty feet above the white sand. Brilliant light spread across the dreamscape like a radiant summer day. The light sparkled off the deep blue-green sea. She closed her eyes and listened to the gentle rocking of the waves.

A prickle of doubt entered her mind. Was this right? Was it right to enter Damien's dreams for her own selfish reasons?

Selene fluttered toward the dunes, pondering her latest thought. She didn't know. As she came near the ground, she spotted something. Her heart sped up again, and she flew toward the light that lay north of where she was.

As she drew closer, the feeling of joy and longing encompassed her being. Down between two dunes of white sand lay an orb of twisting flames of white light.

Damien's soul.

Selene landed and changed into her human form. As she watched the tendrils of his life-force dance like a thousand tiny flames, the hunger inside of her leapt forward, drawing her closer.

She held back, watching the pulse of light. Moments later, she lowered her body toward the sand and lay down.

She curled on her side, one arm beneath her head, and watched the orb. It reminded her of those moments when the sun would enter her room just so and leave a pool of light on her bed, inviting her to curl up in the sunbeam and fall asleep.

Yes. She closed her eyes. It felt just like that. Warm and peaceful. Her body relaxed. She felt like she could stay forever. Right here, next to Damien's soul.

Damien slowly opened his eyes. The pale light of morning shone through the crack between the shutters at the end of the room. He blinked and looked again. Selene lay a foot away, on the very edge of her bed, one arm tucked beneath her head, the other hanging off the side. If she moved any closer, she would topple off the mattress.

He lay still and watched her. She breathed in and out gently, her lips slightly open, her eyes shut, but not tightly. There was a faint color to her cheeks, and her hair hung across her shoulders and body in silky strands.

She was dressed in a simple, faded beige tunic much too big for her. Probably one of Mildred's.

It softened her, made her appear like a young woman and not the cold lady he was used to. He lifted himself up onto his elbow. If Selene were a flower, she would be a rose. Beautiful, but unattainable, surrounded by thorns.

How could he draw this woman out? How could he speak to her? How could he get past her icy shroud?

Light, I have no idea. But I'm willing to try.

Damien quietly got up and made his way around the beds to where his tunic lay. It was still slightly damp, but at least it smelled better, unlike the rest of him. He shrugged into the tunic, pulled on his boots, and headed out.

His men were already downstairs, dressed and ready, except for Sten, who'd had guard duty last night and was now sleeping.

"Good morning, my lord," Taegis said with a bow. The other men greeted him in similar fashion. "Cohen and I were about to head out and see what we could find for provisions for the trip to Nor Esen. I think it will be best for us to be on the road before noon."

Damien nodded. "Good idea." The young monk grinned. No doubt he was excited to see Rone. Once again, Damien was glad he had brought Cohen along. The more the young man saw of the world, the more prepared he would be to take over for Father Dominick and lead Baris Abbey.

"Karl will stay here with you."

Karl stood on the other side of Taegis, his arms folded, his hair wet and slicked back.

As Taegis and Cohen left, Mildred came into the main room through the back door, black clothing over one arm. "My lord," she said and bowed her head. "I have Lady Maris's clothing for her."

Damien frowned. *Lady Maris?* Then he balked. That's right. Selene was now Lady Maris. He fought the urge to run a hand across the back of his neck. Hearing that title was going to take some getting used to. "Her clothing?"

"Yes, I washed them last night. I'm afraid you were gone when I came back downstairs, or else I would have been happy to serve you as well."

"Thank you."

Mildred bowed again and headed for the stairs to deliver the clothes to Selene. Damien let out a sigh of relief. He would let Mildred be the one to wake Selene up. He wasn't sure she would appreciate a man waking her up if all she had on was a tunic, even if that man was her husband.

His stomach fluttered, and he pinched his nose as another thought came to him. Where exactly would Selene room when they reached Northwind Castle? His room? Separate quarters? There was the spare room next to his, but was that really the precedent he wanted for their marriage? He had a feeling Lady Ragna and Caiaphas did not share a room. Most of the Great Houses did not share

79

bedchambers with their spouses. But his parents had.

Damien pushed the thought aside. He would have time enough to think about it later. Right now, he needed to get ready to leave.

Damien helped Karl retrieve the horses and saddlebags. After securing their mounts, bags, and swords, he returned to the inn just as Selene stepped off the stairs and into the main dining area. Sunlight filled the inn with a soft glow, and the smell of baking bread spread across the room.

Her hair was back in a long braid, and she wore her usual black clothing, complete with her cloak and boots. The icy lady was back, the young woman from this morning gone. She studied him. Her expression was guarded, but there was a hint of thoughtfulness—and something more—in her face. And the circles beneath her eyes from the last few days were gone.

"Sleep well?" he asked as he crossed the room.

She hesitated, then answered, "Yes."

"Good. I had hoped you would find rest here, in a real bed."

Before she could answer, Karl stepped inside, along with Taegis and Cohen.

"Cohen and I were able to secure more food and another waterskin. We should have enough provisions to see us to Nor Esen." Taegis turned his attention to Karl. "Go wake up Sten and let him know it's time to go."

Karl nodded and headed for the stairs.

Not long after, everyone was mounted and riding through Rone. Sunlight streamed through the bare trees that grew between the buildings. Leaves of red, yellow, and orange lay scattered across the cobblestone street. Green ivy clung to the stone homes, adding color to the grey. Wisps of smoke rose from narrow chimneys. The air held a cool, crisp feel to it.

As they rode toward the other end of town, men tipped their hats to the party, while women held rugs out of second-story windows and beat the dust from them. Children in faded tunics or dresses laughed and ran through the streets, dogs nipping at their heels.

Damien glanced at Selene from the corner of his eye. She seemed to be taking it all in with a sense of wonder. Her eyes were wide and her lips parted. A little girl in a blue dress with a white cap over her auburn hair stopped beside a tree and watched Selene for a moment, then waved.

Selene hesitated, then lifted her hand and waved back.

Damien brought his horse next to Selene's. "These are your people now. I hope—no, I believe—you will come to love them as much as I do."

"They remind me of my own people. I wish . . ." She looked down at her hand and clenched it into a fist.

"You wish?"

She took a deep breath and opened her hand. "Nothing."

No, it wasn't nothing. He had heard the passion in her voice. Did she regret leaving her home and her people behind?

Damien stared past Sten to the gate ahead that led northward out of Rone. Of course she did. If he was in her place, his own heart would be grieving for his homeland and people.

Would he have made the same choice she ultimately did? To forsake everything in order to save someone from another house?

He wasn't sure.

They left Rone and continued along Trader's Road north toward Nor Esen. The day waned and night came. Camp was made, horses cared for, food consumed, and then the party slept.

When the sun rose, they did as well and continued along the road. For two days the cycle continued, with little talk between the company. Each morning, Damien would wake up to find Selene an arm's length away, on her side, one arm beneath her head, the other stretched out toward him. He would almost swear two women lived inside of Selene: the cold one who kept herself isolated from the others, and the quiet woman with hidden beauty who he found at daybreak, moments before she awoke.

On the third day, it began to rain. Oiled cloaks were pulled out of saddlebags, and everyone rode at a slower pace. The air grew cold and a biting wind whipped raindrops across Damien's face. No one spoke as they rode through the mud and downpour. When it grew too dark to see, Taegis led them to an outcropping of trees just off Trader's Road.

It was drier beneath the branches, but not by much. The horses huddled on one side beneath the trees as Sten tried to get a fire going. After a few minutes, he was able to produce a small flame, but there was only enough dry wood to last a short time. Everyone sat around the fire and ate stale bread and dried meat.

Damien laid out two wool blankets between the nearest tree trunk and fire. "Selene," he said quietly. When she looked up, he pointed to the blanket near the fire. "For you."

She nodded and came over. "Thank you." She lay down without hesitation, wrapping her cloak and the other half of the blanket around her. Days ago, she would have been wary about sleeping near everyone else. It appeared she was becoming more comfortable with their small party—and with him in particular. Good.

The fire burned down low as the others prepared for bed. Damien lay on his back, looking up through the thick array of tree branches. The rain had stopped, but a cold wind still blew. Selene was already asleep nearby, Cohen curled up on the other side of the fire. Sten started snoring and Karl grunted. Taegis kept the first watch.

Just as Damien's eyelids started falling, Selene gasped and sat up, clutching her cloak. She looked around as if to see if anyone had spotted her. Damien kept his eyes as slits and watched her. She twisted around and slowly lay back down, her face toward him.

Minutes ticked by; the only sounds were the last few snaps and crackles from the dying fire and the *drip-drip* of rainwater through the forest.

Damien shut his eyes.

And felt something touch his hand.

He yanked his hand back and opened his eyes. He glanced to his right and found Selene staring at him, her hand stretched out, her fingers mere inches from where his had been.

"Selene?" he whispered, frowning. Had it been her fingers that touched his hand?

She quickly drew her hand back to her chest.

"Are you all right? Do you need something?" he whispered.

"No." The word came out strangled.

"Did you touch me?"

There was a pause. "Yes."

"Were you trying to wake me up?"

There was another pause. "No."

His frown deepened. Then why had she touched him?

"I'm sorry, I didn't mean to wake you." She began to shift around.

"Selene. Stop."

She glanced over her shoulder.

Damien spotted Taegis on the other side of the camp. Either he could not hear them, or he was ignoring them. The other men slept on. Damien looked back at Selene. "Is something wrong?"

She lay down on her back, her face toward the sky, her fingers curled around the edge of her blanket. He could barely see the contours of her face in the dying firelight.

Just when he thought she wasn't going to answer, she whispered, "I can't sleep."

Damien blinked. That didn't explain why she had reached over and touched him.

"The nightmares won't stop. Every time I close my eyes, they're there. I've barely slept since we left the Hyr River."

Damien knit his brows. "What about the inn? You seemed to sleep fine there. Is it the strain of traveling? Or the newness of everything?"

"I don't know."

She still hadn't explained why she had reached out to him. Did she find comfort in touch? That was the last thing he would have expected of her. Or had it been an accidental brush of her fingers? "Can I do anything to help you?"

He heard her quiet intake of breath.

"Selene?" he whispered.

She rolled onto her side so she was facing him. "Can I . . . touch your hand?"

His eyes went wide and every notion of sleep disappeared. Selene wanted to hold hands? His heart started thudding inside his chest and his mouth went dry. Why was he nervous? He'd touched the hand of a woman many times. He'd even held Selene's hand when they were running toward the river. Was it because they were now married? Because she was his wife and unlike any other woman to him?

Slowly he pulled his hand out of his oiled cloak and reached forward.

Selene lifted her hand, then hesitated. "Damien," she whispered.

"Yes?" he answered, surprised at her use of his name.

"You know what I can do."

What did she . . . Oh. Her dreamwalking gift. He started to say the word but found no sound came when he moved his mouth. Apparently he was too close to the other men to speak of it. "I know only a little."

"I'm afraid I cannot explain it here. But I want to be honest with you. I . . . that is . . ." She sighed. "I've held your hand every night since the inn at Rone."

"You have?"

"Yes. I should have asked before I did it. But I was desperate. And so tired. You . . . you help me sleep. The nightmares cannot follow me there."

"I don't underst— Wait." He sat up and stared at her. Out of the corner of his eye, he spotted Taegis turn in their direction. He leaned toward Selene until there were only inches between their faces. "You mean when you hold my hand . . ."

"Yes." Her eyes turned downward. "I shouldn't have done it."

He didn't understand what being a dreamer meant or how her gift worked, but however she did it, she just admitted she had been doing it to him. He tried to recall the last few nights. Could he see her inside his mind? Was that how it worked? He couldn't remember. He couldn't remember any of his dreams since leaving Rook Castle.

He ran a hand across his face. He wasn't sure what to do. She had entered his dreams without his consent. Part of him felt betrayed. How could she use her gift on him? He would never do that to someone else. The very thought made his pulse beat faster. An overwhelming desire to turn around and lie down with his back to her surged inside of him.

But another part of him felt for her as he gazed at her shadowed face, full of fear and vulnerability. He had seen how exhausted she was. And she'd been honest about what she had been doing the last few nights even though she could have kept it a secret. Was it really that bad that somehow, someway she had found it possible to find rest through him?

If only he knew more about what she could do . . .

Selene withdrew her hand. "I understand," she said quietly. Then she rolled over onto her side, her back to him, and pulled her cloak up around her neck.

Damien lay back slowly. No, this was not the kind of man he wanted to be. If it helped Selene—if it helped his *wife*—to hold his hand in order to sleep, then he would do it, even if he didn't yet understand how or why.

Damien reached out and ran his fingers over her shoulder. "Selene."

She tensed at his touch. A moment later, she twisted her head around. "Yes?"

"You can hold my hand," he whispered.

She froze. He could almost see the battle inside of her, the same one he had experienced moments ago: to turn around or to turn back. Just when he was sure she was going to keep her back to him, she turned to face him instead.

"Are you sure?" she whispered back.

"Yes," he said, drowning out his own concerns and focusing on her needs instead.

She hesitated again, then pulled out her hand. Their fingers meshed, his warm ones between her cooler ones. He laid their hands on the edge of her blanket, right between them.

He let out a long breath and relaxed. This felt right. "Good night, Selene."

He swore he heard a strangled sob from her. "Thank you," she said, almost inaudibly.

Damien rolled onto his back, keeping his hand in hers. Her fingers were so small compared to his, but they fit perfectly in his hand.

He stared up at the canopy of darkness, then closed his eyes. He had no idea what the future held for them. And he still hardly knew the woman whose fingers were intertwined with his.

But perhaps reaching out his hand was a first step in getting to know her more.

7

Selene slowly woke to a clear sky above and something warm between her fingers. She blinked and looked over to find Damien still asleep, his hand in hers. She listened to his soft breathing while studying every contour of his face. Her throat tightened. She almost didn't tell him last night. He would never have known she dreamwalked inside his mind to find peace.

But the longer she was with him, the more the guilt of her deception had grown until she finally spoke last night. If she was going to put the past behind her, including the Ravenwood secrets, then she had to speak up, even if he turned away from her.

But he didn't.

She swallowed as she gazed at him. More than anything she wanted to know this man. Damien was unlike any other lord she had met. And his soul . . .

Sten sat up and rubbed his eyes. Grey stubble covered his chin, and his hair was even messier than usual.

Selene yanked her hand away and tucked it inside her cloak, hoping he didn't see. Her gaze traveled across the rest of the camp. Karl sat on the other side of the camp with a bored expression on his face, his dark hair almost covering one eye. Cohen snored near one of the trees. Taegis sat with his back against a nearby tree trunk, his arms folded and his eyes closed.

Damien blinked and shifted onto his back. Cohen started moving as well, which meant soon everyone would be awake and it would be time to get on the road again.

Selene stood. After smoothing out her clothes, she reached for the blanket and headed for the trees to shake out the dirt and leaves. Behind her, she could hear the men speaking in soft tones. When she returned, she found Damien sitting up and conversing with Taegis, while Sten dug around in their supplies. Karl stared at her from across the camp, his lips tight.

"Good morning, my lady," Cohen said as he walked in her direction.

"Good morning," she replied as he passed her and headed into the trees.

At the sound of her voice, Damien turned.

Her heart leapt into her throat as he gazed at her. Her body alternated between hot and cold, and adrenaline raced across her nerves. Selene swallowed nervously. What was wrong with her?

Sten broke their connection as he passed out small loaves of brown bread and a waterskin to share. After a quick meal, the horses were loaded and the small party was back on Trader's Road. The air was muggy from yesterday's rain, but already a cool wind was blowing the humidity away, leaving a fresh, clean feel to the bare forest. Small insects thrummed beneath fallen leaves, and the occasional squirrel chattered overhead.

Sten led the way, Cohen beside him. Selene rode alone between the men, the beige mare rocking gently beneath her saddle. She knew where Damien was behind her. It was as though every part of her was attuned to him. She could hear his words as he spoke to Taegis and could almost feel his gaze upon her back every few minutes.

"We should be to Nor Esen by midday tomorrow," she overheard Taegis say to Damien.

Nor Esen. The famed capital city of the Northern Shores.

After hearing her father describe the coastline and the city built along the cliffs overlooking the sea, Selene had always wanted to visit Nor Esen. And if her time in Damien's dreams was any indication, the coast was lined with white sand, rocky cliffs, and water as far as the eye could see. A country far different than her own home in the Magyr Mountains.

But these were not the circumstances by which she had ever thought to visit Nor Esen. She would have come as an envoy of House Ravenwood on some diplomatic mission. She would have enjoyed the luxury of a visiting dignitary. And afterward, she would have returned to Rook Castle.

Instead, this city would be her home.

Selene gripped the reins tightly between her fingers as her stomach began to churn. What would the people of the Northern Shores think of their new grand lady? She had a feeling she was not what they were expecting. It was likely thought that House Maris would align with a more agreeable house, like House Luceras, or that Damien would marry someone from a lesser house within their own nation. Not the Lady of Ice of the mountain people. What would she do if they didn't accept her?

What I've always done, she thought, lifting her head. She would survive by burying her heart.

"Watch out!"

Selene barely had time to register the words when an arrow zipped by her head, missing her by inches.

Her training took over.

She was already off her horse opposite the side of where the arrow had come from, using her mount as a shield. Shouts went up between Taegis and Sten as the men went into action. More arrows flew through the woods, this time from the front and back of the road, but still on the same side. That meant that the tree line behind her was the safest place at this moment.

With a sharp twist, Selene turned and dashed for the trees. Out of the corner of her eye, she saw Cohen doing the same. Seconds later, she crouched behind a thick tree trunk and pressed her body as close as she could. Her heart thrummed inside her ears.

Selene moved her head to the right and looked out. Taegis and the other guards had their swords out and were surrounding Damien. From the other side of the road, a handful of men dressed in black stepped out of the forest, with dark pieces of fabric tied around their heads that hid all but their eyes. Each one carried a simple sword.

"What do you want?" Taegis said, his sword in position, as Sten's eyes swept the tree line and noted Selene's and Cohen's positions. Karl stood on the other side of Damien, his sword drawn, facing the bandits on the other side of the road.

Selene scowled. They were outnumbered, and she didn't have her swords with her. And could Cohen even fight?

The tallest highwayman stepped forward. "We want all your valuables," he said, his voice muffled by the cloth.

"Is that it?" Taegis said.

"Yes."

"If that is all, then we will accommodate your request."

As Taegis took a step back to confer with Damien, the leader spoke up again. "Oh yes, and one more thing."

Taegis's body tightened as he faced the leader again. Selene pressed closer to hear.

"We also want the woman."

For one second, the world stopped as Selene stared at the man in black. A trickle of fear spread across the back of her mind, but it disappeared in a wave of anger. Her eyes narrowed and she clenched her hands. Did that highwayman think he could take a lady of Ravenwood? Dart'an! She had come too far, given up too much to be taken by some men hiding out in a forest. These bandits would discover she would not go so easily.

She barely heard Taegis's answer before the fight started. Her eyes roved across the forest floor as the sound of clanking swords filled the air. She may not have her dual swords, but she still had her skills. All she needed were two medium branches roughly the size and length of her swords. . . .

There. She picked up one stick from between the fallen leaves, then spotted another half hidden in the dense foliage. As she bent down to retrieve it, Cohen yelled, "Lady Selene, behind you!"

Selene jumped to her feet, twisting around with her makeshift swords in full swing.

One of the highwaymen barreled toward her with a rope in hand, but no sword. Good. That meant they wanted her alive.

Selene smiled. The man had no idea what was coming.

She positioned her feet, then brought the wooden weapons in front of her. The moment the man stepped within her reach, Selene swung her right arm down across her body, catching the man across the cheek and sending his face flying to the side. Without stopping, she brought her left one over and struck the area below his rib cage.

The man went down with a groan.

Selene looked over her shoulder. "Cohen! Tie him up."

Cohen sat frozen, his eyes wide as he stared at her.

"Now!"

He blinked, then moved.

Selene wasted no time to see if the monk was following her orders. Taegis and the others were being overrun and needed her help.

Selene stepped from the tree line, her weapons ready.

Taegis was engaged with the leader and another bandit across the road. Karl pushed another man down the road with a flurry of hits, his height and youth giving him the advantage.

Damien was holding his own against a burly man with thick black hair. The black fabric slipped down from the man's face to reveal a jagged scar across his cheek and a crooked nose.

As Sten subdued his man, another arrow flew from the forest. Sten swore loudly and took off for the tree line, no doubt after the archer, his thick, powerful legs pumping as he ran.

As Sten disappeared into the forest, another

bandit emerged from the trees up the road and headed for Damien. Taegis was currently engaged in a fight, and Karl was even farther away.

Damien needed her help.

Selene dashed along the road, bypassing Damien, and met the man as he made his way along the dirt path. She stopped halfway between Damien and the approaching highwayman and repositioned her makeshift swords to have her right arm up and across her body, her left ready to swing.

The bandit stopped just outside her reach. "Move," he snarled through the black cloth across his face, his green eyes narrowed. "Move and you won't get hurt."

Selene answered by standing still, ready to strike the moment he took another step.

His eyes crinkled as he studied her weapons and laughed. "You come at me with sticks?"

Selene remained motionless. Though his voice was muffled through the cloth, she thought she detected an unfamiliar accent.

His eyes narrowed again, and he gave out a shout. The moment he stepped forward, Selene swung her right sword down at an angle, catching his jaw with a powerful swing and ripping the cloth away from his mouth.

He staggered back, but she gave him no time to recover. She moved into the empty space and thrust her left stick hard into his gut, then swung her right stick across the other side of his face, sending his head flying in the other direction. Then she brought her leg up and kicked him in the same spot she had hit moments before with her left stick. The man stumbled back, one arm across his stomach as he moaned and spit up blood.

There was a shout behind her.

Selene spun around. Damien was hunched over, one hand on his thigh as he held his sword up to block an incoming hit from his opponent. Taegis was far away now, along the tree line, and Karl down the road.

Damien's sword sagged and his face twisted in pain. The man prepared for another blow—

Breathing hard, Selene sprinted toward the bandit. As she approached, she suddenly jumped and rotated her body, using her momentum to swing her whole body around and bring both sticks in concussive cracks across the man's neck. If the sticks had been her swords, she would have severed his head. Instead, he dropped to the ground, unconscious.

Selene landed a few feet from Damien and gulped in a lungful of air. It was one thing to practice on a dummy, or her mother, or Amara, and quite another to actually fight. Adrenaline coursed through her body, but already her limbs were growing weary.

"I've been hit," Damien said through clenched

teeth as he clutched his leg. Sweat poured down his face. An arrow stuck out from his thigh, above the knee. It looked like it was lodged in the muscle. Still, it was a wound and—

He looked up. "Watch out!"

Selene swung around, bringing her branches with her, and caught the incoming sword on her right stick, directing the sword's trajectory away from her body. Her stick cracked under the blow, sending a fissure up the wood. Not good.

"Damien! Toss me your sword!" Selene yelled, glancing back as she threw down the broken stick.

He didn't even hesitate. He pitched the sword to her, blade up. She caught it by the hilt with her right hand just as the man's blade came down on her other stick.

Crack.

Without missing a beat, Selene threw the other stick aside and brought both hands along the hilt of Damien's sword. She had very little experience with a single sword. That was Amara's area of expertise. But she would do whatever she could to keep herself and Damien alive.

She readjusted her grip on the unfamiliar—and heavier—weapon. Sweat soaked into her hair and stung her eyes. Her arms shook slightly. Her vision narrowed until all she could see was the man in front of her and the burning need to stay on her feet long enough to defeat this opponent.

The bandit laughed as he swung at her again.

Selene brought the sword up and caught his blade with her own. Each time he tried to find an opening, she blocked him. But that was all she could do. She breathed hard, her face hot, her arms shaking.

Another hit sent her stepping back.

I can't do this much longer, a part of her mind screamed.

She gritted her teeth. *I have no choice. I won't die today. And I won't let Damien die either.*

She barely had time to block his next swing.

"Your companions should have given us what we wanted," the man said, panting. At least he was tiring as well.

Yes, he definitely had an accent. She could hear it now that the cloth was away from his face. "I don't think . . . you know who . . . we are," Selene replied, breathless.

"Argh!" The man went for another swing—

And Taegis intercepted it. Within two blows, the man was on the ground with a deep cut along his arm.

"Tie him up with the others," Taegis barked. Karl was already moving forward with a long piece of rope.

Selene stumbled back, the tip of the sword down on the ground. The forest spun around her.

"Selene!" She heard Damien call out. "Quick! Someone help her!"

She collapsed on her side, and the sword slipped from her fingers.

Cold water touched her lips as someone held her head up. Selene took a sip and slowly blinked her eyes. Her body shivered as a cool wind blew across her sweat-soaked body.

"Are you all right?" Cohen asked, hovering over her.

"Yes." She sat up and rubbed her face. "I just overexerted myself."

"I had no idea a lady like you could fight."

Selene didn't answer. She did what she had to do. But the others had seen what she was capable of. Would they still trust her?

A couple of feet away, Taegis talked quietly with Damien, who sat on the ground, holding his right leg gingerly. Only a small part of the shaft stuck out, but from the way he was moving, it seemed the arrowhead remained. The older man's hair had come undone from the leather tie and hung around Taegis's shoulders in an array of dark blond and grey. A cut ran across his cheek. Over to the right, eight men were tied up, with Karl and Sten standing watch over them.

Taegis straightened and turned around. "There is a village east of here, about a half day's walk, called Clonah. We can leave these men in the custody of the local authorities until they can be brought to Nor Esen. Sten, Karl, you will be in charge of delivering them."

"Why are we not taking Lord Maris to Clonah if it's closer than Nor Esen?" Karl asked with a scowl. Selene wondered the same thing.

"I don't know if there is a healer there. And even if there is, I don't trust anyone but our own court healer," Taegis said.

That made sense. If they arrived in the village and found no healer, Damien would be worse off.

"I know the way to Clonah," Sten said. Karl nodded.

"I will escort Lord Damien and Lady Selene to Nor Esen. If any of these men give you trouble, slay them." Taegis let his gaze fall over the small group sitting sullenly on the ground. "It is by the mercy of Grand Lord Maris that you are still alive. If you try to escape, then you forfeit his good favor."

As Taegis turned around, Selene approached him. "Sir Taegis," she said quietly.

"Yes, my lady?" he asked, seemingly surprised by her address.

"You may want to question these men. I heard one speak when the cloth fell from his face. He has a foreign accent. I'm not sure from where, but certainly not from our lands."

"I see." He looked over his shoulder, concern on his face. "I will question them when they are delivered to Nor Esen."

"Up, you rascals," Sten said as he pulled on the end of the rope with one hand, holding his sword in the other. Karl flashed the group a wicked smile, looking even more menacing with that one lock of dark hair hanging over his eye, almost daring any of them to get out of line.

The men grumbled and stood. One kept glancing at the forest, then spotted Karl and seemed to change his mind. Selene had no doubt Sten and Karl would do what they needed to deliver the bandits to Clonah, or whatever that village was called. They were fortunate that Damien was kind enough to let them live. If it had been her mother they had attacked, they would all be dead.

Taegis watched the two guards herd the highwaymen east, then turned. His shoulders sagged, and he wiped his forehead before pulling his hair back and securing it at the nape of his neck.

His eyes focused on Selene. "My lady, I have not had a chance to ask if you are hurt."

Selene swept her braid back over her shoulder and straightened her back. Already she was feeling much better. "No. Not even a bruise." No one had come near enough to her to even scrape her skin, although the last bandit had come close. Taegis watched her a moment longer, studying her.

Seemingly satisfied with her answer, he turned to the monk. "Cohen?"

Cohen glanced up. "I'm all right."

Taegis nodded. "Then I will need you to assist me in helping Lord Damien. We cannot remove the arrow in his leg. The arrowhead missed the bone, but it seems to have a hook at the end. We will need a skilled healer to remove it."

Selene grimaced. She had seen such arrowheads before; their curved sides hooked the head into flesh, making them hard to remove. She couldn't imagine what it felt like. Then a sudden thought struck her. "The arrowhead isn't poisoned, is it?"

Taegis shook his head. "Not that I can tell. But the sooner we arrive in Nor Esen, the better." With that, he gathered Sten and Karl's mounts and secured them to his and Cohen's saddles. "All right, let's go."

Selene watched as Taegis and Cohen assisted Damien up into his saddle. Damien let out a grunt of pain and his face paled for a moment, then he gripped the reins and straightened.

Her eyebrows drew together. Could Damien really ride for over a day with an arrow in his leg? She turned and mounted her own horse, a whisper of worry shadowing the back of her mind.

8

The four travelers stopped as dusk settled across the forest and only a few more minutes of daylight remained. Taegis gathered what dry wood he could and set about making a fire right there in the middle of the road, the only place where there was no brush or foliage.

Selene pulled a blanket out of her saddlebag and laid it near the small blaze Taegis was coaxing to life, while Cohen helped Damien from his horse.

"Here," she said, patting the blanket.

Damien groaned and panted as he hobbled over with Cohen's assistance. "Thank you," he said and lay down.

Selene looked around. Surely there was something more she could do. She spotted Karl's saddlebag and proceeded to retrieve the guard's blanket as well. She rolled the woolen cloth up, then brought it back over to Damien.

"For your head," she said as she knelt down.

He opened one eye. "Thank you." He lifted his head, and she pushed the makeshift pillow beneath.

"How are you feeling?" she asked quietly.

"It hurts."

Her eyes wandered over to his leg. It appeared

swollen beneath his pants. Blood crusted around the wound, but the arrow seemed to be stopping any further blood flow. Keeping the arrow in had been a good idea. "Is there anything else I can do?"

He looked up at her. "Water, please."

As Selene went for a waterskin, Cohen brought over one of the last rounds of bread and gave half to Damien. He broke off a piece and slowly chewed without sitting up. She brought the water back and knelt beside him.

She popped off the cork and held the skin close to his chest. Then she placed a hand beneath his head. "Here you go."

He sat up with her assistance. She tipped the skin up, and he took a long drink. "I feel much better," he said, his lips curving upward in the corners. His blue eyes looked deeper in the weak firelight.

Something fluttered inside her middle as she brought his head back down. "Let me know if you need more."

Damien nodded and went back to eating his bread. After they all finished the simple meal, Cohen and Taegis took a few minutes for their personal needs.

Selene laid Sten's blanket out near Damien's and proceeded to lie down.

"Where did you learn to fight like that?" he asked quietly.

Selene froze, her mind racing for an answer. "My mother," she said finally. "It's a style that's been passed down for generations."

He turned his head and looked at her. "Why does your family fight? The only houses I know of who teach their ladies to fight are House Merek and House Luceras."

Selene lay down on her back and looked up at the stars. A sliver of a moon hung low across the horizon and a dozen stars shone overhead. Damien still didn't know about the missions, or the deaths. So many deaths. All he knew was the Ravenwood gift still existed.

"We fight to defend ourselves. Men are not the only ones who can die by the sword." How would he react when he finally found out what she had been trained to do? That her gift was one born of blood and fear?

"I see."

There was a rustling sound. Selene glanced over to find Damien extending his hand toward her. "Good night, Selene," he said, his hand resting on the ground between them. Then he closed his eyes.

Selene's throat tightened. After all he'd been through, she hadn't expected this gesture. And yet here he was, holding his hand out toward her, waiting.

She swallowed and slowly moved her own hand until her palm lay on top of his and their fingers were intertwined. His hand was warm, warding off the autumn chill in the air.

Minutes later, Taegis and Cohen returned to the camp, talking in low tones.

Selene watched them from the corner of her eye. For a moment, she considered letting go of Damien's hand. This small touch felt too private for the eyes of others. But the thought of facing her nightmares alone made her leave her hand where it was, and she closed her eyes instead.

Soon the camp grew quiet, with only the soft snap and crackle of the fire and the occasional hoot from a nearby owl. Selene snuggled down deep within her blanket and let out a long contented sigh, ready to find her way inside Damien's dreams.

Hot.

So hot.

Damien's dreamscape was a whirlwind of memories, feelings, and shadows. Selene could barely maintain control of her raven form along the currents of his mind. Every time she brought him back to the coastline of white sand and calming waves, his dreams would take a sharp turn, thrusting her into a new place.

People from his past flashed across his mind: a loving couple who looked vaguely like Damien; a boy with unkempt hair and a mischievous smile;

a trio of children with light blond hair gathered under an ancient oak tree; Damien standing on the beach on a stormy day, watching tiny boats put out to sea.

Over and over they flashed by at dizzying speeds. And the heat inside the dreamscape was almost unbearable. Even when she was flying above the stormy sea, it felt like she was inside a fire.

A low moan echoed inside her head, then Selene found herself flung from the dreamscape.

She woke with a start and sat up. Darkness still lingered across the forest and road, but the first rays of dawn were spreading across the sky. A brisk cold wind swept across her body, sending shivers over her skin.

As she wrapped the blanket around her shoulders, there was another moan to her right. She looked over. Damien's face glistened in the dim light. His brows were pressed together, and his lips moved as if he were speaking. Then he jerked to the side and moaned again.

Suddenly Taegis was there, kneeling beside Damien, his hand along his forehead. "Hot," he muttered. He looked at Selene. "Can you be ready to go in five minutes?"

Selene didn't even need to think. "Yes," she said, standing. She shook out the blanket and went into the forest while Taegis woke Cohen. By the time she was back, both men were packing the horses. Damien lay on the ground, oblivious to the movement around him.

Once they were packed, Taegis turned around. He stared at Damien and frowned. "I'm not sure Lord Damien can ride by himself. We will need to take turns holding him up and switching horses. That way we can make our way back to Nor Esen as fast as possible. I'll go first. Cohen, I'll need your help getting Damien up onto my horse."

Selene headed toward her horse while the men placed Damien up on Taegis's steed. Minutes later, they were on the road again, traveling north toward Nor Esen. The sky had brightened, and birds sang in the trees overhead. Sten and Karl's horses were attached to Cohen's saddle.

Selene rode ahead and caught up to Taegis. "Is it poison?" she asked.

"I don't think so. I think his wound is infected. Hence the fever."

Damien's head lulled to the side, then his eyes blinked. "Wh-where am I?"

"On the road to Nor Esen," Taegis said.

Damien turned his head. "Why am I riding with you?"

"Do you feel like you can ride by yourself?"

Damien paused, his face still glistening and now pale. "No. I feel weak all over."

"I thought so. Let us help you, my lord. We should be to Northwind Castle by midday."

Damien nodded, then closed his eyes.

An hour later, Cohen took his turn riding with Damien on a fresh mount, the other horses attached to Selene's saddle. The sky was clear overhead and the trees thick, with conifers set between the naked oaks and maples.

Midmorning, Taegis took Damien again. Selene almost offered but wasn't sure how well she could hold Damien and guide her horse at the same time.

Just as the sun reached its zenith, there was a break between the trees and a city came into view. Selene's eyes went wide, and she sucked in a breath. A collection of multistoried houses, slate-colored tile roofs, turrets, ivory towers, and round domes rose in tiers along high cliffs, above a thick grey wall. Light blue banners emblazoned with the symbol of House Maris snapped against the salty wind on the topmost poles. Trees of every color and type were scattered throughout the city. And the entrance to it all was an enormous double gate made of pale wood, with waves carved along its surface.

Nor Esen. The famed city of the Northern Shores.

It was magnificent, incredible . . .

And foreign.

A heaviness settled over her as she followed the men toward the large gate. To the right of the city, the trees grew sparse and beyond them, she could see endless blue.

The sea.

The thought lightened her mind for a moment before she sunk back into the hollowness inside her chest. Suddenly, she wanted to go back home, longing for what was familiar, what she knew and loved—the open sky above the Magyr Mountains and the pine-scented air. The open walkways that let the crisp, cold mountain winds flow through Rook Castle. Deep snows and the howl of the timber wolves.

But there was no going back. There was only forward.

Selene straightened in her saddle and held the reins tightly between her hands. She was Lady Maris now, wife to the grand lord of this land. As such, she would enter her new home with pride and dignity.

She buried deep the feelings of homesickness until she felt nothing. Then, with her chin raised, she watched the gates open up to Nor Esen.

People gathered in the streets as the small party entered the city. Taegis kept one hand near his sword, the other wrapped around Damien's waist and holding the reins. Selene rode beside him, her eyes forward. Most of the glances sent their way were focused on Damien, usually followed by gasps and whispers. A few curious stares landed on her as she rode along the cobblestone street, but she did not turn. Inside, her heart beat like a trapped bird.

The street wove along the tiers of the city, first left, then right, as it made its way to the other end of Nor Esen, where a castle of grey stone stood at the edge of the wall. She recalled Damien saying his room overlooked the sea.

A smaller wall surrounded the castle, and the street led up to gates made of similar grey wood. They were open, with a guard on either side. The guard on the left waved them inside, a frown on his face as Damien rode by, assisted by Taegis.

The courtyard to Northwind Castle was small compared with Rook Castle. A wide stairway led up to ornate double doors, while a narrower staircase followed the right side up along the wall. Walkways with arched windows lined the second and third stories. Two guards marched across the courtyard, dressed in leather with a blue tabard.

Taegis pulled up on the reins and stopped his mount in the middle of the courtyard. "Jenkin! Bryce! I need your help."

The two men rushed over. "Jenkin, help me get Lord Maris to the court healer. Bryce, run ahead and make sure Healer Sildaern is there. If not, find him immediately."

"Yes, sir," the men responded, the shorter one running toward the double doors, taking the steps two at a time, while the taller one stood beside Taegis's horse and lifted his hands.

Damien blinked his eyes and looked around. "Northwind?"

"Yes," Taegis said as he placed one of Damien's arms over his shoulder. "We're home." The other guard did the same, and between the men, they assisted Damien up the stairs and through the front doors.

Selene started after them, leaving the horses and Cohen in the courtyard. She had no desire to be left behind, and deep down she was worried about Damien. What would happen to him? What would happen to her if he . . .

She clenched her hands. *No, I'm not going to think about that now.*

No one met her at the front doors, so she walked in.

The walls, ceiling, and floor inside the castle were also made of cool grey stone. A large circular rug made of light blue encompassed the main floor. Three hallways led away from the room, each one lined with light blue runners trimmed in silver. A decorative railing graced the second floor where the three hallways met above and circled the open entrance hall. Windows were interspersed between the second-floor corridors, letting in natural light. At the very top hung an intricate silver chandelier, ready to light the area at night.

She paused for a moment, taking it all in. She had imagined a cold, dark castle, similar to how she had first envisioned the Northern Shores. Instead, there was a cool beauty to this place. Then it hit her. This . . . this was her new home.

Taegis, Damien, and the guards disappeared along the hall to the right on the first floor. She hurried forward, her cloak swishing behind her.

There were no pictures on the walls. Instead, images of the sea were carved into the stone: waves, fish, turtles, and creatures and plants she had no names for. So beautiful. And so different than Rook Castle, with its dark stone and open airways. Part of her wanted to reach out and touch the uneven surface, but she held her hand in place. She had no time, not if she wanted to keep up with Taegis—

Selene crashed into a short, stocky man coming around the corner.

She stepped back and rubbed her chin where his head had connected with her.

He massaged his head, a scowl on his plump face. "What in all the sand hills—" His eyes settled on Selene and his scowl deepened. "Who are you? And what are you doing in Northwind Castle?"

Selene pointed down the corridor, her heart sinking as she realized Taegis and Damien had disappeared. "I'm here with Lord Damien."

He glared at her. "His lordship is not here today. Now turn around and leave."

Selene narrowed her eyes. "No. I said I'm—"

"Who do you think you are that you can

say such a thing to me?" He crossed his arms, drawing her attention to his fine blue tunic and sleeveless jacket with a golden chain around his neck, a dozen keys attached to the end. His grey hair was thick and curly, and his eyes were a pale blue.

"I'm—I'm—" A flush crept up her cheeks as she remembered her own attire: torn black pants, tunic, and stained cloak. Not the usual garments for a woman of her stature. Not the garments for any woman, really. She lifted a hand and touched her hair. They had been in such a hurry this morning she hadn't taken the time to redo her braid and could feel the stray hairs tickling her face. She looked anything but a lady.

Dart'an! What could she say? *I'm Lord Damien's wife? Ha! Like he'd believe that.*

"As the steward for House Maris, I am telling you to leave this castle before I call the guards."

A sliver of anger trembled through her body. "I told you, I'm with Lord Damien."

"All right, then. The guards it is. Guards!" he yelled. "We have an intruder."

Selene breathed through her nose, flexing her fingers as she tried to figure out what to do next. Part of her wanted to tell the steward off. He had no jurisdiction over her, a lady of Ravenwood and now wife to his own lord. Mother *never* would have allowed a common man to treat her in such a way.

But just as she went to speak, she paused. Was this how she wanted her first interaction to be at Northwind Castle? Escorted from the castle by the guards or attempting to force her way inside? Neither would reflect well on Damien.

Her shoulders fell. This was not the reception she had imagined, not by any stretch of the imagination. But this was her home now, and as such, she would respond how she imagined a lady of House Maris would. She held up a hand. "Wait."

The steward stopped yelling and eyed her warily.

"I will go," she said with as much dignity as possible. She would wait in the courtyard until Taegis or someone came back for her.

"Good choice." The steward remained where he was. A guard appeared from another hall, his sword drawn.

"Steward Bertram?" the guard said, his eyes on Selene.

"Please escort this woman from Northwind Castle."

"Yes, sir."

Selene kept her chin lifted as she turned, but humiliation, anger, and loneliness pounded within her heart. She clenched her hands, pressing her fingernails into the soft part of her palms, and took each breath slowly.

"My lady?" Boots pounded along the hallway.

Cohen appeared seconds later, his burgundy robes flying behind him. "My lady," he panted as he crossed the corridor. "You left, and I couldn't find you—what's going on?"

"Do you know this woman?" Steward Bertram asked. The guard paused, a look of confusion on his face.

"I do. This is—"

"Lady Selene!" Taegis's voice rang out behind the steward. The steward turned and dropped his arms. The guard gave Taegis a small bow as he approached.

"Thank the Light you're here," Steward Bertram said, taking a step toward Taegis. "This woman was prowling the castle. I was going to have one of the guards escort her away, but now that you're here—"

"This woman is Lady Selene, Lord Damien's new wife!" Taegis's voice boomed across the corridor.

The steward froze. Slowly, he glanced back, his face pale.

"I can attest to that as well," Cohen said, "since I performed the rites of matrimony myself."

The guard looked between the three men, and then at Selene. He bowed. "My lady."

Steward Bertram opened his mouth and closed it, like a fish out of water. "I . . . I . . . I had no idea."

Taegis shook his head and closed the gap

between him and Selene. "My lady, I did not mean to leave you. My first thought was to get Lord Damien to the healer."

"I know. But I want to see him. And don't try to stop me."

The corner of his mouth quirked, and she could have sworn Taegis was pleased by her words. "My lady, I'll take you there now. But first"—he turned toward the steward—"Steward Bertram, let me present to you Lady Selene Maris, wife of Lord Damien, formerly lady of House Ravenwood."

Bertram bowed low, sweat coating his forehead. "My lady, please forgive me. I didn't know who you were."

The former lady of Ravenwood reared up inside of her. Mother would have expected her to coldly reprimand a man like him, one who dared to lord over a lady of a Great House. But then she remembered how Damien had treated the people they had met so far on their journey with kindness and grace.

She took a deep breath and let the anger from moments earlier wash away. "I understand. There was no evidence that I was Lady Maris."

He lifted his head, a red sheen to his cheeks. "You are most gracious, my lady."

Taegis cleared his throat. "Steward Bertram, would you please see to arranging the room next to Lord Damien's for Lady Selene's use?"

"Next to his lordship's room?"

"Yes, until other arrangements can be made."

"Yes. Right away." Steward Bertram turned and hurried down the hall.

Selene sagged forward, the whiplash of emotions leaving her drained.

Taegis was by her side in a flash. "I'm sorry, I shouldn't have left you behind. Here, take my arm and I will lead you to his lordship."

"Thank you, Taegis." Selene tucked her hand in the crook of his elbow, thankful for something to hold on to.

"Healer Sildaern is taking the arrowhead out right now, then he will treat his lordship's fever."

"Good."

Taegis sighed. "I apologize for Steward Bertram's behavior. He can be a bit gruff, and sometimes he forgets his place in his effort to protect the young lord, but deep down he has a good heart. I'm sorry you had to meet him this way." He turned and looked at her. "Why didn't you tell him who you were?"

"He never gave me a chance." Selene raised an eyebrow at Taegis. "And I certainly do not look like a lady in this attire."

He shook his head. "You're right. Yet another reason I shouldn't have left you. I don't think anyone was expecting Lord Damien to come home with a bride. There were alliances with other houses in the works."

Selene wondered if Taegis meant something more with that statement or if he was simply stating the facts. She was sure House Ravenwood was the last house anyone thought would align with House Maris, and yet here she was. The circumstances behind their rushed union might lead some to doubt the validity of the marriage, save that it was enacted by a monk and witnessed by others.

She sighed and continued along the corridor with Taegis. Not only was she entering this castle and Great House as a stranger, she was entering as a potentially unwanted stranger.

9

Taegis took the hall to the right on the first floor and led Selene down the corridor. Silver sconces were attached along the supporting pillars between the walls, each with a single candle inside, ready to light the hallway. Closed doors stood every twenty to thirty feet, made from the same greyish wood as the outside doors. The air held a cool feel to it and smelled clean.

After two turns and another corridor, they neared the end of the hallway, where a guard stood near the last door.

"Sir Taegis," the guard said with a dip of his head.

"Cedric."

The guard glanced curiously at Selene.

"Cedric, may I present to you Lady Selene, Lord Damien's new wife."

Cedric's eyes grew wide, and he bobbed his head. "My lady."

"She wishes to see Lord Damien."

"Of course. Healer Sildaern is with his lordship right now." Cedric opened the door and stepped back. Taegis entered first, Selene close behind.

The room was medium sized, with a roaring fire in the stone fireplace against the right wall. Steam rose from the spout of a black kettle hung over the fire. In the middle of the room stood a long rough wooden table covered in old books, jars, an array of dried herbs and flowers, and a stone mortar and pestle. A strong herbal scent filled the room, but Selene could not place the smell. Against the left wall were three beds. Damien lay in the nearest one, a wool blanket pulled across his body.

His eyes fluttered, then opened. "Taegis?" he said in a raspy voice.

A longing spread within her. She hadn't expected to feel such a strong pull toward him. Was it due to the connection she had made during her dreamwalks? Or something more?

Taegis and Selene crossed the room. "Yes, my lord. I brought Lady Selene here."

"Selene?" He turned his head and focused on her, his face glistening in the candlelight.

Her heart quickened at her name. "I'm here," she said, approaching the bed. "How do you feel?"

He gave her a wry smile. "Terrible. But glad to be home. I'm sorry I'm in such poor condition for your arrival here."

"Taegis and Cohen are taking care of me." She was not going to share how the steward had first treated her. Damien didn't need to know.

His eyes shut. "Good."

After a moment, it appeared Damien had passed into a restless sleep.

A man walked into the room seconds later, dressed in long green robes with a wooden tray in his hands. His hair was black and smooth, with the upper half tied back at the crown of his head while the rest fell to midchest. He looked almost like the male version of Lady Ayaka Rafel, and Selene wondered for a moment if the man was related to the Great House of Rafel.

"Healer Sildaern, this is Lady Selene, Damien's new wife. She insisted on seeing him."

The healer's intense gaze turned to Selene. "My lady," he said a moment later with a bow.

"Healer," Selene replied.

"I'm about to remove the arrowhead. It appears to only be a flesh wound, but the arrowhead is barbed. It's good that it was left in until I could attend to it. If it had been pulled, his lordship would have lost a lot of blood."

"Is the wound infected?"

Healer Sildaern left the tray on the long table and came to Damien's side. "I will know soon enough, and I will send word of what I find." He looked over at her with that intense stare again. "Be assured that I will do everything I can to help Lord Damien."

Selene bowed her head. "Thank you."

"Now then," he said brusquely, "I need room and space to do my work."

Selene and Taegis backed away as the healer turned and prepared his instruments on the table.

"There isn't much we can do here," Taegis said. "Why don't I show you a place you can wash up while your room is prepared?"

"Yes, that would be nice," she said distractedly, watching as Healer Sildaern measured a couple of wooden rods and nodded to himself. A set of tongs, a jar of honey, and linen lay on the tray he left on the table. Part of her wanted to stay and see how he removed the arrowhead and part of her wanted to get as far away as she could.

Taegis gently took her arm and led her out into the hallway. A moment later, a yell filled the room behind them.

The sound pierced her heart. Selene twisted around, ready to fight her way back in. Her thoughts caught up to her body, and she stopped herself, again surprised at her strong reaction to Damien's pain.

"Don't worry, my lady. Lord Damien is in good hands." Taegis tugged on her arm and started walking again. "All we would be is in the way."

There was another yell. Selene bit her lip and forced herself to keep walking. Taegis was right.

"Healer Sildaern is a cousin to House Rafel and a very gifted healer. He came two years ago in response to our desperate situation when the plague swept across the Northern Shores. Unfortunately, it was too late for Grand Lord and Lady Maris, and Lord Damien's brother, Quinn. However, Healer Sildaern chose to stay and has been with us ever since. His lordship's wounds will heal fast under Sildaern's supervision."

So she was right—the healer was related to House Rafel. Perhaps he even had a touch of healing left in his blood. She glanced at Taegis. "That's why you wanted to bring Lord Damien here instead of to that small village."

"Yes. I knew he would recover better and faster with Healer Sildaern than with a village healer."

Near the end of the hall, Taegis turned left and opened a door into a large room with a round bath in the middle of the floor. The bath was enclosed by white tile, and steam rose above the rippling water. Three windows on the far wall allowed in sunlight, and a table with linens, ointments, and soaps sat on the left.

"I thought you would like to clean up after traveling so far," Taegis said. "This bath is fed by natural hot springs here along the Northern Shores."

Selene inhaled the humid, warm air. A bath would take her mind off of Damien and the events of today. Not to mention she was ready to be rid of her travel-worn tunic and pants. They could burn these clothes for all she cared. "A bath sounds wonderful."

"I'll send in a maid with fresh clothing."

Selene nodded without turning. "Thank you, Taegis."

"I should know more about how his lordship is

doing soon and will relay that news to you." The door closed moments later.

Selene looked over the soaps and ointments, then chose simple lavender and placed it beside the circular bath, along with clean linens.

After tossing the ragged, stained clothes to the side, she stepped into the pool and let out a deep sigh. Niggling thoughts pressed against her skull, but she held them back. There were many things she would be facing in the upcoming days, but those troubles could wait. Right now, she would enjoy the water.

Minutes later, the door opened. "My lady?"

Selene jerked her head up from where she had been lying on the tile and looked back. A young woman shut the door and turned with her head bowed and dark clothing over one arm. Her nut-brown hair was gathered beneath a white cap and hung in a single braid over her shoulder.

For a moment, all Selene could see was her maidservant Renata in her baggy grey dress and hear her stutter as she spoke. She gripped her throat with one hand, her heart beating rapidly at the vision. Where was Renata now? Who was taking care of her? "I shouldn't have left her. I shouldn't have left any of them," she whispered, staring into the distance.

"My lady, are you all right?"

Selene blinked, bringing her vision back into focus.

"Yes, just . . . remembering," she said through a thick throat.

The young maidservant stared at her with big brown eyes. "I brought you clean clothes and will place them on the table here. Do you need anything else?"

"No, I don't think so."

The girl walked across the room and laid the clothing near the folded linen. "Would you like me to have your other clothes washed?"

"No. They did well for traveling, but I think they have served their purpose." More than served their purpose. She never wanted to wear them again. She couldn't help but catch the girl's look when she picked up the black clothes. Not the usual traveling attire for a lady of a Grand House. She wondered what the young woman was thinking.

"Yes, my lady," the maidservant said a moment later and bowed again before turning for the door. Then she paused and looked over her shoulder. The girl had such a fresh, young expression to her face. She couldn't be more than fourteen or fifteen springs. "Are you—are you really Lord Damien's new wife?" she said, her face growing red.

"Yes." Selene raised her hand from the water and looked at her wrinkled fingers as if to assure herself. "I am."

"Welcome, your ladyship," she said hurriedly.

Before Selene could respond back, the servant girl was gone.

She stared at the door, her heart moved by the girl's words. *Welcome.*

Her first welcome here at Northwind Castle.

It wasn't much, but it gave her the courage to get out of the bath and step into her new way of life.

The same servant girl met her outside the bathing chamber. She was shorter than Selene, with a constant smile to her lips, reminding Selene of her little sister Ophie. She already liked her.

"This way, my lady."

Selene followed the young woman along the hallway. The long dress that had been provided for her was loose, but at least it was clean. And she liked the simple lines. The undergarments were also loose, and she wondered whom they had belonged to before her.

They passed several doors before the girl stopped before the second-to-last one. At the end of the hall was a large arched window. Already the sky was growing dark outside, bringing night swiftly along.

"Here is your room, my lady." The servant girl opened the door to a bedchamber half the size of Selene's at Rook Castle. It contained typical bedroom furniture: a four-poster bed with a coverlet of light blue, changing screens with pictures of the sea embroidered along the front, a wooden chest, and a matching wardrobe. A small stone fireplace stood opposite of the bed. One large arched window graced the far wall. A door of grey wood stood near the bed.

"The seamstress will take your measurements tomorrow for your new clothing. And I will be your new maidservant."

Selene nodded as she took in the room. "What is your name?"

"Essa, my lady."

"Thank you, Essa."

Essa bobbed her head and stepped out, closing the door softly behind her.

Selene stepped farther into the room and looked around. Her eyes kept returning to the door by her bed, and she wondered where it led. Was it an additional room? A private washroom?

She looked at the handle, then pressed down on the metal lever. The heavy wooden door opened without a sound. On the other side was an even larger bedchamber, with more lavish furniture and décor. The bed alone was twice as big as the one in the room behind her, with a thick blue coverlet trimmed in silver and a dozen pillows. A bearskin lay across the stone floor in front of an ornate fireplace—much fancier than her own—along with two stuffed chairs and a small table in between. A painting hung above the fireplace. A man stood behind a pretty woman, his hand resting on her shoulder. An older boy stood to her left and a young boy to her right.

There was something about the people that triggered familiarity. But before she could think on it more, the three large windows to the right caught her attention.

Selene approached the windows and looked out.

Her heart stopped.

Water spread out below and to the north as far as she could see. The sun was setting to the left, the brilliant colors in the sky reflecting across the water's surface. White waves crashed against the rocky cliff upon which the castle stood.

The sea.

She leaned toward the glass, her breathing fast. So beautiful. Even more beautiful than Damien's dreamscape. She wanted to reach out and touch it, to soak in the beauty and let it encompass her being.

She watched the waves below, and the colors in the sky turned from bright to deep and brilliant. The sun sank to the west, and streaks of red and purple filled the sky.

The first star came out, hanging over the horizon.

"Lady Selene?"

Selene gasped and stepped back from the window. Taegis stood in the doorway between the two bedrooms, a candle in hand. "I came to check on you."

"Whose room is this?" she asked, turning away from the window. Even as she asked the question, she knew.

"Lord Damien's."

Of course it was. Her stomach tightened and fluttered at the same time. "And how is he doing?" she asked, keeping her feelings behind her mask.

"The arrowhead has been removed. There is an infection, but Healer Sildaern feels confident he will recover quickly. In fact, they plan on moving him here tonight. Healer Sildaern believes his lordship will feel more comfortable in his own bed."

Selene nodded. Behind Taegis, she noticed that her room had already been lit for the evening. A reminder of how much her life had changed in a fortnight. She was married now, with separate rooms, separate quarters, perhaps even separate lives, like her father and mother.

"I ordered dinner to be brought to your room. I figured you would want some time alone this evening instead of being surrounded by strangers."

"Yes. Thank you, Taegis." Selene straightened her shoulders. *I can do this. Don't look at the years ahead, focus on the here and now. Just like a mission.*

He gave her a warm smile, the first one she'd

seen from him. "If I may, my lady, let me be the first one to welcome you to your new home."

His smile and words comforted her. But they weren't enough to dispel the lump in her throat or the fear in her heart.

10

Selene.

Selene tossed one way then the other across the bed.

Selene.

It wasn't so much a voice, but a feeling. A feeling that pulled on her as strongly as if the person were calling to her.

Selene.

She opened her eyes and sat up. A weight sat upon her chest like a stone. She rubbed the area and looked around. In the dim light she could make out the furniture of her new room and the beginnings of a half moon outside the window. The gentle *whoosh* of the sea waves was barely audible and reminded her of the wind.

She sighed and dropped her hand. At least she hadn't experienced a nightmare tonight, nor seen that shadowy creature. The very thought made her shiver, and she looked around, almost expecting to see something standing in the corner.

Nothing.

She rubbed her chest again, feeling that same pull. What was this new sensation, this new . . . feeling? Was it another aspect of her dreamwalking gift? Was someone calling out to her?

Or was she just dreaming?

Selene lay back down and stared up at the canopy that surrounded her bed. She couldn't remember the last time she had actually dreamed, minus the constant nightmares. Maybe this *was* dreaming. The young maid Essa had reminded her of Renata, which brought to mind all the people she had left behind. Perhaps the guilt was weaving its way into her mind.

She turned onto her side and pulled the coverlet up around her neck. *I did what I had to. I made the best choice I could. I have a chance to make things right in the future. I'll discover exactly why House Ravenwood has been given this gift and free my sisters. Maybe I'll even find a way to save Renata.*

A sad smile crossed her lips. *I hope so.*

She closed her eyes and gripped the coverlet between her hands. As she started drifting off, the feeling was back.

Selene.

She sat up again and looked around. There was no denying it. Somehow, someway, someone was calling to her. A soft moan drifted through the door on her left, the one that led into the bedroom with the windows that overlooked the sea.

She stared at the door, her heart pounding. There was someone in there—

Damien. Taegis had said Damien would be moved to his own chambers tonight.

Another soft moan floated through the door.

An ache filled her throat. He was in pain. Before she knew it, she slipped from her bed and moved toward the door. She stared at the handle, debating whether or not to walk in.

Was it possible he was the one calling to her?

"But that's impossible," she whispered. The only way a Ravenwood woman could enter another's dream and make that kind of contact was through touch. And there was a wall separating her from Damien.

But what about the pull she felt toward Damien earlier that evening inside the healer's room? Was it the same pull she felt right now?

She clenched her hands. *I don't know.*

And she couldn't ask her mother either.

She was on her own.

Selene took a deep breath and pressed down on the handle. She stepped inside. The palest of moonlight spilled through the windows. To her left was the great four-poster bed, with a figure on top.

Silently she slipped across the room, the action as familiar to her as the night. Damien lay on the bed, dressed in a loose tunic with a coverlet pulled up to his chest. As she approached the bed, he turned his head back and forth. "No," he moaned, his eyes fluttering beneath his lids. It appeared he was in the thralls of a nightmare.

Selene came up to his side and reached out her hand. She brushed his hair back and pressed her palm against his forehead. So hot. Just like yesterday. The fever had not broken yet and was probably feeding into his dreams.

She bit her lip as she studied him. Her fingers moved from his face to the hand that lay on top of the blanket.

Was it possible she could help him? If she could bring forth nightmares, then she could change his dreams to more pleasant memories, right? It made sense. If nothing else, maybe it would soothe his mind.

It was worth trying.

Selene lay down on the coverlet facing Damien, her heart hammering inside her chest. She took a deep breath. *I can do this.* Then she closed her eyes and wrapped her fingers around his wrist.

Selene.

It was Damien's voice inside her head.

Before she could process that, the dreamscape rushed past her as she was pulled into the fiery memories filling his heat-filled mind. Selene spread out her arms and within seconds had transformed into a raven. She recognized many of the memories playing below her: the sick couple lying in a bed, three large wooden boxes dropped into the sea, and the stormy day when Damien used his power, amongst others.

A young man with dark hair and deep blue eyes who looked similar to Damien lay in a four-poster bed, his face gaunt, almost skeletal, and glistening with sweat. "Damien," he rasped. "Father . . . Mother . . ."

Damien sat near the bed. At his words, Damien reached over and grabbed his hand. "Shhh, Quinn. Healer Sildaern said you need to rest."

"I-I don't want to be alone."

"You're not alone. I'm here. And the Light is with you as well."

Sunlight moved across the window as time turned, and still Damien remained beside the bed. As the sun began to set, Quinn opened his eyes again. "I see it," he whispered, his eyes bright and feverish.

Damien lifted his head from where he had laid it on the edge of the bed. "What do you see?"

"The Light." He let out a long breath, a content smile on his face. "It's beautiful, Damien, just like Father said it would be. So . . . beau . . . ti . . . ful." His lips stopped, and the life faded from his face.

Damien sat up. "No," he whispered. "Quinn, you can't leave me." He shook Quinn's hand. "Do you hear me? Quinn! *Quinn!*"

Damien bowed his head and broke into uncontrollable sobs. Selene had never seen a man cry like that before, but instead of being repulsed, she wanted more than anything to wrap her arms around him. She could feel his deep and piercing grief through the dreamscape. Such love. Such anguish.

Beyond the dream, she heard Damien moan.

I need to change this. I need to find good memories. Happy memories.

Selene spread her wings and flew up along the wind current, high above the nightmares flashing across Damien's mind, and searched.

She dove down toward a memory, pressing her power against the dreamscape, changing the scene from that dark bedroom to this new one, full of light and laughter.

Three children stood below an ancient oak tree. The trunk was wider than a doorway, with thick branches spreading high above, its leaves forming a canopy of green over what appeared to be a city square. The sun shone brightly overhead, surrounded by a blue sky.

Selene recognized two of the young people. Only one family had that shade of blond hair. As she circled down, she realized the third was a younger version of Damien, on the brink of manhood.

The girl clasped her hands together as she stared up into the tree. "Quinn, be careful."

Damien folded his arms and laughed. "See, Tyrn, I told you Quinn would beat Elric."

The other boy—with that pinched look of adolescence—scowled. "I think they're both foolish and should come down before someone catches them."

A burst of laughter came from high above. Selene landed on the closest branch and looked into the tree. Two boys were making their way up, laughing along the way. One with dark hair, the other with the telltale blond.

"I'm almost there, Elric," shouted the dark-haired boy.

"Think again, Quinn!" Elric yelled as he gathered speed and climbed the next few branches in a flash. By now, the two boys were nearing the top, where the branches were thinner and sagging slightly under their weight.

"All right," Tyrn hollered from below. "Time to come down before one of you falls."

"He's right, Quinn," Damien shouted. "I don't want to be the one to tell Father that you broke your leg."

Quinn glanced down. "But I'm almost to the top."

Adalyn—Selene was sure that's who the girl was—clasped her hands even tighter. "Please, Quinn."

Selene studied her for a moment. Long flowing blond hair with a slight curl to it, bright blue eyes, and a gown of white that made her appear almost ethereal. The youngest Luceras was just as pretty when she was a child as she was now as a young woman. Once again, Selene felt that slow burn inside her chest, but then crushed it. That feeling had no place here.

Quinn shook his head with a smile. "Fine, fine, I'm coming down."

"Then are you declaring me the winner?" Elric grinned.

"No, I'm simply doing what the lady asked of me."

Adalyn blushed but continued to look up.

The two boys scrambled down almost as fast as they had climbed the old oak tree. A bell rang in the distance, bringing moans from the two boys. "I was hoping to explore the glen in the gardens before dinner," Elric said with a pout.

Tyrn sniffed as he led the small party along the road past the city square. On either side were narrow two-story buildings with shutters of every color. A few of the windows were open and curtains fluttered through the openings. "You're lucky you were able to leave the castle grounds," he said. "You're supposed to be practicing with Paladin Emeran and improving your polearm."

"Father said it is good to build relations with House Maris." Elric winked at Quinn.

"By climbing trees?"

"It was all good fun," Damien chimed in. "But now it's time to remember who we are."

"Yes." Adalyn bobbed her head and stole a glance at Quinn, who didn't seem to notice.

The five young people made their way along the street toward the open gate ahead that led into the castle grounds. Beyond it stood an elegant building of white with the banner of House Luceras fluttering in the wind.

Selene watched them leave from her perch along the oak tree, her heart twisting. Was this really what Damien's childhood had been like? Laughter and camaraderie?

Her own memories filled her mind as the young people passed the castle gates. Memories of training, Amara's jealousy, Mother's constant reminders of the importance of House Ravenwood, and the overwhelming weight of her destiny. The only happy times she could remember were in the castle garden with Petur and times spent talking with Father, sipping tea and reading in his study. And even some of those memories were now bitter ever since she had dreamwalked inside Petur's mind.

She closed her eyes and breathed slowly, her wings folded against her body. She wasn't here to stoke the fires of jealousy; she was here to help Damien. And she could already tell this memory had soothed his mind. It was a happy memory. One of Quinn.

Again, her throat tightened. Damien and his brother had been close, whereas she and Amara were anything but. She shook her head and spread out her wings. Up into the bright blue sky she rose, drifting along the wind current and searching for another memory to soothe Damien's mind.

11

Damien blinked as the faintest light of morning trickled in through the large windows to his right. He felt tired, but the heated headache and nightmares were gone.

What the—

There was a lump on the bed beside him, pinning him beneath the covers.

He turned his head, a frown on his face. It was a body. In a . . . nightdress?

His mind sped up as he fought the urge to throw back the covers and leap from the bed. Who in land's end would be in his bed?

The figure shivered, then rolled over on top of the coverlet, her black hair long and tangled around the pillow on which she lay.

Selene?

He carefully pulled back the covers, then lifted himself up on his elbow. Even with her head facing the other direction, there was no mistaking that hair, so black that there was a blue sheen to it.

What was she doing here? In his room? *On his bed?*

She shivered again.

He rubbed his brow, then reached over and lifted his covers and draped them across her body. She didn't wake up.

Slowly, so as not to jostle the mattress, Damien sat up and turned toward his side of the bed. A blast of pain shot through his thigh, and he bit back a gasp as he reached over and grabbed one of the bedposts. Now he remembered. He had been shot during the attack, then somehow Taegis had gotten him to Nor Esen and to Healer Sildaern. He looked down and found his leg bandaged up. The pain was more achy than anything else, which meant the arrowhead was gone, and his leg was on the mend. But *ouch!*

He was fingering the bandage when he heard Selene stirring behind him. All he had on was a tunic and undergarments. He stood and limped over to the changing screens as fast as he could and reached for a pair of pants. Whatever the reason Selene had come into his room, he doubted she was ready to see him in this state of undress. His lips quirked at the thought, but then he pushed it back down.

Pulling on the pants sent another gasp through his lips, but he got them on and secured a belt around his waist, then pulled a sleeveless jacket over his tunic. He had a lot to do now that he was back at Northwind Castle—writing letters to the other Great Houses, collecting what information he could about what happened back at Rook Castle, and starting afresh with the alliance.

He brought a hand to his forehead. Not for the first time he wished his father were still alive. He felt so alone in leading his people and influencing the other Great Houses.

You're not alone.

The dream from last night came back to him, the day he lost Quinn. He had told his brother he was not alone, but sometimes he himself forgot that. The Light was with Quinn and his parents. And it was with him now as well.

Damien closed his eyes. His body was still weak from the attack and the ensuing fever, and his chest was heavy with burdens, so he did what he had seen his father do during moments like these. He spoke to the Light.

Words intermingled with the feelings flowing from his heart. He moved his lips, but no words came. He wished he could go out along the cliffs today and raise the waters, but there was no time, and Healer Sildaern would come after him with threats of bed rest. Instead, he stood there behind his changing screens and prayed.

Eventually, Damien bowed his head and took a deep breath. Time to step back into the role of grand lord. He exited the screens carefully and spotted Selene still lying upon his bed, and the door that led to the next room stood ajar.

Quietly, he approached her. Once again he was struck by the realization that he had married a woman from House Ravenwood. And here she lay, the heir to the House of Dreamers. A dreamwalker.

His wife.

In slumber, the coldness that was usually etched across her features was gone. Her long hair lay in dark strands across the pillow, her face now flushed with warmth from the thick cover he had placed over her body.

He cocked his head to the side and watched her. Why had she entered his room? Even though they were married, no doubt Taegis had set her up in the room next door. Did she come in to hold his hand again? Was she having nightmares? And he still didn't even know how she used her gift. How did one dreamwalk?

A conversation he wanted to have with Selene. Soon.

Speaking of . . .

Damien rubbed his temple and turned toward the door. He would also need to announce to his people about his recent nuptials. The sooner the better. Like as in today or tomorrow. He would be sure to arrange that with his steward and council.

Yes, he had a long day ahead of him.

Damien put the small rolled piece of parchment to the side of his desk and sighed. It hadn't taken Caiaphas long to write and update him on what happened after he left. It appeared Lady Ragna was spinning a tale of lies and deception and casting doubt on his own allegiance. The false accusations left a bitter taste in his mouth. He could put up with a great many things but not the tarnishing of his house. He would need to let the other houses know he was alive and share what he could.

Damien glanced back down at the parchment. Caiaphas had also inquired about Selene.

He could almost hear the fear and worry in Caiaphas's words. Not just from a father, but from a leader of the coalition. They needed her. And now Damien knew why.

He ran a hand through his hair and glanced out the window. A grey sky hung over the city, and to the left, the sea stretched out past the cliffs to the unending horizon.

His leg began to protest from sitting too long. And the wound area was still tender, even though Healer Sildaern had used a special salve that had done wonders already. Once again he was amazed at what Sildaern was capable of and wondered if the man carried a hint of the Rafel gift of healing.

Damien slowly stood and stretched out his leg. He should check on Selene. She would be up by now and likely overwhelmed by a new place and new people. Taegis assured him that she was looked after when they arrived, but maybe seeing a somewhat familiar face would put her at ease.

Then again, he was the reason she was here in the first place. He ran a hand along his face. Life could be so complicated.

As Damien made his way down the corridor, he overheard two servants talking as they cleaned.

"Did you see her?"

"Who?"

"That woman yesterday. The one in black."

Damien slowed near the corner, listening.

"I did. She looked mysterious."

"I heard she's Lord Damien's new wife."

"Her? She doesn't look like a proper lady at all."

"Someone said she's from Ravenwood."

"Ravenwood? I've heard bad things about Ravenwood."

Their voices drifted down the hall until they disappeared.

It was just gossip, but it still gave him a picture of what Selene would have to overcome. There was distrust of other houses amongst his own people, especially toward unknown houses like Ravenwood.

A heaviness settled across his chest.

Damien continued down the hall toward his own room, past the long windows that overlooked the sea. He slowed, then paused beside one of them. A memory came flooding back from the first time he met Selene, almost a month ago, during their first meal. She had asked him questions about the sea with excitement in her eyes. Maybe he could show her his home before dinner.

Correction. Their home.

The thought lightened his heart a little, and he moved forward again.

Once he reached the door next to his own room, he stopped and knocked. "Selene?"

There was no answer. He waited a moment, then knocked again. The door opened, but it was a young maidservant with a white cap over her head and a simple blue frock who greeted him, not Selene.

Her eyes went wide. "My-my lord!" she said and bowed to him.

"I'm looking for Lady Selene."

"She is with the seamstress, my lord."

Damien blinked. Of course she would be. She had brought no clothing with her. "When will she be finished?"

"By dinnertime, my lord."

"I see." Well, that changed his plans for the rest of the afternoon. "Would you tell her I will see her at dinner tonight?"

The maidservant bowed again. "I will, my lord."

"Thank you."

His leg began to ache again, and he cast a glance at his own bedroom door. Perhaps he would take the healer's advice and actually rest.

Damien eased into the chair at the head of the dining table later that evening. Seated along either side were members from the lower houses, along with his councilors and people of note, including Taegis.

The room was rectangular, with windows that overlooked the sea at the other end. Darkness filled the glass as night descended upon the castle. A fire had been lit in the fireplace, and candles burned in the round metal chandeliers that hung above the dining table. The hum of conversation filled the room as those assembled waited for food to arrive.

A servant came by and placed a goblet beside his plate.

"How are you feeling, Lord Damien?" Taegis asked beside him as Damien lifted the cup to his lips.

"Tired. Caiaphas informed me of what happened when I failed to show up for the treaty signing," he said quietly and took a sip.

"You've already heard from him?"

"Yes. It didn't take him long to send a message. We can talk about it later."

"And how is your leg?"

Damien let out his breath. "Much better. Amazing how such a tiny thing like an arrowhead can cause so much hurt."

"So no fever?"

Damien snorted. "Do you think Sildaern would let me walk around if I had one? The man found me only minutes after I left my room this morning and grudgingly acquiesced to letting me get back to work."

Taegis laughed. "That's Healer Sildaern for you. And how is Lady Selene?"

Damien took another sip before responding. "I'm not sure. When I went to find her, she was with the seamstress. So I have not seen her all day—" He choked on his words as his eyes went wide and his mouth fell open.

Selene stood in the doorway to the dining room as if summoned by the mention of her name. Her black hair was pulled back to the crown of her head, then spilled down across her shoulders and back. She was dressed in a dark blue gown with silver accents along her fluttering sleeves and neckline. The light caught the edges of her face, accentuating the rare beauty of House Ravenwood within her features.

His heart beat faster as he gazed at her.

"By the Light, who is that beautiful lady?" someone whispered.

"I'm not sure," someone else answered.

"Is it the woman I heard one of the guards talking about?"

It was then Damien realized the whole room had grown quiet as every eye turned toward Selene.

Damien stood and held out his hand.

Selene spotted his movement and made her way along the path between the table and diners to where Damien stood. Murmurs broke out amongst the guests. Selene did not appear affected by the sound. Her eyes were only on him, which quickened his breath.

She placed her hand in his, then Damien turned toward those gathered around the table. "Because of an injury on my way back from the Assembly of the Great Houses, I was unable to formally introduce you to Lady Selene of House Ravenwood."

The word *Ravenwood* spread across the room, and both curious and suspicious looks were sent toward Selene. Damien tightened his grip on her fingers. No doubt they were wondering why a member of House Ravenwood was here in Northwind Castle when the two houses had very little to do with each other. *Well, until now,* Damien thought. *Now they would have a lot to do with each other.*

He looked over the room again and held Selene's hand up. "Lady Selene is now my wife."

At the word *wife,* eyes widened and hurried whispers spread across the dining hall. It sounded more like shock than excitement, although some people seemed to already know, probably from the gossip around the castle. Not the reception he was hoping for, but not surprising. There were some who had made known their own thoughts on whom he should marry.

"I will be making an official announcement tomorrow. Thank you."

Damien ignored the conversation around him as he pulled out the chair on his right for Selene. "You look lovely," he whispered as she sat down.

She stared up him, her look unreadable. "Thank you."

Was she discomfited by his words? Or was it the whispers around them?

"My maidservant, Essa, and the seamstress found the gown for me." Her face softened as she dipped her fingers in the washbowl. "They were very thoughtful to have found something for me to wear this evening."

Damien took in the gown again, his mouth dry. It wasn't just any gown—it brought out every beautiful thing about Selene. She looked even more stunning than she did at the gala back at Rook Castle.

She glanced at him while she dried her fingers. "Is everything all right?"

"Yes." He fought the urge to tug at the collar of his tunic. He took his seat instead and reached for the closest goblet. Their fingers met at the stem and both drew their fingers back.

"I'm sorry, I didn't realize you wanted to take a sip first," Selene said.

"No, that is . . ." His lips quirked upward, and he laughed. "I believe we ran into the same situation when we first met."

"We did?"

"Yes. It was the first time we ever spoke, during

the first dinner at Rook Castle. We both reached for the goblet at the same time."

Selene tilted her head in thought. "I believe you're right. That was only a few weeks ago." She placed her hands in her lap and stared at the plate before her. "So much has happened since then."

Yes, so much had. More than he could have ever imagined. He glanced around the room from the corner of his eye, trying to gauge what the other diners were thinking, but everyone had fallen into quiet, guarded conversation.

At that moment, servants began to bring out platters of seafood, ranging from cod and herring to mussels and crab, each served with sauce and spices. Damien helped himself to the platters using his two-prong fork, then realized Selene had not moved.

"Are you not hungry?" he asked as he glanced over.

Her eyes were wide as she looked over the table. "I don't recognize anything here, except maybe that fish."

Of course. She probably had very little experience with food from the sea. "Here, try this," he said and placed a piece of cod as well as two mussels in the shell onto her plate.

She picked up her own fork and tried the fish first. Then she studied the mussels.

"Like this," Damien said, picking up a mussel from his own plate. He split open the shell, dug the meat out with his fork, then dipped it in the broth bowl.

"Fascinating," Selene murmured as she followed his instructions.

Damien popped the mussel into his mouth and chewed while he observed Selene. He spotted Taegis covertly watching the whole procedure next to him with a small smile on his lips.

She dipped the mussel into the broth, then tentatively brought it to her mouth. She chewed slowly, then swallowed.

"Well?" Damien asked.

"It's . . . different. Like a light and fluffy mushroom, only it tastes like . . ."

"The sea," Damien finished.

"Is that it?"

"Yes. Do you like it?"

The corners of her mouth turned up slightly as she reached for her other mussel. "Yes, I do."

Damien smiled as he placed the empty shells on a nearby plate, dipped his hands in the wash water, then moved on to the crab. As the meal went on, platters of bread were brought around for sopping up broth, and goblets were refilled. Conversation filled the room, with glances sent toward the head of the table every now and then. Most of the looks were tolerable politeness, but there were a few who appeared to be as captivated with Selene as he felt.

Damien stopped, his bread halfway to his

mouth, the temperature in his body rising, suddenly aware of what he had just thought. He glanced at Selene out of the corner of his eye. She was finishing the fish on her plate and talking quietly with one of the councilors—Isak from the lesser house of Norred—who was sitting next to her.

Surely it was right to be enamored with one's own wife, wasn't it?

Damien stared down at the piece of bread, strongly aware of his own heart beating.

Dinner finished up shortly after. Damien stood to excuse himself. Between these new burgeoning thoughts of his and lingering weakness from his recent fever, he didn't want to stay and talk.

Selene looked up at him, and he felt like he had stumbled off a walkway. "Are you leaving?" she asked.

"Yes," he said, grateful his voice didn't crack. "I'm afraid I'm not quite myself yet."

Selene stood and gathered her gown. "May I go with you? I feel the same way."

He could see it all over her face that she did not want to be left alone in a room full of strangers. He extended his arm and smiled, his heart suddenly full. "Of course."

Turning, he addressed the room. "Good night, everyone." He bowed his head, and the rest did likewise.

Damien led Selene around the room to the

exit and walked out into the cooler corridor. "I stopped by your room today, but you were with the seamstress. I had hoped to show you the sea. I remember how enchanted you were when I spoke of my homeland."

Selene turned toward him, and a smile slipped across her lips. "I would like that."

Damien faltered onto his next words. "Also, I should let you know that tomorrow I will present you to Nor Esen. Usually a union of this sort is announced ahead of time, and the ceremony a public affair. This is the first time in a long time that House Maris has had a marital arrangement like the one we have."

"You mean one of circumstance."

Damien let out his breath. "Yes."

"I understand." The smile fell from her face.

He frowned. Did he say something he shouldn't have?

"I also heard from Caiaphas today," he said quickly, trying to restore the pleasant mood.

She turned her head sharply. "Father?"

"Yes. He sent word almost immediately after we escaped. He inquired after you."

Her face softened slightly. "That was kind of him." She said nothing more, nothing about missing her father, or even asking how things were back at Rook Castle. Perhaps it was too soon, and the pain of losing everything still too fresh. Damien chose to remain silent the rest of the way.

They arrived at the door that led into her room. As he turned toward Selene, he was strangely reluctant to let her go, even though he was feeling the aftereffects of his injury and could probably use another dose of Healer Sildaern's medicine. And she appeared ready to retire for the night.

He reached for the door and opened it for her. He wanted to reach for her hand as well but held back, a part of him wondering at these sudden thoughts and impulses. "Good night," he said softly as she headed inside.

She turned back briefly within the doorway. In the candlelight cast by the sconce on the opposite wall, he caught sight of a single tear in the corner of her eye.

"Selene?" he whispered, his heart twisting inside his chest.

"Good night, Lord Damien." Then she bowed and entered her room.

Damien stared after her before slowly closing the door. He remained there, staring at the wood grains and patterns along the surface.

Was it possible she regretted this marriage?

He swallowed the lump in his throat and headed for his own door. Yes, it had been an arrangement of circumstances. But it had the chance of becoming more. He was open to the idea. Did she not feel the same way?

Damien entered his room, the candle near his bed lit for the evening, along with a fire in the fireplace. He walked toward his changing screens, his heart and mind still mulling over Selene and the marriage announcement tomorrow. He stripped off the day's garments and pulled on a clean undershirt and pants.

He stumbled over to his bed and found a vial of medicine and a glass of water waiting for him, sent by Healer Sildaern. After drinking both, he put out the candle by his bed and slipped under the covers.

He stared at the fire across the room. By marrying Selene, had he condemned himself to a loveless marriage? His chest tightened, and he rolled onto his back. He always wanted to marry for love. Instead, he married to save a woman he barely knew.

What if she never loved him?

Light, what do I do?

The fire popped and crackled in the fireplace.

Love her.

Damien heard the words as clearly as if they had been spoken in his ear.

Love her.

Could he do that? Could he learn to love Selene, even if she never returned his love?

12

Amara sucked in a breath as she emerged from the old gardener's mind. Petur groaned and turned on his side, curling his legs up to his chest. Pale moonlight shone through the small window, leaving a square of light across the ground. She clenched her hand into a fist and punched her thigh. Why couldn't she do it? Why couldn't she change the dreamscape?

Her mother emerged moments later, and Amara could feel the heat of her anger. She stood to her feet and glared down at Amara. "Come, Amara. Morning is almost here."

"Yes, Mother." She stood and followed her mother outside of the small hovel and across the servants' quarters. She clenched her hands again, so hard that her nails dug into her palms. What did Selene have that she did not? She worked harder and wanted this more—much more than Selene ever did. And yet her elder sister was the gifted one.

And then she threw it all away when she left with the grand lord of House Maris. Amara clenched her hand. Why?

Her mother led the way back into Rook Castle, moving along the corridors like an apparition. When they reached the west wing, she stopped.

"You will continue your physical training. And you will continue to dreamwalk every night. I expect to see a better performance than I saw tonight in two weeks from now. You will prove to me why you deserve to inherit the mantle of House Ravenwood. Do you understand?"

"Yes, Mother." Amara carefully concealed her features, but inside she burned.

Her mother turned and left without a word, leaving Amara standing in the middle of the dark and silent hallway.

A lump filled her throat as her shoulders sagged. Was it like this with Selene? Mother pressuring her to achieve more and more with their gift? Amara snorted and headed for the secret training room below the castle. Probably not. Everything always came easily to Selene. She was able to dreamwalk the first time flawlessly, and she still had Mother's respect, even after leaving in disgrace.

She slipped into the sitting room and headed for the fireplace. She placed her fingers in the three small indents beside the stone mantel, twisted her hand clockwise, and listened to the gears deep within the wall as the hidden door opened.

Like a cat, she slid into the narrow passageway and closed the door behind her. Pitch-black pervaded her senses, but she was used to it. With practiced hands, she lit the first torch, then used it to light the other torches along her way.

As she headed into the bowels of the castle, her mind churned with questions. With everything at her fingertips, why did Selene run away? Did she secretly love Lord Damien? Perhaps. She had seen the way her sister's face had changed when she looked at him. But the cold, calculating sister she knew would not simply throw everything away for an infatuation. There had to be something more that had caused Selene to make such a drastic decision.

But what? And why?

"And why do I care?" She seethed as she entered the training cavern. She finished lighting the room, then placed the torch in one of the brackets. Her sword sat on the table, next to an array of weapons. Noticeably empty on the table was the place where Selene's twin blades used to lie.

Amara harrumphed as she grabbed her own sword and went for the dummy. Whatever the reason, Selene was now gone, allowing her to gain Mother's favor.

I will become the heir to Ravenwood.

Whack.

I will learn to control my dreamwalking and become stronger.

Whack.

And I will take Selene's place in Mother's eyes.

Amara attacked the dummy with her single blade, dancing in and out, swinging her blade and slicing into the dummy until an hour later only straw, shreds of cloth, and the wooden skeleton was left.

She wiped her brow and let her sword hang down at her side. She would have to drag another dummy down here, but it was worth the effort. Already she felt much better. She walked over to the table and placed her sword down. She had enough time to quickly bathe in one of the hot springs and visit her little sister, Opheliana, before resting until later this evening and dreamwalking again.

That was another benefit to Selene's absence: she had Opheliana all to herself.

Amara stepped into the nursery. She breathed in the scent of lilac and smiled, remembering her own childhood. Opheliana must have recently finished bathing.

"Opheliana," Amara said quietly as she stepped into the room. She shut the door behind her and walked across the crimson rug that lay across the stone floor. A cozy fire burned in the fireplace, and a handful of wooden toys sat on the round table in the corner.

A voice hummed from the other room, out of tune, but comforting just the same. Amara peeked into the bedroom. Maura, the nursemaid, stood by the wardrobe to the right, her back to Amara, as she folded clothes and placed them inside. The two beds on either side were made, thick furs placed on top to ward off the coming winter chill.

The metal bath was still in the room, though no steamy wisps emerged from the opaque surface. The smell of lilac hung heavier in here.

Movement to her left caught her eye. Amara turned and spotted Opheliana standing on a stool next to the narrow window, her face pressed against the glass as she stared out across the rocky mountain expanse.

Another smile spread across Amara's face, and the tension and frustration from last night ebbed away. "Opheli—"

She snapped her lips shut, and her eyes went wide. Opheliana stood on her tiptoes, her blue dress rising above her bare feet, exposing her ankles. Her sister must not have heard her because her back remained to Amara, allowing her full view of the mark just below the hem of her dress.

It can't be.

Amara silently entered the room, her eyes pinned to the reddish mark above Opheliana's ankle. Her heart raced, leaving her breathless. *It can't be, it can't be!*

But there was no denying the flaming birthmark on Opheliana's ankle.

The mark of House Friere.

There was a gasp behind her. "Lady Amara, I didn't hear you enter."

Amara spun around, anger replacing the shock from moments before. "What is the meaning of this?" she shouted and pointed at Opheliana.

"What do you mean, your ladyship?" Maura slowly edged around the room, putting herself between Amara and Opheliana.

Opheliana turned around on the stool and stared at Amara with her head cocked to the side.

"That mark on my sister's ankle!"

Maura's face paled as she sidestepped over to Opheliana and used her body to shield the little girl, which only made Amara angrier. What did the nursemaid think she was going to do? Hurt her little sister? "Explain, Maura."

The nursemaid's lip began to tremble. "Please, my lady. No one was supposed to know—"

"Know what?"

Maura tugged on the apron around her waist. "If I tell you, she'll kill me."

Amara folded her arms and held tight to her elbows, her nostrils flaring. "Who, my mother?"

Maura nodded her head, her eyes so wide the whites showed.

"I won't tell her. But I do want an answer. Why does my sister have the mark of House Friere?"

Maura looked down and let go of the apron, wringing her hands instead.

Amara clenched her teeth. "If you don't tell me, then I *will* go to my mother."

Maura's hands worked faster. "Lady Opheliana

is part of House Ravenwood . . . and House Friere." Her last words were so quiet Amara barely caught them.

She let out her breath in one quick whoosh. "How is that possible?"

Maura shook her head, keeping her eyes down. Opheliana stepped down from the stool and came to stand beside Maura.

Amara narrowed her eyes as she stared at her little sister, taking in every feature. Opheliana had the same dark hair as her mother and Selene, with a red tint to the curls. But on closer look, her eyes resembled Lord Ivulf's shape and amber color, and her lips were thin, like Lord Raoul's.

Dart'an! How could her mother . . . ?

Amara spun around, still gripping her elbows. The longer she thought about it, the more it made sense. All the trips to Ironmond. The close relationship between Ravenwood and Friere, particularly between Mother and Lord Ivulf. The hints dropped by Lord Raoul.

All that talk of House Ravenwood and preserving their house purity, only to have the evidence otherwise on her sister's ankle. A person could possess only one house gift, and apparently the mark of House Friere had been passed on to her sister. What did that mean for Opheliana? Was that why her mother kept her little sister cloistered away like an invalid?

A hand tugged on her dress. Amara looked

over to find Opheliana standing behind her. For a heartbeat, she thought her sister would finally speak. But she never opened her lips. Instead, she gazed up, her eyebrows drawn together as she tugged on the fabric again.

In that one second, all the rage inside her fled at the look of innocence on her sister's face.

Amara knelt down and gathered Opheliana into her arms. Her hair and clothing smelled like lilac. Like the purity of childhood. She pressed her face into the small crook of her sister's neck. "No, Opheliana, I'm not angry with you. I could never be angry with you." It was not her sister's fault that she carried the mark of Friere on her body. And if Amara was honest with herself, she didn't care. It didn't change how she felt about Opheliana.

What hurt was knowing that if her mother's indiscretion was found out, it would be Opheliana who would pay for it. Opheliana could never be an heir to House Ravenwood, not with that mark on her ankle. Would House Friere take Opheliana in if Lord Ivulf found it?

The thought made her sick. Amara had her own ambitions, but she was not stupid. She knew Lord Raoul was an unforgiving, cruel man. And Lord Ivulf was as cold as his power was scorching. That kind of influence would break her tender little sister. So would their mother's.

Amara looked up and scowled, ignoring

167

Maura. No, no one would find out. She would make sure of it. She would do as her mother wished. She would work hard, harder than any other Ravenwood woman had before her, and she would become heir to House Ravenwood and the grand lady of the mountain people. Then Opheliana could remain as she was, an innocent little girl, and live in Rook Castle forever.

Yes, she would protect her sister. At all costs.

13

Selene's nightmares were different that night. Instead of visions of past dreamscapes, her dreams were her own. She clutched the coverlet to her chest as the sun rose outside her window, her body tense, her chest aching.

Over and over she heard Damien's words inside her ears.

I never wanted to marry you. I only married you to save myself.

She knew it was only a nightmare. He'd never said that. But deep down, it was what she feared. That someday the truth would come out: he married her so she could never fulfill her mission. The nightmare had been so strong she was tempted to search her mind for a raven in the background, watching.

Selene sat up and growled. "Why does it matter?" She flung the covers away and stood. House Ravenwood never married for love. That had been drilled into her, along with the importance of house loyalty, ever since she was a little girl. In some ways, she was still fulfilling her duties. By marrying Damien, she had the opportunity to search out the truth behind Ravenwood's gift, a truth that would hopefully free her family.

There was a knock on her door, then Essa walked in. "Good morning, my lady," she said with a smile that looked like pure sunlight. She held a tray in her hands. On top was a mug of steaming liquid and a brown egg resting in an eggcup. She placed the tray on the table near the bed, then headed for the wardrobe. "The seamstress is almost finished with the gown you will be wearing for the announcement today," she said as she pulled out a simple green dress with flowing sleeves. "The rest of your new attire will be ready in a couple of days."

Selene watched the young woman brush out the gown, then walk across the room and place the gown on the other side of the changing screen.

"Thank you."

Essa smiled and bobbed her head. "My pleasure, my lady. I will be happy to do your hair once you're dressed."

Selene disappeared around the screens. Essa was the complete opposite of Renata. Her hands trembled as she took off her nightgown and pulled on the dress.

Renata.

Selene took in a shaky breath and finished dressing. She ate the simple food, then sat down for Essa to finish the last of her grooming. As her maidservant put the finishing touches on the small braids wrapped around her head, there was a knock at the door. Selene turned back to her tea as Essa went to answer.

"Is Lady Selene here?"

Damien's voice drifted into the room. Her body went rigid at the sound, her nightmares flashing once again across her mind.

"Yes, my lord."

Selene stood and walked toward the door. Damien looked over Essa's shoulder and spotted her. "Lady Selene."

Essa backed away with a bow as Selene approached Damien, her heart thumping inside her chest. For what reason could he be here?

"I was wondering if you would like to take a walk with me. I would still like to show you my home—our home—here, in the Northern Shores."

Her eyebrows shot up. Oh. That was not what she was expecting. His words and the genuine earnestness on his face disarmed her a little. "I would like that."

If she was going to be living here for the rest of her life, she wanted to know more about this place. And she couldn't deny how much she had longed to see the sea. She retrieved her cloak and walked out the door, leaving Essa behind to straighten up the bedroom.

He started with a tour of Northwind Castle, pointing out paintings and sculptures along the corridors. The castle was about the same size as

Rook Castle, but unlike her former home with open airways, steep ravines, and tall mountain peaks, Northwind Castle stood on the highest cliff above the city of Nor Esen, and every architectural detail was made of smooth lines and waves, almost as if the castle itself was the sea.

"How are you finding your accommodations?" Damien asked as they started down a windowed corridor along the second floor.

"The room is nice. And comfortable." What more should she say? It was just a room like any other—

Her breath hitched in her throat as she caught sight of a wide expanse of deep blue-grey. Selene stepped toward the windows, her heart held in suspension inside her chest. Even though she had seen the sea the other night outside Damien's windows, it still left her in awe. The water appeared unending, melding into the grey sky above, with a flock of white birds soaring along the stone cliffs to the west, and tall pine trees to the east.

As wild and free as the Magyr Mountains.

Her heart started to beat again.

She pressed her fingers against the glass, her eyes riveted on the scene before her.

Damien stepped beside her. "Incredible, isn't it?" There was pride in his low tenor voice. "Would you like to go outside and stand along the cliffs?"

"Yes," she answered without turning.

"Then follow me."

He directed her toward the end of the corridor, where a door led to the outside ledge and cliffs that lined this side of the castle. As Selene walked beside him, she caught his scent, a strange scent, almost like the ocean itself.

Damien opened the door, then waited as she exited the castle. A cold wind blew across the jagged stone cliffs, sending her hair flying to the side. The gap between the castle and the edge was about twenty feet, ending abruptly in a sheer drop-off with white crested waves far below. To her left, a narrow ledge jutted out over the sea like a finger pointing north.

Her cloak fluttered behind her as Selene came to stand near the edge and looked over the sea. "It's even bigger than I had imagined."

"Yes." Damien stepped beside her, a soft smile spreading across his lips.

"All I could picture was one of the crystal lakes in the Magyr Mountains, but this is different. It's like a whole land unto itself, only made of water. Do you go out to sea often?"

"Not as much as I would like. But I do have my own ship that I use to travel up and down the coast, or to the other lands. Most of the cities and villages of the Northern Shores are located near the coastline. The majority of our trade consists of fishing and transport."

Selene clasped her hands together as another gust of wind grabbed ahold of her cloak and sent it flying, along with her hair. She closed her eyes and took a deep breath of the salty-sweet air. She stood there, letting the wind and the waves block out everything else.

"I wish we had a bit longer," Damien said eventually. "But there is some business I need to attend to before this afternoon."

The public announcement of their nuptials. Selene dropped her hands and opened her eyes as reality came crashing back. "I understand." She let her mask slip back over her face. Yes, this had been a thoughtful gesture on Damien's part. But it didn't silence the whispers inside her mind. *I only married you to save myself.*

"I'll have Taegis escort you to the throne room when it's time."

Selene nodded without saying a word, the weight of fear latching back on to her chest.

"Selene?"

"Hmm?"

"Are you nervous?"

Selene glanced over at him. "I was raised knowing I would marry someday out of duty. Our marriage . . . it's not what I was expecting."

He nodded and glanced at the sea in thought. "It's not what I was expecting either."

At least they were being honest with each other. "It will take time for us to adjust and get to know each other." He turned back toward her. "I promise I will give you all the time and space you need."

"Thank you." But she wasn't sure if time or space would help.

Storm clouds rolled in across the city as Selene made her way to the main audience chamber, escorted by Taegis. Earlier, Essa had delivered an exquisite silk gown of white, with waves embroidered along the neckline and sleeves, along with a matching light blue cloak. After brushing her hair out, Essa had insisted she should wear it down. The black strands hung over her shoulders and fell to the embossed belt she wore around her waist.

Her fingers were cold as she grasped the inside of her sleeves. Taegis led her to a part of the castle she had not visited yet. He stood before the double doors, each side stationed with a guard, and glanced at Selene.

"Are you ready, my lady?"

Selene raised her chin. A kernel of fear burned deep within, but she held it at bay with the same iron determination that had seen her through the last few months. "I'm ready."

Taegis opened the door.

She wasn't sure what she was expecting. Maybe a chamber similar to the one back at Rook Castle, which was a large cavernous room with the denizens of lower houses and wealthy elite standing around a platform with a raised throne.

Instead, the audience hall was a long narrow chamber made of light grey stone, with stairs at the end that led to a throne made of glass. On either side of the throne were two large fish heads from which water flowed in a cascading waterfall to the waiting canals below. The canals wove between the columns and disappeared in grates near the double doors. The sound of rushing water reminded Selene of the mountain streams back home.

Behind the throne were three large windows the length of the wall, with a view of the wide-open sky, currently filled with the grey clouds of a brewing storm.

On the throne sat Damien, dressed in a deep blue tunic and sleeveless jacket, all covered by a bright blue cloak trimmed in silver. He stood the moment she walked in and held out his hand.

Selene made her way across the hall, noting the tiled pictures of the sea, sky, and beach across the floor. Her boots barely made a sound, and as she passed each column, she spotted people standing in the wings. It appeared the chamber had been constructed so that the focus of the person entering was on the throne and not those gathered.

She gathered her dress in one hand at the bottom of the stairs and made her way up to

Damien. He gave her a soft smile that reached his unusually blue eyes.

In his gaze, the rest of the room vanished. All she could see was depths of blue, and she felt herself drowning inside of them.

The moment he touched her hand, a sizzling arc flashed across her fingers, causing the hair on her arms to rise. The sizzle intensified as he brought her hand up to his lips and kissed her knuckles.

Heat flooded her being, burning away any trace of icy coolness from minutes ago.

"Ready?" he asked quietly, warmth in his eyes.

Selene nodded dumbly, unable to speak. Dart'an! Where was her iron will? Her strength? She felt like a newborn foal on wobbly legs.

Damien stepped around the throne, her hand still in his, and led her behind the platform where a door stood beneath the windows. A guard stood on either side of the door, backs straight, hands at their sides.

As they approached, one moved and opened the door with a bow. "My lord. My lady," he said.

Damien nodded toward the man and led Selene out onto a slim balcony that overlooked the city of Nor Esen. A salty wind picked up, tugging on her cloak and dress.

Selene looked down, her mind retreating into a numbing fog. Every street, every window, every tree was filled with people. Thousands of them.

She couldn't even see the cobblestones along the roads.

At their appearance, a roar broke out across the city. Articles of blue waved in the air, from kerchiefs and cloaks to blankets, banners, and even tiny ribbons.

A huge grin erupted across Damien's face as he approached the stone railing and waved with his free hand. The crowd grew even more boisterous.

Selene watched in amazement. Due to Rook Castle's location high up in the Magyr Mountains, special announcements were delivered to the villages and announced to a select few in the audience chamber. Never had she seen such a large crowd gathered before. And they seemed happy. Delighted. Even ecstatic to see Damien.

They loved him.

Selene felt like she had been punched in the gut. No one had ever reacted this way when meeting her mother. House Ravenwood was respected by the mountain people, yes. But it was also feared. Not loved. Not like this.

And Damien loved them back.

She could see it in the way he looked over the crowd, in the way he waved, in the smile that illuminated his face.

A rush of adrenaline washed over her, leaving her knees weak. She reached for the railing and clutched the top. Her head began to spin.

Damien's hand tightened around her own. "Are you all right?" he asked as he finished waving.

"Yes." Selene forced herself up, ignoring the cold sweat collecting across her back. The wind blew again, pulling her hood from her head and letting her hair fly around her face.

Damien watched her a moment longer before turning to address the crowd. "People of Nor Esen and the Northern Shores." The people quieted and Selene wondered how much of Damien's words they could actually hear.

"Let me present to you Lady Selene of House Ravenwood, my new wife."

It took a moment for Damien's words to spread across the crowd. The cheers began again, although not quite as loud. Selene reached up and tucked her hair behind her ear, unsure if she should wave or just stand there. She opted to stand there as Damien spoke for a little longer.

A few drops of rain splattered across the stone railing, and one hit the tip of her nose. She glanced up. It looked like the heavens were about to burst open. Damien finished his speech, waved again, and turned, his hand still in hers. A few more drops fell from the sky, and the wind picked up.

The door was open and waiting for them. Damien stepped back and motioned for her to enter first. As she walked by, he placed his hand on her back and gently guided her. Every nerve

179

inside of her felt his contact, as if his hand was a hot poker pressing into her back.

"There is a special dinner tonight in our honor. Some of the same people you met last night will be there."

"And who are they?"

Damien led her down the stairs, following the path of water that ran along either side of the walkway toward the doors ahead. The people in the wings were already filing out. "Members from a handful of lesser houses, some wealthy families whose source of income is trade, and people handpicked by me. And Taegis, of course. Do you need anything, or are you ready to head to the dining hall?"

"No, I'm ready."

He kept his hand on her back, guiding her along the lit corridor. Two guards followed.

"So who exactly is Taegis?" Selene asked, still feeling the pressure of his fingers along her back. "A councilor? Captain?"

"He's my guardian. And he was my father's guardian before me. He acts as a personal bodyguard, counselor, and friend."

"I see." In some ways like Mother's Hagatha, although Hagatha served more as a servant than a guardian.

"I don't know what I would have done without him when my family passed away." There was a hint of sadness in his voice. He cleared his throat.

"By the way, you looked radiant standing there on the balcony." His smile was back. "I think the people of Nor Esen approve of you."

"Thank you," she said as they turned a corner. But did *he* approve? She clenched her hand against her side as doubts flooded back into her mind. Did Damien want her? Now wasn't the time, but eventually she was going to ask him, even if the answer was the one she feared, the one that haunted her nightmares. At least then she would know the truth.

I never wanted to marry you. I only married you to save myself.

14

Damien stood up from his desk and stretched his arms over his head, giving each elbow a tug before dropping his hands. It had been two days since he had made the official announcement about his marriage to House Ravenwood and three days since he had sent messages to Houses Vivek, Luceras, and Merek. He didn't expect a response for at least a moon cycle, given how far each house had to travel from Rook Castle back to their lands, but it was hard to wait. He wanted to know what had happened in their own words, and he wanted to confer with each house on what to do next. And the fact that both Lord Rune and Lady Runa had been assassinated by Lady Ragna Ravenwood needed to be worked through as well.

Speaking of . . .

He sighed and looked down at his desk, barely seeing the scattering of parchment across the wooden surface. It was time for him to approach Selene about her gift and find out what he could. He only hoped she would be willing. She had become cold and silent over the last couple of days, and he wasn't sure why.

He shook his head and carefully stacked the parchments into one pile, then placed them on the right side of his desk. Perhaps she was in a state of grief and missing her home and family. Or perhaps the nightmares had returned.

"My lord?"

Damien looked up and found Taegis standing in the doorway. "Do you need me for anything this morning?"

"Yes." Damien stepped around the desk. "I need a break. Would you care to spar?"

"How is your leg?"

Damien glanced down and rubbed the fabric above the area. "I'm still amazed at what Healer Sildaern can do. It's completely healed, save for a small scar on my thigh."

"That's good to hear."

Damien straightened up. "And he's given me leave to go back to my usual routine, including exercise."

Taegis took a step back and motioned for the door. "You lead and I'll follow."

The two men headed down the corridor toward the training room. "How is Lady Selene doing?" Taegis asked as they walked.

Damien let out a long breath. "She's been quiet the last couple of days."

"Ever since the announcement?"

"Yes."

"Have you spoken to her?"

Damien shook his head. "I think she is grieving. I didn't want to intrude."

They entered the training room. Three guards were exercising near the back, beneath the high windows above. The smell of sweat and steel filled the air, along with the occasional grunt and pant. To the left of the doorway stood a table with practice swords and a jug of water.

The guards paused in their training and bowed toward Damien, who nodded in return. The guards resumed as Damien chose his sword and held it up in the air, inspecting the nicks along the wooden surface. The wooden weapon was not the same as his own sword, but it would do for today. Taegis chose the one next to it. Then they took up their position on the wooden floor, away from the guards.

It didn't take Damien long to fall into the rhythm of sparring. With each move, his muscles grew warm and limber and his chest expanded. It felt good to exercise, to give his mind a break and feel the strength of his body.

"Have you thought about sparring with Lady Selene?" Taegis asked after acquiescing to one of Damien's moves an hour later.

Damien lowered his sword and blinked. "Lady Selene?"

"Yes." Taegis wiped his brow before continuing. "Do you remember seeing her ladyship exercise in the small training area when we were at Rook Castle? Perhaps doing something familiar would help her with her loss. And it would give you a chance to spend time with her." He eyed Damien as he spoke those last few words.

Heat filled Damien's face. Why hadn't he thought of that? It seemed Taegis was more aware of the needs of his wife than he was. "You're right," he said, swallowing down his hurt pride. "But what would the servants or guards say if they saw Selene fighting?"

Taegis snorted. "Does it matter?"

No, it didn't matter. What mattered was Selene. "I'll see if she is interested. In fact, I'll look for her once I've had a chance to wash up. Do you know where I can find her?"

"She was in the library this morning."

"Then I shall head there shortly."

Taegis bowed his head. "Very good."

Damien headed toward the table, then stopped beside Taegis and placed a hand on the older man's shoulder. "Thank you, Taegis. I sometimes feel like I have no idea what I'm doing when it comes to this marriage." He hadn't meant to be so open, but with Taegis it was easy to do.

Taegis turned and looked at him. "As you know, I have no experience with that kind of bonding. But I imagine that for any marriage to work, it's about the relationship. Study her, know what she likes, dislikes, what makes her heart race, and what would make her heart break. You cannot work or fight alongside someone you do not know and care for, and that goes for marriage as well."

Damien laughed and dropped his hand. "Why didn't you marry, Taegis? I think you would have made some woman very happy."

Taegis smiled and shook his head. "My desire has always been to serve House Maris. And I always will, wholeheartedly."

Damien let out his breath. "I'm thankful for your service. I don't know what I would have done without your advice and guidance."

"You would have been fine. You have a good and strong heart, my lord. Just like your father. And you have his faith."

His father's faith? Damien mentally shook his head. Hardly. Father had believed in the Light more than anyone he knew, and it had showed. If he could have half the faith his father did, then perhaps he would not worry so much about leading his people.

Damien quickly washed up and changed his clothes before crossing Northwind Castle to the first-floor library. At the door, he spotted Karl.

"My lord," Karl said with a quick bow of his head.

"Karl, I didn't realize you were back."

"Yes, my lord. Sten and I returned last night. We reported everything to Captain Baran."

"And the men?"

"Locked up in Clonah until Captain Baran can send a contingent of soldiers to pick them up."

Damien nodded. "I'm interested in finding

out who exactly they were. Let Captain Baran know I would like to be informed the moment he discovers who those men are." He glanced at the door. "Is Lady Selene in the library?"

"Yes. I was assigned to her today." His face remained passive as he reached over and opened the door.

Damien entered the room. Rows of bookcases stood on either side of the room. Ancient parchments rolled up in protective metal tubes, thick tomes, and leather-bound books lined the shelves. Between the shelves were narrow windows, allowing a small amount of light into the room— enough to see by, but not so much that it would damage the books. The room was cool and smelled of wood and parchment.

It was a small library compared to the one owned by House Vivek, but it did boast of a rare collection of sketches and research conducted along the Northern Shores, information privy only to House Maris.

A blue runner ran between the bookcases, leading to the other side of the library. Damien silently walked along the runner, glancing down every row, searching for a familiar head of black hair and feminine features. At the end of the rows, he stepped off the runner and looked to his left, where a small alcove was built into the wall and four arched windows overlooked the cliffs to the north of the castle. Selene sat on a blue cushion next to one of the windows, her legs drawn up beneath her simple gown, her face pressed against the glass, the book in her hand forgotten. Her hair was pulled into a braid that hung over one shoulder down to her waist. She didn't appear to have heard him.

Damien stood still. His eyes traveled from the book she held—curious as to which volume it was—to the way her face was pressed to the window and wondered what held her interest. Then his eyes trailed to her hair. He wanted to untie the end of her braid and touch the long black strands and see if they felt as silky as they looked. And the curve of her neck . . .

Damien glanced away and cleared his throat, both to alert Selene to his presence and to tear his mind away from the path it was traveling down. Now was not the time. Eventually, when things weren't so cold and awkward between them. Not that he was feeling very cold at the moment . . .

He looked up and caught Selene staring at him, leaving his mouth dry.

"I didn't hear you enter," she said as she closed the book and stood.

How could that one movement look so enticing?

"Lord Damien?"

"I wanted to ask you something." Words poured out of his mouth as he reeled in his thoughts.

"Yes?"

"What were you reading?" he blurted out.

"Reading?" Selene looked down as if seeing the book in her hands for the first time. She turned it around and glanced at the cover. *"The Campaigns of Tolrun."*

Damien frowned. "You were reading a book about Commander Tolrun?"

"Yes. I wanted to know more about the man who led the first razing of the Dominia Empire. We do not have this volume at Rook Castle. I had no idea about the acts of brutality he committed against the eastern side of the continent. Large-scale slaughters, wiping out local populations . . . It's a miracle most of our people and lands survived." Selene rubbed her forehead, her eyes still set on the book in her hand. "If the empire was that dangerous then"—she locked eyes with him—"what are they capable of now?"

Damien turned his gaze away from Selene and stared out the window to her right. Even hundreds of years later, Commander Tolrun was still seen as a hero to the people of the Dominia Empire. Commander Orion was walking the same path as his predecessor, gaining the accolades and prestige of the people of the empire. Orion elevated the common man, allowing his soldiers to retain the spoils of war and have a part in how the empire was governed. In a way, Damien understood Commander Orion's methods. Damien wanted the same rights and respect for his own people, hence the coalition his father had started and that he continued. But not at the expense of other people. Never that.

He turned his attention back to Selene. "That's why I'm doing what I can to bring the Great Houses together, so we can be ready for when the empire comes. Does this have anything to do with House Ravenwood's gift?"

Selene froze, the book between her fingers. "Why do you ask?"

"Because it was during the Dominia's first razing that House Ravenwood was wiped out and the gift of dreaming thought gone."

Selene looked as if she wanted to flee. But then her face changed. She lifted her chin and squared her shoulders. "Are you asking me about House Ravenwood's gift? And why we still have it?"

"Yes."

She looked around as if confirming the absence of others, then heaved a sigh and sat back down on the bench built into the alcove. She placed the book on the cushion next to her before starting. "You may not like what you hear. But I cannot keep it from you forever. After all, our lives are now linked together."

Damien sat down on the other side of the bench and leaned forward, his elbows across his knees. "I promise to listen."

Selene glanced at him, then proceeded. "As you are aware, House Ravenwood was not completely destroyed during the first razing by the Dominia Empire. My ancestor Rabanna Ravenwood was taken back to the empire as a little girl. From what I know, the empire only saw her as spoils of war, never realizing that instead of a servant, they had taken the last daughter of Ravenwood. Rabanna grew up on the other side of the wall, as a slave within the empire's palace. When she came into her gift, she began to practice dreamwalking, honing it until there came a day she was able to use it to escape the empire and make her way back to our lands."

"How?" Damien asked.

"You'll see." Selene held her arms across her stomach as if in pain.

Damien frowned and nodded for her to continue.

She looked out the window. "She was able to find passage on a boat back to our lands. Once here, Rabanna traveled to the Magyr Mountains and Rook Castle, entering into the good graces of House Remyr, the lesser house that took over as House Ravenwood after the razing. She eventually married the grand lord, raised two daughters, and taught them how to use the Ravenwood gift of dreamwalking. Her husband was bound to house secrecy, and so it has been ever since. Every Lady Ravenwood passes on the gift of dreamwalking to the next generation of daughters, who then marry and bind their husbands to secrecy. Only the head of House Ravenwood can free them from this secret. That is how we have kept our gift hidden for all of these years."

"But why? Was your family afraid they would not be welcomed?"

Selene glanced back with such sadness and weight in her eyes that Damien was thrown off guard. "Naturally it would be difficult to trust those who allowed your house to be sacrificed. But there is more. The women of my family found a better purpose for our gift, one that brought power and gold to House Ravenwood, and ensured that our house would never fall again."

The hairs along his arms and neck rose. "What was that purpose?" he said quietly.

"We use our gift to kill through dreams."

Silence filled the library. The tingling along his neck and arms expanded across his entire body, sending a shiver up his spine as his mind tried to comprehend Selene's words. The Ravenwood gift of dreaming . . . had been turned to killing?

Assassinations . . . random deaths over the years . . . the rise of House Ravenwood . . . Caiaphas's veiled hints . . .

"Is that how your ancestor Rabanna was able to escape the empire? By . . . by . . ."

"By killing? Yes."

Damien swallowed. "And when you say power and gold, you mean . . ."

She curled her lip. "There is a lot of money to be made in secrets and assassinations. Enough to help our people when the mines dried up."

"Secrets?"

Her eyes grew hard. "Dreamwalking allows us to reach inside a person's mind and memories. Powerful people are willing to pay a great deal of money for that kind of information."

"I see." Damien's mind was spinning. Not only could House Ravenwood enter a person's dreams, they could see the person's thoughts—or kill them. Their gift could well be one of the most powerful ones amongst the Great Houses. And no one knew. Except Caiaphas and now himself, and whomever else Lady Ragna might have told.

Selene let out a sorrowful laugh and tugged at the corner of her sleeve. "Now you know our secret."

He looked up. "So that night, when I found you beside my bed, you were there to kill me. Not with your swords, but with . . ." He couldn't say it. He couldn't wrap his mind around it.

"Yes. I was there to assassinate you. Inside your dreams." Her voice was cold and quiet.

Dear Light! Damien held his head in his hands. Their bonding had only revealed that she could dreamwalk, not what House Ravenwood had done with that gift. This was not at all what he had been expecting when he asked her about her gift. How should he respond? What should he do? None of the other houses were so malevolent and vile as what Selene had revealed about Ravenwood—not even House Friere, for all of its pride and aggravating ways. To use one's house gift in such a way went against the whole reason the Light gave the seven houses such gifts! It was perverted. It was wrong.

Selene must have seen the shock and disgust on his face because she suddenly stood. "I'm sure you have a lot to think about," she said in a low tone. "After all, not only did you end up marrying a woman you do not love, you married a murderess."

His head shot up. "You've used your gift to kill?"

"No, but I might as well have."

"What do you mean?"

Her nostrils flared, and her hands tightened into two fists. "I—" She looked away. "I shattered a young woman's mind during a dreamwalk. She cannot move, she cannot speak. She lies in bed all day, staring at the ceiling. She's as good as dead. And there is no way to undo what I did." Her voice cracked. "So there you are. Behold, the gift of the Dreamers." Before Damien could say another word, Selene spun around and left.

Damien stared at the empty space where Selene had been standing moments ago, her words replaying inside his mind like a song in minor tones. House Ravenwood killed with their gift. And had kept it a secret for hundreds of years.

He pressed a fist to his mouth. How many had they killed? How many secrets had they uncovered? He thought back to those nights when he held Selene's hand. What exactly was she doing? Searching his mind? Using her gift to uncover every covert part of his being? Not that he had that many secrets, but still.

He dropped his hand and frowned. However, there was something missing from Selene's explanation. Something she failed to mention. Something he remembered from that night when they escaped from Rook Castle.

"I couldn't do it."

Those were her words.

She had been sent to kill him, and she couldn't. Did that mean that she had been unable to do any of the other things she just shared?

He looked out the window and swallowed.

Selene had woken him up that night and told him he wasn't safe. She'd risked her life to lead him and his men to the borders of his land, knowing that she was forfeiting her life in doing so. And she'd saved his life on Trader's Road when she fought off those bandits.

So who was Selene really? The one he had witnessed for himself or the one she had painted during her confession? Yes, she had admitted she shattered a person's mind, but the way she said it reeked of guilt and shame, not pride. It was almost as if she had used that memory as a shield to keep him away.

Damien stood. He needed time to sift through what Selene had shared. There were considerations to be made, the foremost being if his people were safe. He ran a hand through his hair. Had he been wrong to bring a member of House Ravenwood back to the Northern Shores?

And what did this mean for his marriage?

15

Why had she shared her past with Damien? Selene hit the wall with her fist, then slid to the floor of her bedroom and held her head between her hands. No more secrets. No more hiding behind the veneer of a noble lady. The mask was off. She was a wicked woman, and now he knew.

A burning bubble of bile rose up her throat, threatening to expel the little food she had eaten that morning. She bit her lip and forced the burning sensation back down. At least she could live with herself. It was too much to carry a lie and wear a mask at the same time. Now she was free to carry only one. The mask could stay in place, but as a way to keep people at arm's length, not to hide the truth. Damien knew everything now. It was too bad he didn't know before he married her.

Selene slowly stood, her body tense and her eyes on the verge of tears. She balled her hands into tight fists. No, no crying. What she needed was exercise. If only she had her dual swords with her and a place to let out all these pent-up emotions. Exercise always had a way of siphoning off restless energy.

She turned and opened the door. The hallway

was dark and silent. Her mind churned. Perhaps she could have new swords forged. And in the meantime, it wouldn't be a bad idea to learn a new skill, like how to use a single sword. It might save her in the future, should she find herself in another fight without her own weapons.

She closed the door behind her. Dark feelings still simmered inside of her, but she had a mission now, and it allowed her to suppress her feelings. She headed for the training room she had spotted the other day. Hopefully she would run into someone she knew, like Taegis. He might be willing to help her out.

A shadow fell into step behind her. Selene glanced back and found Karl a couple of feet away. She frowned. When had he returned?

At her look, he bowed, his face holding just a hint of contempt.

She turned around and continued along the hall. Her annoyance at the guard grew with each step. She could almost feel his disdainful stare as she moved across the castle. He still did not approve of her marriage to Lord Maris. Then again, perhaps he was right.

Selene gritted her teeth. *Well, no changing that now.*

She politely nodded to those she passed, barely aware of the servants' stares and bows. She stopped at a familiar door. This looked like the right place. She opened it and found a handful of guards across the room, practicing with wooden swords or engaging in hand-to-hand combat.

"My lady?" said a voice to her left.

Selene spotted Taegis standing near a long table covered with a variety of training weapons. He wiped his hands on a rag and left it on the table as he made his way over to her. "Do you need something?"

"Yes. That is . . ." Why was her face heating up? She straightened her shoulders and pushed on. "Where would I inquire about having a special sword forged?"

Taegis frowned. "I don't understand. . . ."

"I don't want to lose the skills I've acquired over the years. And—" she swallowed—"it would help me to have something to do. I am unfamiliar with other ladylike habits such as painting or weaving." It was hard to admit that she was a failure when it came to being a proper lady. None of that would have mattered if she had taken her place as Grand Lady Ravenwood, married a lesser lord, and remained as head of her house. There, she would have had the luxury and freedom to train below Rook Castle and rule her castle as she saw fit.

"Hmm. Lord Damien left not too long ago to talk to you about possibly sparring."

It was her turn to frown. "What?"

"Did he not find you?"

Selene pressed two fingers to her forehead and

turned away. Was that why he had sought her out in the library? But then why had he asked her about her book and subsequently her gift?

"My lady, are you all right?"

"Yes, yes. I just . . . Yes, Lord Damien found me. But sparring was never brought up."

"Odd," Taegis said behind her. "Well, in answer to your question, yes. The weaponsmith will need to speak to you. He will need details about your previous swords. Come, I will take you to him."

"Thank you," Selene breathed as Taegis came around her and opened the door.

"Sir," Karl said, his posture rigid and upright.

"Karl, I will be accompanying Lady Selene. Go ahead and take your midday meal."

"Thank you." He bowed toward Selene. "My lady."

"Karl," Selene acknowledged.

The dark-haired guard turned and left.

"This way, my lady."

They followed another hall along the second floor lined with windows that overlooked the sea.

Selene slowed as she passed by a set of windows. She knew this place. It was the same corridor where Damien had taken her days before.

She glanced out one of the tall windows. White-capped waves rolled in from beyond, crashing along the cliffs below. The sky was a dull grey, painting the water below the same color. The cliffs were bare, with only wisps of yellow grass and rugged stone—

She came to a stop. There, along the narrow precipice that jutted beyond the rest of the cliffs, stood a lone figure.

A man stood on the edge, moving his arms in front of him, his knees bent, his back straight. The wind pulled and tugged on the cloak whipping around his body. He raised his hands up to chin level, palms up, sending the cloak flying to his right side like a banner, leaving his light tunic exposed. The wind pressed his clothing against his body, and she could almost see the contours of the muscles along his back move in conjunction with his arms. A spray of water shot past the edge of the cliff, washing over him. Whoever he was, he was in excellent physical condition—and had to be cold.

"Who is that? And what is he doing?"

Taegis paused and looked out. "It's his lord-ship."

"Lord Damien?" Selene glanced back. Yes, she could see that now: the hair, the height, the body build. She held her breath, mesmerized as another wave crashed up over the edge of the cliff, sending a wall of seawater up into the air in front of him. A tingling sensation spread up from her back to her neck and face.

A smile touched on the older man's lips. "It

has been a while since Lord Damien raised the waters. Members of House Maris have stood on that cliff for hundreds of years, practicing their gift of raising the waters and communing with the Light."

"The Light?"

"Yes. This is Lord Damien's time when he intercedes for his people and offers his gift up to the Light."

What a lovely concept. "Like worship," Selene murmured.

"Yes."

So different from the cold sanctuary and solemn words spoken during the new moon service to the Dark Lady. Selene closed her eyes, but she could not erase the image of Damien standing on the cliff, his body moving in perfect harmony with the water and the waves in supplication to the Light. Just the way she imagined a man with a soul like his would.

So unlike herself.

She opened her eyes and clutched the front of her dress, remembering their conversation from this morning. What did he think of her now? Disgust? Revulsion? Her cheeks burned at the thought.

"Lord Damien, like his father before him, is a follower of the Old Ways. Using his gift is one way he worships the Light."

It took Selene a moment to realize Taegis was

referring back to their conversation. She glanced back at the window. "Why does he follow the Light?"

"Well, that's a question you'd have to ask him. But one thing I do know: the Light gave him his gift, and so he offers it back to the Light."

Was it possible the Light also gave her the gift of dreamwalking? Was there a way to find out? It couldn't be as simple as asking. Or was it? After all, her mother communed with the Dark Lady. Perhaps the Light was like the Dark Lady, a being of higher power. But the Dark Lady only spoke to the priest and her mother. How did one speak to the Light? And would he even speak back to her? She was nothing like Damien.

"My lady?"

Selene blinked, bringing her mind back. Damien still stood on the cliff outside, his legs spread front and back, his hands high. White spray flew up across his boots. He looked like a grand lord of House Maris, standing there with his arms raised and waves bursting across the cliff's edge, his muscles bulging at the effort.

A strange heat filled her belly.

Selene turned away from the window and swallowed.

"Are you ready, my lady?"

"Yes. Please lead on, Taegis."

He nodded and started down the hallway, Selene close behind.

• • •

That night Selene lay curled up on her side and stared at the door that led into Damien's room. Whenever she closed her eyes, she could still see him standing on the cliff, raising the water with movements that looked almost like a dance as seawater sprayed up around him.

It was beautiful. So achingly beautiful.

Did the other houses use their gifts in similar ways? She could imagine House Luceras, with their gift of light, worshiping *the* Light with their power. And House Vivek filling books with the wisdom granted to them. Even House Friere could use their gift of fire and earth to make items of worship.

But what place was there for a dreamwalker? What purpose was there in visiting a single mind? Yes, she had been able to soothe Damien when nightmares had invaded his feverish mind. But that was only one person. And it wasn't that amazing.

She rolled over and sighed. Perhaps the only true power of a dreamwalker was in secrets and death. If it was true that the Light gave the Great Houses their gifts, then what purpose was there in hers?

Selene curled up into a tight ball, pulled the covers up close to her neck, and squeezed her eyes shut. A sudden burning desire filled her chest, a desire to speak to the Light. To ask him or it or whatever this being was about her gift. But how?

Wait. Cohen was a monk. Was it possible he could intercede on her behalf? Or maybe Damien could as well.

But then she remembered the shock on Damien's face in the library. No, not him. She would go to Cohen instead. But how to find the abbey where Cohen lived . . . ?

Sleep crept across her eyes until darkness took hold.

She moved in and out of dreams, soaring along the dreamscape, visiting cities and places she had never been before until she found herself in an empty hallway of Northwind Castle. Moonlight streamed through the windows, casting the corridor in shadows and pale light.

Selene landed on the stone floor and changed into her human form. She raised her hand and held out her fingers. Her skin appeared hazy and translucent, like the images of those whose dreamscapes she visited. White fabric fluttered at her elbow. She glanced down. A simple nightdress covered her body, but she didn't recognize the garment. She vaguely recognized the hall she was in. It was on the other side of the castle, the part she had barely visited, and not enough to know how to make her way back to her room.

Selene looked around again, then back at her

hand with a frown. Whose dreamscape was this? And why did she appear as a dreamer?

A yellow light appeared at the end of the corridor, like the glow cast by candlelight.

She took a step forward. "Hello? Is someone there?"

The light moved away, down the other hallway.

"How did I get here?" she whispered. *Am I visiting my own dreams? It has to be. I'm not touching someone.*

"Little raven," spoke a raspy voice behind her.

Selene froze, except for her heart, which began to pound frantically inside her chest. Slowly she turned. As she moved, the dreamscape began to morph. A chill swept across her body as tall obsidian columns rose in place of the walls. The hallway and Northwind Castle disappeared in a mesh of grey and darkness until the room settled and she found herself in the Dark Lady's sanctuary back at Rook Castle. Ten feet away, near the front of the sanctuary, a dozen candles burned in the retable, providing the only light.

Selene took a step back. *I don't want to be here. Not here.*

Before she could turn, she spotted a figure draped in black approach the retable. A pale gaunt hand reached out from beneath the robe and pinched each twinkling flame until only one remained. It was the same shadowy figure that had been visiting her almost every night since she left Rook Castle.

Run! Her mind screamed, but she was still frozen, her gaze fixed on the scene in front of her.

"Little raven." The figure's hood hung low, covering everything but the lower half of its face. Lips painted black were all that was visible. A hand rose and the robe's sleeve fell back. Long pale fingers beckoned her. "Come with me."

Her heart raced inside her chest until it felt like it was going to explode. She couldn't breathe, couldn't speak. Was this . . . was it the Dark Lady?

The finger beckoned again. "Come."

Selene shook her head, finally free of her paralysis, and took a step back. "No." She spun around, her power exploding inside of her and transforming her into raven form. With a caw, she flew toward the doors and out of the sanctuary.

The dream morphed again, back to Northwind Castle. A last flicker of light disappeared at the end of the corridor. Selene soared down the hallway toward the light. Just as she reached the corner, the candlelight disappeared around another bend. Glancing back, she spotted the black-robed figure gliding toward her.

She rounded the corner and flew with all her might. *Is the Dark Lady pursuing me? In my dreams?*

She focused on the area around her as she flew.

Yes, this was definitely a dreamscape. She could feel it along the edges of her being. And it was a strong one, connected to a strong mind. Was it really hers?

The rustling of cloth along the stone floor drew closer. She beat her wings harder and took another corner, careening along the shadowed corridor. *I need to do something. Anything!*

She landed on a windowsill and closed her eyes. She pictured the hallway, then her bedchambers back at Rook Castle. Drawing on the power inside of her, she pressed against the dreamscape, willing it to morph into her room. Harder, harder, until the walls were shuddering under her force. But the moment she let up, they resumed their position.

"Little raven."

Selene spotted the cloaked figure and lifted from the windowsill, flying in the opposite direction. Only a sliver of the candlelight remained at the end of the next corridor. Why didn't the dream change? Was it because it was hers? Was she trapped here, like she had been in Damien's dreamscape?

Could she be wrong? Was this *his* nightmare?

It couldn't be. Why would he be dreaming of the patroness of House Ravenwood? He followed the Old Ways. There was no reason he would dream of such a sinister being.

But then who?

Selene continued flying, putting as much distance as she could between herself and the robed figure, all the while chasing after the small glimmer of light that continued to move through the hallways. One thing filled her mind, one emotion kept her going when her wings began to burn and she could barely catch her breath: if she stopped, the Dark Lady would overtake her.

16

Salty wind pulled at Selene's cloak as she walked along the cliffs overlooking the sea west of Nor Esen days later. The nightmare never came back. She still had no idea whose dream she had visited or what the dream meant—or if that had really been the Dark Lady. Selene shivered and drove the thoughts from her mind. Best not to dwell on them or she might find herself back in that dreamscape.

The landscape around her was grey, both the sky and the water, with a hint of rain in the air. A dozen ships lay in the bay below the city, moving with the waves coming in from the open water. A small figure stood on the precipice jutting out from Northwind Castle, barely a pinprick against the grey sky, but the rise and fall of the water along the cliff wall gave him away. Damien was practicing his gift.

Selene pulled her cloak closer to her body and watched as wave after wave crashed against the rocky cliffs. There was no secret to what he was doing; everyone in Nor Esen could see him practicing, if they wanted.

She brushed her hair aside and wondered what it was like to have no secrets. Everyone knew Damien's power. And they knew he used it for their protection. He held his people's respect and admiration. She had seen it on the journey here and in the way those around Damien treated him in the castle and within the city.

Would the people of the mountain nation have treated House Ravenwood the same way if they knew what she and her family could do and that her family used their gift for the benefit of their nation? No secrets, just open honesty between the mountain people and her house? Was it possible that a long time ago, back before they were dreamkillers, House Ravenwood was respected?

Selene sighed and turned away. She didn't know. She continued to pick her way along the trail that ran along the top of the cliffs toward Baris Abbey. She hoped to find Cohen and ask him more about the Light. She wanted to know more about this being Damien followed and even worshiped with his gift. What was the Light like? Did he work for House Maris like the Dark Lady did for House Ravenwood?

Did the Light illuminate Damien's soul?

Was there a connection between the Light and her new nightmare?

Tall pine trees lined the trail on the right, and light-colored grass grew on the left, right before the ledge gave way. The air grew more dense and misty the longer she walked, coating her face and exposed fingers in tiny droplets. Twenty paces behind, she could sense Karl following her, a shadow to her every movement. At least he was quiet and unobtrusive. He had even dropped his unpleasant expression and now appeared impassive.

As she rounded the bend, a lone stone building came into view near the cliffs beyond a field of tall grass. Baris Abbey. Cheery light shone from the huge arched windows lining the first and second story. The roof was steep and angular, with blue tiles covering the top. A trail led through the waving grass to a set of tall wooden double doors that led into the abbey.

A bell rang, its dulcet tones ringing out across the field and cliffs. Then a second bell. Moments later, the soft sound of chanting filled the air.

Selene stopped and stared at the abbey. The low, deep voices were coming from the far side, where the face of the abbey overlooked the sea. As she listened, the chant began to blend with the soft wind and gentle sound of the waves. The hairs along her arms rose at the sound. The music, although it was much more, seemed to spread across her body and move toward her heart, warming her entire being along the way.

She wanted to join the voices. She wanted to raise her hands and close her eyes and let forth this incredible, enchanting power filling her on the inside. She didn't even realize she was crying until Karl stepped beside her.

"It's the Chant of Light."

Selene worked her mouth, trying to form words. "It's beautiful," she whispered. "I've never heard anything like it."

"Very few have. The Baris Abbey monks sing to greet the coming winter, to remind us that even though the days will be short and cold, the light will come again."

The light will come again.

"Do you follow the Light, Karl?" Selene asked as the wind whipped the tears from her cheeks.

"I believe he exists, but nothing more. Not like the monks. Not like his lordship, Lord Damien."

"Why?" She hadn't meant to ask the guard such personal questions, but at the moment, it was like her heart was flung open.

Karl glanced away, his arms crossed. "I've seen too much darkness."

Selene wiped her eyes with her fingertips. "I understand." And yet there was something inside of her that longed desperately for the light. If there was such darkness in the world, then there could also be immense light . . . right?

That was what she was determined to find out.

The last notes of the monks' chant lingered in the air like a fading wisp before being washed away by the sound of the sea. Selene started again along the path, her dress and cloak rustling through the long grass, her eyes focused on the double doors ahead. A mist began to rise from the trees, and a gull called out nearby.

Her fingers were numb with cold when she reached the doors. There was a large pewter knocker on the left door, which she lifted and let drop with a loud bang. Karl waited silently behind her.

Moments later, the door opened with a creak. A stout man dressed in mahogany robes stood in the door, a beard covering the lower half of his face. A golden pendant of the sun hung from his neck. "May I help you?" he asked in a deep voice.

Selene folded her hands together and raised her chin. "I am Lady Selene Raven—er, Maris, and I am looking for the monk Cohen."

His eyebrows shot up. "Lady Maris? His lordship's new wife?"

"Yes." She could feel his perusal but could not tell what he thought of her.

"This way, my lady," he said, motioning her inside.

Selene stepped into the long hallway. The entrance area was two stories high, with a stone staircase on the right that led up to the second floor. Thick wooden beams held the steep ceiling in place, and arched windows lined the far wall, allowing natural light into the sacred building. An enormous fireplace stood against the wall opposite of the staircase, a long wooden table in front of it.

Everything was made from soft-colored stone, almost the same color as the beach near Nor

Esen. There were no other colors: no tapestries, no rugs, not even a painting.

Doors lined either side of the main hall, each one opening into smaller rooms. The air was cool and smelled like aged herbs and wood. Soft voices echoed through the hall, and every once in a while a monk would emerge from one of the rooms, carrying a tome or a scroll. They would glance at Selene, then carry on with their work.

"This way," the stout monk said, and he led Selene and Karl to the other side of the abbey. Beneath the staircase was a set of doors unlike the others. The monk opened one of the doors and ushered them in. "Cohen is with Father Dominick today."

The room was bare, with only a wooden table in the middle and a bench on either side. Two men sat at the other end, near three arched windows overlooking pine trees.

Selene recognized Cohen's thick, wheat-colored hair. The other man was old and thin, his head mainly bald save for a couple strands of wispy white hair. Both were dressed in the same mahogany robes and wore golden chains around their necks. They glanced over as the door opened, and Cohen smiled broadly the moment he spotted Selene.

The stout monk bowed. "Father, please excuse my interruption. Lady Maris has graced us with her presence today. She said she wished to see Brother Cohen."

Cohen and Father Dominick stood. "Lady Maris," the older man said. "Welcome to Baris Abbey."

Selene walked across the room. "Thank you, Father Dominick."

His warm brown eyes studied her. "Yes, yes," he said quietly. "You have the makings of a great lady and will be a strength to Lord Damien in the days ahead."

Selene blinked, but before she could say anything, Father Dominick stepped around the bench. "You may visit with Brother Cohen in here. I am needed in the repository. I look forward to seeing who you become, my lady." He glanced at the stout monk. "Brother Maelor, please follow me."

"Yes, Father."

Selene watched the two monks cross the room and leave through the door before turning toward Cohen. "What did Father Dominick mean?"

Cohen shrugged. "There are times Father Dominick speaks in riddles, as if he can see more than we can but cannot share exactly what he sees."

Selene cocked her head to the side. "Is that because of his position as abbot?"

"Yes. The Light speaks to him."

Her eyes lit up. "Does the Light speak to you as well?"

Cohen ran a hand through his hair, causing it to stand on end. "Kind of. But not directly, not like Father Dominick. Anyway, welcome, Lady Selene, to our humble abbey. I'm afraid we don't have much to offer, but if you wish, feel free to take a seat, and I will procure some tea from the kitchen."

Selene dipped her head. "Thank you, Cohen."

He gave her a wide grin as he bobbed his head and left the room.

Selene gathered her dress and held it to the side as she took a seat on the bench. Mist gathered along the windowpanes, coating the glass with condensation. Karl coughed softly behind her, then took up his spot by the wall.

She frowned as she leaned forward and held her chin in her hand. What did Father Dominick mean? Had the Light given him a glimpse of her future, much like how the dark priest had warned her mother of the threat from the north? What did he mean that she would be a strength to Damien? How was that possible when they weren't even speaking—not since she had shared about her gift?

Her chest tightened at her last thought. It wasn't that she had spent a lot of time with Damien since their vows, but he hardly spoke to her now. He was never at dinner, and she barely heard him at night on the other side of the door. Then again, she was sure he was busy. Between the assassination of House Vivek and their escape from Rook Castle, no doubt the Great Houses had been thrown into disarray and were ripe for an invasion by the Dominia Empire. The Damien she knew from the assembly was most likely working fervently to form a fledgling alliance before the empire appeared.

All the while, she sat alone, day after day, reading what she could find, and wandering the castle, looking for purpose.

And I will continue to look. She set her lips resolutely. *For the sake of those I left behind. And because I want to know . . . who is this Light?*

Minutes later, there was the rustle of robes and the aromatic smell of tea. Selene glanced over to find Cohen carrying a wooden tray bearing an earthen teapot and two small cups. He placed the tray down on the table and took a seat on the bench on the other side, almost knocking the tray over with his knee.

His face turned bright red, almost matching his robes as he tucked his legs under the table, bumping the table in the process. "I apologize. I sometimes have trouble with these long legs of mine."

Selene gave him a reassuring smile. "There is no need to apologize." Cohen looked nothing like the other monks. He was tall and gangly, with unruly hair and a boyish face. Perhaps that was why she had felt so comfortable around him ever since they left Rook Castle.

He lifted the teapot and poured the tawny liquid into one cup then the other. "Here you go. This is Brother Sammus's special blend." He held out the tiny cup, the size of which he could have easily palmed. Selene took the cup between her fingers and blew across the top, savoring the warmth as it spread across her hands.

"We are honored that you came to visit our abbey, Lady Selene. Is there anything we can do for you?"

Selene ran a finger around the rim of her cup. "Yes, I have some questions. I know very little about the Light. Taegis said something the other day that I have been wondering about ever since." She looked up. "Did the Light give all of the Great Houses their gifts or only House Maris?"

Cohen blinked in surprise, then coughed to clear his throat. "That is an interesting question coming from . . ." He hesitated.

"Coming from me, since I am from House Ravenwood."

"Yes, my lady. It is my understanding that your house follows another way."

Selene shifted uncomfortably and waited.

"To answer your query," Cohen continued, "yes, every Great House was given a gift in which to rule and support their people."

"By the Light?"

"Yes."

"Why?"

"When the nations first formed under the Great Houses, they were small and weak, so seven families were given a way to help their people. House Maris protects the people of the Northern Shores with the power of water. House Merek was able to earn the trust of the wyverns with their gift of courage. House Luceras wields weapons of light offensively and defensively."

"Are you sure the Light and not some other higher power gave every house their gift?"

Cohen rubbed the back of his neck. "Are you referring to the Dark Lady?"

Selene turned her attention back to her cup. "Yes."

"The, uh, Dark Lady is capable of many things." His voice grew more confident. "But the giving of gifts is not one of them."

Interesting. Cohen conceded that the Dark Lady was real and had power. But not that kind of power. That was reassuring, in a way. "So the Light also gave House Ravenwood our gift?"

His face fell. "Yes. But much has not lasted since the birth of the Great Houses. I'm afraid your gift is one of them."

Selene pursed her lips together. She could neither tell Cohen, nor wanted to tell him, that her gift still existed. However . . . "How do you speak to the Light?"

His brow furrowed. "Speak to the Light?"

"Yes. You said the Light doesn't speak to you directly, but he does speak to you, correct?"

A flush crept up Cohen's cheeks as he ran his hand through his hair again. "Yes. We have many sacred texts passed down by previous monks. Through those the Light speaks to us. And sometimes he speaks directly to the abbot, Father Dominick."

Like the priest and the Dark Lady. But there were times her mother was able to speak to the Dark Lady. And Taegis said Damien prayed to the Light. "Can anyone speak to the Light?"

"The library is open to everyone. But the texts must be handled carefully and can only be read here in the abbey since some are very old."

"I understand. But what about actually talking to him? I want to ask him a question."

"I see. What is the question? I might know the answer, or Father Dominick might."

Selene shook her head. "It's a private question."

"Oh. Well, you could look through our texts."

"But how will I know if I've received an answer? What if I miss it? Or"—she laced her fingers together on top of the table and leaned forward—"what if he doesn't answer?" That was what she feared the most: that the Light would have no reason to answer someone like her.

"He'll answer. But sometimes his words are as quiet as a soft breeze, and his light like the first rays of dawn. Only those looking for it will find it. You must listen and watch, and quiet your heart within. Then your answer will come."

Selene stared at Cohen. Those were profound words coming from the awkward monk. "So listen and wait?"

"Yes. And study. Come by the abbey whenever you want and read from our library. Perhaps your question was asked by another."

Selene nodded. "I will." She stood up. "Thank you, Cohen."

"My pleasure, Lady Selene. I hope you find what you are looking for."

"As do I." She turned to find Karl looking inquisitively at her before he glanced away, his blank façade moving back into place.

Cohen led the way across the abbey to the outer door. "Farewell, Lady Selene."

Selene stepped out into the chilly mist with Karl by her side. "Good-bye, Cohen. Thank you again for seeing me today."

The monk bowed his head. "We live to serve the Light and House Maris."

Selene turned and started down the path back to Nor Esen and Northwind Castle. Questions once again filled her mind. Who was she? Why was House Ravenwood given the gift of dreamwalking? And who was the Light?

Cohen had given her ways to find out. And she would do just that.

17

Snow fell on the second day of winter. Damien watched as snowflakes collected along the edge of the glass pane, coating the windowsill in white. A fire burned brightly in the fireplace on the other side of his desk. Three long letters lay open on the wooden surface, one each from House Luceras, House Vivek, and House Merek. The first two were inquiries addressed to his steward, asking if he was at Northwind Castle. He had a feeling it was impressed upon the other houses that he, too, had been murdered or defected, and the letters that he had sent when he arrived at Northwind Castle, the ones letting them know he was alive, must have crossed theirs in the air. The last letter, the one from Lady Bryren, gave him the most information.

Grand Lord Damien,

More than ever I hope this letter finds you in good health, contrary to what Lady Ragna shared with us when you were discovered missing and Lord Rune and Lady Runa found dead. I might have even believed her explanation, save for the question you asked me the night of the gala about the mysterious murders amongst the lower houses and the death of my father. Because of that, I am sending you this letter and implore you to answer back quickly.

The entire assembly was in disarray the moment the news broke. Lady Ragna claims the assassination was carried out because of the assembly, that we provoked the empire and the deaths of House Vivek were a warning. Given the way Lady Ragna spoke of what was found, it would seem possible, and I think some present even believed the accusations.

But how did an assassin enter Rook Castle with all of the security? And why did the empire go after House Vivek? And covertly, no less. This is not how Commander Orion operates. He is not the kind of man to hide behind secrecy and duplicity. Something else is going on. And I believe you disappeared because you know what is happening, not because you ran away or were murdered.

Please write as soon as possible. Whether the empire was involved or not, Commander Orion will take advantage of this situation and most likely go for the wall near House Vivek. We need to act before it is too late.

Grand Lady Bryren of House Merek

Then it was true beyond a shadow of a doubt. Lady Ragna had succeeded in killing Lord Rune and Lady Runa. Damien clenched his hand into a fist. She murdered them in their sleep using her gift, just like Selene said her mother would. Just like Selene herself could.

His nostrils flared, and he spun around and picked up the letter. Lady Ragna used their deaths and his disappearance to plant seeds of doubt and fear, destroying any unity the seven houses could have achieved and allowing the empire an easy way into their lands.

And the Dominia Empire would come. Already the empire had sent out scouts. The highwaymen they had caught during their trip here had indeed been from the Dominia Empire, confirmed after Captain Baran interrogated them. And the empire was working with House Ravenwood and House Friere. Even now Commander Orion's army could be crossing the wall.

And we are in shambles, unprepared for the onslaught.

He breathed through his nose, scoured the letter again, then placed it down. No, the empire would not cross yet. It would be foolhardy to invade in the winter, especially since this year was predicted to be especially snowy. There was still time. Very little time, but at least they could formulate a plan.

Damien sat down and pulled his quill from the

jar while reaching for a fresh piece of parchment. "Well, I am definitely alive and well," he said as he began to write. "And there is no longer a question as to if there will be a war. The real question is, will we be ready to fight?"

His pen flew across the page, detailing what he could share of Selene's revelation and the duplicity of House Ravenwood and House Friere, his hand only stopping when a house secret prevented him. At the end of the letter, Damien wrote,

> We need to arrange a meeting. This kind of planning cannot happen through letters and needs to be done in person. Winter will keep the Dominia Empire at bay, but once the last frost melts, war will be upon us. If you are still for signing the treaty, then let us find a central location and determine our course of action. If we do not, then I fear the worst for our people and our lands.
>
> Grand Lord Damien of House Maris

He finished all the letters, including one to House Rafel, in hopes of changing Lord Haruk's mind. He wasn't optimistic that the elder grand lord would change his position, but there was always a chance. They would need the healers of

House Rafel when the war started. If the empire's previous campaigns were any indication of what was to come, there would be death. So much death.

Damien rubbed his forehead. *Light, what do we do? Can we survive such a war? Or has the time of our demise finally come?* He leaned forward and prayed as the fire crackled, warming his body against the cold winter chill.

As he finished his prayers, his thoughts turned toward Selene. He had been avoiding her ever since she had revealed why House Ravenwood had hidden their gift. The very thought of that conversation made his body tense. And writing these letters didn't help.

Damien stared at the fire. But was she really like her mother? Was Selene capable of the same actions as Lady Ragna?

He didn't think so.

Still, the very fact that the Ravenwood gift of dreaming had been used in a way so completely opposite of its intention made him sick. House Maris protected people. House Ravenwood murdered people. How could he resolve the two? They were polar opposites.

He leaned forward and placed his head in his hands. A headache was coming on behind his eyes. He knew what he needed to do. He needed to talk to her again. No more avoiding her.

Weeks ago she said she couldn't kill him. If

that was truly the woman she wanted to be, the kind who wanted more from her gift than what her family had offered her, then he should give her that chance. Maybe he could even help her. But he would not know until he asked.

An hour later, Damien found Selene standing in the second-story hallway, the one that ran the length of the castle with windows that overlooked the sea. Her hand was pressed against the glass as she looked out across the watery expanse. Snow fell gently outside, and he could see her breath collecting on the glass with every exhale. Her black hair matched the cloak around her shoulders.

"Selene."

She slowly turned. He could almost see her shields slam into place. "Damien."

A small part of him was surprised that she had used his informal name. "I would like to speak with you."

Her body went rigid, but she answered in a clear voice. "As you wish."

"Somewhere private."

She tilted her head but made no comment.

He scanned the hall. The best place was his bedchambers. There they would be far away from listening ears so they could speak freely. "Follow me."

He walked past her down the hall until he reached the door that led into his room. He pressed down on the latch, then stood back and motioned for her to go first.

She hesitated for a moment, then entered. Selene glanced over the room before making her way toward the sitting area near the fireplace. The fire from that morning was almost gone, so Damien crouched down, picked up a few logs from the firewood rack, placed them over the embers, and blew across the hot coals until the flames caught.

He watched as the fire spread, starting with the bark and making its way through the logs, and used the time to figure out where to start the conversation.

After a moment, he slowly rose and turned. "I've been thinking about what you shared, and I have one question."

Selene sat in the chair to the right, her hands folded across her lap. "Just one?"

"Yes. You shared that House Ravenwood has been using their gift of dreaming to steal secrets and kill others." Her face blanched as his bluntness, but he went on. "However, when you had the chance to kill me, you didn't. Your words were, 'I couldn't do it.'"

She raised her chin. "Yes."

"Then you want nothing to do with House Ravenwood, or your past?"

She wavered, then looked down. "No matter what, I will always be a Ravenwood, and I will always have my past."

Damien rubbed the back of his neck. "What I mean is, who do you want to be? Do you want to follow in your mother's footsteps? I've received letters from the other houses. They confirmed what you and your father said happened: your mother murdered Lord Rune and his sister and lied about their deaths. Is that the kind of woman you want to become?"

Selene stood to her feet. Her nostrils flared and her hands tightened into two tight fists. "No."

Damien felt like all the air had left his body. He sagged against the side of the fireplace and rubbed his face. "I hoped you would say that."

"What?"

He looked over at her. "I had to know. It was eating at me from the inside."

"I don't understand."

"I've had two voices warring within me: one said that you were just like your mother. And another that said you were different. What you said the night you woke me and told me I was in danger were not the words of an assassin. They were the words of a woman who wanted to save life, not take it away. But I had to know for sure that is the woman you still want to be."

Her hands twisted the fabric of her gown. Her dark eyes were wide as she stared back at him. "It is. I want to find out the real reason I was given the gift of dreaming. I believe there is more to it than I was taught, that there is something good in it."

He let out a huge breath. "Then I want to help you. And I believe you can help me. Help all of the houses." He could see the war of emotions across her face. He had angered her. Perhaps if he'd had more time, he might have found a better way to couch his words, but he no longer wanted to wait. He needed a partner.

He could see anger give way to confusion as her face furrowed and she looked away. She still gripped her gown with tight fists, but slowly her fingers began to release. He had taken a step of faith to trust her. Now it was her turn to take a step of trust and believe he wanted to help her.

She let out a shaky breath as her gaze met his. "I would like that. I've started searching and have already visited Baris Abbey and talked to Cohen. I've read everything I could find, but the answer still eludes me. Who were the Ravenwoods before Rabanna? How did our gift help our people?" She raised a hand and pressed it against her chest. "Who am I?"

For the first time, Damien was touched by her honest words. He had grown up knowing who he was, what he could do, and how to use his power to help his people. But from what Selene had said, her upbringing had been much different.

"I'm sorry," he said quietly. "I didn't know that you felt that way. I can't imagine what it is like." He had been so appalled when she first shared that he hadn't been able to see past his disgust and spot the hurting woman beneath the mask of words she had used. "And I am sorry too for how I acted when you first told me."

"It was understandable. I'm ashamed of my family's secrets. I want to find a better way for me, for my sisters, and for my people. I want to change. That is why I left with you when you offered me sanctuary in your land. And I saw something inside of you that I hoped might help me."

Damien raised an eyebrow. "You did?"

"Yes, when I walked in your dreams."

"What did you see?"

Her eyes came up and met his. "Your soul."

He looked down and touched the area above his heart. "My soul?"

"Yes. Sometimes we meet the soul of the sleeper when we enter a dreamscape. When I first dreamwalked inside your mind, I saw yours."

"You can really see a person's soul?" His eyes widened. There was more to the Ravenwood gift of dreaming than he had imagined.

"I can, if it presents itself. The dreamscape is made from your thoughts, consciousness, and memories. And once in a while, the very essence of who you are will appear as well. Your soul."

"What do they look like?"

Selene sat down. "I've seen souls as dark as night, and souls surrounded by chains. But yours . . ." She looked out the window. "It was very different."

Damien sat down in the other chair. "How?"

"Your soul is the most beautiful thing I've ever seen."

Heat slowly spread from his neck, up across his cheeks, and to the tips of his ears. He opened his mouth to say more, but his throat was dry.

She continued to stare out the window. "Your soul is full of light."

He looked down again at his chest and pressed a finger against his tunic. His soul . . . "But how?"

She turned and looked at him. "That's what I want to know. How are you different? And can others have that light?"

Damien blinked, his mind going over what Selene had just shared. She could see his soul— *his very soul*—and it appeared like light. Was it because he followed the Light? That somehow his faith manifested itself? "I . . . I don't know why I am different, since I'm not sure why my soul looks like that."

"I think it has something to do with the Light."

Damien sat back and tugged on his chin. "That could be true. It's worth looking into."

"I hope to find out more from Baris Abbey."

"That's a good place to start. The monks have been studying the Old Ways since before the Great Houses were formed. In fact, Baris Abbey was here long before Northwind Castle."

Selene hummed thoughtfully. "Sadly, they

didn't seem to know much about House Ravenwood's gift—not that I could tell them that it still exists."

"Their library is vast. There are rooms upon rooms beneath the abbey. I'm sure there is something there."

She looked up. "You think so?"

Her face—a mixture of hope and apprehension—tugged at him, leaving a fluttery feeling inside his chest. "I believe so. And like I said, I want to help you." He stood up and held his hand out to her. "In the meantime, I would like to get to know you more, and perhaps ask your advice on working with the other houses. After all, you are the heir to a Great House too."

Selene took his hand and stood. She narrowed her eyes and studied him, then seemed to come to a conclusion. "Yes, I would like that. We are married, and I would like to know the kind of man I will be living with for the rest of my life."

Damien pursed his lips. He felt the same way.

18

"What's happening to me?" Lady Ragna stared down at her palms as if the lines across the surface would answer her question. Her hands looked as they always did. But inside, where her eyes could not see, she could feel it. A change. It was subtle, but it was there, a small trickle. Slowly, her gift was fading.

She clamped her hands shut and looked up at the portrait of Rabanna Ravenwood that hung above her fireplace. Bloodlines could weaken. It had happened before. Rumors were, House Merek was not the power it used to be, due to the dilution of their blood.

But how could that be true in her case? The Ravenwood women had carefully protected their line for hundreds of years. Never had there been a change in power from one woman to the next, except when the matriarch died and the next Ravenwood woman took her place as the grand lady.

"Maybe I'm imagining it," she whispered to the darkening room. Night was quickly coming, and the only light came from the burning embers in the fireplace. A servant would be by soon to tend the fire for the night. "Then again . . ."

She stood and brushed her gown aside and

turned toward the door. She would consult the dark priest. Perhaps the Dark Lady knew what was happening to her—*if* something was happening.

Lady Ragna swept down the corridors of Rook Castle, ignoring the looks from guards and servants. Snow fell outside the windows, and a chill began to take hold of the castle as winter settled in across the Magyr Mountains. As she walked along the halls, she turned her focus on her plans for the weeks ahead. It was time for Amara to take her final test with her dreamwalking gift. The girl was ordinary and mediocre when it came to her gift, but she would suffice for the upcoming missions. She wasn't the first Ravenwood woman to simply carry the gift and nothing more. Unlike Selene . . .

Selene.

Her lips turned upward in a snarl. So much power. So much potential. And that traitor threw it all away.

She took in a long draught of air and let it out slowly. Nothing could be done about it now. She would finish training Amara and ensure that this time the job was finished and death was dealt. Not like that mistake with that servant girl, whatever her name was.

Then there was the empire.

A raven arrived yesterday with a coded message that Commander Orion was preparing his troops for when spring came, and the few men and women who were on this side of the wall were already arranging for his arrival. All she needed to do was keep the Great Houses in disarray and make sure they didn't band together.

That's where Amara would come in handy.

She reached the outer doors to the sanctuary and walked inside. The air was even chillier in here, like the ice caves to the south, where even on a hot summer's day ice still formed along the ground and walls. She half expected to see ice adorning the obsidian pillars, but they were as black as ever without a glint of moisture. Twilight trickled in from the high windows above, pooling on the stone floor below. The platform ahead was empty. But not for long. She knew the priest came here every evening to light the candles for the Dark Lady. He would be here soon.

Sure enough, as she approached the platform, the small door to the right opened, and a lanky robed figure exited. He held a thin stick in one hand with a tiny flame at the top. He never glanced her way. Instead, he crossed to the retable, stopped, and began to light the candles.

Lady Ragna pulled her skirts back and went down on her knees before the platform, her head bowed in submission.

"Lady Ragna," the dark priest said after a moment. "What brings you to the sanctuary?"

"A question," she said, eyes on the stone floor. "And wisdom from the Dark Lady."

The priest did not answer.

Lady Ragna looked up. The priest continued to light the candles along the retable. Silence stretched across the sanctuary. Only once all the candles were lit did the dark priest finally turn around. His hair was hidden beneath the cowl of his robe, and his face appeared gaunt within the shadow of the hood. "What is your question?" he asked as he brought his hands together within the folds of his robe.

"Is there a change going on within me?"

He stared at her with pale blue eyes—so pale he almost appeared as a blind man. Then his eyes shifted above her, trance-like. Was he speaking to the Dark Lady? Lady Ragna wanted to turn around and see her patroness for herself, if the Dark Lady was indeed behind her, but reverence cautioned her to remain where she was. The Dark Lady was powerful, and Lady Ragna wanted that power on her side.

The priest's eyes came back into view. He looked down at her, his hands still clasped in front of him. "The downfall of your house has begun. Your eldest daughter now surpasses you in power."

Lady Ragna kept her head level with the platform as she glanced up at the priest. "What do you mean?"

"There has been a shift in authority. The headship of House Ravenwood has changed. It no longer belongs to you."

Lady Ragna felt like her breath had been knocked from her chest. She reached up and clutched the front of her dress, her mouth gaping like a fish left on the dock, gasping for air. "Wh-what do you mean? Headship can only change when the previous grand lady passes away."

The priest looked down from his place on the platform. "Or when someone with great power— greater power than yours—comes into her gift. That has always been the way with the Great Houses."

Selene . . . was more powerful than she? Of course Selene was powerful; Lady Ragna had known that since the moment she laid eyes on the mark on her infant daughter's back. But powerful enough to interrupt the natural flow of power within a house?

What did this mean for her? For House Ravenwood? For her alliance with the Dominia Empire? "Does Selene know?"

"No. Your daughter is ignorant of the change. At this moment, the Dark Lady is in pursuit of your daughter. Perhaps not all is lost."

The Dark Lady was pursuing her daughter? The thought sent a chill down her spine. Deep inside, even she feared the patroness of her house, despite the power the dark one provided for Ravenwood. But if the Dark Lady could bring Selene—and her powerful gift—back to their cause, then it was worth it. But . . .

"What if my daughter chooses another way?"

"Then your house will fall."

The fire that had been ebbing away within her chest came roaring back to life. Lady Ragna slowly stood, drawing on the power and strength not only of her own will, but that of every Lady Ravenwood who had served before her, all the way back to Rabanna. "That is not an option."

The priest bowed in acquiescence, a slight smile to his thin lips. "It is the strength of the Ravenwoods—your desire to survive, no matter the cost—that drew the Dark Lady to your ancestor hundreds of years ago. Hopefully your strength will prove greater than that of your daughter."

Lady Ragna gazed back at the priest. "It will. Because if Selene doesn't turn back"—she clenched her jaw—"then I will take care of her myself."

19

W ho are you?"
Only silence answered Selene within the dreamscape. The candlelight moved along the corridor of Northwind Castle until it faded around the corner.

What was that light? And why did it always leave her?

Selene watched it disappear, then lowered her head and stared down at her translucent body. Why was she here again? As she moved her fingers, she stretched out her senses, feeling along the dreamscape, searching for the sleeper.

It felt familiar. And powerful. Cool, like the mist that covered the Magyr Mountains on an early spring morning.

It felt like . . . her.

Her head shot up, but before she could think on it further, there was a rustling sound behind her.

Selene froze.

Swish. Swish. Like a dress across the stone floor.

Slowly, she looked back.

The Dark Lady moved between the patches of moonlight along the corridor, her body and face covered in dark fabric. The hood fluttered for a moment around her face, revealing lips black as night. "Little raven," she whispered.

Selene stared at the ghoulish figure. She opened and closed her lips, but she couldn't speak. Only one word entered her mind.

Fly.

She twisted around, burst into her raven form, and flew down the hall where the light had disappeared moments ago.

She was caught between the light and the Dark Lady as she raced within the halls of Northwind Castle—never catching up to one, barely escaping the other. Never a moment's rest.

Right when it felt like her lungs would burst and her wings were on fire, Selene collapsed to the floor in her human form and watched the last of the light vanish around another corner.

"Why am I here?" She curled her fingers against the floor. "Why does my mind keep bringing me to this place?" But it wasn't just her. The Dark Lady was here too. Was she keeping her trapped here?

She only had a few moments before the Dark Lady appeared again, but she couldn't move. Every breath she dragged in through her lips felt like glass shards inside her lungs. *Why can't I escape?*

Escape . . . Escape . . .

Selene sat up with a gasp and opened her eyes. She was back in her room, with the first few rays of dawn filtering through the window. She pressed a hand to her cheek, feeling as though she was going to vomit. Cold sweat met her fingertips. "What is happening to me?" she whispered. Was something changing with her gift? Why couldn't she escape this dream or change it?

What did it mean?

There was rustling in the room on the other side of her wall. Selene stared at the door that led from her room to Damien's. He must be up. Just hearing the sound of another human being made her heart slowly return to its normal beat.

She lay back down and stared up at the ceiling, her thoughts returning from the dreamscape to the present. She listened to the movement on the other side of her wall.

Was Damien always this early of a riser?

She frowned. It was something a wife should know about her husband. And yet the only time she had spent in his bed was when they had first arrived, and she had helped him with his fever-induced nightmares.

They had been married for a month and yet nothing had happened between them. She sat up as heat spread across her cheeks. Her stomach felt like she had fallen down a flight of stairs. She wasn't sure if she was ready for anything yet. They were only now speaking to each other again.

However . . . She remembered her declaration from a few days ago. *I would like to know the kind of man I will be living with the rest of my life.*

The rest of my life.

There was no place for fear in her future. She threw back the quilts and furs and stood. The cold floor and air swept across her exposed feet and thin nightgown. The sun appeared through the window with the pale light of winter. Today was the first day when she would learn more about Damien Maris. He said he wanted her advice on the other houses, and she was ready to hear what had transpired after they left Rook Castle.

And . . . she wanted to know more about him. Perhaps in her study of Damien, she would discover why his soul was the way it was. She might even discover how to change her own soul.

If that was possible.

After Essa brought her morning meal of tea and an egg, Selene headed out of her room and spotted Karl standing across the hall. "Good morning, Karl."

He looked up. "Good morning, Lady Selene."

"Where is Lord Damien this morning?"

"In his study."

"Could you take me there?"

He frowned slightly, then nodded. "This way, my lady."

Selene followed Karl along the hallway,

passing by the windows that overlooked the sea and the cliff where Damien raised the water and communed with the Light. For one brief moment she glanced outside the glass panes and wondered if he would be out there today. And if so, would it be possible to join him sometime? If only to see how he did it, how he used his gift and spoke to the Light.

Ten minutes later, Karl stopped in front of a door on the other side of the castle and knocked.

"Yes?" came a muffled voice.

Karl opened the door and looked in. "Lady Selene wishes to see you."

A chair scraped across the floor. "Please send her in."

Karl stepped back while holding the door open. "My lady," he said with a stiff bow.

"Thank you, Karl."

Selene stepped into the study, her gaze moving across the room. Bookshelves lined both sides, each filled with books, tomes, artifacts, and small sculptures. In front of her stood a massive desk with one large arched window behind, filled with light blue sky.

Damien stepped around the desk and reached his hand out as he crossed the room. Before she could move, he swept her fingers up and kissed her across the knuckles, sending a jolt through her body. "I was not expecting you," he said as he let go, a gentle smile across his face.

Her hand dropped to her side, but she could still feel the soft coolness of his lips across her skin. Her heart fluttered inside her chest, and her throat was suddenly tight. "You said you wished for my advice concerning the Great Houses." Her voice came out higher than usual. She glanced at Damien, wondering if he had caught the strange pitch of her voice.

"Yes, I did. Let me see if I can procure a chair for you."

Selene turned and watched Damien head to the door and speak to Karl outside.

He had changed from the man she had left in the library after revealing the vile secrets of her house. Damien had been more cordial ever since their more recent talk. He could be hiding how he really felt inside, but even if he was, he was at least trying.

The tension from that morning slowly slipped away, allowing her to relax a little as Damien turned back around. His eyes met hers, and her mouth went dry again. Such a stunning blue.

Dart'an!

Selene spun around and grasped her hands together and stared out the window ahead.

"I'm glad you came this morning." Damien's soft tenor tone carried behind her. He came around and stood by his desk. "I was going to find you today. I have a surprise for you."

Her heart started thumping again. "A surprise?"

she asked, thankful that this time her voice remained even. What was going on with her? She was acting like a shy young maiden.

"Yes. Taegis told me about your conversation with the weaponsmith, and I just received word that your swords are done."

Her mind latched onto his last words. "Swords?"

Damien leaned against his desk and ran a hand along the back of his neck. "Yes. You had mentioned to Taegis that you didn't want to lose your skills. I'll warn you, though, it's not common for a woman to use a weapon here at Northwind Castle."

Selene went rigid. Was he going to tell her to behave like other ladies? Like how she imagined Lady Adalyn Luceras or Lady Ayaka Rafel did?

He looked up. "But I know this is important to you. And I said I would help you. Taegis thought doing something familiar would help you adjust to your new life here at Northwind Castle, and I agree."

Selene blinked. Her first thoughts were wrong. Even though women training with weapons wasn't something done here, he would encourage it anyway. To help her. Just like he said he would.

"Would you like to see them now? Maybe even test them out? I could use a break. I've been here all morning."

Selene spoke before she could think. "Yes,

I would like that very much. I would need to change first though."

"I'll escort you back to your room, then to the training room. How does that sound?"

A smile crept across her face, the first one in a long time. "You lead and I will follow."

Damien smiled back and headed out of the study. Selene followed, her spirit light. Could they really make this union work? Was it possible that Damien believed she wanted to be a different woman?

Selene was surprised to find a loose tunic, pants, and soft-skinned boots hanging over her changing screen. After changing and redoing her braid, Selene emerged to find Damien waiting for her, clothed in a similar fashion. "Ready?" he asked.

"I am." Her fingers were already itching to hold her new blades and feel the strength of her muscles. She followed Damien down the hall, then a flight of stairs to the first floor, around a corner, and down another hallway. "Should we have let Karl know where we are going?" she asked, her voice echoing along the stone corridor.

"No, I assume he'll leave the chair in my study. I'll need that extra chair there anyway since you'll be coming now." He smiled at her before stopping at a set of doors, sending another whooshing sensation through her belly. He opened the left one. "Here we go."

Selene stepped inside, the smell of sweat and wood greeting her. Three dummies stood near the far wall, but the rest of the room was wide open. On the weapons' table, right near the edge, were a set of twin blades that looked almost exactly like the ones she had to leave behind the night she left Rook Castle, only less ornate than the originals.

Selene walked over to the table and fingered the hilt of the blades. They looked to be about the right length and width. She picked one up, then the other, then hoisted both into the air. In the next movement, she swung the blades, getting a feel for the weight. The weaponsmith got the lengths right, with her lead sword longer than her other, a must for her technique. They were also a little heavier than her old blades, just slightly, but not enough to throw her off. But the curve to each blade was exactly how it should be.

"Well?" Damien asked behind her.

Selene turned around, a smile on her face. She couldn't help it. These swords were the first thing that made Northwind feel like home. "A little heavy, but otherwise perfect."

Damien leaned against the doorway, his arms folded across his tunic. His hair had been trimmed recently and his face shaved, giving him a pleasing, clean appearance. "Good. The weaponsmith worked hard to finish them. And

I'm glad the seamstress was able to make you something loose and comfortable to practice in."

Selene looked down again at her clothing. "Yes." Damien must have ordered them for her. She couldn't remember Essa saying anything about training clothes when the maid was instructing the seamstress about her wardrobe. His thoughtfulness touched her.

"Would you like to try your swords out after you've had a chance to warm up?"

She looked up and raised one eyebrow. "Are you asking me to spar, Lord Damien?" The joy inside of her spilled out across her face and words.

He seemed taken aback for a moment by her playfulness before he returned her look with a grin. "I am. I've seen you practice against dummies and highwaymen. I would love to test your skills against my own."

His smile made her heart do a weird flip inside her chest. Selene turned around and headed for the closest dummy as her face heated up. "I would like that," she said without looking back and began her drills on the straw-stuffed canvas.

The familiar rhythm came back to her, the flow between her body and her blades. Her muscles had grown soft over the weeks, but they would be strong again soon. She hit the dummy with consecutive moves, each hit emitting a muffled sound.

From the corner of her eye, she spotted Damien warming up nearby. But instead of using a practice dummy, he first stretched out his body, then went through a couple of motions with his own sword in the middle of the room. Her heart did that weird flip again. His physique, while not necessarily muscular, was certainly athletic. His moves were controlled, smooth, and potent—not wild with brute power.

Selene went back to her warm-up and wondered if Damien's fighting style would be similar to Amara's one-sword technique or different. Her lips quirked to the side. She was looking forward to this.

"Ready?" Damien asked ten minutes later.

Selene turned around, sweat beginning to form along her skin. "Yes." She joined him in the middle of the training room and raised her right hand and longer blade and held it above her head while she staggered her feet, the majority of her weight along the back leg. Her left hand, holding the shorter blade, was held out in front of her.

Damien gripped his sword between his hands and held it between them, point up, his feet apart and knees slightly bent. "Ready?"

Selene nodded. "Ready."

She blocked Damien's first move with her shorter blade, then brought her longer blade around. He caught it with the side of his sword, pushed her blade away, and went for the opening. She blocked again.

The strength of her style was in her dexterity while Damien's power came from strength itself. She danced and weaved around him, moving in when she could, bouncing back and blocking when he went for an opening.

He was strong. Stronger than Amara. Stronger than her mother. Stronger even than the highwaymen.

Selene sucked in another lungful of air. Heat radiated off of her body like a warming brick. She blocked again, but her movement was a hair slower. Did he notice?

Damien wiped the side of his face, then brought his sword up again.

This time, Selene attacked first, charging with her shorter sword and catching his as he lifted his own up to block. She went to jab him with her right as she pushed his sword away with her left, but he pulled out of her grasp, angled up, and knocked her sword to the side.

Before she had a chance to reset her swords, he was pointing his blade at her heart.

They stared at each other, panting, with sweat streaming down their skin. His dark hair glistened, and his eyes appeared even bluer next to his flushed cheeks.

Damien slowly lowered his sword, his eyes still on her. "You're very good with your blades.

For a moment, I thought you were going to best me."

Selene dropped her hands, letting her new swords hang at her sides. "Apparently I haven't lost all of my skills. But I was still defeated. You're the strongest opponent I've ever fought."

"So it wasn't because of the blades?"

Selene held the right one up and looked across the edge. "No, they are well made. Thank you."

Damien wiped his brow with the side of his sleeve. "Feel free to practice anytime you want."

She glanced up. "Are you sure about that? I'm not like other ladies, Damien. My time at Rook Castle was spent training to fight, dreamwalk, and infiltrate a room at night. I have no idea how to embroider or paint or serve tea—"

Damien closed the gap between them and cupped her chin, lifting her face to meet his own. "Those kinds of things don't matter to me."

Selene couldn't move or breathe. It was like her body had forgotten how.

He raised an eyebrow. "If you want to learn any of those pastimes, feel free. But they are not what make a lady." His thumb stroked her cheek. "All right?"

"Yes." The room was beginning to spin, and there was a rushing sound inside her ears.

He opened his lips as if he was going to say something more, but then he froze. Selene stared back, her heart beating inside her head, her chest, her entire body. His eyes grew more intense. The pull between them was like lodestone and iron. His head moved slightly forward, his lips parted—

Then he dropped his hand and took a step back.

Selene stepped back as well, confused by the sudden rush of emotions inside of her. She'd wanted to kiss him, and not, at the same time.

"I'm going to wash up in the baths and head back to my study. Join me if you like." His face turned bright red. "In the study, that is."

She blinked, confused, then her own face heated like a thousand suns.

There were muffled sounds behind her, and the door to the training room opened.

". . . and then this raven appeared in my dream—Lord Damien!"

Damien looked over her shoulder. "Sten, Cedric. It is good to see you both."

"My lord, we didn't realize you were in here. Would you like us to come back later?" Sten asked.

Damien walked past Selene, his eyes firmly ahead and not on her. "No, Lady Selene and I just finished our routine. The room is all yours."

Selene turned toward the table with the weapons to place her own down. She could feel the heat of her own face still blazing.

"You can take them with you," Damien said.

She glanced over her shoulder and spotted him between the table and outer door.

"I also had a scabbard commissioned, but it is not done yet. In the meantime, feel free to store your swords in your room."

There was still a tinge of red to his face, causing him to look more like a young man than a grand lord.

Suddenly she wanted to laugh, both to ease the awkwardness from moments before and at the look on his face. But she refrained, although the corners of her lips twitched. It was good to know Damien was an ordinary man, despite his title. "Thank you."

He gave her a small bow and left the room.

After exchanging pleasantries with Sten and Cedric, Selene left the training room. For the first time since arriving at Northwind Castle, she felt hope for the future burgeoning inside her heart.

20

A week later, Selene held her heavy cloak close to her body as she trudged through the snow toward Baris Abbey. Snowflakes fell thickly from the sky, coating the pine trees in blankets of white. To her left, the sea was grey, barely moving below the cliffs.

As she walked, her mind drifted like the white snow around her. She had spent the last few mornings with Damien in his study, catching up on the news from Rook Castle and the responses from the other houses. She wasn't really surprised about what had all come to pass, given the secrets she knew, but it still saddened her: the assassination of House Vivek, the lies her mother had spun about Damien's disappearance, the call for each house to mind its own business and not provoke the empire. Now the question was, what would her mother do next? And what about Amara? Had she come into her gifting? Was she training to be a dreamkiller?

Had Selene's escape been for nothing?

Then there was Damien. She thought there had been a breakthrough between them. They had talked, even laughed, during those times in the study. And they had sparred again. She'd even caught him looking at her from the corner of her eye when he thought she wasn't paying attention. That kind of look sent her mind and heart spinning.

But then the last two days he seemed more and more lethargic: the blank stares, the shuffling of papers even though he hadn't looked at them, the repeated questions. No more spark to his eyes, no smile tugging at his lips. This morning Taegis told her Damien wasn't feeling well and would be in his room all day.

Was Damien really ill, or was it something else?

She rubbed her nose and sighed. Moments later, the cheery lights from the abbey windows appeared through the snowfall. Selene walked faster, and she could hear the crunch of Karl's boots behind her. No doubt he was as cold as she.

Selene reached the door, pressed down on the metal latch, and pushed inward. A blast of heat and light greeted her as the door creaked open. Monks stood in the main room, conversing or reading near the massive fireplace. She spotted Cohen, talking to a shorter monk. Then again, everyone was shorter than Cohen.

Both men looked over, and Cohen broke out in a huge grin. "My lady, you came to visit today."

"Yes." Selene stepped inside and stomped out her boots as Karl shut the door behind them.

Cohen and the other monk walked over. "Lady Selene, let me introduce you to Brother

Aedan. He leads us in our morning and evening chants."

"My lady," the older man murmured and bowed his head.

"Brother Aedan, it is nice to meet you. I heard the Chant of Light not long ago, and it was beautiful."

"Thank you. It is one of our oldest chants."

"Can I get you some tea?" Cohen asked.

Selene rubbed her hands, not quite ready to remove her gloves. "Yes. I was also hoping to read anything you might have about the birth of the Great Houses."

Cohen wrinkled his brow. "I might have to look around, but I'll see what I can find. I know there are some old tomes in the vault below, but many of those are sealed until we can copy them and preserve them."

"I understand."

Aedan spoke up. "I will be happy to make tea for Lady Selene if you would like to find what she is looking for, Brother Cohen."

"Thank you. I will start with Pallion's writings. Lady Selene, feel free to take a seat at the table near the fireplace, and I will bring you what I can find."

She took a seat at the end of the long table, then removed her cloak and gloves and laid them beside her. Karl stood by the fire, his body turned so he could keep an eye on her and warm himself at the same time. Not for the first time she wondered why Karl had been assigned to her since her arrival at Northwind Castle.

The gentle hum of conversation combined with the snap and crackle of the fire. Selene leaned forward, her body slowly thawing from the trek here.

"I heard Lord Damien is feeling ill today." One of the monks spoke softly.

"Not surprising. He was the same way this time last year as well."

Selene remained still as she tuned into their conversation.

"Do you think he'll ever recover from the death of his family?" the first monk said in a low voice.

"His parents, perhaps. But it was Lord Quinn's death that hit him the hardest. They were close."

"Ah yes, Lord Quinn." There was a sad chuckle. "He was the sun to Lord Damien's moon. One fiery and hot, the other cool and level-headed. And now the sun is gone. I sometimes wonder why the Light allowed the young lord to pass."

"One of many questions that humankind has been asking for a millennia. I think even if we were able to stand in the presence of his brilliant light, we would still not be able to comprehend the ways of the Light."

"You speak truth, Brother Eoin."

Selene stared wide-eyed at the fire. Was today the anniversary of the passing of Damien's brother Quinn? A vision of a dark-haired young boy climbing an oak tree with Elric Luceras filled her mind. His laughter, his smile, his adventurous attitude. Then her memories switched to the pale young man in a bed much too big for him, with Damien kneeling nearby, his head bent. And the way Damien wept when Quinn breathed his last. Such a bond between siblings, unlike anything she had experienced, even with Opheliana.

When Quinn died, it was as if part of Damien had died with him, a severing she had felt within Damien's dreamscape.

Even now, she could feel Damien's sorrow swelling up inside her own heart. Selene pressed a hand against her chest. No wonder Damien had seemed listless.

She watched the flames flicker and dance in the fireplace across from her. Should she do something when she arrived back at Northwind Castle? Was there even anything she could do?

And why do I care?

She turned her gaze to the table surface. There was this deep and powerful urge to comfort Damien, something she had never experienced before.

Strange. What did it mean? Now that she no longer hid herself behind an icy shroud, was it possible her heart was returning to her? Or was it something more? Some kind of connection that had formed from her dreamwalks?

"Here you are, my lady." Cohen carefully placed a leather-bound book as thick as three fingers on the table in front of Selene. "These are the writings of Pallion, one of the first scholars to write about the Great Houses."

A leather cord held the tome closed. Selene fingered the tie, then began to work the loop. "So his work is set before the razing of the empire?" she asked as she undid the knot.

"Yes. I'm not sure how far back since I have not personally read or copied any of his work. But it might give you a starting point."

Selene pulled the leather cord away from the tome, then paused. She looked up at Cohen. "Could I also see any books you have on the Light? Perhaps something that explains who or what he is?"

"Certainly. The best place to start is with Father Dominick's personal essays. His are the most easy to understand. He wrote them in conjunction with the sacred texts as a way to help young monks learn the basics of the Old Ways. I've also seen him share his work with some of the people from Nor Esen."

Selene nodded. "That would be wonderful. Thank you, Cohen."

Cohen grinned as he bowed. "My pleasure, Lady Selene. If you have any questions, please let me know."

"I will." Selene slowly opened the tome,

careful to keep her fingers on the very edges of the parchment. The calligraphy was superb, each letter exact and straight. She began to read, but in the far back of her mind the shadow of Damien's sorrow over Quinn's death hung over her.

Selene and Karl made their way through the snow hours later, reaching Nor Esen's gates just as they began to shut. The sky grew darker by the minute as the wintry night came and more clouds gathered, plump with snow.

The tip of her nose and her fingers were numb, despite the gloves. She pulled her cowl farther down her face and pushed on through the streets with her head bowed. No one was out this evening. And probably hardly anyone would be venturing out once this storm hit. She was grateful she had been able to visit the abbey and read before more snow came and kept her bound inside Northwind Castle.

Her toes were as numb as her nose by the time they reached the inner gate and entered the courtyard. Karl opened the front door for her and spoke to the guards inside. Selene stamped out her boots, then headed toward her own room to change into warm, dry clothes.

"Lady Selene."

Selene turned around and found Taegis approaching from one of the other hallways.

"Hello, Taegis. Karl and I just arrived from Baris Abbey."

"Good. I was about to head out and escort you back."

Selene began tugging at the tips of her gloves. "How is Lord Damien doing?" she asked, hoping Taegis would tell her more about what was truly ailing Damien.

Taegis stopped in front of her. "He is still in his room. But he should be better in a day or two."

"I see. Thank you for letting me know." Selene finished pulling off the gloves and turned just as Taegis called out again.

"My lady."

Selene turned back.

Taegis opened his mouth, then closed it, then opened it again. "If I may say, you might be able to help him."

"Help him?"

Taegis stepped closer. "Two years ago today Damien lost his brother and parents and became grand lord of House Maris."

Selene stared down at her gloves. "I overheard the monks talking about it."

"Forgive me for not telling you beforehand. Damien wishes to be left alone during this time. A dual loss and responsibility like that is a heavy burden. The people know he is grieving today, but it is more than sorrow. There is a hole inside of him he keeps hidden away from everyone."

She lifted her head. "Everyone but you?"

"I've known Lord Damien since he was a little boy. There is very little he can hide from me."

A hole inside of Damien. Selene recalled the hint of darkness she sensed within his luminous soul in his dreamscape. Was that the same hole Taegis spoke of? The loss of his family?

"I'm not sure what I can do." She knew nothing of this kind of hurt or love. Still, that same powerful urge from the library swept over her again, the desire to comfort him. But how?

"Be with him. I've talked to Damien before, but I am his counselor and guard and can only do so much. Perhaps, as his wife, you can speak to his heart in ways I cannot."

Speak to his heart? Selene almost laughed. Taegis knew nothing of her past. What did she know of speaking to someone in pain? She only knew how to hurt others and find their weaknesses in the dreamscape.

However, she had helped Damien during his fever when they first arrived at Northwind Castle. But he wasn't sleeping at the moment. And neither of them had spoken of that night.

"Please, Lady Selene," Taegis implored. She could see the love in the older man's eyes for his lord, and it touched her heart. So many people loved Damien and cared about him. So different than the mountain people's reaction to House Ravenwood.

"I'll see what I can do."

His shoulders sagged, and he gave her a small smile. "Thank you, my lady."

Selene turned and headed down the hallway, her emotions a tangled knot inside of her, causing her stomach to clench. *What do I do? How do I help someone? Do I talk to him? Dart'an, I don't even know what to say! Maybe I should head to my own room.*

But she couldn't do that. The weight of that thought was even heavier. So she bypassed her own door and stopped in front of the one that led into Damien's room.

She stared at the thick grey door while the candles flickered in the sconces along the corridor. Her heart pounded inside her chest, a constant thump.

No, no more fear. She clenched her sweaty hands. *I may not know what to say, but I want to help him, just like he offered to help me.*

Before she could change her mind, Selene opened the door. The room was dark, save for a fire burning in the fireplace to the left, casting a warm orange light across the room. Damien stood on the other side of the room in front of the three large windows that overlooked the sea. His clothing and shadowed figure blended in with the darkening sky.

"Damien?" Selene said quietly, her fingers still curled around the edge of the door. He didn't say a word or turn around. She stepped inside and closed the door behind her.

Selene swallowed and took a step. "I heard you were not feeling well." Another step. "Taegis told me why."

His body tensed.

"I . . . I don't know what to say." She bit her lip and looked down as she took another step. "I've never lost someone I loved." Well, that wasn't totally true. When she escaped from Rook Castle, she left those she would consider loved ones behind: Ophie, her father, the servants, her people, even Amara. Her mother's face flashed before her eyes, but she blinked the image away.

What she wouldn't give to have another nightly talk with her father in his study or to bring Ophie her favorite flower. Even to spar with Amara again.

Selene sniffed and rubbed her nose with the back of her hand. Her eyelids grew hot as she continued—one step at a time—across the room.

She stopped a foot away from him and stared at the firm lines of his back, the way his dark hair slightly curled along his neck, his arms that were strong and yet gentle.

Something moved inside her heart.

She wanted to help this young lord who led the people of the Northern Shores with the power of his gift, this person who laughed and treated all people as his equals, this man who gave up the chance to marry all others in order to save the life of the very woman who had tried to kill him.

Selene closed the distance between them and snaked her arms beneath his, lacing them across his chest, and laid her cheek against the crook of his neck. "I'm sorry," she whispered. "I wish I could take your pain away. I wish—" Her words were choked off by a sob. It felt like her heart had broken open, like a frozen river cracking beneath a spring sun and running again.

She pressed her face tighter against his neck and gripped the front of his shirt with her fingers. No matter how hard she squeezed her eyes shut, hot tears still trickled down her cheeks. If only she could take away the pain in this world. Pain brought by death, sickness, war, even the hands of others.

If only she could heal instead of hurt.

Before she could react, Damien turned around. "Selene," he said in a hoarse voice.

She looked up, tears coating her lashes, her arms still beneath his.

His blue eyes were dark, reflecting only a speck of light from the fireplace. His mouth opened and closed, then he leaned forward.

Selene's heart leapt into her throat. She could feel his warm breath across her face.

Was he going to kiss her?

He paused, his lips near hers, then he lifted his head and kissed her forehead instead, then pulled her in close and placed his head next to hers, his chin resting on her shoulder. His scent of clove, cinnamon, and sandalwood filled her nostrils. She could hear the comforting sound of his heart beating beneath his tunic.

"Thank you," he said, his warm breath brushing past her ear.

They stood there next to the windows, the wind pounding against the glass as the winter storm blew in. Her fingers and toes were no longer cold. Damien had warmed her entire being.

21

No matter how hard Damien had tried to face the day, the anniversary of his parents' and Quinn's death still hit him like a fist to the gut, stealing his breath away and leaving a hole in the middle of his body. As the day drew near, the chill of sorrow siphoned away his strength and will until he finally succumbed to it and isolated himself. And it didn't help that he was already feeling the weight of the two water barriers he had left up in protection of his people.

Then Selene had showed up, just when it hurt the most.

"I'm sorry. I wish I could take your pain away."

The feeling of her arms wrapping around his middle, the warmth from her body, the dampness of her tears at the base of his neck. He couldn't remember the last time he had been held close.

He could barely speak her name when he turned around. Her eyes glistened with tears, and his heart hammered inside his chest. Suddenly he wanted to kiss her, to show her how he felt, because there were no words he could say.

But a warning bell went off inside his head. She wasn't ready yet. So instead he had leaned forward and pressed his lips to her forehead, then pulled her closer and breathed in the scent of her hair and skin.

In that moment, Selene quietly moved into that empty place in his heart left by the death of his family.

Minutes ticked by. The room was silent except for the wind outside and the crackling of the fire.

"Is there anything I can do?" Selene said, breaking the silence. She lifted her head from his chest.

"No. Your presence is enough." More than she knew. "Thank you for coming."

"I haven't lost someone, but I did leave behind people who I love. It . . . hurts."

He rubbed her back, his heart aching for her loss. "I know." He wished he could say more, to tell her that she would see them someday, but he couldn't. Given the way House Ravenwood and House Maris were divided, who knew when she would be able to see her family and loved ones again?

Her chin dipped down, and she slowly took a step back. "I'm glad I came. Taegis was concerned about you. And I was too." Her eyes shifted to the window.

His lips quirked. Apparently Selene was not one for long episodes of physical touch. Then again, given her family background, he wasn't surprised. He sobered at the thought. His family had been overwhelmingly loving and generous with their words and affection, something he greatly missed when they passed. Perhaps he could share that part of his family with Selene someday, if she was willing.

She took another step back. "I'm afraid I haven't had a chance to change yet. I visited Baris Abbey today, and the hem of my dress and boots are still wet from the snow."

He could almost see her scurrying back behind the cover of her invisible mask. It was still too early for her to feel safe away from her barriers. He understood, even if he desired otherwise. "I've asked for my meal to be brought to my room. Would you join me this evening?"

She looked up, and the mask moved, even if only for a moment. "I would be happy to join you."

"Thank you." He hadn't meant to sound so relieved. Selene's presence helped with the deep ache inside his chest, but he wasn't ready to leave his room and be around other people at the moment. But he didn't want to be alone either. "I'll see you at seven?"

She gave him a small smile that made his mouth go dry. "Yes. I'll be here." Then she turned and headed for the door that led to her own room.

His brow furrowed as the door shut behind her. It almost seemed to represent one of the other barriers between them, and he wondered if there would come a point where she would no longer have her own room, but would share his instead.

· · ·

Damien lay in his bed later that night and stared at the ceiling. With Selene gone, the hole was once again expanding across his heart, bringing with it dreary and shadowy thoughts. As much as he tried to push them away, the memories pressed against his mind, forcing him to relive the death of his parents and Quinn.

The plague had spread like a wildfire across Northwind Castle and Nor Esen until both resembled ghost towns. The streets and hallways stood empty, save for the few who seemed immune to the fever. Even now he could remember how eerie the castle felt, so silent and vacant.

Damien rolled over to his side. Father and Mother did everything they could, while he and Quinn had been sequestered in a room at the far end of the castle. Messages were sent to House Vivek and Rafel in hopes for a cure. Fires burned both day and night as those who succumbed to the illness passed on and their bodies were burned. There were moments when he wondered where the Light was in all of this.

Why didn't the Light save them?

Damien squeezed his eyes shut. Others might think his faith was strong, but he still had doubts and fears. He would have given everything to save those around him. So why didn't the Light?

Then Father and Mother fell ill. He left his

room to be with them, but his presence did nothing. Then Quinn—

He swallowed and closed his eyes. *Why was I the only one left alive?*

Quinn went from a robust youth to a skeleton within days as the fever ate away his body. Father and Mother passed on with hardly a whisper. Then Quinn followed them, leaving him all alone, the last of House Maris.

Damien's heart beat faster, and his entire body tensed. He clenched his hands and brought his knees up. The pain hurt so bad he wished he could pull his heart out of his chest.

"You want to save everyone, my son."

His father's words came back to him.

"You have a big heart. And it hurts to see the pain in this world. But that's not a weakness. It is your hidden strength. Never forget that."

His father was wrong. It was both his strength *and* his weakness. He couldn't let go of his crippling grief, even two years later. He didn't know how. What good was having a heart if it was chained by sorrow?

Damien fell into a restless sleep filled with moans and feverish dreams. He was kneeling again at Quinn's bed, watching his brother succumb.

I don't want to be alone.

He couldn't tell if that was Quinn speaking or himself.

I don't want to be alone. I don't want to be alone. . . .

His bed moved.

Damien woke up but remained still. He glanced to his right without moving his head, peering into the darkness through a slit in his eyes.

A small figure lay down near him—above the furs—and let out a quiet sigh. Moments later, warm fingers felt along his arm, then stopped at his wrist and wrapped around the narrowest part.

What in the . . . Selene?

He could make out the head now, barely, hair as black as night. What was she doing here? Even as he thought that, a strange peace settled across him like a warm blanket, loosening his tight muscles and causing his eyelids to grow heavy. His mind focused on the warm spot where her fingers connected with his skin. His breathing leveled out, and his heart no longer hurt.

Sleep took him under. His mind wandered along pleasanter dreams: searching for shells along the beach with Quinn, reading at Baris Abbey on a rainy afternoon, watching the sunrise with his father as they practiced their water-raising gift together.

Every time his dreams ventured toward those bleak memories, they were blown away, as if by a wind, and he would settle again amongst pleasing thoughts. Once in a while, he thought he spotted

274

a raven watching him from a boulder along the beach or a corner of the abbey.

The raven did not frighten him. It was more like a comforting companion, a familiar presence.

It was still dark outside when he opened his eyes, but light enough to declare it was morning, despite the heavy falling snow outside the windows and the clouds spread across the winter sky. He let out a sigh, then felt the weight of another body pressing the blankets and furs down across his own.

Selene lay nearby, a single fur pulled over her body, her face toward his, her hand stretched out toward his arm but no longer touching him. Her black hair lay tangled around her head, and her cheeks were red. She made a small noise, then curled her fingers and drew her knees in closer to her body.

Damien blinked away the last vestiges of sleep, willing his mind to wake up. He felt refreshed, for the first time in a long time. A sense of tranquility hung across his spirit, so different from the heavy shadows of yesterday. The darkness was still there, but it had sunk back out of sight, far enough that he could only feel a sliver of its chill.

He looked again at Selene. Was this her doing? He recalled the raven watching him inside his dreams. Was that her?

Damien sat up carefully, so as not to disturb her, and rubbed his face. She had revealed so much about her gift, and yet there seemed to be even more to learn, like how she could change her appearance. And he had a feeling it was Selene who had chased away his nightmares and given him peace.

What an amazing gift. What more could she do?

He leaned forward and whispered, "Thank you, Selene."

She never moved, just continued sleeping with even breaths.

Damien turned toward his side of the bed and stood, taking care not to move the mattress. After dressing, he glanced at Selene one more time, feeling something stir inside his heart. Was it possible that waking up next to Selene could become a familiar sight? That they could face the day together, live life together, like his parents and his grandparents had?

Was this something she desired also?

22°

Amara gasped as she sank back into her body. Her heart raced like a horse inside her chest, threatening to burst forth. Her knees were numb from kneeling on the cold floor while she was in the young stableboy's dreamscape.

She sucked in a lungful of air and looked up. The boy lay still across the sleeping mat inside the tiny room. A faded quilt was pulled up across his chest, his fingers fanned along the edge. Pale moonlight streamed through the narrow window to the left. His face . . .

Amara turned away and pressed a fist to her mouth. But the image of his face was forever imprinted on her mind. The way his glassy eyes stared up at the ceiling in horror, the curve of his mouth, open in a silent scream.

She shut her eyes. She was going to be sick. She was going to retch right there, next to the boy's body. *No, I can't.* She breathed in through her nose and out through her mouth. Breathe in. Breathe out.

"Good. Very good, Amara." Her mother spoke next to her, her low alto voice carrying across the small room like a whisper. "You've finally come full circle with your gift."

Amara curled her fingers into her palms,

forcing away the horror from moments ago, washing it down with a much hotter emotion. "Thank you, Mother," she said as she turned to face Lady Ragna. But inside, she seethed. She'd always wanted Selene's place as firstborn, but never did she imagine what that would entail, including the death of the boy before her. If she were any weaker, she would run. But if she did, Opheliana would be left unprotected.

Selene, you coward!

Amara stood to her feet. Anger allowed her to look down on the stableboy again. She would do what she needed to do to keep her sister safe. All she had to do was what Mother told her and she would become the heir to Ravenwood. As grand lady, it wouldn't matter that her sister carried the mark of House Friere on her ankle. No one would need to know. And if someone found out, well . . . She lifted her hand and stared at her palm, then crushed her hand into a fist. She would do the same thing she did to the boy at her feet.

"It is time that we left. We will leave the boy for someone else to find. Follow me to my bedchambers. There is something we need to discuss."

Amara turned back toward her mother and nodded. The two of them silently left the room near the stables, making their way along the wall toward a secret door at the other end of Rook

Castle. A horse neighed beyond the wooden stalls, and a cat darted around the corner. A bitter wind sprang up, and not for the first time Amara was thankful for the thick cloak as she pulled the edges closer to her neck to keep out the chilly air. The sun was starting to come up, painting the sky in purple and pink, when they reached the small door and went inside.

Amara followed her mother across the castle to her bedchambers. Only a handful of servants were awake, and they were easy to maneuver around. The air was cool inside the castle, but not biting like it was outside. Once they reached the thick oak doors, her mother pressed down on the metal handle and let Amara inside first, then shut the door behind them.

A low fire burned in the fireplace below the picture of Rabanna Ravenwood, who seemed to look over the room with an air of condescension. Amara glared back at her ancestor before crossing the room and warming her hands near the fire. Her mother removed her cloak and hung it over the changing screens in the corner before disappearing behind the colorful canvas to change.

She wondered what Mother had to speak about this time. The last time she had invited Amara to her bedchambers, it was to reveal their secret connection to the Dominia Empire, not that it came as a surprise. When that stranger had visited her mother days after the assembly, he had planted the suspicions in Amara's mind. House Ravenwood were traitors, but she found she didn't care. As long as she was able to retain Rook Castle and become the grand lady of House Ravenwood, she could not care less about the other houses or the empire's desires. She had her own plans. She just needed to be strong enough with her gift to carry them out. And she was becoming stronger. Perhaps not as strong as Selene, but strong enough.

Her mother emerged from behind the screens, dressed in a dark gown. Her hair was still in a single braid, but Hagatha, her maidservant, would be along soon to finish Mother's attire.

"First, I have news from the north. It would appear your sister has married Lord Damien Maris."

Amara felt like she had been dropped from the battlements and was falling toward the rocks below. "Married? To Lord Damien?"

"Yes. Which means Lord Damien now knows about our gift."

Amara was still stuck on the idea that Selene had married Lord Damien. Selene . . . married? How? Why?

"I tell you this since it could impact your upcoming mission."

She looked up, her thoughts still hazy from her mother's news.

"As you know, we will be helping Commander Orion move his forces across the wall near the border between House Friere and House Vivek. However, we must wait until spring. In the meantime, I have a mission for you. Ever since your sister disappeared into the lands of House Maris, I've had the border between our lands watched. Lord Damien continues to keep his water-wall up, preventing us from crossing over into the Northern Shores. But eventually he will desire to meet with those houses who oppose the Dominia Empire, which means he will either need to leave his lands or bring the wall down so the other houses can cross. That is when your first mission will start."

Amara narrowed her eyes. "And what mission is that?"

Her mother crossed the room and placed her long fingers along the back of one of the chairs near the fireplace. "You will finish what your sister did not: the assassination of House Maris. Shortly before the Assembly of the Great Houses began, the Dark Lady sent a message to me that there was a threat to our house from the north and if it was not dealt with then it would mean the end of House Ravenwood."

"And the threat was House Maris? Then why did you dispose of House Vivek?" Amara bit her lip. She should have worded her questions in a less accusatory way, but her mother didn't seem to notice.

"The only information I had was that the threat was from the north. So I took House Vivek and Selene was assigned to House Maris. And the rest you know."

Yes. Instead of killing Lord Damien, Selene had gone and married him. "So this threat still exists?"

"Yes. The Dark Lady confirmed it."

Amara frowned. Then why hadn't the Dark Lady specified which house was the threat in the first place? But she wasn't about to ask Mother that, as she was sensitive to matters where the Dark Lady was concerned. "So my mission will be to kill Lord Damien Maris."

"Yes. When the water-wall goes down, you will need to be prepared to go, whether that will be traveling to the capital city of Nor Esen or elsewhere."

Amara crossed her arms. "And what about Selene?"

"What about Selene?" her mother said in a low, dangerous voice.

"If I go after Lord Damien, surely I will meet up with Selene. Should I kill her as well?" Although how she would do that she wasn't sure. She could barely keep up with her mother in the dreamscape; going against Selene would be suicide. Perhaps she could use poison or her sword. If Selene didn't know she was coming, she couldn't protect herself.

"You will do nothing to Selene."

Amara's nostrils flared, and she gripped her forearms. "Why? Are you hoping to bring that traitor back?"

Lady Ragna stood still, so still that she seemed as though she were a statue. Except for the cold rage that burned in her eyes. Amara quivered inside, but she didn't show it on her face. To show Mother fear was to invite verbal abuse.

"No," she finally answered, "because I want to take care of Selene myself. A Ravenwood has never killed another Ravenwood. But there are other ways to deal with her. Selene is a traitor—a traitor to our house. So I will be the one to take care of her. Not you." There was finality in her voice.

Amara narrowed her eyes and stared at her mother. Was this her final test to see if she was worthy to be Grand Lady Ravenwood?

"This mission will not be easy. Lord Damien has a deep and influential mind that will be difficult to maneuver. You will need to practice and hone your gift every night until the time comes for you to leave."

Amara straightened up and uncrossed her arms. Was that why Selene had failed? Had Lord Damien somehow influenced her? Maybe Mother had overestimated Selene's power.

"I will have the Vanguard Garrison alert us when the wall goes down," her mother continued. "Then it will be up to you to trail Lord Damien and finish your sister's task. Do you think you can do that?"

"Yes." For once she was thankful she looked more like Father than Mother. It would be easier to hide her connection to House Ravenwood.

"Good." Her mother pressed a hand to her forehead and looked away.

Amara studied her mother in the dim light with a raised eyebrow. Was that worry she saw in her mother's face? What in all the lands would cause her mother to be anxious?

"After the last snow melts, I will be traveling to Ironmond to make my own preparations and meet with Lord Ivulf." Her hand dropped and tightened into a fist. "We will usher in a new era, one where House Ravenwood is in power. Then the other houses will taste of our bitterness."

Amara watched her mother but didn't speak a word. Hatred ran deep within Mother, so much so that if she were cut, Amara was sure hate would flow from her veins. Would she become like that someday?

"Now go. I need to rest."

Amara bowed, conflicting thoughts tumbling through her mind. "Yes, Mother."

She mentally shrugged as she left the bed-chambers and her mother behind and followed the hall to her own room. If that was what it took to keep her sister safe, she didn't care. Opheliana was the only person who mattered to her. She would become as dark as she needed to be.

23

I've received letters from Houses Merek, Luceras, and Vivek."

"When?" Selene sat on the other side of Damien's desk. Snow continued to fall outside from the storm that started the previous night. But the inside of Damien's study was warm, thanks to the thick quilt over her lap, the fire nearby, and a cup of hot mulled cider.

"Sometime yesterday. We're lucky the carrier birds were able to make it before the storm began."

"Wait, House Vivek sent a letter? Who answered for them? Have they chosen a lesser house to fill the role of Great House?"

"No," Damien said slowly and held up the creased parchment. "Lord Rune's son, Renlar. Now Grand Lord Renlar."

Selene blinked. "Lord Rune's *son?* When did he have a son?" This didn't make sense. She looked down and rubbed her forehead. Did her mother know about this son? If so, what was the purpose in taking out Lord Rune and Lady Runa if there was still a successor to House Vivek? Was House Vivek still a threat to House Ravenwood?

Ugh, and why do I care about that? I turned my back on Ravenwood when I left my family and home.

"As dual rulers of House Vivek, it was always assumed one sibling would continue on after the death of the other. I don't know all the details behind Lord Rune's secret marriage, only that it resulted in the birth of a son."

She looked back up. "How come I've never heard of Lord Renlar?"

"Very few have. He was raised away from the palace as a scholar in one of the great libraries. Lord Vivek disclosed information about his son to very few people. My family was one of them."

"I see." So he had been hidden away for some reason. More house secrets. "House Vivek is not without a leader."

"No. Lord Renlar has chosen to step forward and lead his people. He is strong in both body and mind. Given what he wrote in his letter, it doesn't appear that he believes the explanation given for the death of his father and aunt."

Selene wrapped her fingers around the warm mug and breathed in the spicy, fruity fragrance, her mind spinning from this new information. "I don't think my mother expected people to believe it forever. Just long enough to sow seeds of doubt and disunity until she revealed her true colors, behind the might of the Dominia Empire." What would Mother do when she discovered House Vivek had endured? Kill again? So much pain, so much death. For nothing.

Damien tapped the top of his desk. "I believe

the Dominia Empire will make its move once the last of the snow melts. Do you think your mother and House Friere will make their alliances known by then?"

She lowered her gaze and stared into the deep amber liquid. "I don't know. I'm ashamed that my family is even part of this."

"When I was at the assembly, Caiaphas told me your mother would never ally with the other Great Houses. He said her hatred runs deep. But he didn't believe that was true of you, and I don't think so either. He said that you might be the ally we were looking for."

"Ally?"

"A representative for House Ravenwood. Someone who would be willing to use her gift for the welfare of all Great Houses and peoples."

Selene blinked. "My father said that? When did you meet with him?"

"The night before the gala. That was the same night I promised him I would protect you." Damien laughed softly. "He was very adamant about that. Now I know why. He knew you were the missing piece to the alliance—that you possessed the gift of House Ravenwood."

"You keep saying alliance. What is this alliance you speak of?" Suddenly, a conversation with her father came roaring back to the front of her mind—the one where she realized he was part of some secret coalition. The one where he revealed why he had married her mother: to find out if the dreamwalking gift still existed.

She stared at Damien, her whole body tingling. "Are you part of some secret alliance?"

Damien gazed back. "Yes. It's a coalition whose purpose is to unite the Great Houses. Your father is part of that group. And so are a number of lesser lords and ladies. When my father died, I inherited his position as the leader of the group."

"The . . . leader?" The room began to spin around her. She raised a hand and placed it against the side of her face in an effort to make everything stand still. Her father's words filled her mind. *There is a group of people who have been searching for a way to unite the Great Houses. This group has existed for many years, quietly working to bring every nation together.* And Damien was one of them. No, he was the *leader* of them.

"Is that why you called for the Assembly of the Great Houses?" Selene asked.

"Partly. Also because we could no longer deny the threat that Commander Orion and the empire pose. I had hoped that the encroachment of the empire would have been a catalyst to unite the Great Houses, but I didn't realize that hatred and greed ran so deep, or that House Ravenwood and House Friere had already aligned themselves with the empire."

"Aren't you afraid for your life?"

"Yes." He looked back at the fire. "Although my position as a grand lord does give me a measure of safety. The others, however . . ." He tapped a finger against his knee. "There are some who have given their lives for the cause."

Selene shivered, despite the warmth of the room. People who were accused of being a part of this group died. Her mother had a man thrown from the wall of Rook Castle last year. And House Friere burned three others.

Damien's fingers stopped their tapping, and he seemed to be thinking. "On the surface is the treaty between the Great Houses. But underneath, real unity between the peoples will require everyone working together: grand lords and citizens alike. The general guides the army, but it is the soldiers who fight. That is why the coalition exists, and why it is made up of more than Caiaphas and myself. It is a treaty, in a sense, that crosses borders and includes all people from all the lands, not just lords and ladies from Great Houses. We have grown over the years. The coalition is large enough now that they could rise up in place of the Great Houses."

"And do away with our gifts," Selene said, her eyes flashing as she remembered her mother's words.

Damien shook his head. "No. That has never been our goal. We want unity. We want to work *with* the Great Houses, if possible. There is a reason the Light gave seven families special gifts. Gifts to help all people, not only the family."

Selene looked away. He'd voiced the doubt that had been lurking inside of her ever since her dreamwalking training had begun a year ago: that the women of Ravenwood, although claiming to help the mountain people, had really only been helping themselves.

"The Great Houses are only as strong as our people," Damien stressed. "And we can help our people become even stronger by the gifts the Light has given us."

There was a knock at the door, interrupting their conversation.

"Yes?" Damien said, glancing at the door.

The guard on duty looked in. "Steward Bertram wishes to speak to you, my lord."

Damien stood. "Yes, I am expecting him. Tell him I will be with him shortly." He turned toward Selene after the guard left. "I'm sorry to cut our time short. One more thing before I leave. Your father believed you and your gift could help unite the Great Houses and their people." He moved around the desk and placed a hand on her shoulder. "I'm still coming to know you. But your father's trust weighs in your favor. And I hope you know that the fact that I have shared about the coalition means that I trust you as well, even though your gift . . ."

"My gift?"

"We have yet to discover what your gift can really do. You've helped me twice with my dreams. But . . ."

Oh. She could see the hesitancy in his eyes. There still seemed to be a shadow lurking inside his mind concerning her dreamwalking. "Because of what it was previously used for," she said softly.

He dropped his head. "Yes."

At least he was honest. "But doesn't my marriage to you already connect me to your coalition?"

"Partly. Although I would prefer you to join of your own volition."

"And my gift?"

"We'll continue to search for other ways you can use your power."

She held his gaze. "I think I want to find out more about my dreamwalking gift before I join."

Damien bowed his head as he pulled his hand away. "I understand. And I am happy to help you in any way I can."

Did he really know what he was offering? Did he mean that he'd be willing for her to use his dreamscape? And would she actually take him up on that?

He reached the door, then looked back. "Oh, and one more thing. Would you be interested in joining me in the breaking of your fast tomorrow morning? There is something I would like to show you."

Selene raised her eyebrows. "I have no obligations tomorrow. I believe I can join you."

He smiled back. "Wonderful. It has something to do with my family, and I would like to share it with you."

Her pulse increased. What could that be?

"Good-bye, Selene."

"Good-bye, Damien."

The door shut quietly behind her, and she sat in silence as the fire burned low and the snow continued to fall.

"There is a reason the Light gave seven families special gifts. Gifts to help all people, not only the family." Damien's words were similar to the ones he said the night of the gala back at Rook Castle: gifts were given to help people. And even those leaders without gifts could serve their people through sacrifice and love.

But what about my *gift? I refuse to hurt anyone else with my power. And I can only visit one mind at a time.* She leaned forward and placed her head in her hands. Yes, she had brought peace those times she visited Damien's dreams. But he was only one man, one dream. Was that truly the extent of her gift? But . . .

She raised her head. Did that matter? If what Damien said all those months ago still proved true, then she could serve people through sacrifice and love.

She stared at her fingers. She was already familiar with sacrifice. But love? How could she still love her people when she was no longer at Rook Castle? Could she love the people here, in the Northern Shores? What was love, really?

Selene stood and headed for the door. *I need to find out more. More about my gift. More about the Light who gave me this gift. More about who I am.*

24

L ittle raven," a cold voice whispered.

Selene stood in the entryway to Northwind Castle. The air was hazy and dim, with that dreamscape-feel. Down the corridor, a light disappeared around the corner, leaving the area in shadows.

"Selene," the voice rasped, using her name for the first time.

She closed her eyes, ignoring the sudden chill, and pressed against the dreamscape with her power, pushing out with her mind until her hands shook at her sides. *Change, change!*

A cold breath blew across her cheek, filling her nostrils with the smell of rotting flesh. "There you are, little raven."

Selene gasped and her eyes flew open. She flung herself away from the Dark Lady. "Get away from me!"

"I cannot," the shadow whispered. "For you are mine."

Out of the corner of her eye, she spotted two people, pale and translucent like spirits, standing beside the broad doors that led out into the courtyard. Taegis and Sten.

She shook her head, confused. What were they doing here?

Before she could find an answer, the Dark Lady glided toward her. Selene spun around, transformed into a raven, and flew off.

She soared along the hallway, passing more and more translucent people. She clicked her beak. Who were these people? Were they real? Or was her mind filling this dreamscape with her own memories?

She rounded the corner and searched ahead for the light. It appeared at the very end of the corridor. She passed by more people, some vaguely familiar. But she had no time to stop and look at their faces, not if she was going to catch up to the light—

Surprised and terrified shouts filled the air behind her. Selene hovered for a moment and looked back. The Dark Lady drifted along the hall, passing the same people she had flown by moments ago. As she passed them, they collapsed across the floor, lifeless.

A frigid stinging filled her chest. What did the Dark Lady do to those people?

The Dark Lady looked up, and her lips spread in a sinister smile.

Selene spun around, soaring toward the end of the hallway. *Dart'an! I can't let the Dark Lady catch me.*

The light disappeared upstairs. Selene flew in pursuit. The light seemed to slow down along the corridor with the windows that overlooked the sea. Selene sucked in a breath of air and winced at the stitch in her side. Not only did the light seem slower, it appeared more brilliant, overtaking the darkness of the hallway.

She stretched out her body and pumped her wings. *I'm almost there. I can reach it. Maybe if I touch it, this nightmare—and the Dark Lady— will disappear.*

But the light swerved around the corner and vanished.

Selene rounded the corner in surprise. What happened? Where did the light go—?

Hands grabbed her feathered body. Selene cawed and fought back with her wings and talons.

"You are mine, little raven," the Dark Lady hissed. "You always will be."

"Never! Damien, help me!"

Selene sat up with a gasp. Her covers were tangled around her body and drenched in sweat. The wind rattled the windows and moaned outside. Grey clouds filled the sky, accentuating the chill inside her bedroom.

She leaned forward and gripped the front of her nightgown, breathing heavily. She could still feel the Dark Lady's cold hands around her and the terror that had encapsulated her.

Why, after all this time, after her supplications back at Rook Castle, was the Dark Lady finally visiting her?

But I don't want her. Not anymore.

She held her face in her hands. Why did she keep dreaming about this? Was this her dreamscape?

The door wrenched open at the foot of her bed, and Damien burst in, his shirt untucked and his feet bare. "Selene, are you all right?"

Her eyes went wide, and she pulled the furs up to her chest. "Yes. Why?"

He leaned against the doorway and ran a hand through his untidy hair. "I heard you yelling and I thought . . ." He looked back at her and dropped his hand. "Are you sure?"

"Yes. It was only a-a nightmare."

"A nightmare? Do you want to talk about it?"

Selene turned away. "No. Not really."

There was a pause. "I understand. Some things are too hard to speak of."

Her head snapped up. Was he referring to the death of his family?

"If ever you want to talk, just let me know."

She had half a mind to tell him of the Dark Lady and her fears, but something stopped her. Was it shame?

"I'll see you soon." He turned and left, closing the door behind him.

Selene frowned. *See you soon?* She pressed a hand to her forehead. She had forgotten Damien had invited her to break their fast together this morning. Something about sharing a family tradition with her.

She dropped her hand and pushed the heavy quilts and furs aside. The cold air helped clear her mind as she stood to her feet. The floor was icy to the touch, sending another jolt of awakening through her body. The thought of spending the morning with Damien lightened her heart, banishing the images from her most recent nightmare. The Dark Lady could not have her. Her mother and sister might worship the Lady of the Night, but not her. She wanted something more. Something new. And her life with Damien could give her that chance.

Selene shivered from the cold, reaching for the wrap that lay at the end of her bed. As she pulled it across her shoulders, she paused. She remembered screaming Damien's name in her dream. Had she yelled his name in the physical world as well?

He had obviously come from bed to check on her, given his state of undress. The thought touched her heart, and warmth spread across her body, reaching her fingers and her toes.

A half hour later, Selene sank down on the rug beside Damien inside his room. Snow fell gently outside the windows, and the fire popped and crackled within the large fireplace a couple of feet in front of them. She eyed the silver platter that sat on the floor on his other side. A round of bread had been sliced and lay fanned out on a plate, along with a small-lidded crock, a pot of tea, and two cups.

Damien grabbed what looked like a poker out of a vase near the fireplace, only there were three metal prongs at the end instead of a metal hook. He took one of the thick slices of bread, pressed the bread into the prongs, then held the poker near the fire.

"Are you cooking the bread?" Selene asked.

"Toasting it. On snowy mornings, my mother would invite Quinn and I into this room, and we would toast bread together."

Selene glanced over to find Damien smiling wistfully. The smell of warm bread began to fill the room, causing her stomach to gurgle. "Sounds like a nice memory."

"It is. And it's a memory I wanted to share with you."

Damien pulled the poker back a minute later. The bread was golden brown now, and crispy along the edges. He blew on it a few times before pulling the toast off. "Here," he said, holding it out to her.

Selene took the toast with a frown. "Now what?"

Damien grinned and reached around. He picked up the small crock and the accompanying knife and lifted the lid off to reveal creamy white butter inside. "Hold out the toast."

Selene held up the toast. Damien dipped the knife into the crock, then spread the butter across the top. The butter melted across the surface, leaving the bread glistening and golden. The smell of toasted bread and butter made her mouth water.

"All right, go ahead and eat it."

Selene took a bite and chewed, savoring the flavors. "This is good!"

Damien laughed as he speared another slice of bread and held it near the fire. "It's one of my favorite foods. Such a simple thing, and yet so comforting and delicious."

Selene munched away on the bread while Damien finished toasting his own. Then they sat in amiable silence, enjoying the simple fare and sipping their tea.

"How often did your mother do this for you and your brother?" Selene asked as she wiped away the crumbs from her dress.

"Many times. We would laugh and talk and eat toasted bread together."

A lump filled her throat. Selene leaned forward and wrapped her arms around her knees while she watched the flames dance across the logs. Time with her mother meant training and discourses on Ravenwood's history and importance. She couldn't even imagine sitting on a rug with her mother and Amara, laughing and enjoying toasted bread. The thought almost made her laugh out loud at the absurdity of it, except for the sudden tightness across her chest.

"What memories or traditions do you have with

your family?" Damien asked, spearing another piece of bread.

The tightness grew. "My memories . . . are not like yours."

"Explain."

Selene had half a mind to ignore his request, but another part of her wanted to share. "We never laughed. And we rarely spent time together, other than for training and House Ravenwood affairs."

"By we, you mean . . ."

"My mother and Amara. Everything we did had one goal: to further the interests of House Ravenwood. If it didn't benefit House Ravenwood, we didn't spend time on it. Ophie, however, is four, and so she has yet to be trained."

"Ophie?"

"Opheliana. She is my youngest sister. She cannot speak, or at least has chosen not to. I think that's part of the reason Mother keeps her sequestered in another part of the castle with Maura, her nursemaid." Selene smiled softly as she gazed at the fire. "She is the sweetest little girl you will ever meet. And so kind."

"I had no idea there were three Ravenwood daughters."

"Most people don't know about Ophie."

"You miss her, don't you?"

Selene tightened her grip around her legs. "Yes." She could hardly say the word.

"I understand the feeling."

Selene glanced over. Yes, Damien understood the feeling all too well. The only difference was she might be able to see her sister someday. Damien would never see Quinn again, at least on this side of the veil.

"So the only memories you have of Amara and your mother are ones of training?"

Selene swallowed. "Yes." The more she grew to know Damien's family, the more she wished she could have experienced what he did, instead of the cold upbringing she had been forced to endure. At least Ophie was free of the weight of House Ravenwood. In some ways, her muteness was a blessing.

"You know, we have a chance to make new memories."

Selene raised one eyebrow.

"Together, you and I. Good ones." He glanced down at his bent knees and spread his hands across the tops. "We both carry heavy responsibilities as leaders of Great Houses, but I don't want that to be the only thing we remember when we are old. I want there to be other memories too. I hope we laugh together, cry together, and enjoy the little things." He motioned to the few crumbs that lay around his boots, alongside his empty teacup, and smiled.

Selene stared at him. It was as if he had offered his hand to her, inviting her to a place of warmth and sunshine. A place like his dreamscape. She bit her lip, her chest aching at his words. "I would like that."

Damien looked up and his smile spread. Her heart fluttered strangely at the subtle shift in the way he looked at her. "Selene, may I ask you something?"

Her heart began to thud inside her chest. "Yes," she said, grateful her voice didn't crack.

Damien paused and leaned in. His eyes grew dark, like the sky at sunset. She could see every tiny scar, every line across his face. The firelight played along his skin, reminding her of the luminescence of his dream world. His face stirred her soul.

"Can I kiss you?" he asked softly.

Her heart missed a beat as her mind went into a free fall. He was asking her for a kiss? Her mouth went dry as her thoughts scrambled for a foothold. "Why?"

He cocked his head to the side. "Why?"

"I mean . . . we're already married. Most couples have already kissed and . . ." Her cheeks lit on fire.

That same gentleness spread from his mouth to his eyes. "Because I will never do anything without asking you first."

Was he saying he would wait if she said no? But did she want to say no? Eventually, if her desire was for this marriage to flourish, she would need to say yes.

She curled her fingers beneath her palms. She wouldn't do that to him. He had committed himself to her. She would not let fear rule her or her relationships.

Selene worked her jaw and lifted her chin. He stared back with such conviction that she felt like she could draw on that alone for strength. If there was someone with whom she could be vulnerable, could open up her innermost heart, who already knew her and still wanted to remain by her side despite her past, it was him. "Yes," she said quietly. "You may kiss me."

His eyes darkened further as he reached up and lightly brushed her cheek with his fingers. His touch sent tingles across her face and down her neck. Then he leaned in, slowly. She felt his breath across her lips and inhaled the earthy scent of tea.

His lips touched hers.

A torrent of feelings flooded her body, filling her with heat. His mouth lingered only for a moment before he pulled back, but it felt longer. And she wanted more. It was as if he had opened up a secret door inside her heart, one she had closed away, never letting anyone close. Until now.

"Thank you."

Selene blinked, and Damien's face came into focus. "What for?"

"For your kiss." He leaned away, a grin on

his face as he turned his attention back to the fireplace.

A bold spirit enveloped Selene. She smiled shyly and reached out her fingers, brushing the top of his knuckles. "I liked it."

His head snapped around. "You did?"

She grinned back. "Yes."

It was Damien's turn to look as if the rug had been pulled out from beneath him as he stared at her with his mouth open. She brushed his hand again, almost laughing. It was odd, and yet thrilling, to know she could make him look as stunned as she had felt moments ago.

He leaned back toward her. "Then may I do it again?"

Selene smiled as the fire danced across the logs and snow fell outside the windows. "Yes."

25

Damien couldn't stop thinking about Selene as he stood inside the massive hall inside Brightforest Citadel days later. The way she had looked sitting beside him in front of the fireplace, the way she smiled as they shared the toasted bread and tea, the way her lips felt when he kissed her the first time. And his surprise when she kissed him again. His whole body warmed at the memory, driving away the chill.

And yet, he couldn't dismiss the fact that he still wasn't sure about the extent of her power. That same morning, a dozen servants and guards were found collapsed across the castle. Healer Sildaern had been able to revive them, but what were the chances this happened at the same time Selene was experiencing a nightmare and had called out to him?

Was Selene using her dreamwalking gift on others around the castle? Was there more to her gift than either of them realized?

Were his people in danger?

He pressed two fingers to the middle of his forehead and closed his eyes. *Light, what do I do?*

He breathed in deeply before dropping his hand. *I said I would give her a chance, and*

I will stand by that until proven otherwise. He had five days before he headed back home to Northwind Castle, just in time for the Festival of Light. Time to think, reflect, and pray. And time to come up with a gift to give to Selene for the festival.

Damien took a step closer to the crackling fire inside the fire pit and glanced around. Like Northwind Castle, Brightforest Citadel was made entirely of light grey stone and stood on a cliff overlooking the sea near the forest for which it was named. However, the building was functional, with none of the decorative etches or stonework of Northwind Castle. It had been built as the headquarters for the Northern Shores navy, the protecting force of House Maris.

The air was frigid except for near the fire pits that lined the floor, one every thirty feet, with three total in the main hall. Thick wooden beams held the ceiling two stories above the room. Banners with the colors of House Maris hung from the beams, light blue with indigo waves enclosed in a white circle.

"I don't remember a winter quite this bitter." Taegis stood beside Damien with his hands fanned out toward the fire and a scowl on his face.

"Neither do I, but it does give us more time to prepare."

"That it does, if the men don't freeze first."

"A little bit of frostbite never killed anyone," a deep voice chimed in.

Damien and Taegis turned to find an older gentleman decked out in leather and the colors of House Maris approaching them. Leather bracers were wrapped around his muscular forearms and thick boots covered his feet and calves. His chestnut-colored hair was pulled back and held in place with a leather cord. The rest of his face was clean-shaven.

Taegis snickered. "Admiral Gerault."

Admiral Gerault bowed. "Lord Damien. Taegis." He lifted his head and grinned at Taegis. "It's been a while, my old friend."

"I still can't believe someone thought it was a good idea to make you an admiral."

"And I can't believe anyone listens to your advice."

"I still have a few good ideas."

"And apparently someone thinks I'm respectable."

The men laughed while Damien looked on and smiled. He didn't know Admiral Gerault as well as he knew Taegis, but he did have fond memories of the older man at Northwind Castle, visiting with his father and sparring with Taegis. He'd lost his entire family during the plague, and yet the man could still smile. He was an inspiration.

"Thank you for coming. While my captains

assemble the men, please follow me to the meeting hall so we can speak privately." Admiral Gerault turned and headed back toward a door at the rear of the cavernous room.

Damien followed, with Taegis beside him. Inside the next room stood a long wooden table, benches, and another fire pit built into the stone floor. Along the top of the table was a map etched out in ink across cream-colored vellum. "I've taken the liberty of bringing a map of the lands here so we could speak first."

Damien stopped in front of the map and peered down. It was detailed, with every location labeled down to the last stream and trail.

"Do you know what the other Great Houses have planned?" Admiral Gerault came to stand beside Damien.

"I don't. I hope with the break between storms that another set of carrier birds can be sent out. But this is what I have in mind: First, every house mobilizes their military and readies their forces to move at a moment's notice. Second, the Great Houses meet again at the end of winter. I am proposing the meeting to take place at Lux Casta."

"Lux Casta?" Admiral Gerault tugged on his chin. "Wouldn't the capital city of House Vivek be a better choice since it's near the wall and border?"

Damien shook his head. "I'm not sure yet where the new grand lord's alliances lie."

"So they found a replacement for Lord Rune and Lady Runa amongst the lesser houses?"

"No. Lord Rune's son is the new grand lord."

"Lord Rune's son?"

"Yes."

"I didn't realize he had a son."

"Very few did." Apparently he would be having more of these discussions as the knowledge of Lord Renlar spread. Damien continued on. "And it is better for the Great Houses to meet farther from, not closer to, the wall and the lands of House Friere."

Admiral Gerault frowned. "Then I take it House Friere is not an ally."

Damien sighed. "No. Not only did Lord Ivulf refuse to sign the treaty, I was made aware later that both House Friere and House Ravenwood are working with the empire."

The admiral's head shot up. "What do you mean?"

Damien glanced around. "It means the Great Houses are divided, and Friere and Ravenwood are our enemies."

"And what about your new wife? Isn't she from House Ravenwood?"

New wife. His heart gave a strange warble at the words. "She's the reason I even know of such matters, as she's defected from her own house."

His eyes widened. "I see. That's quite a risk she took."

"Indeed." Damien smiled softly down at the map. "The more I come to know her, the more I am convinced she will be a capable ally in the upcoming conflict."

"That is high praise coming from you, my lord."

Across the table, Taegis smiled.

Yes, Damien missed Selene. But now was not the time to dwell on her. He needed to focus. "Going back to the map, here is what I need from you, Admiral Gerault: I will be bringing the sea barrier down. It has been siphoning my strength, and I will need my power elsewhere in the coming months. I also require the barrier down in order to travel to Lux Casta. So I will need the naval fleet to start patrolling our shores. I will also need our forces to be ready to move inland when the empire invades."

"How is the empire going to cross into our lands with the eastern wall in place? I know small forces here and there have climbed the wall and fought along the border. But no large force can enter without the wall coming down."

Damien tapped a finger on the table next to the map. "I'm not sure. But if I were Lord Ivulf and working with the empire, then I would find a breach in the wall and use my power to crack it open. It took both of our houses to create the wall, but all he needs is a small opening that he can widen by himself with his own power."

"And let Commander Orion and his forces in."

Admiral Gerault let out a whistle. "What made House Friere and House Ravenwood turn from the rest of us?"

Damien lowered his head and flexed his fingers across the table. "Hatred and greed. Two of the most dividing forces amongst humankind."

"I see. And there is no persuading them otherwise?"

"That was the purpose of the assembly. Unfortunately, I failed."

"You did not fail, my lord." Taegis came to stand beside him. "Every man and woman must make their own decisions and live with the consequences. House Friere and Ravenwood made theirs. You did not make it for them."

Damien nodded. "You're right. All we can do now is work with what we have and pray to the Light."

The men fell silent, with the only sounds coming from the adjoining hall where the naval soldiers of House Maris were gathering.

Damien stared down at the map, his heart heavy. What made Lord Ivulf and Lady Ragna think the Dominia Empire could be trusted? Did they really think Commander Orion would let two of the Great Houses remain? Even one Great House would mean a potential future uprising. Commander Orion would be a fool to let anyone survive who could undermine his rule. Why couldn't they see that?

The door opened on the other side of the

meeting hall. A man dressed in a uniform similar to Admiral Gerault's looked in. "Admiral, the men are ready."

Admiral Gerault looked over his shoulder. "Thank you, Captain Mercer."

Captain Mercer bowed and left the room, closing the door behind him.

Admiral Gerault straightened. "Thank you for the information you provided, Lord Damien. I will be sure to set up a patrol of our shores and have our men ready. In the meantime, the men would like to see their grand lord, and then afterward we can continue our conversation and discuss strategies about the upcoming war."

"Very good, Admiral."

Admiral Gerault bowed, then headed for the door, where muffled conversation flowed from the room beyond. Damien's throat tightened as he followed the admiral. Why did it have to come to this? Why did there have to be a war? If only the Great Houses had united . . .

He stepped out of the meeting hall to thousands of eyes set upon him. Voices lowered, then vanished. Damien looked upon the men present: each one was a brother, a son, a father. His heart twisted, tightening his throat even further. If only there was a way he could go in their place.

Instead, he would be sending them to war, and some would not come home.

What kind of man did that make him?

• • •

Damien wished Admiral Gerault and his captains farewell before boarding the *Ros Marinus* three days later. The air was clear and bitterly cold, without a cloud in the sky. Slabs of ice floated along the dark blue waters. If it were anyone other than Captain Stout, then he would be hesitant to travel back to Nor Esen by sea. But the captain was an excellent seaman and the *Ros Marinus* a fast and nimble ship, able to navigate icy waters in winter.

Despite the cold, they made good time and arrived in port two days later, just as the sun was setting. Damien stood at the prow and stared up at Northwind Castle, above the city of Nor Esen. Lights twinkled along the windows, creating a warm and inviting picture. *Home.*

He breathed out the word, his breath a wisp in the cold air, and pulled his fur-lined cloak closer to his neck and ears. How many times did he come back to Nor Esen and long for the comfort of Northwind Castle? And even more so now after long, grueling days of talks and strategies with his naval personnel? All he wanted was to shed his heavy cloak, sit in front of the fire inside his bedchambers, and kiss Selene again.

He gripped the railing tighter at his last thought. Had she missed him as much as he had missed her? He rubbed the side of his face. His thoughts reminded him of a smitten young man, not those of a grand lord. And yet he was both.

"It's good to be home."

Damien started and looked to his left. Taegis had silently joined him at the prow. "Yes. I never tire of seeing the lights around Northwind Castle at night."

"Neither do I. But perhaps there is another reason you are happy to be home?"

Damien smiled and looked back up at the castle, despite his earlier misgivings. The sky was dark now with a sprinkling of stars. The ship lurched, then grew still as it settled next to the pier. "Yes. It's been a while since I had family to return back to."

"Family? Does that mean you see Lady Selene as your family now?"

Damien paused, then answered, "I believe it does."

"Good," Taegis said. "I'd hoped you would find comfort in a life partner. I wasn't sure at first if Lady Selene would be that person, but from what I've witnessed over the last two months, she seems like she is a good match for you. It will be interesting to see what the next few months bring."

"Yes, it will be," Damien said softly.

"Will you be giving her a gift for the Festival of Light?"

"Yes. She's had many questions about the

Light and the gifts of the Great Houses. I want to introduce her to both."

"You'll take her to raise the waters?"

"Yes, at the same place my father taught me, as long as another storm doesn't come in."

Taegis slowly nodded. "I think that would be special."

Damien looked back up at Northwind Castle. The torches, candles, and fires were the only light against the backdrop of grey stone. "I think so too."

The smell of pine and spices filled his nose the moment Damien stepped into Northwind Castle. Already the servants were preparing for the festival by hanging garlands made of pine branches and satchels of spices along the stairways and corridors of the castle. There was humming along the hallway to the left as a maidservant swept, an old familiar tune about the first light on winter's morning.

"We have just enough time to change and join the others for the evening meal," Taegis said.

"Yes." Damien had hoped to find Selene before dinner, although he wasn't sure what he would say. He simply wanted to see her again.

What an odd thought. And what a change from over a month ago. He hurried up the stairs and down the hallway toward his own bedchambers.

As he passed the library, he paused. Perhaps she was in there. He opened the door. Candles were lit, and down at the other end of the room, past all of the bookshelves, a cheery fire burned in the fireplace. He made his way between the books and looked around the last bookshelf toward the built-in nook beneath a set of windows.

Selene sat on the cushions, dressed in a simple gown of blue, with her legs pulled up and tucked beneath her skirt. The light from the fire bounced across the glass behind her, creating a background of orange and midnight around her body.

She was so focused on her book that she didn't hear him as he approached.

He took in the sight of her: the blue sheen of her dark hair as it hung over one shoulder, her lips moving silently as she read, the smallness of her fingers as they held the tome.

Just when he thought he should alert her to his presence, her head came up and her eyes met his. The silence of the library felt magnified as they stared at each other. "Damien," she finally whispered.

"Selene."

"You're home."

He closed the distance between them and sat down on the other side of the nook, a foot away from her.

"I thought you wouldn't be back until tomorrow."

"We finished early and left."

"How was your trip?"

It felt like they were having a casual conversation over a light dinner instead of seeing each other for the first time in over a week. He wanted to reach over and hold her, smell her hair, kiss her lips. But he wasn't sure that's what she wanted. "I shared with Admiral Gerault and the captains the ideas and plans we came up with. I also shared with them all of the information I knew so we could plan a course of action."

Selene looked down with a small sigh. "So it has come to this. War will really be upon us."

"Yes. But we will be ready, the best way we can be."

"Still, there is no guarantee of victory."

Damien glanced away. "No, there isn't. But at least we have the gifts of five of the seven houses."

"Five?"

Damien looked back. "Yes. House Rafel declined signing the treaty. So that leaves my house, Luceras, Merek, most likely Vivek. And you."

She raised one eyebrow. "I'm not sure what help my gift will be, unless you plan on using my abilities in the same way my mother employs hers."

He shook his head. "No. There is another purpose for your dreamwalking. Perhaps we can discover it together." More than anything he had faith in that, despite the shadow across his heart. A muffled bell rang beyond the walls, signaling dinner would be served soon. They both glanced toward the aisle that led to the door and stood. Selene placed the book on the table and headed for the exit.

"Wait, Selene." He reached out and gripped her elbow.

She turned around, a puzzled look on her face.

"I missed you."

Her eyes softened, and a smile crept across her lips. "I missed you too."

Before he could stop himself, Damien gathered her into his arms. She stiffened for a moment, then slowly moved her arms around his waist. He turned his head and breathed in the scent of her hair, some kind of attractive smell he could not place. Floral, maybe? His lips followed her cheek and jaw, but never touched her skin until he found her mouth, then he pressed his lips to hers.

She responded by tightening her hold around him and kissing him back.

He never wanted to let go. Her body was warm and solid within his arms, as if she had been made to fit there. And her lips tasted like sweet wine. This was what he'd dreamed of during his absence.

The bell rang again.

Reluctantly he pulled away. He didn't want

them to be late. And he hadn't had a chance yet to change. "We should probably get ready for dinner."

Her eyes appeared even darker in the dim firelight. "All right. I'll see you then."

She slowly drew away and slipped around the corner like a spirit. Damien stood there, staring at the edge of the bookshelf where she had disappeared, a trembling inside his chest.

Yes, Selene was filling the hole inside his heart his family had left behind. But there was still a fear there, a fear of losing those he loved. There was a strong possibility that could happen. Selene had a mark on her set by her own house. He doubted Lady Ragna would give up her hunt for her eldest daughter. And when war broke out, Selene would be a target—both as a member of House Maris *and* House Ravenwood.

But he couldn't leave her here, in the safety of Northwind Castle. He felt certain she had a part to play in the upcoming conflict. Every house would be needed in order to push back the empire. The coalition would need her gift of dreamwalking, if they could figure out the original purpose of the gift. And when that moment came, he would have to let her go and leave her in the protection of the Light.

Damien shook his head and started for the door that led out of the library. Others thought his faith was strong, but he knew better. They didn't know how much he struggled with letting go of others.

Death was the ultimate separation. He couldn't stop it. And when it happened, it tore him apart.

Not right now, he thought, running a hand through his hair as he left the library. *I'm not going to dwell on what I can't change. I don't know the future. All I have is the present. And I'm going to be grateful for every moment.*

26

Night after night the Dark Lady visited Selene in her dreams. And each morning she woke up in a cold sweat, her heart pounding. No matter how hard she ran or flew, she couldn't escape the Dark Lady or lay hold of the light. She was trapped between both inside the dreamscape.

Selene lay in her bed and watched the morning light trickle in through the window on the other side of the room. The smell of baking bread drifted beneath her door and filled her room with a sweet aroma, making her stomach gurgle. The last few days had filled her eyes, ears, and nose with the most delectable senses: pine wreaths, savory smells from the kitchen, the bustling of the servants as they cleaned the entire castle, painted glass balls hanging from windowpanes so the sunlight could catch the colors and spread them throughout the castle. She smiled as a guard walked by her room, humming an unfamiliar tune.

Absolutely enchanting. And a welcome repose from her nightmares.

Selene slowly rose from her bed. She still wasn't sure what this Festival of Light was, but it appeared to land on the same day as the Turn of Winter and the start of the new year. Given how much thought and care was going into the preparation of this festival, it looked like it was a highly regarded celebration.

Despite her dreams each night, Selene couldn't help but catch the feverish excitement spreading around the castle and Nor Esen. And best of all, Damien was home to be a part of it.

Damien.

Selene paused behind the changing screens, her fingers curled around the simple tunic she wore for training. He had found her in the library last night and admitted he had missed her. And she had missed him.

And that kiss . . .

Even now her lips tingled from the remembered touch. He was strong and yet gentle at the same time. That thought sent a flutter of emotions through her body as she pulled her sparring tunic over her head and tied the front laces.

Then she paused, her hands still on the ties. What was this feeling growing inside of her? When he was gone, it felt like part of her was gone too. And when he was near, it was like a fire burned inside of her, brightening even further when they touched.

She turned and glanced at herself in the mirror, her heart thumping. That was good, right? She had hoped someday that the man she married would be someone she respected and loved. Perhaps her hope was coming true.

So what was next?

The room suddenly grew hot. Selene tugged at the edge of her tunic above her collarbone as her face flushed. Their marriage was still in name only. Was she ready for more?

"I will never do anything without asking you first." Damien's words came back to her from that morning when he first kissed her.

She stared directly at her image and dropped her hands to her sides. "Do you want this marriage or not?" Her lips moved with her words in the reflection. "There is no place for fear, remember?"

She would keep telling herself that. Besides, what did she have to be afraid of, other than the unknown? Sure, there was the chance that Damien might prove to be a different man than she thought he was, but she was almost certain she knew him. After all, she had walked in his dreams and seen his soul.

The new year was almost here. Selene lifted her chin and stared herself straight in the eye. She could make it a new start to their marriage as well.

Remember, no fear.

After she finished dressing, she stepped out of her room, surprised to see Sten standing guard at her door. Selene had only seen the older guard in passing since their arrival at Northwind Castle. He must have been the one she had heard humming out in the hallway.

"Sten, it's good to see you."

"My lady," he said with a bow.

As they walked to the training room, Selene asked, "What can you tell me about the Festival of Light? I've never heard of it until now."

Sten smiled. "Ah yes, our Festival of Light. It is a time when the people of the Northern Shores come together and remember hope and light. And eat good food." He winked at Selene. "It is also customary to give gifts."

"Give gifts?"

"Aye. When I was young, every year my mother would craft mittens for me and my brothers from rabbit fur. They were the softest gloves I've ever worn."

"And what do you do now for gifts?"

"If I'm not on duty, I spend the day with my brothers and their families and usually bring something I've whittled from wood. Gifts given during the Festival of Light are to come from the heart, from one person to another."

"I see." She wrinkled her brow in thought.

"Along with the gifts, the monks from Baris Abbey visit Nor Esen and bring their own kind of special gift."

"What is it?"

Sten smiled again. "You'll see. I don't want to spoil it for you."

Puzzled, she made her way into the training room. Sten whistled a tune as he headed back down the hall.

Her mind turned back to Sten's comment about gifts. What kind of gifts did people give each other? He said they were heartfelt. Did Damien plan on giving her a gift? She had nothing to give to him, nothing in her possession that could be offered as a gift. And even if she did, what could she give that came from her heart?

Inside the room, four guards were sparring, leaving the area with the practice dummies available.

Selene ignored the surprised and cautious glances sent her way as she drew her swords from the double scabbard around her waist and stood before the straw dummy. She seemed to be getting more of those glances over the last fortnight, even more than when she first arrived at Northwind Castle.

Perhaps it was her presence in the training room that made them uncomfortable. After all, this was her first time coming here alone. But Damien had encouraged her to follow her own pursuits, and she was finally following his advice.

She focused on the unpainted face of the dummy, breathed, then went through her first set of motions. Then the next. And the next.

Her body grew warm beneath the practice clothes she wore, her hands and arms moving of their own accord, while her mind moved from one thought to the next: the upcoming war, the festival, the gifts. Damien.

Suddenly, she sensed something was off. Selene paused midswing and looked over her shoulder. The four guards had stopped and were watching her. She lifted her chin and stared back, waiting.

Two glanced away, but the other two stepped forward. "Excuse me, my lady," one of them said, his head bobbing in embarrassment. "We've never had a woman join us in the training room before."

"Nor have we ever seen a fighting technique like yours," said the other guard who was still watching her. "Sir Taegis said we might see you. Welcome."

Her chin dropped, and her mouth would have too if she hadn't stopped herself in time. She had expected veiled inquiries about her place here. Even with her position as Damien's wife, she had anticipated uncertainty from others when she came to practice in the training room. Instead, she was greeted with quiet respect, at least by some of them.

She bowed her head toward the men. "Thank you."

"If you ever need a sparring partner, I would be happy to oblige," the first guard said.

"If you don't mind, I'll be the first one in line to spar with my wife." There was a note of humor in that tenor voice.

The two guards bowed their heads while the other two spun around and did likewise.

Damien walked toward the other side of the training room and talked with the guards while Selene watched, a very different kind of warmth spreading across her body. Then he turned and smiled at her, raising the temperature inside of her to blazing—hot enough to burn away the coolness from those two guards who still regarded her warily.

"I was hoping I would find you so I could ask you something," Damien said as he approached. His hair was wet, and his cheeks and the tips of his nose were ruby colored. His eyes were the brightest blue, matching the cloak he still wore over one shoulder. She wondered if he had been out practicing his gift.

"Yes?"

"I have a gift that I want to give you tomorrow."

"For the Festival of Light?"

"Yes."

Selene dropped her arms and looked away, her swords at her sides. "I'm afraid I don't have anything for you. I'd never heard of the Festival of Light until a few days ago and—"

A finger pressed against her lips.

"I do not desire a gift, only your presence. Meet me tomorrow morning outside our bedchambers. All right?"

She nodded.

"In the meantime, I think I'll do a little sparring myself. Care to join me?"

The corners of her lips twitched as a playful spirit took hold of her. Who cared what the guards thought of her? Only Damien mattered at this moment. "Yes. And I will beat you this time."

Damien grinned as he unhooked his cloak. "We shall see."

27

Selene stepped out into the hall to wait for Damien outside their bedroom doors. She smiled as she remembered her duel with him yesterday. It was a long fight, but in the end she made it past his sword and won with her blade just below his chin. But he didn't seem put out by his loss. Rather, he congratulated her amongst the applause and whistles from two of the guards inside the training room.

Her smile ebbed away. She was slowly finding acceptance here in Northwind Castle, but there were still those who were suspicious of her. The other two guards had watched their sparring with hesitant expressions.

"Did you hear? There are more people in the infirmary. Passed out with no explanation."

Selene inclined her head to her left, listening to the voices coming from the other direction.

"Did they also have that strange dream? That one with . . . Lady Selene?"

"I don't know. Have you had it?"

The men's voices faded down the other hallway.

Selene stared at the wall across from her, stunned. People were in the infirmary? And having dreams about her?

She leaned against the wall for support, her

arms across her middle. Were her nightmares affecting those around her? But how? She stayed in her own room and never had contact with anyone during her sleep. It wasn't possible.

Or was it?

She shook her head as if to shake away the morbid thoughts clinging to her mind like cobwebs. It couldn't be. But then why were they dreaming about her?

No.

She squeezed her arms as she firmly set her thoughts aside. She would not ponder such things today. This day was for gifts, for celebration, for light. A day with Damien.

She breathed again, the heavy weight lifting from her chest. She dropped her arms and sighed. Damien. Over the last few months he had become a friend and companion. He understood the struggles of being the head of a Great House, he had a quiet strength about him, and he accepted her for who she was, with all the damage and fears she carried.

She loved him.

Wait, what?

Selene shot away from the wall. The truth of her last thought slammed into her, taking her breath away.

She loved Damien. Someway, somehow, her heart had thawed, and he'd found a way inside.

She held a hand against her chest, her pulse racing again.

The door opened beside her, and Damien emerged from his room, wearing a heavy cloak, thick boots, and gloves. "Are you read—Selene, are you all right?"

Adrenaline washed over her, leaving her limbs tingling. "Yes." She shook her head, drawing on every ounce of strength to bring these wild emotions under control. "I am. I was just thinking . . ."

He lifted an eyebrow. "About what?"

She dropped her hand. "Things. Life." She wasn't about to confess her newfound discovery with him. Not yet.

He eyed her again before exiting his room and shutting the door. "All right. Well, are you ready to go?"

Selene adjusted her thick cloak around her shoulders and nodded. "I am."

"Then follow me."

Damien nodded to the guards they passed as they walked, and they in turn bowed to him and Selene. At the end of the hall, he opened a door that led to a balcony outside Northwind Castle on the cliff side. A narrow stone path from the balcony wove between boulders ranging from the size of a horse cart to a small house and led toward a small opening in an overhang thirty feet away.

"This way." Damien glanced back. "And be careful. The path might be slippery."

She nodded as a sudden blast of frigid wind blew through the doorway. Pulling her hood over her head, she turned her face away from the wind and followed him along the path toward the entrance ahead. The cave opening was carved into the stone and wide enough for two people.

At the entrance, Damien held out his hand to her. Selene took it without a word, and they slipped into the tunnel. The passage led downward, toward a small light at the end, most likely the exit. The sound of rushing waves filled the area. Selene held her hood in place with her other hand and wondered where he was leading her.

At the bottom, the cave opened up. Roaring, frothy waves spilled across the pebbly beach, surging toward the walls, then dragging the lightest stones back to the sea, only to crash into the next set of waves coming in. Gaps along the ceiling let in pale wintry light. Cold sea spray filled the area, leaving Selene thankful for the oiled cloak across her body and her warm boots.

Damien let go of her hand and crossed the gravel to the edge of the waves and stood there with his hands on his hips. As he looked over the waters, his hood flew back and the bottom edge of his cloak rippled in the wind.

Selene watched from the bottom of the

passageway. She could feel the power of the sea swirling inside the cavern, and in that moment she felt like one of the small pebbles at her feet. The raging water was vast, potent, and living—a force to be reckoned with. The ability to harness such power had been given to House Maris by the Light.

Amazing.

Damien looked back at her, then motioned for her to join him. Selene picked her way across the gravel as another wave came crashing in. She came to a stop beside him, clutching her cloak close to her body. The mist froze across her face, leaving her nose chilled.

Damien didn't seem to notice the spray or the cold. Instead, he gazed out over the water with a satisfied look on his face. "This is where I first learned of my gift. My father brought me here and told me the history of my family. We were given the gift of the waters to protect our people. But it's more than that; it's how I worship the Light. What he gave me I give back to him."

Damien bent his knees and brought his hands up until they were level with his chest. He inhaled deeply, then slowly raised his palms again. This time, the waves moved with the motion of his hands. Instead of crashing along the pebbles, the water rose in a thick sheet.

He kept one hand in the air, brought a leg back, then pushed out with his other hand. The water mimicked his movement. The wall of water moved out toward the wide cave entrance like a wave, only much bigger.

"When I move the water, I feel a connection to the one who gave me this power." Damien changed his stance and slowly brought the wall of water back. "I feel peace. I lift the days left to me to the Light in service, then I pray for my people. In the same way I move the water, I want the Light to move me, to use me and my power for the benefit of others."

"But how did you come to know the Light in the first place? How do you know he's real? And what is he?" Selene gripped the front of her cloak closed to keep out the cold mist.

"My father and my mother taught me. Then I explored the Light myself. I read all I could at the abbey. He gave life to everything that was created, and his very being brings light to everyone. That is why he is known as the Light. No other title is needed."

"But where is he? Can I see him?"

Damien chuckled and brought his palm down as if he was going to pat the water. "He dwells in light, and he is Light himself. One of the oldest manuscripts says his light is so immense that mortals cannot approach him. Yet he is near to all."

"You speak in riddles."

"Perhaps the sun is a better comparison. It is

bright and hot in the summer, but cool and dim in the winter. It is the same sun but can be both blistering and a comfort. The Light is both."

"And you follow this Light? This being? This—this God?"

"I do. It was my decision to make. After my search, and feeling the power I have been given within my own body, I could see no other path I wanted to take. Following the Light does not mean there is no darkness. Rather, it means there is light *in* the darkness, even if it is only a single flame. I've never been alone. The one who made me and gave me my power has always been with me."

Selene crossed her arms and looked down. "But what if we've already lived in the darkness . . . and maybe even brought darkness to others?" Her voice hitched as she thought of Renata. How could the Light accept someone like her, someone who had misused her gift so terribly?

"Does the sun disappear when clouds come?" Damien brought his hand up, palm facing the sea, and pushed out. The water followed. "Or is the sun still there?"

"It's there, hidden."

"Just as the clouds cannot quench the sun, the darkness cannot quench the Light. We are not bound to what we've done. There is always a choice: to stay in the shadows or to step into the Light."

"So I can change?"

"Yes. Any time. But the moment you step into the Light, you'll never be the same. It will permeate your entire life."

Selene watched the wall of water move toward the front of the cave with the same motion as Damien's palm. "Is that why your soul is full of light?"

Damien grew silent. He moved his hands up, bringing the water almost to the ceiling of the cavern. "Perhaps. Perhaps it is a reflection of the one I follow." He shook his head. "I doubt my soul is full of light because of who I am alone."

She glanced at him sharply. "But you seem so good and always make the right decisions."

Damien laughed and dropped his hands. The water-wall came crashing down in a mix of waves and foam. He turned toward her. "I don't always make the right decisions. There are times I doubt and let anger get the best of me." He lifted one of his hands and looked at his palm. "And I have a hard time letting go of things. Any good you see in me is the Light. The rest is just . . . well . . . it's just me."

Selene stared at him. "Well, I like the man I see."

His eyebrows flew up into his hairline.

She could feel heat spreading across her cheeks, but she gritted her teeth and kept his gaze. She was not embarrassed of what she had said. It was the truth.

His eyes moved back and forth across her face as if confirming her words. Then he stepped toward her and reached out his fingers and lightly touched her cheek. "And I like the woman I see before me." Then he kissed her.

His lips were cold and wet from the mist and tasted like salt. His hand trailed to her braid, and he pulled her hair over her shoulder, following the braid to the end while his other hand went around her back and pulled her closer.

The kiss was short and quick and took her breath away. When Damien drew back, she wanted to grasp the front of his cloak and pull him toward her again. But he spoke before she had a chance to act on the impulse.

"Thank you for coming here with me today. I wanted my festival gift to you to be memories. This place is special to me, both because of my gift and because of the Light. And since you are also special to me, I wanted to share it with you."

Selene's throat grew tight as she gazed into his eyes. "Thank you." If only she had something to share back.

He smiled, and it was like the sun breaking through the clouds. "Always. Now, we should get back to the castle before we freeze—and before Taegis realizes I'm gone." He winked at her.

She nodded. He took her hand and started

toward the path at the back of the cavern. Behind them, the waves resumed their natural ebb and flow.

Once again she felt like her heart would burst inside of her. It was the same exhilaration she felt the first time she changed into a raven and flew within the dreamscape. Never had she imagined she would end up with a partner like Damien. The best she had hoped for was a man whom she could at least respect. And she got so much more.

They exited the tunnel and walked toward Northwind Castle. Selene turned her mind back toward Damien's words about the Light. When he was raising the water and speaking of the Light, it was almost as if his very soul had shone through his body, like a flame in a paper lantern. He was beautiful, inside and out.

It was something she longed for as well. She wanted the same thing he carried inside of him. And yet . . .

And yet it was terrifying. His description of the vastness and the glory of the Light had made her heart tremble. How could a person like her enter such a presence, especially when she had misused her gift in such a terrible way? She felt stuck between the darkness of her past and the light of her future.

She furrowed her brow. Was it possible her recurring dream was a manifestation of her vacillation? Was her dreamscape a threshold of sorts? A part of her wanted to find the light, and yet a part of her was afraid to take that next step. And so the light was always out of reach.

Was she stopping herself from finding the light in her dream? If so, what would happen if she actually let go and gave herself over to the Light?

28

As the evening of the Festival of Light approached, the excitement around Northwind Castle and Nor Esen grew. Lights were lit all over the castle and the smell of roasting meats, bread, and spices filled the hallways. Everyone had a smile on their face, even Karl, which caught Selene by surprise as the usually surly guard greeted her in the hallway with a bow. It changed his features, softening his face, and made him appear younger than usual.

"Good evening, Lady Selene."

"Karl. Good evening."

"Lord Damien awaits your presence in the audience hall."

Selene dipped her head. "Thank you."

She gathered the thick folds of her burgundy gown and headed down the hallway. The buzz of conversation filled the corridors, interspersed with laughter. Candlelight twinkled everywhere she looked. Garlands made of pine branches and pine cones were draped across mantels, doorways, and banisters.

It was all so different from her life back at Rook Castle. Winter was the darkest month, and not only because of the shorter days. It always felt cold and lonely. And when she started training to be a dreamkiller, her entire being felt like it was encased in ice—frozen, unable to feel, unable to breathe.

Here, there was light and laughter and life, even in the middle of winter. In fact, they celebrated it. Selene smiled. She couldn't wait to see what else was in store.

At the audience hall, Karl reached forward and opened the door for her. The tall columns with streams of water weaving between the pillars, the walkway that led up to the glass throne with a waterfall on either side, and Damien standing at the head, waiting for her with his hand extended. It was just as it was the day when Damien had publicly announced their marriage, only this time candles were lit all over the hall, their lights flickering on the surface of the water and glass. The sky beyond the throne was almost dark, with a bit of grey streaking across the horizon.

A sense of wonder overtook Selene as she headed for the throne. Damien's smile grew as she approached, causing her heart to race. His blue eyes matched his regalia, his dark hair brushed back and falling to one side of his face, his entire ensemble proclaiming him to be the lord of a Great House.

"Good evening," he said as he took her hand. In his usual fashion, he lifted her fingers and brushed his lips across her knuckles. Such a simple gesture, but it sent shock waves across her body. "Welcome to the Festival of Light. As soon as night falls, Baris Abbey will present Nor Esen with their gift. Come, we will watch from the balcony." He grinned, and his eyes sparkled in the candlelight. "You don't want to miss this."

Selene followed Damien around the throne to the door that led out onto the balcony that overlooked the city of Nor Esen. Thousands of lights flickered across the city, and the gentle sound of the sea provided the background music.

Selene pulled up the hood of her dress and came to stand beside Damien at the balcony. There was hardly a breeze tonight, as if the Northern Shores was holding its breath for what would happen next. Then, one by one, the lights began to go out across the city. It started at the far end where the gates were, then moved upward toward Northwind Castle.

"What's going on? Is something wrong?" Selene leaned over the balcony, trying to see who or what was putting out the lights.

Damien's hand gently gripped her elbow. "No, this is part of the festival."

"The lights disappear for the festival?"

"Yes. Just watch."

Soon, all the lights were gone across the city. Then the lights began to disappear within Northwind Castle itself. There was no moon and no stars because of the cloud cover, so when the last candle was extinguished, the world fell into darkness. Silence descended upon the city.

Selene took a step back. She wasn't sure she liked this. It reminded her too much of home, of dreamscapes and nightmares.

"It's all right, Selene." Damien's hand moved from her elbow, and he entwined his fingers between her own. "Watch and listen."

His grip was reassuring. Slowly, her body relaxed. First she could only hear the waves. Then a low melody could be heard, just above the sound of the sea. Lights appeared at the far end of the city, where the cliffs and forest separated Nor Esen from Baris Abbey. The chant grew louder. Moments later, an assembly with lanterns emerged from the forest. Selene could not see each individual, but she knew who they were. The monks from Baris Abbey.

Their voices rose and fell as they approached the city, their lanterns appearing like tiny fireflies from her spot on the balcony.

As they entered the gates, the torches along the wall were lit. The monks began their trek through the city. Each time they passed a house, the candles were relit. A bell was rung, then they started their chant again.

Selene watched, her gaze on the lanterns, her ears full of the voices of the monks. They spoke of the darkness, and the light that came when all was lost. A light that spread across the lands. A light that darkness could not extinguish.

The words seemed to seep into her very soul, touching the deepest parts of her being, filling her to the brim, until her only reality was the lights reappearing across the city and the story the monks told through their chant.

"It's beautiful, isn't it?" Damien said quietly.

Selene took a deep breath, realizing cold tears had slipped down her cheeks. "Yes," she said as she quickly wiped her face. For a moment, she thought she would break down and sob right there. Instead, she bit her lip and clutched her hand to her chest.

Nor Esen twinkled again with the light of thousands of candles and torches. It was like the city had died for a moment, then come back to life.

"Every year we remember the Light during the darkest day. We were not left in darkness, to flounder about in this life. Instead, humankind was given hope." He squeezed her hand. "We have hope, even with the threat of the empire."

"Does that mean we will win?"

"No. Sometimes we lose, for reasons I don't understand. But he does."

"The Light?"

"Yes."

"Then why trust him?"

"Why indeed?" He chuckled. "I'll be honest. I've asked myself that before, especially when my parents and Quinn passed away. But there is this anchor inside of me, this knowledge that even though I cannot understand the reason why, I know the darkness will not prevail. The light shines in the darkness, and the darkness can never extinguish it."

Selene frowned in thought. Those words were familiar. She'd read them a while ago from a small book Cohen had let her borrow from the abbey. But before she could ask more questions, a bell rang as the monks reached the gates that led into Northwind Castle. Within seconds, lights filled the castle, and the monks changed their chant to a song as they entered the courtyard. Across the castle and city, others joined the song, until the chorus of thousands of voices rang out across the night.

Damien began to sing beside her, his tenor voice blending in with the others. Once again, a familiar lump filled her throat as she listened to her husband sing with his people. Deep down she wished she could be a part of this, but she still felt like a stranger, a foreigner from a very different world. Welcome, but still separate.

It was not because of Damien or the people of the Northern Shores, but because of her. Every night reminded her of this as she walked the dreamscape, searching. Always searching. She was Lady Selene Ravenwood, heir to the House of Dreamers, and she always would be.

The last note faded into the night, then the city broke out in shouts, laughter, and excitement. Damien squeezed her hand again before giving her a quick kiss on the cheek. "Now it's time to celebrate the Festival of Light. Follow me."

Selene nodded and let him guide her back into Northwind Castle, her mind and body a storm of emotions.

She removed the hood of her gown once they were inside the throne room, freeing her long black hair to fall across her shoulders and down her back. She caught Damien watching her from the corner of his eye, and it made her grow warm all over.

"I don't think I told you how stunning you look this evening," he said as he pulled her closer to his side.

"Thank you."

"And I'm glad you left your hair down. I like it that way."

Selene brushed the side of her face with her hand, the warmth spreading again.

At the bottom of the stairs, they followed the stone path that led between the pillars and streams of water to the audience hall.

Taegis greeted them in the corridor. "My lord. My lady." He dipped his head in their direction. His hair hung along his shoulders instead of gathered at the nape of his neck like usual. And in place of his simple tunic and leather jerkin he wore a strikingly embroidered surcoat in the colors of House Maris.

"Join us, Taegis. We were just heading to the dining hall for the feast."

His head came up. "Thank you." Taegis walked on the other side of Selene as the three of them headed toward the other side of the castle. "What do you think of the Festival of Light so far, Lady Selene?"

She smiled back. "I've never experienced anything so wonderful before. The way the city looked and the chant from the monks was mesmerizing. I had no idea winter could hold such a celebration. We observe the spring Festival of Flowers, but it's nothing like this." She wasn't about to mention the new moon worship. She didn't want shadows of the Dark Lady haunting her thoughts this evening.

"The Festival of Light has been around as long as Baris Abbey. The first abbot wrote the chant they sung this evening thousands of years ago, even before House Maris ruled the Northern Shores."

"Amazing," Selene murmured. Did Rook Castle or the Magyr Mountains hold such history? She only knew as far back as Rabanna and the imperial razing, but nothing earlier. But there had to be more. House Ravenwood had existed as long as the other Great Houses. Even with all her research, she still had not been able to find the rest of their history.

They reached the formal dining hall. Taegis opened the door and ushered Damien and Selene inside. The hall was exquisitely decorated for the festival. Thick candles were set in glass tubes along the wide table, surrounded by pine branches and small red berries. Plates trimmed in silver sat before each chair, alongside matching goblets and two-pronged forks. Dipping bowls were ready for finger washing, and the servants were already pouring the wine.

Voices filled the hall as members from lesser houses, wealthy sea merchants, and those of importance entered the dining hall, including Healer Sildaern, whom Selene hadn't seen since her arrival at Northwind Castle. His long black hair hung around his shoulders, and he wore deep green robes trimmed in silver, the colors of House Rafel. He glanced at Selene with a curious expression before turning away.

Selene frowned as Damien pulled out the chair to the right of his. As she sat down, his fingers brushed her shoulders, then he pushed the chair back in. Taegis took a seat on Damien's left. Damien settled in between them and gazed around the room, nodding and smiling.

Food was brought in minutes later: tureens of cream soup, platters of meat, including venison and poultry, and various dishes of fish and seafood. Roasted root vegetables were served along with dried fruits baked in puddings. Bread was provided to mop up the extra broth and sauce. Wine and honeyed mead was poured into common goblets set around the dining hall.

Conversation filled the air as those gathered washed their fingers and began to fill their plates. Selene helped herself to a small portion of fish and vegetables but found even with the array of tantalizing dishes and atmosphere of merriment, she wasn't hungry. Instead, her entire being was focused on Damien beside her. She listened to the words he spoke, noticed every smile he gave, and felt the strange warble of her heart when his eyes captured hers.

She took a sip from the goblet between them and appreciated the smooth, sweet taste of the honeyed mead but was careful not to drink too much. She had no desire to lose her sense of judgment, one of the many lessons her mother had drilled into her from her training, and one to which she still adhered. A dreamer must always be in her right mind.

"You've barely eaten. Are you all right?"

Selene stared once again into his deep blue eyes and felt a whoosh inside her middle. "Yes. I'm afraid I'm not that hungry tonight."

He raised an eyebrow. "Can I get you something else?"

"No, but thank you."

He gave her a smile before turning to Taegis and starting a conversation. Selene continued to take small bites of her fish, interspersed with light talk with the stout older woman who sat next to her, a Lady Morvand. However, whenever there was a pause, her gaze would return to Damien.

She remembered their time that morning, how he had shared his special spot and heart with her as his festival gift. She still had so many questions, but seeing his faith had answered some of them. His words were like his soul: beautiful.

And she hadn't given him anything in return.

If she were at Rook Castle, maybe she could have had a sword commissioned by the weaponsmith or searched over the wares brought in by traveling merchants. She couldn't embroider, so a handkerchief was out of the question. Same with a painting. She couldn't cook or sew.

She mentally shook her head. Those gifts weren't from the heart, anyway. And he'd said he didn't need a gift, but she wanted to give something back to him. Something as special as he had given her—

Selene paused, her fork hovering over the last bite of fish. Her heart began to beat faster, and her mouth grew dry. Only days ago she'd looked in the mirror and told herself she wanted to make this marriage work. There was one thing she could give him. One thing only she could offer.

Heat crept up her cheeks, and the hair along her arms rose. He said he would never do anything without asking. Did she really want to wait for that? She glanced at Damien from the corner of her eye. He was laughing at something Taegis had said. The way he smiled lit up his entire face and showed such joy. How could she not love a man like him?

Her heart pounded at the thought, and her palms grew sweaty. There was a mixture of trepidation and anticipation circling inside of her. Did every woman experience these contrary feelings? She reached for the closest goblet—

Damien's hand stretched out at the same moment and their fingers met. He grinned, his fingers still touching hers. "We need to stop meeting this way."

That one touch sent every nerve flying. Her lips twitched while her heart hammered even harder inside her chest. "Perhaps I would say we need two goblets, but I don't mind sharing,"

Damien chuckled, then pushed the goblet toward her. "Ladies first."

Her throat was so tight she wasn't sure if she would get the liquid down. She breathed in, forcing a trained calmness across her body, and took a sip. She raised her eyes and found Damien studying her, the lightness from moments earlier gone, replaced with an intensity. She stared back, pulled into his gaze until the liquid began to burn at the back of her throat, forcing her to swallow.

After taking another drink, she handed him

the cup, then spotted a couple across the table watching them with knowing smiles. Her cheeks flushed as she glanced away, but she couldn't hide her own smile.

A half hour later, Damien stood and thanked those present for coming. Everyone else stood and bowed toward Damien. Selene dropped her lap cloth and stood as well.

"Would you like to stay for a bit?" he asked her as half of the room sat down, while the other half mingled or headed for the doorway.

"No, I'm ready to leave."

He held out his arm. "Then let me escort you back to your room."

Selene took his arm, her senses swimming with his essence, smell, and presence as he led her out into the hall. It felt like she was about to open a new chapter in the book of their lives, and she looked forward to the days ahead with eager expectation.

Damien stopped beside her door and turned toward her. His face glowed in the candlelight, his lips slightly parted, his eyes dark and full. "May I kiss you good night?" he said quietly.

Selene took a moment to compose the sudden rush of emotions inside her by slowly placing her hands on his chest. Then she looked into his eyes. "Yes."

He leaned forward and brushed his lips across hers. But that wasn't enough for her. She reached up and pulled him closer, deepening the kiss.

Damien followed her lead and wrapped one arm around her waist, running his fingers through her hair with his other. The feeling stirred her.

He finally pulled away, his breathing heavy, and placed a hand on her cheek. "I don't want to say good night."

"Then don't."

He halted, a frown across his lips. "What do you mean?"

Her heart beat rapidly inside her chest but she pushed on. "I don't want to leave either. I want to be with you tonight."

He pulled back and studied her face. "Are you saying . . . ?"

She nodded. Adrenaline, not unlike a fight, sped through her veins.

His thumb began to stroke her cheek. "Selene, are you sure?"

"Yes. I want this marriage. When we first bonded, it was a marriage of circumstances. Since then, I've changed. I want it to be more." She pressed her hand against his chest. "This is my gift to you. My heart."

His thumb stopped. His gaze moved along her face, sending another wave of adrenaline and heat through her body. "I told you I don't need a gift, and I don't want you to feel obligated—"

She pressed a finger to his lips. "This is what I want. And this is what I want to give to you. Will you accept it?"

She could feel his breath across her finger as he stood silently before her. Then he lifted his own hand and removed her finger, leaned forward, and kissed her again.

This time he did not hold back. He kissed her more thoroughly than he ever had before, and she rose to meet his passion. His smell, his touch, his taste filled her.

Then he pulled back once more, his fingers still entwined in her hair. "I said I would never do anything without asking you first. So, one last time, are you sure?"

A light smile graced her lips. This was the right choice, the right time. The man she loved. "Yes."

His eyes seemed to grow more intense as he reached past her to the left, and a moment later, the door opened to his own room. The corners of his lips turned upward in a mischievous smile. He bent his head toward hers. "I'm glad I don't have to say good night," he whispered before sweeping her up into his arms and walking inside.

29

Everything was warm and hazy as Damien awoke. He looked over at Selene next to him and studied her in the morning light. She was still asleep, her body rising and falling with each breath as she lay curled on her side. Her hair was scattered across the pillow and bed in long black strands. He reached over and felt a lock between his fingers, then spotted a bluish mark beneath her hair along her back.

He moved onto his side and gently moved her hair away. His eyebrows rose. Along her back, right near the shoulder blades, were bluish-grey wings spreading from her spine, like a bird's.

Amazing.

His finger trailed one of the wings.

Selene gave a start and sat up. She glanced over her shoulder at him, then her face blossomed into the deepest red as she reached for the coverlet.

"Is this your mark?" he said.

She nodded, her eyes wide as she stared back at him.

He pushed up on an elbow and brushed her back again with his fingertip. "It's beautiful. Like two wings across your back." His gaze moved from her back to her face, then he reached over and brushed her hair from her shoulder.

Her eyes trailed down his chest, stopping at his upper hip. "Is that yours?"

He glanced down at the familiar mark. "Yes. Three waves for House Maris."

She hesitated, then reached over and lightly brushed his skin. His muscles tightened under her touch. "So different than mine," she murmured. "When did your gift appear?"

Damien lay back down, his hands behind his head, remembering the day when his gift came. It had rained all day and night and into the next day. "When I passed sixteen harvests."

"So young."

He glanced at her. "Really? How old were you when your gift came?"

"Eighteen winters."

"And how old are you now?"

"Almost nineteen winters. I was born a fortnight after the Turn of Winter."

He hummed thoughtfully. "So you've only had your gift for a year?"

Selene smoothed out the blanket in front of her. "Yes."

"And yet your dreamwalking ability appears powerful. It took me years to master raising the waters. Is that common for all dreamwalkers?"

She shook her head. "No. My mother said I was special since the day I was born. My mark is not small like my predecessors and has not faded. And it didn't take me long to control my gift."

"Interesting." Damien grew quiet as he stared up at the canopy. Just how strong was Selene's gift with a mark like that? Then he calculated their ages. "I'm twenty-four harvests. So we're not far apart in age compared to most couples."

"That's true." He could feel her eyes on him and looked over. "You became grand lord at twenty-two, my father said. That's young."

"Yes." He let his breath out. "It's not been easy."

She placed a hand on his shoulder and smiled down at him. "I know."

His heart beat faster at her touch. Sunlight filled his bedchambers, casting a warm glow across the room. He didn't want to leave. He wanted to stay here and spend the morning with Selene. To talk. To share their lives. To be a married couple. But there was much that needed his attention.

He sighed and sat up. "I wish I could stay with you this morning, but I'm afraid I have a lot to do today. Soon most of the ice will be gone and we'll need to be ready to leave for Lux Casta. And the navy will need to be ready for when the empire moves."

Selene gave him another smile. "I understand."

Her look made his stomach turn inside out. "I

would love for you to join me again tonight. Or every night if you want. I know most grand lords and ladies have separate rooms, but perhaps you would consider something different?"

He held his breath. Maybe it was too soon to ask.

Her smile widened. "I would like that."

He felt like he had been hit upside the head with the blunt end of the sword, knocking his thoughts out of his head. "I-I will have Steward Bertram see to it that your belongings are brought to our room today." Did he really just stammer? Like a youth? Then what he had said hit him.

Our room.

There was something right about those words. "Let me know if you need anything. I'll be with Taegis or in my study." On impulse, he leaned over and kissed her, savoring the feel of her lips. Reluctantly, he pulled away. "I'll see you tonight."

"Yes," she said breathlessly, her eyes shining.

He stared at her, mesmerized. She was so beautiful. Never did he realize what they would become when they stood beside the Hyr River and said their vows.

Move, Damien, his mind demanded.

He mentally shook his head, rolled to his own side of the bed, and stood. Compared to the comfort and warmth in his room, he had no desire to head out and plan more strategies or talk to his naval personnel or prepare for a war. Why couldn't things have remained peaceful? Then again, he would have never married Selene if the times had been peaceful. They probably would have never even met.

Life could be both bitter and sweet.

Damien headed outside into the frigid cold. He stood upon the cliff outside Northwind Castle and raised his hands, then began his usual morning routine of raising the waters and praying for his people.

His oiled cloak whipped around his boots as his hands grew cold inside his thick gloves. But he needed this. He needed this time to commune with the Light and to continue to strengthen his gift. He had grown used to the pull of both water-walls on his power, but he would be happy when he could take the sea barrier down when they left for Lux Casta.

As he went through his intercessions, he paused on Selene. The water roared in a wall reaching the edge of the cliff he stood on, spraying his boots and cloak with salty mist. His heart swelled with love and thankfulness. He closed his eyes and breathed in the cold air. *Thank you, Light. Thank you for my wife.*

The corners of his lips turned upward as he resumed his exercises. What would his family have thought of Selene? Would they have been shocked that he had married a Ravenwood?

Would they have accepted her? Would Quinn have joked with her in his usual manner?

His throat thickened as he raised the waves again. They would have come to love her as he had.

30

Snow covered the city of Nor Esen in a thick blanket of white. Damien stared out the window of his study, lost in thought. The sweet scent of Selene still lingered in the air even though she had left a half hour ago.

Had it really only been a fortnight since the Festival of Light? So much had happened. It was hard to believe there was a time when they barely knew each other, dancing around each other as strangers, sleeping in separate rooms, going their separate ways each day. Now they broke their fast together each morning and worked together in his study, talking and sharing ideas. Each night they fell asleep together.

She was a partner in the truest sense. And yet . . .

He ran a hand through his hair and turned back. She never spoke of the night terrors she experienced every night. When he asked her about them, she seemed to almost physically retreat behind a mask. Was she hiding something? Or did she feel like she couldn't share?

There was a knock at the door, and then it opened behind him. Damien frowned and turned around.

"My lord, may I speak to you?" Taegis said.

"Yes, come in. I finished my writing a short time ago."

Taegis shut the door behind him and approached the desk. Damien's frown deepened at the serious look on his guardian's face. "Is there something wrong?"

Taegis let out a long breath. "I'm not sure."

"You know I value your words and thoughts. You can share whatever you need to with me."

Taegis paused, then answered, "It has to do with Lady Selene."

Damien stiffened. "Lady Selene?" This was not what he was expecting.

"Yes. Do you remember the dreams you had when we were at Rook Castle during the assembly?"

The hair lifted along the back of his neck. "Yes. I dreamed a lot about my family."

"You also dreamed of a raven, remember?"

There was something in Taegis's voice that triggered a warning in the back of his head. "Yes, I do remember." He now knew it had been Selene in his dreams. "Why?"

"It would seem a dream raven has been visiting Northwind Castle. Apparently for a while now."

"What do you mean?" He consciously forced his body to relax.

"I've heard the guards talking about a raven in their dreams." Taegis looked keenly at him. "Perhaps you brought something back from Rook Castle without knowing it."

Damien stared back. It couldn't be Selene. She was now with him every night, so she wasn't visiting others and dreamwalking. But only Selene could dreamwalk. Was Taegis referring to events before the Festival of Light? Was it possible Selene had been dreamwalking in the minds of those who lived here without him knowing? "Tell me more."

Taegis sat down with a sigh. "It's more than just the guards. The servants have also experienced this dream." He glanced at Damien. "And so have I."

"Tell me all of it. Leave out no details."

"At first, it started with dreams of a dark figure and a raven. Then, if you'll recall, a handful of people were found unconscious around the castle before the Festival of Light."

"Healer Sildaern found nothing wrong with them."

"Nothing wrong, yes. Other than they'd all had the same dream. And Lady Selene was in it."

Damien gripped the arm of his chair. "Why wasn't I told about this?"

"I didn't want to alarm you. At first I thought the people here were simply adjusting to Lady Selene's presence, hence why she was showing up in their dreams. I've had dreams about new people I've met. But when I overheard two of the guards talking about the exact same dream, and not on different nights but on the same night,

I began to wonder. After investigating more thoroughly, I've come to believe that the same phenomenon that haunted your dreams back at Rook Castle has come to Northwind Castle."

Damien shook his head. "I don't understand." Selene said she had to be touching a person to use her gift. But how could she be touching so many people at the same time and entering their dreams? It wasn't possible.

Or was it?

What about her mark? And what her mother said about her power? Was it possible her gift had expanded?

A cold chill swept across his body. There were varying degrees of giftedness within each house. His gift was on par with his father's. Quinn's had not been as powerful. His ancestor who helped build the wall along the empire border had been very powerful.

Was Selene more powerful than she or even her own family knew? So much so that her power had broken the known confines of her gift?

"I'm assuming by your silence that this has something to do with Lady Selene, doesn't it?" Taegis said quietly.

Damien pressed a fist to his lips. "Yes."

"Can you talk about it?"

He shook his head. "No." He paused, trying to find the right words, but they tumbled from his mouth. "It would be so much easier if I could just tell you that Selene is a dreamwalker." No loss of voice, no stopping of the tongue.

Taegis stared at him, his face changing from disbelief to shock. His brows pressed together, and his lips went tight. "What did you say?"

Damien's mouth was agape. "What did you hear?"

"I thought I heard you say that the dream-walking gift still exists. And that Selene has it."

Damien had done it. He had shared House Ravenwood's secret, the one guarded by the matriarch of the house. But did that mean . . .

Was Selene the new grand lady of Ravenwood? Had her power surpassed that of Lady Ragna, and the ancient power of House Ravenwood now recognized her as the new head?

He stared down at his desk. A change in the head of house due to the presence of a vastly more powerful house member was rare, but it could happen. Long ago, House Friere had experienced such, and there were a few other records of this occurrence. If these dreams were indeed Selene's doing—that somehow she was dreamwalking in multiple minds without touching them—it meant that she was more powerful than even she knew. And Damien himself had seen her mark and experienced her power.

"I think the shared dream with the raven and the dark figure are Selene's doing," Damien said slowly, looking up, "but I'm not sure how."

Taegis shook his head, dazed. "I thought the original members of House Ravenwood were wiped out. The dreamwalking gift gone."

"Not quite." He still couldn't believe he was sharing this.

Taegis seemed to catch on to that. "I don't know much about house secrets, but isn't this one of them? How are you telling me these things?"

"I'm not sure yet, but I have a feeling I know why." Damien held his head in his hands, a jumble of thoughts scattering through his brain as if a great wind had come and torn through his mind.

Selene was the new head of House Ravenwood. Did Lady Ragna know? And what were these dreams about? Who was this dark figure, and why were people collapsing from the dream? Was Selene's burgeoning power a threat to him and his people?

He stared down at his palms. He now held in his hands a potent secret, and he wanted to be very careful with what he did with this information—not for the sake of House Ravenwood, but for the sake of Selene. The dreamwalking gift had not been seen publicly since the first razing of the empire. This kind of secret exposed could cause distrust and fear if not handled carefully, even amongst his own people.

Even within his own heart.

He loved Selene, but the safety of his people came first. He would need to see to that. However . . .

This new development meant that House Ravenwood's secrets were theirs. This could change everything, both with the coalition and with the Great Houses.

Maybe even the war.

31

By the time Damien finished speaking to Taegis, it was close to midnight. Too tired to eat, he headed for his own room for the night. The hallways were quiet, with only the occasional guard on his nightly watch.

With the secrets of House Ravenwood under Selene's control now, they could share with the other houses at Lux Casta that the dreamwalking gift still existed, what it had been used for in the past, and what Ravenwood's role had been in inciting the events that had led to the invasion of the Dominia Empire. He wanted to be careful to navigate the talks in such a way that it did not color House Ravenwood in a bad light, but rather provided a cautionary tale. Yes, Ravenwood had become a bitter and hateful house, but it began when the other houses left Ravenwood to be ravaged by the empire during the first razing. It was a warning of what not to do in the upcoming war.

Then there was also the question of what Selene was potentially doing with her growing gift to those around her. Did she know? Was that the source behind her nightmares?

Damien rubbed the back of his neck as he opened the door to his bedchambers. So many questions. So many decisions to make. But it would have to wait until tomorrow. At the moment, he could barely hold his thoughts together.

The fire across the room had burned down to glowing embers. The room was still warm, but a chill clung to the corners.

He shut the door quietly and made his way to the changing screens. As he passed his bed, Selene moved beneath the mound of quilts and furs.

"Damien?" said a groggy voice.

"Yes, it's me." Just hearing Selene's voice did things to his heart. *Light, what do I do if her gift is hurting others?* His throat tightened at the thought. She must have fallen back asleep because moments later, there was the soft sound of metered breathing. He sighed and stepped behind the changing screens.

Shortly afterward, he crawled beneath the thick covers and furs. Sleep was already pulling at him. But before he succumbed, he reached over and felt for Selene's arm underneath the covers.

Her skin was warm and soft to his fingertips. He smiled in the darkness and settled down across the pillow, his hand along her arm. "Good night, Selene."

She didn't answer.

Damien closed his eyes and let go of the physical world.

Images began to play across his mind: the gentle waves of the sea on a summer morning, bits of conversation with Taegis, camping under a starry night. His body relaxed in sleep's embrace.

Suddenly, an invisible rope tightened around his waist and hauled him forward, sending his head and legs flying back. He flew through the darkness, dragged by the invisible rope. Then the pressure around his waist disappeared, and he found himself plummeting down, down, down—

He landed in a crouch on the balcony outside the throne room in Northwind Castle. At least, it looked like Northwind Castle. The edges of his vision were hazy, as if going in and out of focus. The area was completely dark, and yet he could still see, like gazing into a bank of fog at twilight. His mind cleared the longer he stood there, going from a dreamlike state to clarity.

What's going on? What's happened to me?

Damien turned and glanced at the door that led into Northwind Castle.

Why am I here? Is this . . . a dream?

He stepped forward and entered the door. The layout of the castle wasn't like he remembered it. The rooms seemed to shift fluidly. First he was in his throne room, then he found himself in the kitchens. The dream changed, and he was standing beside Taegis near the dining hall.

"Taegis?"

Taegis lifted his head, his eyes half-lidded as if

he were sleepwalking. Then he slipped away like an apparition. Others appeared and disappeared around the castle in the same way Taegis had.

Damien lifted his hand and gazed at his palm. His appearance was solid, more flesh than spirit. He was different than those he met. Like he was more cognizant of the dream than the others he encountered.

A woman screamed inside the castle.

Damien twisted and ran toward the sound. He rounded the corner, then staggered to a stop. On the ground lay an elderly woman, her eyes wide and lifeless. Ahead, a robed figure disappeared at the end of the corridor.

He knelt down beside the woman. One of the kitchen staff. He brought his hand up and went to place his fingers on her neck, only to have his hand pass through her before she faded seconds later.

What the—

He stood and stared at the spot. What just happened? He looked around, then back at the spot. *What is this place?* It was Northwind Castle—and yet not—at the same time.

There were more shouts ahead where the robed figure disappeared. Damien turned and dashed down the hall. Answers. He needed answers. As he reached the end, the dream shifted, and he found himself right inside the main doors.

A dim light moved down the hall to his right,

like someone holding a candle. He headed in that direction when something large and black brushed his head and soared along the hallway, disappearing around the corner with the light.

A raven.

Wait. Was Selene dreamwalking in his mind? But what about that feeling, the one that felt as if he were being pulled . . . ?

The temperature dropped inside the hallway. A sudden shiver swept across his body. Damien sucked in a frigid breath and rubbed his arms.

What now?

Long tapered fingers spread across his shoulder as a putrid smell filled his nostrils. "What do we have here?" a hoarse voice whispered in his ear.

Before he could look back, the castle changed. He was now in his bedchamber near the fireplace. The room was swathed in shadows. Selene stood by the window, dressed in a simple white nightgown. She lifted her head and spotted him. Her mouth fell open and she flinched slightly. "D-Damien?"

He glanced down as if to confirm his own body. "Yes." He looked back up. "What's going on? Are you dreamwalking inside my mind?"

She slowly shook her head. "No. This is my dreamscape. You shouldn't be here." She placed both hands along her temples. "What's going on? Did she bring you here? And the others?"

"She? Who is 'she'?"

"Damien, you need to run. You're in danger. This is not a safe place—"

The door burst open to his right, and a dark figure drifted in, draped in black from head to toe. It was the one he had spotted in the hallways. The air froze within seconds, then filled with that same overpoweringly foul smell as before. Another shiver erupted down his back.

The figure turned toward him. The hood covered the upper half of its face, leaving only the black lips and jaw exposed. White pinpricks peered out where the eyes should be. "You again," she whispered in a raspy voice.

The figure glided toward him. His breath froze in his lungs as adrenaline washed over him. His heart crashed against his rib cage, the only thing that seemed to be moving in his entire body.

"Don't touch him!" Selene yelled.

The figure laughed as she raised a bony hand and held out a single white finger toward his chest. "You think *he* can help you? Is that why you brought him here?" The figure spun around and laughed again, her voice high-pitched and cackling. "No one can help you, little raven. Certainly not some mere man. You are mine."

Selene . . . brought him here?

"What do you mean?" Panic laced Selene's voice.

"My dear little raven, you still do not understand the power you possess. I am not the one bringing these mortals into the dreamscape. You are. You have the ability to pull sleepers into your own dreams. I haven't seen this power since the first dreamwalker came to be."

Selene shook her head. "No . . ." she whispered.

So he was right. Selene's gift was more powerful than anyone knew. More powerful than even she knew.

The figure then pointed her bony finger at Selene. "And I will have that power."

Selene was as white as her nightgown. Damien glanced at the dark figure, then back at Selene, a fire growing inside his chest, erasing the chill across his body and spreading a deadly calm across his mind. Who was this being who was saying such things to his wife? He straightened and tightened his fists. "No, you will not."

The figure hissed as she looked back at Damien. "You have no power in this place, Light-follower. This is *my* domain."

The calmness spread across the rest of his body, slowing his heartbeat and banishing the last of the chill within his bones. "I may not have any power here, but the one I follow does."

The figure hissed again. "She is mine. Her family has been mine for generations." The figure vanished, then appeared next to Selene and clutched her arm. "I will not give her up."

"She has a choice."

"I am the one who gives her power."

"No, her power comes from the Light. Now let go of her."

"Never!"

Damien sunk down on one knee and bowed his head. The dark one was right. He had no power here in the dream world. But the Light did.

Light, I need your help.

There was no place, no power that could overcome the Light. He knew this more than anything else. "I bend my knee to the Light and intercede for my wife." He clutched his hands together. He still didn't understand Selene's power, or know who this sinister being was, or know if his people were in danger because of the struggle going on in this dream. All he knew was that Selene needed his help. "Help us, Maker of Worlds. Please free Selene."

A small slip of light began to burn between the dark one's hand and where she gripped Selene. Brighter and brighter it grew, like a ball of white flame.

The figure screamed, dropped Selene's arm, and backed away, clutching her burned hand to her chest. "I will be back." She seethed, her teeth bared between her black lips. "I will return for my own." With a twist and flutter of black fabric, she disappeared.

Selene dropped to the floor in a heap.

Damien exhaled and closed his eyes, his hands

shaking from the encounter. When he opened them, he was no longer in the dreamscape. Instead, he was in his bed, lying on his side and facing Selene. She lay beside him on her back, staring up at the canopy with wide eyes, her skin pale and clammy.

"Selene?"

At first she didn't seem to hear him. Then she slowly turned her head and stared at him. Her eyes were dilated and darker than usual.

He sat up and placed a hand on her cheek. "Selene?"

"Damien?" she croaked.

"Yes."

"I-I . . ."

"I know. You had a nightmare."

She stared back up at the canopy. "The Dark Lady wants me. There is no escaping her."

The Dark Lady. So that's who the figure was. "She does not hold power over you."

"That's what you said, but . . ." Her eyes moved as if she were thinking. Then she slowly sat up. "You. You were there. But how?"

"You brought me there." And not just him, but everyone around Northwind Castle—perhaps Nor Esen itself.

She brought a hand to her face. "How is that possible?" she murmured. "Such a thing has never been heard of within House Ravenwood. But the Dark Lady said . . . But how? Sten,

Taegis, Karl, the servants and other guards . . ."
She shook her head. "Were they really there?"

"Yes."

Selene ran her hand down her face, dazed.

"Taegis spoke to me last night. There has been talk around the castle about a shared dream, one involving Northwind Castle, a cloaked figure"—he stared at her—"and you."

"Why? How?"

"I don't know." He leaned in. "You've admitted yourself that you know very little about your gift. Is it possible that this is an aspect you never knew about?"

She gave a small, humorless laugh. "If my mother had known we could bring people into our dreams, I'm sure she would have trained me to use my gift in that way. After all, it would have made our missions much safer if we could bring our targets into our own dreamscapes."

Hearing Selene speak so openly about what her family did with their gift reminded Damien of exactly how sinister House Ravenwood had become. And how different Selene was. Damien tugged on his chin and narrowed his eyes. "The Dark Lady mentioned the first dreamwalker. Do you know who that was? Maybe your mother doesn't have this ability, but it sounds like an ancestor did?"

Selene studied her fingers. "That's possible. But why wouldn't Mother have said something?"

"Maybe she never knew. Selene, how strong do you think your gift is?"

She looked up and their eyes connected. Damien had forgotten how intense her soulful eyes could be.

"It's strong," she whispered, pulling away from his gaze.

"Strong enough to connect people within the dreamscape?"

She didn't respond. He could tell his words frightened her.

"Strong enough that the Dark Lady will do anything to have that power?"

She clenched her hands and breathed harder. "But that's not what I want."

He reached over and touched her arm. "I think I'm beginning to understand. There is a war going on inside of you. You are facing a choice between the Dark Lady and the Light. You have a choice in who you will follow. I don't know much about the Dark Lady. But I can tell you this: the Light will never force you or coerce you, but he is always there, waiting."

She glanced over at him. "But then why is the light always moving away from me?"

He thought back to the dreamscape. "Is it really moving away from you? Or are you afraid to move toward it? Perhaps your dream is revealing how you really feel inside. You're afraid to approach the light, and so it is continually out of reach."

She let out a shaky sigh. "This is a lot to think about."

"I'm sure it's overwhelming. I felt the same way when my family passed away and I was named grand lord. So much responsibility, so many things I didn't know or feel strong enough to do."

"Yes. All of that."

"And there's more."

The tone of his voice must have alerted her because she looked up again, bracing for what he had to say next.

"Selene, it would appear you are the new head of House Ravenwood."

Her eyes narrowed. "What do you mean?"

"Your mother is no longer the keeper of Ravenwood's secrets."

"And how would you know this?" But he could see she was already putting the pieces together.

"I was able to tell Taegis about your gift."

Selene pressed a hand to her temple. "Why me?" she whispered. "I was content to never dreamwalk again, to live a normal life here as Lady Maris. My only desire was to discover the original reason we were given this gift in hope of helping my sisters. Not this. Never this."

His heart broke as he watched a tear slip down her cheek. Damien closed the space between them and pulled her to his chest. "I believe there is a reason you are a strong dreamwalker:

because you also have a strong heart and a strong spirit. We know you can use your gift within the dreams of other people. Perhaps you will be able to help them. Maybe even influence them toward the Light."

"Or the darkness."

"You are not bound to the Dark Lady, whatever she may say. The Light is greater than the darkness. It's your choice. Not hers."

"I'm still not sure I believe that. My family has followed the Dark Lady for many generations."

"It only takes one person to change the future." Selene lay silently with her head pressed against his chest. Damien slowly ran his fingers through her hair. "If you want to talk, I'm here."

"Thank you," she said in a small voice. "Right now, I just want to figure out who I am—*what* I am—and I need time to think."

"I understand. I will give you all the time you need. I only ask one thing: May I share what we know about your gift when we meet with the other Great Houses in Lux Casta? I believe that knowledge could help us."

"Yes." There was no hesitation in her voice. "I'm done with secrets. I'm done with the hurt they cause."

Damien leaned down and placed a kiss on the top of her head. His entire body filled with love for this woman in his arms. "I need to go," he said quietly as he pulled away. "But I'll see you tonight."

He went to move from the bed when Selene reached over and grabbed his hand. "I'm not sure what you did in my dream, but thank you."

He frowned as he looked back. "What I did?"

"When you went down on your knee. You made the Dark Lady go away."

Damien sat back down. "I didn't make her go away. The Dark Lady was right; I have no power in that place. I only interceded for you. The Light is the one who released you. Only the Light has the power in the dream world. The Light . . . and you. "

She nodded and let go of his hand, her gaze in some faraway place.

Damien reached over and kissed her again before standing. As much as he wanted to stay here, there was much to prepare for the future and their departure for Lux Casta. And this was not his battle. He would stand beside her, but in the end, this was Selene's fight. She had to choose for herself whom she would follow.

32

Amara stood within her mother's bed-chambers, a scowl on her face as she looked up at the painting of Rabanna Ravenwood that hung above the fireplace. The elder Ravenwood's cold stare seemed to disapprove of her. Instead of cowering, Amara glared back at her ancestor, as if daring the woman to come down and fight her.

The door opened and her mother walked in, her dress swishing around her. There was a sprinkling of silver amongst the strands of her hair, and for the first time, Amara detected faint purple circles beneath her mother's eyes.

Lady Ragna's gaze came to rest on her. "Amara," she said as she closed the door behind her.

"Mother."

No affection, no warmth between them. Just a courteous acknowledgment before business commenced. It had always been that way for as long as Amara could remember. The only hint of emotion she had ever seen in her mother's eyes was always for Selene, and never for her.

Selene.

She clenched her hands at her sides as she thought of her older sister. She'd always held an admiration for Selene that bordered on jealousy. She couldn't disregard how powerful Selene was and how much Selene could hold her emotions in check—two things Amara sorely lacked, and her mother never missed an opportunity to remind her.

And then Selene left, leaving her to care for Opheliana and bear their sister's secret heritage, and fulfill the duties of a Ravenwood dreamkiller.

I hate you, Selene.

Her mother came to stand near the fireplace. "I have information. It appears that Lord Damien and your sister will be leaving the Northern Shores. There will be another meeting between the Great Houses in Lux Casta."

"Lux Casta?"

"Yes, which means Lord Damien will be leaving the protection of his water barriers. You will be parting shortly for Lux Casta to finish your sister's mission, disguised as a pilgrim making her way to the Temple of Splendor. While you are in Lux Casta, I will travel to Ironmond to meet up with House Friere."

Amara narrowed her eyes. "If the Great Houses that oppose the empire will be meeting in Lux Casta, why am I only assassinating Lord Maris? Wouldn't it be better if two of us went and we eliminated all of the heads of the Great Houses at once?"

"Think, Amara." Her mother's voice dropped

a couple of degrees. "We already spoke of this. The houses will be expecting something. Security will be tight. Yes, I could disguise myself, but there is too great of a risk I would be recognized. It is better to succeed in taking out one house than to try to eliminate all of them and fail. Besides"—she waved her hand—"there is strategic reason to take out House Maris apart from the warning the Dark Lady has given us. Without Lord Damien's power to raise the water, the wall that divides our lands from the Dominia Empire cannot be repaired and the rivers cannot be raised between our lands. Out of all the Great Houses, it is his power that could slow down or even stop the empire's advancement."

Amara crossed her arms. She was spoiling for a fight and couldn't stop the words from tumbling from her lips. "And why exactly are we helping the Dominia Empire? What has the empire done for us?"

Her mother's face darkened as she moved slowly and deliberately toward Amara. Anyone else would have backed away from Lady Ragna, but Amara was feeling particularly reckless today, and the hatred inside of her steeled her nerves. She stared boldly at her mother.

"The empire will help us rebuild our house's name and power. As a lady of Ravenwood and future heir, you should understand the importance of these matters." She lifted one eyebrow, and her eyes seemed to glint. "I would think you would be intelligent enough to understand. Your sister Selene did."

Amara drew her lips back and bared her teeth. Warning bells went off in her head, but she said it anyway. "Yes, I can tell Selene understood. She understood it so well that she up and ran off with an enemy of House Ravenwood—"

Slap.

Amara blinked back the stinging tears as she brought a hand up to her throbbing cheek.

"You might be my daughter and a Ravenwood, but you will never be what Selene could have been: great. Never forget that, Amara. If you want to at least rise above mediocrity, you will do as I say."

Her mother's words were sharp and piercing. Amara knew that she wasn't like Selene. But never had her mother said she was weak and dense before. She dug her fingernails into her palm, drawing strength from the pain as she slowly turned back. "I understand." Only too clearly. No matter what, Selene would always be the favored daughter, even after she had turned her back on her family.

And Amara was the leftovers.

Endure. Amara gritted her teeth and concentrated on that one word. *I will be grand lady of Ravenwood someday. I just need to outlive*

Mother and endure. Then I will be the one with power.

Lady Ragna waved her hand at Amara dismissively. "Pack your things. Be ready to ride out within the hour. Captain Stanton and two guards will escort you to our border. And Amara"—her eyes came up—"if you fail, don't come back."

Amara lifted her chin. "I won't."

But her mother was already crossing the bedchambers to the adjoining room.

Amara watched her go, seething as the last of Lady Ragna's gown swished out of sight. Her fists shook beside her.

I hate you too, Mother.

The road to the border between the mountains and rolling hills ruled by House Luceras was cold and wet. Snow coated the roads, and there was a steady, frigid drizzle. Captain Stanton and the other men spoke little on the journey, and the horses appeared as miserable as their riders felt. The landscape was still bare and dead, save for the occasional green shoot poking up from the ground.

The small company didn't stop at any inns, choosing instead to find shelter beneath the towering trees that lined the road or in the small caves that dotted the mountainside. Captain Stanton and the two guards were coarse and vulgar around the fire at night, leaving Amara fuming beneath her furs. But she chose not to say anything. If she couldn't handle a few uncouth men, then she was as big a failure as her mother imagined her to be.

After three miserable days, the hills of Serine emerged between the trees. Captain Stanton pulled up on the reins of his horse and motioned for the other two men to do the same. "This is where we were instructed to leave you, Lady Amara."

Amara pulled back the hood of her cloak and surveyed the land. Her first mission, and her first time in the lands of House Luceras. After a moment, she dismounted and started to remove her leather satchel from the saddle. As a pilgrim, she would walk the rest of the way, joining others on their journey to the Temple of Splendor. The very thought of spending time with devout peasants left a bitter taste in her mouth, but it would get her into Lux Casta and closer to fulfilling her mission. And the map her mother had drawn from her memory of Palace Levellon would help her get inside.

After securing the satchel across her body, she checked the sword at her side, then pulled her cloak over her scabbard, hiding the blade. She might be disguised as a pilgrim, but there was no way she was going to travel without a weapon.

Now for the last act that would complete her disguise: she would have to cut her hair. She slipped out a small blade from the side of her satchel, held it in her hand, then began to cut away her dark auburn hair.

Reddish curls fell to the ground with each slash. Deep down, away from where anyone could see, she grieved. Her hair had been a source of pride. Now it littered the earth.

Why did the pilgrims have to cut their hair? As a sign of humility? Submission? Mutilation? Just another thing she didn't understand about religion.

Once the ends of her hair graced her shoulders, she placed the knife back in her satchel. Her head felt light and her neck naked. She refused to look down. Instead, she moved toward the converging dirt road that would lead her to Lux Casta.

"Is there any message you would like me to take back to Lady Ragna?" Captain Stanton said behind her.

Amara stopped and looked back. There was a smirk on the older man's face. For a moment she imagined wrapping her hand around the captain's wrist and entering his dreams. It wouldn't take much to wipe that sneer off of his face, only a fear or two. She savored the thought, allowing it to burn away the anguish of losing her hair before responding. "No. I will deliver my own message when I arrive back at Rook Castle."

"So be it. May the Dark Lady be with you on your journey, Lady Amara."

Amara rolled her eyes and turned around without repeating the farewell. She didn't believe in the Dark Lady. If the dark one really existed, she had done little to help Amara. She did not believe in the Light either. Or any other being of higher power. If there really were gods, they had little to do with mortals. They did their own thing, and she did hers. Religion was a foolish pursuit.

Without a second glance back, Amara left the tree line and started along the King's Highway that led through the hills to Lux Casta.

33

Selene stood on the prow of the *Ros Marinus*. The sea wind whipped through her hair and pulled back her heavy cloak. Pale blue sky covered the waters, and the sea . . . the sea was more magnificent than she had ever imagined. From the sound of the waves hitting the front and sides of the ship, to the occasional misty spray, to the salty scent in the air, it encompassed all of her senses. It was almost enough for her to forget the nightmares of the past few weeks, but not quite.

She took a step back and pulled her cloak around her body as if retreating back into herself. It had taken her a long time to adjust to the fact that she was now head of House Ravenwood. Even now, weeks later, her stomach churned at the thought. Other lords and ladies might desire the ultimate position of a Great House, along with the power that came with it, but she did not. But she couldn't deny how useful the position was now. The other houses would soon know the truth of House Ravenwood, for better or for worse.

She breathed in the cold, salty wind and closed her eyes. The Dark Lady had not visited her dreams since that night she had drawn Damien into her dreamscape. In fact, she had not dreamed at all. Perhaps the Dark Lady was finally gone, but she doubted that. She had a feeling her subconscious was fighting her body's natural inclination to dream in order to protect her mind. But the longer she went without dreaming, the more fatigued she became. It was almost as bad as having the recurring nightmares.

And the servant, the one who was in her dream during her last confrontation with the Dark Lady, hadn't woken up yet.

Selene pressed a hand to her chest.

Damien remained aloof when she questioned him, only stating that he would continue to help her discover her gift. But she could see it in his eyes: his concern over the conflict around her power and the presence of the Dark Lady.

Was she an invisible danger to those around her?

Then I need to keep from dreaming, no matter what. If I don't dream, I can't hurt anyone.

A hand wrapped around her waist, startling her. Her heart settled back in her chest as she realized it was Damien behind her.

He leaned in and kissed the base of her neck, then moved his lips toward the bottom of her ear and jaw. She turned and let him pull her in close, kissing him fully on the lips. Everything was forgotten but the feel of his arms around her and the warmth of his face. When they were like this, she could forget everything and just be herself.

"What are you doing?" he asked as he pulled away.

It took a moment for her mind to reengage. "I was thinking."

"I could tell by the faraway look on your face." His thumb caressed her jaw. "This is where I like to stand when I'm thinking too. The wide expanse of the sea seems to help my heart and mind open up."

She placed her head in the crook of his neck. He understood.

"We will soon reach the water barrier." His voice rumbled through his body. "I thought you might like to watch me take it down."

Her mind went back to the day when Damien raised the river-wall. If she thought that was impressive, what was the sea-wall like? No matter how much she was learning about the dreamwalking gift, she felt it was nothing compared to Damien's ability to raise the waters. A small part of her was intimidated by her husband's gift, and yet she was proud of it at the same time. "Yes, I would like that."

He rubbed her back with his hand. "In the meantime, would you like to warm up? It's a bit chilly out here."

"Yes." Her fingers and toes were growing numb, despite the fur-lined boots and gloves. They had left before the Northern Shores had completely thawed, in hopes of preparing for the moment the empire breached their lands. The trace of snow and ice were reminders they still had time—but only a little—before war was upon them.

"Let's go. A cup of tea should help with cold hands and a cold face." He stepped back and held out his gloved hand. She took it and followed him toward the stairs that led to the main part of the upper deck.

Night was falling when the *Ros Marinus* reached the water barrier on the western side of the Northern Shores. Selene gasped as she gazed at the towering wall that stretched from the coastline as far as she could see. The sunset shone through the rushing water in a colorful array of oranges and yellows on a deep blue background. The first evening star shimmered high above the wall. The sound of the constant rush of water reminded her of one of the waterfalls back home, only much larger.

"You did this?" she whispered beside Damien. She knew he had, but it still filled her with awe. A terrifying awe.

"Yes." His answer was sober. His lips were pressed together as he stared ahead, and she wondered if he was remembering that day as well.

"I know what happened," she said quietly.

He turned and looked at her, his eyebrows raised.

"I saw it in your dreams. You destroyed a convoy of ships. I saw the damage . . . and the sailors."

He was silent for a moment. "It was not something I enjoyed. I wish there had been another way."

She glanced down. "I know. After seeing that day, I realized you feared your gift as much as I did mine. It was one of the first times I connected with you. You weren't just a grand lord—you were a person with fears and regrets, who felt the same way I did. I believe that connection partly led to my change of heart about my mission."

Damien looked back at the raging wall of water. "Being a leader—a good leader—is difficult. Ever since my parents died, I've struggled with being the leader my people need. It has cost me a great deal. Sometimes I wish I could walk away, in the same way you sometimes wish to never dreamwalk again."

He didn't know she was already suppressing her gift for the safety of others. But this was not the right time to tell him. He needed reassurance, not an added worry. "Your people need you. And I'm a dreamwalker. That will never change. The Light has given us these gifts, right?"

Damien reached over and pulled her hand into his own without looking. "You're right. Thank you for reminding me."

Selene gave his fingers a squeeze.

They stood on the prow, hand in hand, as the *Ros Marinus* approached the water-wall. "Dropping anchor," the captain yelled. There was a splash, and the ship began to slow. The captain continued to shout orders to the sailors, and out of the corner of her eye, Selene spotted Taegis and Karl come to stand behind them.

The sun sank even lower, sending rays of red through the falling waters. "Will it be hard to lower the wall?"

"Yes. But it will also be a relief. It's been consuming my strength a little each day to keep this wall in place."

"Is the one along the Hyr River still up?"

"Yes. I've become strong enough to hold two in place, but three would be taxing. Admiral Gerault, the commander of the Northern Shores navy, has a patrol ready to take the place of the wall."

They were five hundred feet from the wall when the ship finally came to a stop. The water roared as it shot to the sky, then fell back to the surface. Foam and waves gathered at the base. The sun was almost gone, the fading daylight a glimmer inside the water-wall.

"I will need all the room around me, so please step back and wait with the others." Damien let go of her hand and moved closer to the railing that followed the prow. Selene moved back until she stood beside Taegis and Karl.

With the dying sun in front of him, Damien appeared as a lone shadowy figure against the wall. He took a deep breath, raised his hands, and then twisted his wrists.

A sudden invisible weight seemed to come down on him, and he let out a grunt. Slowly, with his palms up, he began to lower his hands. Beyond him, the water-wall began to move, starting with the area directly across from the ship.

Although he held nothing in his hands, Selene could see the exertion of his power as sweat began to form along Damien's temples and his arms began to shake. However, he never lost control of the wall. Slowly, bit by bit, the water-wall lowered toward the sea's surface until the last of the foam and waves disappeared. The sun sank beyond the horizon. Damien wavered for a moment, then fell to the deck.

"Damien!" Selene and Taegis rushed to his side. She fell to her knees, unsure of what to do. "Damien?" She could barely see his face in the dim light. His eyes fluttered, then rolled up into his head.

Taegis knelt down on the other side, a concerned look on his face. "I wondered if taking the wall down would drain him." He checked Damien's pulse, then paused with his hand over Damien's mouth.

Captain Stout approached, holding an oil lamp.

In the lamplight, Damien appeared pale. The sight squeezed at Selene's heart.

"Is Lord Damien all right?" the captain asked.

"Yes," Taegis said.

Selene looked up at him. "Are you sure?"

"Yes. His heart is beating, and he still draws breath. He's spent. Lowering the water-wall took more out of him than any of us were expecting. Even me."

"So that's all? He's just exhausted?"

"More or less. Let's move him to your cabin." Taegis waved to Karl. "Help me move his lordship."

Karl was already there, at the ready. "Yes, sir."

Selene stood and moved away as Taegis and Karl worked together to lift Damien, then started across the deck. The captain and Selene followed. They made their way inside the ship, along the narrow corridor, before reaching the cabin where they were staying.

Taegis opened the door, then headed in.

The room was small, with a double bed nailed to the floor, built-in shelves, a single lamp that hung on one side, and a port window on the other. With Damien, Taegis, and Karl, there was hardly space for anyone else. Selene waited outside the doorway, her chest and throat tight as they lowered Damien onto the bed. The rational part of her knew Taegis was probably right that Damien had overexerted himself. But that didn't stop her stomach from churning with worry.

Karl lit the hanging lamp nearby while Taegis checked on him once more before turning back toward the door.

Captain Stout stepped beside Selene. "We don't have a healer on board. Do we need to stop at Lucent?"

Taegis shook his head. "No. He simply needs rest. His father, Lord Remfrey, also passed out a time or two after using his gift."

"That doesn't make me feel any better," Captain Stout mumbled.

Selene agreed. Sometimes she felt shaken after dreamwalking, but she was never so fatigued that she passed out. It reinforced her opinion that Damien's gift was the greater one.

Taegis looked at her. "My lady, I would feel better if I could stay with his lordship for a while. I still believe this is caused by fatigue, but I want to stay with him, just in case."

"Of course."

He bowed his head. "Thank you. I will stay with Lord Damien until the evening watch, unless something changes."

Selene nodded. There wasn't enough room for both of them in the small cabin, and even though she was concerned about Damien, she would let Taegis take the first watch. "Thank you, Taegis. In the meantime, I will be on the deck."

Taegis bowed his head. "Karl, help me make his lordship more comfortable." He began to remove Damien's boots while Karl undid Damien's cloak.

Selene left the cabin and closed the door behind her. She ate very little dinner in the galley, then wandered along the top deck, watching the moon rise and stars come out over the water.

Why did the Light give them these gifts? Gifts powerful enough to knock a person out or steal someone's life? She ran her fingers along the railing as a cold wind blew across her face. Damien would say their gifts were given so they could help people. But to wield such power almost cost too much. More pain seemed to come from these gifts than good.

Would it have been better if the Light had left humankind alone?

Selene sighed. So many questions, so many burdens.

What she longed for was freedom and peace.

An image of Damien's soul entered her mind. She hadn't visited Damien's dreamscape in months. An intense longing filled her being to see his light again, a light so powerful it took her breath away. Just a glimpse of that brilliant, peaceful place.

Selene shook her head.

The Dark Lady was hunting her now. And it didn't feel right to enter Damien's dreamscape without his knowledge. That was his place. Perhaps the deepest part of him that was connected to the Light.

Selene watched the moonlight flicker across the waves. If she chose to follow the Light, would her soul look the same? Would her dreamscape become a place of peace and light?

Or was she too far gone, despite what Damien had said?

Could a person like her ever step into the light?

34

Damien still looked pale days after he had lowered the water-wall. Selene cast another sidelong glance his way as she stood by the rail and watched the waves. His mannerisms were the same: he would smile and speak with the sailors, exercise with Taegis or herself, and practice his gift early in the morning at the back of the ship, but Selene could tell something had changed. He ate less than he did back at Northwind Castle, and there was a hint of forcefulness behind his smiles, a small difference that hardly anyone seemed to notice. But she saw it. And when he came to bed, he barely said a word before he rolled on his side and went to sleep.

Yes, something was definitely different.

Selene sighed, leaned over the railing, and watched the blue water ripple along the side of the ship. Perhaps she should have entered his dreams afterward and made sure his old memories didn't haunt him.

No. She gripped the railing. She would not dreamwalk again. Not if she could help it. The cost was too high, and too many people were involved. *I'm tired of people getting hurt because of me, because of my gift.*

Selene squeezed her eyes shut. She remembered

the way Damien spoke to the Light when he raised the water, and when he went down on one knee in her dream. She hesitated, then whispered, "I don't know if I can pray to you, or if you even hear me. But I ask for you to watch over Renata if she is still alive. And that woman at the castle. Perhaps even heal them. And watch over my sisters as well."

She slowly opened her eyes. If the power of the Light could drive back the Dark Lady from her dreams, then he could protect her loved ones, right? She wasn't worthy of asking for anything on her behalf. But perhaps the Light would listen if she interceded for others.

Footsteps alerted her that someone was approaching.

"We should reach the port of Lux Casta by noon," Damien said as he came to stand beside her.

Selene drew back into the real world. "Did you visit Lux Casta often?"

"Yes. House Maris and House Luceras have been close for years, partly because of our borders, partly because of the sea, and partly because both of our houses follow the Old Ways."

"You mean the Light."

"Yes."

"What is Lux Casta like? And House Luceras?"

Damien smiled—genuinely smiled—for the first time in days as he leaned across the railing and looked out over the sea. "You will never meet a place more devoted to the Light anywhere this side of the continent. Pilgrims come from all lands and nations to visit the Temple of Splendor and pay homage to the Light."

Selene swallowed uncomfortably. "Hmm." She remembered her mother's words that even House Luceras had employed House Ravenwood's unique abilities on occasion without knowing it was House Ravenwood they were working with. Perhaps Damien only knew of the bright side of House Luceras. In any case, she wasn't going to tell him what she knew, at least not at this moment.

"And the city itself is beautiful," he continued. "It's set amongst the rolling green hills of Serine. When you come into port, the sun shines on the city, causing it to look like gold."

"And House Luceras?"

"They are like siblings to me. I grew up with Lords Leo, Tyrn, Elric, and Lady Adalyn. My brother and I—" His voice hitched for a moment and a shadow passed over his face. "We would play together. Leo was the serious one, usually off training. Tyrn, the second oldest, and my age, was always reading. And Elric, Adalyn, and Quinn were always together, whether in the castle gardens, or exploring the city, or off traipsing across the hills." He let out a slow breath. "I miss them. It will be nice to see House Luceras again."

Selene wondered if by *them,* he also meant Quinn. In fact, she was sure of it. Despite coming to know Damien more than ever, she still had not pinpointed what the shadow was that hovered behind the light of his soul, like a cold wind that was felt but never seen. Was that the cause of his doldrums? Was it the death of his brother? Or more?

"I hardly know House Luceras, and I have never visited Lux Casta."

Damien turned to her and smiled. "Then I look forward to introducing you to both."

Selene gave him a gentle smile back, but deep inside, she wasn't so sure. The way Damien spoke of the Luceras siblings left a strange pulling sensation in her gut.

Hours later, as the sun reached its zenith in the sky, the city of Lux Casta came into view, just beyond the natural harbor that protected its port. Selene stared at the grand city, its beauty capturing her senses. Damien was right: it looked liked the personification of the Light itself. The buildings were made of white stone with orange-tiled roofs. The city curved around in a circle, with each ring higher than the first, until it reached the castle that sat in the middle of the city, higher than any other building. Hills of green and a bright blue sky were the backdrop for the magnificent city. It was clear that winter had lost its hold on the land weeks ago and spring was in full bloom.

Even the wind felt warmer and carried a sweet fragrance. So different than Nor Esen and her own home in the Magyr Mountains.

Captain Stout expertly maneuvered the *Ros Marinus* into port, bringing the ship alongside one of the wooden docks that connected to the wide boardwalk that lined the shoreline. There were dozens of other ships moored in the harbor, ranging from two-story warships to small fishing vessels. White gulls flew overhead as the banners of House Luceras—white with a shining sun in the middle—snapped in the wind.

The boardwalk was crowded with men moving crates and barrels from ships while women looked over fish lined up on tables, recently caught that morning and ready to be sold. Conversation hummed across the port. Children laughed as they ran between the cargo and ship workers. The smell of smoke, fish, and sea filled the air.

Selene took it all in, her hands clasped in front of her. Though both were port cities, there was a wildness to Nor Esen, whereas Lux Casta felt civilized and was at least twice as big as the capital of the Northern Shores.

The *Ros Marinus* came to a stop. Two of the sailors hauled out a wooden plank, while another opened the railing. The plank was placed within the opening, and all three sailors disappeared down the ramp. The other sailors scurried across the deck, securing the ropes and sails as Captain Stout and his first mate shouted orders.

She looked back at the door that led to the cabins. Just when she thought about searching for Damien, he emerged from the narrow door with Taegis and Karl.

"Selene." Damien crossed the deck and stopped beside her. He wore a blue cloak embroidered in silver and a matching vest. Her own gown matched his, as they both wore the colors of House Maris. He placed his hand around her waist while he motioned toward the city ahead. "Welcome to Lux Casta."

He seemed almost completely relaxed. Almost. His smile almost genuine. The sparkle in his eye almost there, but not quite reaching all the way. A darkness still hung over him, the smallest shadow, like when the sun is shining brightly and one's shadow is only a shade beneath one's feet.

But it was there, and she could see it. The light inside of him had dimmed, and she wanted to know why.

After the ship was secured, the small party left the boat. It took Selene a moment to adjust to the solid ground after being at sea for a fortnight. Taegis led the way, with Damien walking by her side. Karl brought up the rear. Others from the ship would join them at the castle, along with their belongings.

The first wall separated Lux Casta from the boardwalk. Immense gates as thick as a man and as high as a two-story building opened the way into the city. Symbols of the sun were engraved in the dense wood. On the other side of the wall, streets spread out around the city, each one lined with white stone buildings, lush trees, and cobblestones. Lux Casta had the feeling of eternal summer, and Selene wondered if it ever snowed here.

Halfway through the city, a contingent of guards dressed in silver chainmail with white tabards and the symbol of House Luceras met them. The tallest soldier stepped forward. "Lord Leo sent us to escort House Maris to the Palace Levellon."

Taegis spoke for the group. "Thank you. Please lead the way."

The contingent split into two, with half of the soldiers in front and the other half in the back. They continued along the streets, following each curve as they went higher toward the palace in the center of Lux Casta.

The second set of gates that led into the courtyard of the palace were smaller than the main gates, but more ornate. Pictures of the sun were interwoven with images of the hills and city of Lux Casta within the wood. Such artistry.

And the courtyard . . .

Selene drew in a breath. Beyond the palace walls was a courtyard of manicured green grass with a stream running through the midst. A path of smooth river stones split at the stream near the gate and ran along either side toward the wide staircases that led into the palace. Past the lush grass on either side were rows and rows of the most colorful flowers she had ever seen. Farther in, near the palace, stood a great marble fountain spouting misty water into the air and into the stream.

It was breathtaking. The most amazing courtyard she had ever seen. It even rivaled the castle garden that Petur attended back at Rook Castle.

The soldiers took the path on the right and led the company toward the front of the palace. Selene marveled at each flower they passed. Beyond the flower gardens were carefully sculpted bushes. There was nothing wild, nothing out of place. Everything was perfectly shaped, each bud, each flower, each leaf in exact position. Selene shook her head. It had to take an army of gardeners to keep such a place.

They bypassed the three-tier fountain and headed up the steps. At the top, the first soldier opened the door. The leader of the unit turned and dismissed the rest, then spoke to Taegis. "House Luceras waits in the audience chamber to greet you. I will take you to them."

Taegis nodded in acknowledgment.

The inside of the palace was as grand as the outside. High ceilings and smooth white stone lined the halls. Stained-glass images of grand lords and ladies dressed in white with golden hair and serene looks on their faces lit the way, leaving pools of color along the marble floor.

Selene studied the images. What was House Luceras's history? How exactly did their gift of light work? Did they truly follow the Light, or was it just a mask they wore, like the one worn by House Ravenwood?

The soldier stopped in front of a set of white doors and opened the nearest one. Taegis stepped aside to let Damien enter first. Damien glanced at Selene. His eyes seemed to ask her if she was ready. She gave him the smallest nod, although her heart was thumping inside her chest. The only other time she had met the family of House Luceras was at the Assembly of the Great Houses, and even then, she never spoke to them. Now she was entering their hall as the new wife of their closest ally—and as the daughter of one of their greatest enemies.

"Greetings, House Maris," Lord Leo said from the dais at the front of the hall, his voice echoing across the cavernous room. "Welcome to Lux Casta and Palace Levellon."

All eyes turned toward the party as Damien led the way between the pillars. The audience chamber of House Luceras was twice as big as the one in Rook Castle and Nor Esen combined. The hall could easily accommodate hundreds of people, and at least one hundred were gathered between the tall columns that held up the high ceiling.

Selene held her head high. She didn't miss the furtive glances or whispers as she walked by. No doubt word of her marriage to Grand Lord Maris had reached more than just the Great Houses. That, and simple curiosity about House Ravenwood, most likely stoked the people's inquisitiveness. She couldn't remember the last time a member of House Ravenwood had publicly appeared in Lux Casta.

Everything was white within the grand hall, from the marble floor to the walls, and the banners that hung from the ceiling to the collection of thrones at the head of the room. At the front, Lord Leo stood with his hand raised toward them. The other Luceras siblings were beside him, their golden hair radiant as the sun's rays poured through the windows around them.

Lord Leo appeared the same as he did back at Rook Castle, with a stern look on his chiseled face. The young man next to him seemed like his twin, only thinner. Must be Tyrn.

On the other side of Lord Leo stood Elric, a bright smile on his face. And beside him . . .

Lady Adalyn, the Lady of Light.

Selene had forgotten how beautiful the youngest member of House Luceras was. Her golden hair hung down her back in soft waves, with a silver circlet around her head. Her dress was white and shimmery, lovely and modest. She was the paragon of virtue and innocence. How could anyone look at her and not love her?

Selene swallowed and caught Damien's face softening as he gazed up at the Luceras siblings, the shadow that had been plaguing him seeming to disappear, but bringing that strange pulling sensation back to her own gut.

"Thank you for opening your city and home to us," Damien said as he stopped before the dais.

Lord Leo dipped his head. "It was my father's wish. Unfortunately, he is not well and unable to greet you personally. In the meantime, the palace servants will see your family and your companions to their quarters."

Damien bowed. "Thank you." Then he stood and motioned toward Selene. "House Luceras, let me introduce to you my new wife, Lady Selene Ravenwood."

At the mention of her name, a dark look came over the two eldest Luceras brothers. Elric continued to grin, while Lady Adalyn appeared uncomfortable.

Selene stood still, her chin raised, and gazed up at the lords and lady of Luceras, burying the feeling of disquiet deep inside of her. She was an equal to them. She had nothing to be ashamed of. But she couldn't help remembering that there had been some negotiations between the two houses concerning Damien and Lady Adalyn.

"Lady Selene, welcome to Lux Casta," Lord Leo said a moment later.

Selene bowed her head. "Thank you, Lord Leo."

She could still feel the animosity from the two older Luceras brothers and wondered if Damien could feel it also. If he did, he didn't show it on his face. She glanced at him from the corner of her eye as he stepped forward to speak quietly to Lord Leo.

A servant came minutes later from one of the side doors, an older man with thick silver hair and light grey eyes. Lord Leo stepped back. "Oswald will escort you to your rooms. If you need anything, please let him know. Dinner will be at seven."

Damien bowed. "Thank you." Then he turned, and Selene followed him until they reached the doors, where Karl and Taegis joined them.

Oswald led the group from the audience chamber and down another broad hallway. As they passed by a wide window, a shadow passed over the sun, darkening the corridor for a moment. Selene glanced out the window, but the sky had brightened again.

They rounded another corner, and once again the sun dimmed outside the windows. A smile tugged on Damien's lips, which puzzled Selene. Did he know what was happening? And why would it make him smile?

After two more corners, the servant stopped in front of a light-colored door and pressed down on the handle. "These will be your quarters during your stay. There are rooms for both your personal use and for your party. I will direct your belongings to be brought here. As his lordship said, my name is Oswald. Let me know if you need anything else."

"Thank you, Oswald."

Oswald gave them a brief bow, then left the same way he came.

Taegis entered the room first, then he and Karl split up to check the quarters. Damien and Selene stood in the middle of the common room. It was nothing like the rooms back at Rook Castle, or even Northwind.

Everything was trimmed in white molding and gold. The furniture was ornate and perfectly positioned. Bright sunlight poured in through high windows surrounded by a curved railing outside. Along the cream-colored walls hung paintings of pastoral landscapes.

It was beautiful, and yet Selene found herself longing for home. For Northwind Castle, with its cool stone, dark furniture, and furs.

She stilled. For the first time, she had called Northwind home.

Damien took her hand, then lifted her fingers to his lips and kissed her knuckles. "I'm glad you're here with me," he said softly.

All it took was that one look from his eyes to release the tension inside of her. She had no desire to be anywhere else but here, with him. Even if she felt like an outsider. "Thank you."

He dropped her hand and pulled her in for a lingering kiss before they were interrupted by a knock at their door.

Taegis left one of the adjoining bedrooms and answered. A woman's alto voice filled the doorway.

"I thought so," Damien said with a smile, Selene still in his arms.

"Thought what?"

In answer, a woman entered their room. Selene stepped back quickly and brushed invisible wrinkles from her gown. She did not like her affection for Damien to be displayed in front of others.

The woman smiled widely as she approached them. "Grand Lord Damien, it is good to see you again."

Damien laughed. "Grand Lady Bryren. I thought I saw wyverns flying over Lux Casta."

"We arrived shortly before you did. It would seem our wyverns are making the city uncomfortable, so a few of my kin are taking them out into the hills."

Selene looked closely at the woman standing in their room as Taegis shut the door behind her. Lady Bryren looked just as she remembered her. There was a wildness to her, with her leather clothing and copper hair decked out in braids. Kohl lined her eyes, accentuating their light brown color.

Her gaze turned to Selene. "Lady Selene." She dipped her head. "I don't think we ever met while I was at Rook Castle. I must admit I was surprised when I received news of your marriage to Lord Damien. I would like to hear more about how that came about. There were many houses pinning their hopes on Lord Damien." Her eyes twinkled with merriment.

Selene wasn't sure whether she liked the brazen grand lady of House Merek or not. She also confirmed what Selene suspected—House Luceras had hoped for a union between Damien and Lady Adalyn. A marriage of that magnitude would have made them powerful allies. Selene glanced at Damien. Would he share the real story behind their marriage?

"It was a union that benefited both of us," he said.

"Spoken like a true lord. But tell me, do you love each other?"

Selene turned back with narrowed eyes. Such bold questions from a woman she hardly knew. And yet Lady Bryren's question struck her like an arrow to the chest. Now that she thought about it, neither of them had said those words to the other. Deep down, she loved Damien. So why hadn't she told him?

Was she waiting to see if he loved her back?

"I believe that is between Lady Selene and myself."

Lady Bryren studied him for a moment. "I understand." She turned back to Selene. "You're a lucky woman. I don't know you or your house well. But I do know the family of Maris. It is a good arrangement for you."

Selene felt like something unspoken had passed between Damien and Lady Bryren and had no idea what it was. Seeing him so relaxed with the wyvern lady, without that shadow that had been following him since he brought down the water-wall, caused that small fire to burn in the pit of her stomach again. "Thank you."

Lady Bryren nodded. "Now that you're here, I believe the talks will start tomorrow. That is, if Lord Warin is doing better."

"Is he still ill?" Damien asked.

"Yes. There is a small hope he might recover, but until then, Lord Leo will act in his father's place."

"I'm sorry to hear that. How are you doing? I'm sure Lord Warin's illness has brought back painful memories."

Selene perked up.

Lady Bryren nodded. "Yes. It's been over a year now since my own father passed away. Although his death was more sudden." Her eyes darted toward Selene before settling again on Damien.

Selene frowned at her look. Did Lady Bryren think her family had something to do with Lord Warin's death? Her eyes widened. Did they?

Lady Bryren continued on. "We have much to discuss."

"Yes, we do. And what of House Vivek?" Damien asked.

"I heard someone is coming, but I don't know who."

Interesting, Selene mused, her thoughts switching over. Did Lady Bryren not know about Renlar, Lord Rune's son?

"Until then." Lady Bryren bowed. "I will see you both tonight at dinner."

Damien and Selene bowed in reply. "Good-bye, Lady Bryren. Thank you for coming," Damien said as he straightened.

Lady Bryren sent one last smile to the both of them before turning and leaving. Taegis followed her out and shut the door behind him. Selene could hear Karl in one of the other rooms.

"Is Lady Bryren always that way?" Selene asked.

"What way?" Damien turned back.

"Asking private questions."

Damien laughed. "Yes. For as long as I've

known her. I think that quality comes with her house. The gift of House Merek is their courage, although sometimes it can border on recklessness."

"Or impertinence." She wanted to ask Damien about the questions Lady Bryren had brought up, both spoken and unspoken, but at the same time wasn't sure if she wanted the answers. What if Damien only cared about her because of his kind nature and adherence to duty? Her shoulders tightened as old fears came roaring back. Had Damien only married her to save himself?

She turned around. "I'm going to wash up before this evening."

"All right. I think I'll join Taegis and walk the castle."

Selene headed inside their private room to the bowl and pitcher she had spotted earlier. The water was tepid and smelled lightly of roses.

She started with her hands, then washed her face and neck. She paused and stared into the bowl, the water dripping from her fingers. This trip was going to be harder than she'd thought. The other houses would soon discover the duplicity of House Ravenwood. On top of that, she was facing her own personal battle inside her dreamscape and . . .

She swallowed hard, and her fingers began to shake as fear spread again across her heart. She clenched them before reaching for the towel nearby.

What would happen in the next couple of days? Where would she stand with the other houses? Who would she choose to be? Who would she follow?

No answer came the next morning. Instead, the city of Lux Casta was greeted by low horns blowing at the first light.

Grand Lord Warin had passed away at dawn.

35

That morning, the banners of House Luceras were brought down and replaced with black standards. Inside the castle, everything was draped in black, from the paintings to the sculptures and statues.

There was a somberness that hung over the castle, similar to the mourning cloth that draped the furniture. Words were spoken in hushed whispers. Tears were shed behind closed doors. The bright sunlight that shone down on Lux Casta seemed irreverent toward House Luceras and their grief.

Selene stood beside the long windows in her bedchambers and watched everything from her vantage point. She never knew Lord Warin and did not feel the same pull of grief everyone else did. Damien, however, appeared mournful, so she let him have his space in the common room.

She sighed and walked back toward the bed. The talks had been canceled for the time being, understandably so. It was unfortunate that Lord Warin had passed on, but the Dominia Empire would not wait. Alliances needed to be officially formed and the nations ready or all would be lost. Selene knew that when news of Lord Warin's death reached her mother, she would not hesitate to use the confusion to her advantage.

She held a hand to her head as a pulsing ache started to form along her forehead. She hadn't dreamed since the night Damien interceded for her, and it was starting to take a toll on her body. The need to dream was almost as vital to her as sleep itself, and yet she had closed off that part of herself as best as she could. But soon, the dreams would come back, like a dam breaking loose. And she had a feeling that when the dreams came, so would the Dark Lady.

The day moved by slowly. Selene stayed to her room as much as possible so as not to intrude on the sorrow of others. Tomorrow was the public memorial and viewing of Lord Warin. Sometime after that, the talks would begin, but who knew when that would actually start?

Dinner came and went, a private affair within their room, with quiet conversation between Damien and their small party. The light was gone from Damien's eyes again.

Was he feeling Lord Warin's death just as intensely as he did his own family's death? After all, their families had been close, and he had experienced the death of his own father only two years ago. He probably understood what the Luceras siblings were going through, while she still felt like a stranger to their grief.

Selene shook her head as she pulled on her nightgown.

Damien came in a minute later.

She finished brushing her hair, then placed the brush on the table. "How is the Luceras family doing?" she asked as she glanced over her shoulder.

Damien finished changing before he responded. "They're grieving. Lord Warin had been sick for a while, but I don't think anyone expected him to pass this soon."

She nodded but felt disconnected from his statement. And that disturbed her. She walked toward the bed and pulled the covers back. Why wasn't she feeling anything? Did she not care? Had her heart slipped back behind iron doors without her knowing?

Selene blew out her own candle and climbed into bed. The covers were cool to the touch, colder than she was expecting, so she curled into a ball and pulled the blankets tight around her neck. Moments later, the bed moved and she felt Damien crawl in beside her.

They both lay there quietly. Then Damien moved and wrapped his arms around her and pulled her close. His breath was warm against the back of her neck, his body like a warming brick, burning away the chill from the bed. He didn't say anything, just held her.

Slowly she relaxed in his embrace. Maybe he needed this. Maybe he needed her. She snuggled in closer and closed her eyes. Even if she wasn't experiencing the same grief he was, she could still comfort him in this small way. If there was one thing she never wanted to lose, it was him.

Crowds of people spilled into the courtyard and Palace Levellon the next afternoon in order to pay their respect to House Luceras and former Grand Lord Warin. The sun shone as brightly as ever over Lux Casta, and a warm breeze blew through the city.

Selene held Damien's hand as they made their way through the crowded halls within the palace and toward the doors to the audience chamber. She caught sight of the scowl on Taegis's face as he kept close to Damien's side, his hand no doubt on the hilt of his sword. Karl followed on her right side, his face grim as his eyes moved to and fro across the crowd.

Once they reached the grand hall, the people stood to either side, allowing the nobles and lesser houses to make their way to the front of the cavernous room. As they walked between the crowds of people, she felt their gazes, felt their questions press against her mind, even as a hush lay over the audience chamber. They were here to mourn their leader, and she was not one of them. Selene's fingers were cold within Damien's hold, but she wasn't sure if it was because of a sudden chill within her or because his hands were always warmer than hers.

The Luceras siblings stood below the throne

where the light from the high windows along the hall converged onto a stone table, leaving a pool of light around the pedestal where Lord Warin lay.

The chill inside her spread.

Lady Bryren stood to the right of the pedestal, dressed in leather and linen, next to a gruff-looking man wearing a similar fashion. They both nodded toward Damien and Selene as they took their place beside the couple. There were no tears on the fierce lady's face, no red eyes or puffy cheeks. Only an intense, solemn look. Was Lady Bryren remembering the death of her own father?

Damien stood quietly as he looked up at the Luceras family, then back at the body of Lord Warin. There were no tears in his eyes either. The only show of emotion was the way he gripped her hand tighter.

Time ticked along as the assembly stood quietly within the great hall. Every so often, Lady Adalyn hid her face and dabbed at her eyes. A sliver of pity entered Selene's heart. She would not want to stand in front of a crowd while grieving for her own father. What were they waiting for? Weren't they there to say farewell to Lord Warin? It seemed torturous to make the family wait in front of all of these people.

Selene kept her gaze to the side. She wasn't ready to look at Lord Warin yet. An undefined fear seemed to hover across her spirit, and she was afraid it would break upon her the moment she finally looked at the body.

Minutes later, a priest dressed in white crossed the dais and stepped down near Lord Elric to stand before the pedestal. His bald head glistened in the sunlight. He gazed across the room before lifting his hands. Then he spoke, his voice breaking the silence of the room.

The corner of Selene's lip lifted in scorn. His words were rote with no heart. Not like the emotions she witnessed when Damien spoke of the Light. It made her wonder if he really followed the Light, or if it was simply a duty to him.

She tuned the priest out, his voice a buzz inside her ears. Her eyes kept roving back toward the pedestal, but she resisted. She had never seen a dead body in real life, only in dreams. But it was like there was a tether between her and the body, and before she knew it, her eyes were upon Lord Warin.

The dead man lay on the stone, dressed in his full regalia of gold and white, with his arms crossed and his eyes closed. His grey hair and beard were combed back. He looked like he was sleeping, save for the pale color of his skin and lips.

The growing chill inside her swept across her body, as if the claws of death had grabbed her by the throat. She could sense the absence of his soulsphere. All there was before her was an empty shell. There would be no more dreams, no more living for Lord Warin.

So where was he now? The real Lord Warin? What was on the other side of the veil? Where did the soul go when the body died? Who was there? The Dark Lady? Another shudder rippled down her back as the image of a lady dressed in black filled her mind. Was that who was waiting for her?

She suddenly realized the priest was reciting the benediction while he made some strange motions with his hands. She let out her breath, ready to leave this place.

But as the priest walked away, a woman dressed like the priest took his place. Selene clenched her free hand. Would they have to endure more empty words?

The woman's white robes rippled across her body as she stood beside the pedestal. Then, with a voice like a clear bell, she began to sing.

Slowly, Selene unclenched her hand as the song filled her mind. The words were in the old tongue, but she could almost understand them, as if they had been spoken in the modern language.

The young woman sang of the Light, of that Selene was sure, and it sounded like waterfalls, flowers, and the songs of birds. As if all of life was raising its voice to the Light.

Like the sun's rays at the end of a rainstorm, the woman's song swept away the chill inside of her, leaving behind a tender warmth.

The song ended on a long, low note. The hall was silent. No one moved, not one word was spoken.

Selene stood there, spellbound. She wanted to hear that song again, to have it fill her, like the song the people of Nor Esen sang at the Festival of Light.

The moment was broken by a quiet sob from Lady Adalyn.

Those around the pedestal stirred and slowly began to move away. The crowd behind them lined up in order to view Lord Warin. Lady Bryren turned and acknowledged Damien and Selene with a tilt of her head before leaving with her consort by her side.

Damien caught the eye of Lord Leo, while Lady Adalyn hid her face in Lord Elric's shoulder. Lord Tyrn looked stoically over the crowd. Damien nodded and the oldest Luceras nodded back.

Then Damien squeezed her hand and turned, leading her out of the grand hall. As they walked back to their room, Selene glanced at Damien. The heaviness that hung across the castle—coupled with the song she had just heard—seemed to have finally penetrated the numbing fog that had shrouded her the past day.

For the first time, death felt real—more real than it ever did inside the dreamscape. Death came to everyone. And with the conflict coming up, there would be more.

But perhaps, like the song seemed to indicate, there was light in the darkness of death.

36

H ere you go."
Amara looked up into the face of one of
the pilgrims she had joined a couple of days ago
on her way to Lux Casta. The young man smiled
at her, his eyes twinkling as he handed her a bowl
of gruel. Morning sunlight filled the meadow
where the small band of pilgrims had stopped the
night before. Dew clung to the long green grass.
The trees had begun to bud, and birds warbled
out their tunes. Spring seemed to arrive earlier
here in the hill country compared to the Magyr
Mountains.

Amara took the bowl and almost grunted
a reply back, but realized it was not how the
pilgrims treated each other, so she put on a smile
and said, "Thank you."

He seemed to take her answer as an invitation
because a minute later, he was sitting beside her
with his own bowl of gruel.

"Name's Breven. What's yours?" he said before
taking a bite of the grainy cereal.

"Mara," Amara replied. It was easier to lie
when the lie was close to the truth, something
Mother had taught her.

"I'm from Shanalona, the capital of House
Vivek and north of Ironmond. I've been on the

road for over a month. Started my journey the moment the snow was passable. How about you?"

Amara paused her spoon before her lips. Not only was she going to have to deal with company, she wasn't going to be able to eat either. She lowered her spoon and licked her lips while mentally taking a deep breath. "I'm from the Magyr Mountains."

"The mountains? Which side?"

Amara stirred her cereal. "The west."

"Then you haven't been on the road long."

"No, I haven't." She took a quick bite, hoping the questions would stop.

"Have you ever been to the Temple of Splendor?"

"No."

"Have you always followed the Light?"

Amara about choked on her cereal. "No."

Breven glanced curiously at her.

"I'm—uh—new to the order." Dart'an! What did they call themselves? Followers? Pilgrims? The faithful? Even though she had been with this group for days, she had tuned out most of their words. Breven was the first one to come and chat with her.

He smiled back, his teeth white against his dark skin. "So am I. I'm glad I'm not the only one. Most everyone here has followed the Old Ways for years and even made multiple trips to Lux Casta."

"They have?" Amara looked around at the ragtag group of people with their dark cloaks, worn clothes and boots, and hair cut short as a sign of their pilgrimage. Amara tugged absent-mindedly on the tuft of hair that curled below her chin.

"Was it hard to cut off your hair?"

Her eyes widened, and she dropped her hand. Breven seemed to have no boundaries to his questions.

"Yes," she said and went back to eating.

Breven tapped his spoon against his bowl. "It was hard for me too."

She glanced at him from the corner of her eye. His black hair was less than an inch long around his face. She tried to imagine what his hair was like when it was longer. Probably very curly and handsome. Once again she wondered at the strange traditions of the pilgrims and shook her head.

Breven seemed content to finally be quiet, and they both finished breakfast in silence. Besides protection against bandits and robbers, at least there was one advantage to traveling with this group: food and someone to cook it. Everybody shared what they had. However, she could do without all the talk about the Light. Then again, it came with the group.

Days passed. Breven seemed to always make his way to her side, chatting away like the songbirds that filled the trees. The first day, she tried to ignore him, but he never got the hint. The second day, he managed to get her to talk a little. The third day, she actually laughed at one of his stories.

"So what was your life like back in Shanalona?" Amara asked, finally curious about the young man who seemed insistent on walking with her.

He shrugged. "Nothing special. I'm the fourth of six children. My father is the curator for one of the libraries, so I grew up always reading. We didn't have much, but we always had enough. I knew once I turned of age that I wanted to make a pilgrimage to the Temple of Splendor, so I did what I could, picking up jobs here and there until I had enough, then I started walking about a month ago."

"Just to see the Temple of Splendor?"

Breven smiled, which made her heart do a weird flip. "I started following the Light two winters ago. And I want to work in the libraries like my father someday, maybe even handling the history of the Old Ways. But before I begin that part of my life, I wanted to see the Temple of Splendor for myself, the place where the Light first revealed himself."

"I . . . see." She had no idea of the history behind the Temple of Splendor.

He turned and looked at her. "How about you?"

She froze. "Well . . . I . . . I wanted to get away.

My family life . . . it's not so good. I hope to make a new start in Lux Casta." It wasn't the whole truth, but in many ways, it was the truth.

He nodded slowly. "Many start this journey running away from something. I hope in the end you find something to run toward instead."

He flashed her that bright smile again, and for the first time, Amara found herself blushing. Dart'an! She needed to guard herself before she found herself falling for his sweet personality and this Light he followed.

A few days later, Amara finished up her breakfast and washed out her bowl the best she could before returning it to Hari, the eldest pilgrim and the one who made them breakfast every morning.

"Thank you for the food," she said as she handed him the bowl. After so long on the road, she was getting used to this role of a pilgrim. In a way, it allowed her to pretend to be someone else.

Do I want to be someone else?

"My pleasure." His smile made the wrinkles across his face crease even deeper. Then he returned to putting out the fire beneath the black pot.

Amara brought her mind back. "How long before we reach Lux Casta?"

"We're almost there. The weather is nice, so I'd say we should arrive by noon."

So close. Only hours away. And then she would no longer be a pilgrim but a dreamkiller on a mission. Her first step in becoming grand lady of House Ravenwood.

Amara turned away and pulled her cloak close to her body. So why did she suddenly feel so torn?

The sun reached its peak as the small group crested the last hill and the city of Lux Casta came into full view. Behind and to the right of the city, blue water stretched out to the horizon, and to the left were the rolling hills of Serine. White birds flew over the orange-tiled homes. The few people she could see beyond the walls were no bigger than a finger from this high up.

"Amazing," Breven said, coming to stand beside Amara. She silently agreed with the young man.

A fresh wind blew across the company, tugging at the auburn curls around her face and cloak. Ironmond, the capital of House Friere, looked exactly like it sounded: a fortification of iron and stone. Part of her was expecting Lux Casta to be the same, a stronghold of sorts for the family of Light. Instead, with all of the white buildings and walls, the city itself seemed to be light. Except for one thing. Black banners flew across the ramparts and from the castle in the midst of the city.

"Black standards," someone murmured. "What does that mean?"

Hari came forward. His grey brows creased as he looked down on the city. "Someone important has died."

"Died?" another person said. "Who?"

"Most likely someone from House Luceras," he replied.

"I heard Grand Lord Warin has been sick for a while," a woman said behind them.

"If it is Grand Lord Warin, then that would be sad news indeed. I suspect we will find out once we reach the city." Hari hefted his pack, his pot swinging from the corner, and started down the path that led toward Lux Casta.

Grand Lord Warin Luceras? Dead? That could work to her advantage. Many houses held the tradition of allowing their people to view their lord or lady before the body was put to rest or burned. She had been Opheliana's age when her own grandmother, Lady Sunna, passed away, and she remembered how crowded Rook Castle became during her grandmother's viewing. If House Luceras operated the same way, then Lord Warin's death could give her a way into the palace—not to mention the chaos it would cause as House Luceras crowned a new leader.

It was almost as if the Dark Lady was smiling on her plans. Almost. Not that she wanted anything to do with the Dark Lady.

A hush seemed to lie across the city as the pilgrims arrived at the gates. Guards met them at the entryway, dressed in chainmail and white tabards. "Are you pilgrims on your way to the Temple of Splendor?" the closest guard asked.

Hari stepped forward, his pot rattling as he moved. "Yes, we are. Many of us have been traveling for weeks, or even months."

The second guard stepped forward and held his spear at his side. "You are welcome to Lux Casta."

"May I ask what the black standards are for?"

Amara leaned in to hear more clearly.

"Our lord passed away early yesterday morning."

"Grand Lord Warin Luceras?"

"Yes. I'm afraid you came at a mournful time."

Hari bowed his head, along with many of the others. "We are sorry to hear that. We will lift up prayers for House Luceras and Lux Casta."

The two guards stepped back to let the pilgrims inside the gates. "You will find the temple near Palace Levellon. Follow this street through the city until you reach the middle."

Amara readjusted the satchel across her body as she followed the other pilgrims into Lux Casta. There were hardly any people out on the streets, and the few they met were dressed in black and barely said a word to them.

The city itself was at least three times as big as Rook Castle, with shops and smiths of every kind. The air was warm and filled with the scent of budding flowers and baking bread, a contrast to the sober state of the people.

Hari led the small group along the cobblestone road that ran in a circular motion around the city. They passed two lower walls and gates before he took a left and headed inward toward the middle of the city, where high above the green trees and orange-tiled roofs stood Palace Levellon.

Amara stared at the palace for a moment before continuing on. It was a lovely building, with its white towers, glittering gold ornaments, and arched windows. But if she had to choose between Palace Levellon and Rook Castle, she would take Rook Castle. Despite all of the bad memories, there was a sense of freedom and ancient power within the grey stone of the Magyr Mountain castle.

At the next corner, a gasp went up from the people in the front of the group. Amara craned her neck to see what had caused their response, then felt a gasp escape her own lips.

Ahead, with the palace on the right, stood the Temple of Splendor.

The entire building was made of white stone and stood three stories high, with buttresses along the sides. Wide steps led up to a portico lined with thick, ornate columns. Above the massive double doors was a circular window made of colored glass in the shape of a brilliant sun. An internal light glowed from within the temple, radiating through the glass sun and spreading rays of orange, red, and yellow across the steps, as if the sun itself was shining through the stained-glass window.

There were more gasps and whispers at the sight. Even Amara felt her heart taken in by the beauty of the temple.

"I can see why it's called the Temple of Splendor," Breven said beside her.

Amara could only nod. Everything about the temple was opposite of the Dark Lady's sanctuary back home.

As the group of pilgrims approached the temple, the doors opened and two women dressed in white robes stepped out onto the portico.

"Welcome, pilgrims," said the first woman. "We are humble servants of the Temple of Splendor. I'm afraid you have arrived during a sorrowful time in our city. Grand Lord Warin Luceras has passed away, and our people are in mourning. However, our temple is always open to the seekers. We will have limited prayers tomorrow in his honor. In the meantime, you can find food and shelter at an inn nearby that serves those who have come to reflect at the Temple of Splendor. Come, we will show you." The two ladies stepped down the stairs and headed to the right. A two-story building stood near the temple, not as ostentatious, but the architecture was similar.

Amara followed the others inside. There was a small common room on the first floor. A handful of people sat at a long, rough wooden table, eating from wooden bowls and drinking from wooden cups. Smoke lingered in the air from a pipe. Stairs on the right led up to the second floor.

A tall, lean man with stringy grey hair approached the party with a dish towel in one hand. "Pilgrims?"

"Yes," replied Hari.

"I have two rooms available with ten beds in each. You'll have to share. Many hill country citizens are starting to arrive for the viewing of Grand Lord Warin, so there's limited space."

Amara looked around. Between the party, both rooms would be filled. "How much for a bed?" one of the men asked.

"Ten copper coins."

"Do you have separate rooms for the men and women?"

"No, I treat all pilgrims the same."

A few of the women shifted uncomfortably as everyone reached for their pouches. She had no problem sharing a room with the men—not that she would be using the bed much. If any man stepped out of line, she had a dagger strapped to her side and another one in her boot. And there was always her sword.

The innkeeper's eyes gleamed as the pilgrims placed the coins in his outstretched hand. Amara curled her lip as she waited to give him her own coins. It only took one glance to see the innkeeper cared nothing for the pilgrims, just for the money.

Typical.

After everyone had paid the innkeeper, he led them upstairs, the coins jingling in the pouch around his waist. There were multiple doors along the second floor. Within each room five beds lined the walls on either side, with a window at the end.

Compared to the beauty and splendor of the temple, these accommodations were plain. It almost seemed as if the dichotomy was purposeful, to remind the pilgrims of who they were compared to the temple. It rubbed Amara the wrong way.

"These are the empty rooms," the innkeeper said, pointing at the two doors at the end of the corridor. "Choose whatever bed you like. Soup will be served this evening for another copper coin."

After the innkeeper left, the pilgrims scattered between the two rooms. Amara chose a bed closest to the door, so as to have easy access to and from the room during her mission. The women took most of the other beds in the room, but she did spot Breven taking the bed across from her.

He saw her glance up and cleared his throat. "I hope you don't mind. I'm used to sharing a room with my siblings and wanted to keep an eye on you. That is . . ." He rubbed the back of his neck as his cheeks darkened. "What I mean is that even in Lux Casta there are scoundrels." He laughed nervously. "I hope you don't mind."

When was the last time she had met such a decent young man? Lord Raoul Friere, although a lord of a Great House, did not compare to the simple pilgrim across from her.

Remember who you are, and why you are here.

Amara shook her head and placed her pack on the bed. "I don't mind," she said without looking up.

She had a limited window of time to form a plan and to gain as much information as she could, including finding out if House Maris had arrived yet. This was not the occasion to be swayed by dark eyes and a warm heart. If any questions arose about her comings and goings from the inn, she could claim she was praying and reflecting. And the viewing would give her access to the palace.

Breven let out a tired sigh as Amara pulled a toy from her pack. It was a tiny bird whittled out of wood and painted red. Opheliana had given it to her before she left.

She gripped the toy in one hand and closed her eyes. No matter what happened, no matter what it took, she needed to accomplish her mission and return home. Nothing could dissuade her from her purpose here. Everything she was doing was for one reason only.

For the sake of her little sister.

37

An hour later, Amara watched the crowds gather outside the gates of Palace Levellon. There would be three days of this. Three days where the palace would be open for the people to view their lord. Three days for her to study the palace and the guards, discover the whereabouts of Lord Damien, and plan her attack.

Grand Lord Warin's death couldn't have come at a better time.

She leaned against the wall of a shop right outside the palace gates with her arms crossed. The overhang from the shop offered some shade, but not much. The one benefit to having her hair cut short was the feel of the afternoon breeze along her neck and through her curls.

Every few minutes, someone would glance her way, their gaze darting to her hair, then away. The corner of her lip quirked upward. Make that two benefits to having short hair. She didn't have to explain who she was. People simply assumed she was a pilgrim here to visit the Temple of Splendor. As much as she hated to admit it, her mother had been right about this disguise. It was perfect.

From here, she studied as much as she could of the palace, then eased into the crowd as a bell rang. The service for House Luceras and the lesser houses had finished, and now the three-day viewing would begin for the masses. She hoped to catch a glimpse of the houses in attendance to confirm House Maris was here. If not, she would have to resort to other ways of finding out, but a glimpse would be the best.

A bell rang again, and the gates slowly opened. The crowd surged forward. Amara partly wondered if some of the people gathered were more interested in seeing Palace Levellon than actually seeing their lord. There seemed to be more excitement than a body viewing would generate.

Amara flowed in through the gate with the crowd into an expansive courtyard surrounded by manicured lawns, blooming flowers, and green trees. The air was filled with a heady floral scent. Servants and guards ushered the people along in a barely controlled manner. Rook Castle had been crowded when her grandmother died, but nothing like this.

Amara took everything in as she walked along the perimeter of the crowd: from the trees and waterway, to the other buildings that surrounded the palace, to the palace itself, noting the architecture and window style, should she need to climb.

At the front doors, the crowd narrowed and slowed down. A line was formed, one for allowing people entrance into the palace, one for the exit. Guards stood at the doors and along the hallway inside, at least from what she could see from where she stood.

Amara sighed and waited her turn to enter. Time passed, and the crowd shuffled forward. The fountain splashed, a pleasant sound amidst the talk of the people. The sun moved overhead, momentarily blocked by a cloud, then reappeared.

Then it was her turn to enter.

She stepped past the guards into a vast entryway. Everything was white, from the walls to the floor to the formal attire worn by the guards. The only color was from stained-glass windows high above, with images of previous lords and ladies of House Luceras etched in the glass.

People whispered and pointed at the glass. Yes, she was right. They were here partly to catch a glimpse of Palace Levellon.

It was a short walk from the entryway, down a wide corridor, to the main audience chamber. Just as the crowd reached the doors, three guards stepped in front of the people and held out their arms. Behind them, men and women dressed in lavish dark clothing exited the chamber.

Amara craned her neck to catch a glimpse of those exiting as she pressed her back against the wall in order not to be jostled. There were at least twenty people between her and the guards, but she could still see who was leaving.

She went up on her tiptoes to get a better view. It looked like the people departing the hall were members of lesser houses taking their leave from the viewing.

Then someone caught her eye. A woman with long black hair with a blue sheen to it.

Her body stiffened and a tingling spread across her limbs.

Selene.

Her traitorous sister who ran off, leaving her to pick up the mess Selene left behind. To try to fulfill their mother's demands. To protect their little sister, Opheliana.

Anger, jealousy, and hatred twisted like snakes inside her gut as she watched her sister exit the audience chamber. Amara clenched her hands, her chest so tight she couldn't breathe. She could barely keep her eyes on her sister as a red haze filled her vision.

No, I will not lose control.

She took a deep breath in, loosening her hands one finger at a time. Then she noticed the man walking beside Selene as they turned and headed down the corridor in the opposite direction of the crowd. Dark hair, slightly taller than Selene, dressed in the blue colors of House Maris.

Her target: Lord Damien.

She stared at him, her jaw set. He was here. The one man who could solidify her position with her mother and House Ravenwood. All she needed to do now was take the next two days to plan out her attack.

Lord Damien and Selene disappeared. Amara sank back down onto her feet, her mind coming back to the present. A man stumbled sideways and bumped into her.

"Pardon me," he muttered.

Amara ignored him. She was already creating a mental list of everything she would need to know in order to pull off her first mission: where Lord Damien was staying, who else was with him, the best way to access his room, his habits, the ins and outs of the palace, and the security and guard rotation of Palace Levellon. She was thankful for the small map her mother had drawn from her memories of Palace Levellon, one less thing she would need to study.

Amara didn't have much time, but with her skills and resources, she felt confident of forming a plan. And when the moment presented itself, she would strike.

38

Morning broke the next day in an array of light. Selene watched the sun's rays move across the stone floor from the large windows across the room from her pillow.

Damien shifted beside her. Moments later, he kissed the back of her head. "I'm going to support the Luceras family today in any way I can," he said. "Would you like to go with me?"

Selene stiffened. "I'm not sure how much help I would be. They barely know me. Perhaps it's better if you go alone, since you've known them from childhood." *And I would have no idea what to say or do.*

"I understand." He sat up, pulling the covers with him and letting the cold air in.

Selene shivered, having half a mind to pull the blankets back and stay where she was. Another dreamless night had left her body fatigued. But if Damien could get up and help others, then she could at least get up.

By the time she had dressed, the chill in the air had turned to a warmer temperature. Damien placed a sleeveless jacket over his black tunic, closed the wooden chest, and looked up at her. The dark tunic matched his hair and caused his eyes to appear even more brilliantly blue in the morning light, sending a flutter across her heart. She would never tire of those eyes.

He walked over to her and held out his hand. "I thought we could break our fast together in the common room before I go."

Selene tugged on a lock of hair. "I haven't done my hair yet."

"Then let me."

She tilted her head to the side. "You?"

He smiled back. "Yes."

Before she could answer, he crossed the bedchamber, picked up the brush she had left on the desk the night before, then approached her again.

Selene blinked and turned around. She had decided not to bring Essa on this trip, as there was no reason to bring the young woman on such a long journey when she could take care of herself. Could Damien really do any better?

He brushed out the long black strands, then pulled all of her hair back and began to braid it. "When my mother was sick, I took care of her hair every morning."

"Why didn't her maidservant do it?"

"Many of the servants, including her servant Breta, came down with the plague. There were only a few of us healthy enough to do anything. It was a way I could serve my mother. By braiding her hair every morning."

A lump formed in Selene's throat. What had

Damien's mother been like that would compel such a loving gesture from her son? Part of her wished she could have known his family.

She closed her eyes and enjoyed the feel of his fingers as he tugged and pulled the strands together. There was something intimate about having her husband do her hair, and it sent another flutter through her heart.

"There," he said a minute later. "Do you have a ribbon to tie it off?"

Selene handed him the thin black piece of satin, then glanced at one of the windows at her reflection. It was a simple hairdo, but she felt like a queen. "Thank you," she said, her voice full of emotion.

He stepped up behind her and breathed in her scent. "I've been wanting to do that for a long time."

Heat flooded her entire body.

There was a knock at their door. Selene brushed her cheek to stifle her fluster. Damien answered it, then looked back. "A servant has brought us food. Would you like to eat now?"

She looked over her shoulder at him. "Yes."

The lighthearted feelings from minutes ago vanished when they entered the common room and she spotted Taegis and Karl dressed in black with somber faces, reminding her that grief still hung over the palace. The solemn mood seemed to have seeped back into Damien as he took two cups of tea and handed one to Selene. Four brown eggs rested in four eggcups and small rolls filled with dried fruit and nuts sat on a nearby plate.

Hardly anyone ate or drank. The egg was difficult to swallow, and the tea tasted bland and tepid. Damien stood shortly after and announced that he was leaving to spend time with House Luceras.

Selene sensed it again—that shroud across Damien's psyche, similar to the shroud that covered the palace. She frowned as she watched him leave. She still had yet to discover what the shadow was that lay across his soul.

Taegis went with him, and Karl stood guard at the door out in the hallway, leaving Selene all alone. Morning passed to afternoon. The silence filled her, opening doors inside her mind she wished would stay locked. Memories and dreams came flooding back. How was little Ophie doing? She would be five springs soon, and for the first time Selene would not be there to give her little sister a violet from the garden. How were the others? Was Hagatha still alive? Was Petur preparing the castle gardens? Was Renata—

Selene swallowed and blinked back the sudden rush of tears, the first stirring of sadness inside her heart. She dropped her head and studied her fingers. Was Renata still alive? Or had her mother done away with the young servant girl after she left?

She crushed her right hand into a fist. If there were any regrets she had about leaving Rook Castle and her house behind, it was the people who could be hurt by her decision.

And yet . . . wouldn't more be saved if the Ravenwoods no longer killed with their gift? If the cycle of hatred was broken?

She stood. These thoughts were too much to bear inside the empty room. Outside, the sun still shone, but evening was already descending. She doubted anyone would mind if she went for a walk along the gardens she had seen around the palace. Exercise had a way of clearing her mind and helping her work through her emotions.

Selene grabbed her cloak, pulled the hood up over her head, and exited the rooms. Karl followed her like a shadow, discreetly enough so it was as if she was alone, but she could still feel his presence behind her.

Every few minutes, she would hear a muffled sob or low whispers echo along the gleaming hallway. With each sound, her heart slowly slipped open to the grief that was pervading the palace. These people loved the family of Luceras. It wasn't the same as the deep love she had seen and experienced Nor Esen feel for Damien, but it was still there, if only a little bit. It only reminded her of how different House Ravenwood and the mountain people were.

How different she was.

Was it possible it could change someday? Would discovering House Ravenwood's true purpose in dreamwalking change both her family and their people?

She hoped so.

She found the entrance to the vast gardens on the first floor. Double doors opened up to a small valley of towering trees, flowers of every color and size, and paths made of river stone that led out into a green forest.

She stood there for a moment and took in a deep breath, letting the beauty soak into her being. The air was cool and held the fragrance of soil and sweetness. She took a step forward, the river stone crunching beneath her boots, her fingers trailing along the leaves from the trees as she walked. The valley was easily three times the size of the garden back at Rook Castle and filled with more flowers than she had ever seen.

Ophie would love this place.

Selene smiled tenderly as she went for the path on the left, imagining her sister laughing as she ran down the trail, stopping to smell every flower and climb every tree.

Sunlight trickled through the forest in rays of pure gold, and the flowers raised their faces to drink it in. Birds sang in the trees, and a light blue butterfly danced along the flower petals.

In this place, she could believe in the Old

Ways, in the Light who gave light and beauty to everything. This garden seemed to almost sing of his presence. Not even the cloak of death could hide the splendor of this place. She remembered Damien's words from the day of the Festival of Light, when he showed her his gift and told her about the Light. *"Does the sun disappear when clouds come? Or is the sun still there?"* It is still there. Just like the Light.

She could accept it as truth as she walked along the path. There was a peace to this place, a tugging of her heart. Even with Karl far down the path behind her, she still felt alone and encompassed by her surroundings.

Ahead, the trail met up with three other trails beneath an oak tree. As she approached the intersection, voices drifted through the trees. She was going to continue along the one she was following when she heard a familiar tenor voice.

She looked to her right. *Damien?*

The path on the right sloped down toward a gentle stream lined with bushes. Hesitantly, she turned right and started back toward the palace along the new path. Yes, it was definitely his voice.

Then she heard another voice. A sweet, bell-like voice answered his.

Selene stopped beside a flowering bush and looked toward the stream. Damien and Lady Adalyn stood on a small wooden bridge that crossed the stream. Lord Elric stood near his sister, his hand on her shoulder, and Taegis and another guard were situated in the shadows, guarding their lords and lady.

Lady Adalyn stood just below Damien's chin, her light hair gathered over one shoulder, her silk dress flowing in the breeze. She appeared agitated by the way she wiped her face and looked down.

Damien spoke, then Lord Elric spoke as well. The three of them reminded Selene of how close House Luceras and House Maris were, and brought back the memories from Damien's dreams, of when they were young and carefree. Before Quinn's death. Before the deaths of Grand Lord Warin and his wife. Even now, they were comforting one another, like family.

Selene turned away from the tender scene and headed back toward the path she had been on. Seeing them together was like a dagger to the heart, reminding her that she was a stranger. She might have married Damien, but she was still a Ravenwood, with a history of deceit and blood. She didn't belong here. Not with people like them.

She held a hand to her throat as she remembered Lady Bryren's words: *"Tell me, do you love each other?"*

Damien was kind to her and had married her to save her life. And he was a man of integrity and duty and would treat their marriage as such. But did he love her?

Would he have chosen Lady Adalyn instead if he had been given a choice?

I only married you to save myself.

Selene walked back to the path on the left, but instead of heading toward the palace, she started deeper into the gardens. The sun was now sinking behind her, and shadows lengthened across the garden. Her tears blurred her vision, and she wiped them away, angry at the swirl of emotions filling her chest.

She heard Karl behind her, racing to catch up. "Lady Selene," he called out. "Are you all right?"

She stopped for a moment and looked back, her mind in a fog.

Karl stepped toward her. "My lady, you don't look well."

Preservation took over, the same iron will that got her through at Rook Castle. She couldn't show her emotions, not here, not in front of Karl. "I need some time alone, to think." Her voice was even and controlled. "Would you give me a moment?"

He looked at her as if he didn't believe her, and she stared back, placing all her strength into her will.

He sighed. "Just for a moment. I will be waiting here if you need anything."

"Thank you, Karl," she said before starting back down the path.

She reached a bend, then pulled up her gown and left the path and headed into the trees, away from people, away from the sights and noise. A numbness stole over her as she silently made her way through the forest. Whether because of all the dreamless nights or the fatigue from the trip, she couldn't seem to fight this overflowing feeling of hurt and loneliness. "Dart'an," she whispered.

A minute later, she veered again, deeper into the trees. By now it was dusk, heading toward night. She moved through the forest with remembered stealth and silence. The nightwalker was back, and she became one with the shadows.

Somewhere far off, she thought she heard Karl call her name, but she pressed on without a sound. The night was an old friend, a place where she could hide. Deeper she went, the air cooling around her, her gown hiked up around her legs, freeing her to move.

She came upon a small opening in the trees and dropped to her knees. Fatigue was causing the emotions inside of her to crash over her like a tidal wave, but she didn't have the strength to fight. She had been fighting for so long: her mother, her power, her feelings. She just wanted to lie down and let the dreamless darkness take her.

The wind brushed her hair around her face. The soil was moist and smelled of plant life. The only sounds were the croaks from nearby frogs and the buzz of an insect.

She squeezed her eyes tight and dug her fingers into the soil. *Who am I really?*

Twilight turned to night. Far off, the muffled hum of human voices came and went. Selene ignored them. She didn't care. She didn't care about anything anymore. The hole inside of her no longer contained her feelings. She was an empty shell, a solitary woman on her knees in a dark garden, looking for guidance.

Soon, the garden dipped into night. Even the moon was gone, for it was a new moon. The stars were hidden above, their light strangled out by the long limbs of the trees around her, leaving her in almost total blackness.

It reflected how she felt.

Selene lay down on her side in the dirt, the low-hanging branches from the closest tree acting as a natural cover, hiding her from the rest of the world. The cold, damp earth pressed against her cheek, the scent of water, flowers, and soil filling her nose.

She could see nothing but darkness.

Was this how the world began? Was it always dark? Where was the Light the monks chanted about during the Festival of Light?

A cool breeze blew through the trees. Selene

ignored the chill as she clenched her hands to her chest.

Sleep began to tug at her. Selene curled into a ball, her hands pressed against her chest, the ground beneath her.

So tired.

The darkness of sleep beckoned her. Finally, she closed her eyes.

And for the first time in weeks, she dreamed.

39

"Where are you going?"

Amara turned around and found Breven standing outside the door to the inn where they were both staying. The sun was setting over the city, leaving the area in twilight. A warm wind blew through the streets, and the sound of voices carried along the back alleys.

Her cloak rippled in the wind. She quickly pulled the edges together, hiding both her dark clothing and sword. "I'm heading to the palace to pay my respects to Lord Luceras." It was a lie; she had already visited yesterday.

"I visited this morning, before spending the rest of the day in the Temple of Splendor," Breven replied. "But if you would like company, I would be happy to go again."

There was such an earnestness in his face that for one moment Amara wavered. The other pilgrims continued to annoy her to no end with their piousness. But not Breven. He was different. She had found him—and his belief in the Light— intriguing, and a strange fondness for him was growing inside of her. He had brought her a bread roll that morning and showed her where to retrieve water at one of the city wells when they had first arrived.

Was it possible there were actually good people like him in this world?

Remember the mission.

Amara hardened her features. "I wish to go alone."

He seemed taken aback by her abrupt answer.

Dart'an! She could have answered him in a softer manner. But what was the purpose? If her mission was successful—and it would be—she would never see him again.

"All right. I'll see you tomorrow. Maybe we can go to the temple together?"

Amara smiled, although her heart twisted inside. "That would be nice." Another lie, this one like a noose around her neck.

The noose tightened as that familiar—and incredible—smile broke out across his face. "I'll see you tomorrow, then."

"Yes. Now I must be off." She hurried down the street, keeping her cloak around her body, hiding her true purpose for that evening.

As she made her way to the palace, a thought struck her. Did Breven like her? For a split second, she imagined a different life, one she had never thought of before. One where her mother did not exist. One where she could make her own choices. One in which this handsome young man with rich dark skin and a gleaming smile was her consort.

Maybe this was why Selene had left. Perhaps

she had grown tired of the lies, the demands of their house, and the shadows across their future.

In that moment, Amara understood her sister completely.

Getting into the palace was easy. Amara simply followed a crowd of people entering the gates. Twilight had spread, but the lights had not been lit yet, providing a perfect cover for stealing away from the mourners once she was inside the walls. She watched the guards as she walked along the path to the right of the water that flowed down the middle of the courtyard, a couple of steps behind the crowd. There were fewer people than yesterday, most likely those who had waited until now or just arrived in Lux Casta.

Her mother's map had indicated that noble guests to Palace Levellon were housed on the southern side of the palace on the second floor. It would mean a climb, and she would have to determine which rooms House Maris was located in, but it was doable.

The moment the guards shifted their attention, Amara stepped to the side and silently stole to the first tree. Once she was behind the trunk, she pulled off her outer cloak, stowed it beneath a flowering bush, and pulled on her face scarf and hood.

Using her training, she made her way through the trees that surrounded the palace to the southern side. It was almost night, and with her dark clothes, she blended in with the shadows. Minutes later, lights began to appear over the palace as servants lit candles for the evening.

Amara stayed out of the light and continued on.

Once she reached the southern side, she stopped and studied the palace. There were three sets of windows with decorative railings along the second floor, each connected to a set of guest rooms. She narrowed her eyes. How to go about finding who was housed in each . . .

As if in answer to her question, a man opened the far windows and stood in the opening. She couldn't make him out in the darkness, so she moved between the trees toward him.

He sighed and leaned across the railing in front of the windows. Her heart beat faster. He had dark hair, like Lord Damien, but that didn't mean it was him. She had to get closer.

Another man joined him, one with lighter hair pulled back at the nape of his neck.

"How was your time with House Luceras this afternoon?" the second man asked, his voice carrying across the palace lawn.

"Lady Adalyn is crushed," the first man replied.

Amara crouched behind a set of carefully manicured bushes near the balcony and listened.

"Between my brother's death, then her mother's, and now her father's, she feels all alone."

"And what about her brothers?"

Amara peeked over the bushes and looked up. She'd seen Lord Damien during the assembly last harvest. He was a strong, handsome man from what she could remember. The young man on the balcony looked almost exactly like him. And the man beside him . . .

Yes. She recognized his guardian. Taelyn, or something. It was Lord Damien.

"The older two are working through their own grief. I'm glad Lord Elric was there helping me console his sister." Lord Damien sighed again and ran a hand along his face. "I wish I could do more."

"I know this is hard for you right now. You never recovered from your parents' death, or Quinn's."

"No," Damien said quietly, in such a sorrowful tone that even Amara was moved. "I miss them all. And I think Lady Adalyn is also reliving Quinn's death. I never realized just how much she loved my brother. I wonder if my presence today was more helpful or hurtful."

"Given what I saw, I think you were able to help both Lady Adalyn and Lord Elric."

Damien turned toward his guardian. "Thank you, Taegis. I know that Lord Leo had hoped there would be an alliance between our houses, but I know it wouldn't have worked out. She loved my brother, and I have come to love

Selene. Deeply. I hope Lady Adalyn finds a husband someday who will love her the way she loved Quinn."

Amara stared up at the men, her mouth open. Lord Damien loved her sister? Deeply? When—when did this happen? At the assembly? Was that what brought their marriage about? And did her sister love him? She couldn't imagine Selene having any feelings. Selene was made of ice, as cold as any woman could be. There had to be some other reason for their arrangement. But she could not deny the emotion in Lord Damien's voice when he said her name.

Lord Damien turned toward Taegis. "By the way, has Lady Selene returned yet?"

"No. But Karl is with her. There is no need to worry."

"I know. But I have this feeling . . ."

The two men walked inside, leaving the windows open.

Amara stayed where she was within the shadows of the trees, her focus on the windows, while the rest of her senses were spread out, ready to move if she needed to. More lights came on as the guests of the other rooms entered their chambers.

A plan started to formulate in her mind. She would climb toward the windows and stay on the ledge that jutted out beneath the railing and get a feel for who all occupied this suite, their routine, and how she could best reach Lord Damien. If an opportunity presented itself, then she would take it. And if not . . .

No. She set her jaw as she stared up at the windows. She would walk in his dreams tonight and look for his fears. Maybe she would get lucky and find what she needed. She only had one more day when the palace would be open to finish her mission. She couldn't afford to fail.

With that thought, Amara stole toward the palace. Ornate molding provided the perfect handholds. A minute later, she slipped over the railing and stood in the narrow area between window and railing, flattening herself against the wall.

She was never one for patience. Selene had always been the patient one. It took everything inside of her to stand there and wait for her opportunity.

Damien bid someone good night, and she heard a door close. A candle provided light within. He sighed, and she could hear him pacing. A trickle of sweat dripped down the side of her face. What was he doing? Was he waiting for her sister to come back?

Did they share a room?

Amara swore inside her head. Most lords and ladies had separate rooms, but there were the occasional couples who shared. This could complicate things.

Finally, the light went out, and there was a soft thump, then silence. She hesitated. She could hardly see anything, but that also meant no one would see her either.

Her heart beat faster as adrenaline filled her body.

Amara glanced inside the room. The tiniest slip of light shone beneath the door, but not enough to illuminate the room. She could barely make out a body on the bed, on the side opposite the door.

She leaned against the wall and figured out her course of action. In a few more minutes, she would move in, then find a place to make skin contact and enter his dreams.

Time ticked by as everything that could go wrong flew through her mind. Selene could come in, or one of his guards. Or she wouldn't have time to figure out his nightmares. Maybe she wasn't strong enough.

She could fail.

She clenched her hand. Failure was not an option.

Amara slipped into the room, silent as the night itself. She followed the wall along the right, then the next wall, until she reached the bed. Selene and her mother might be more powerful than she was, but she had worked hard and her power was at least sufficient enough for this task. And what she lacked in power she more than made up for in stubbornness, something her mother had noted during their dreamwalks together. She would hold on to her target until she had accomplished her mission. Tonight would be no different.

She knelt beside the bed opposite of the main door. She could hear Lord Damien's breathing, steady and soft. Perfect. The bit of light from one of the side doors let her see where his hand lay across the mattress. Slowly, carefully, she reached for his wrist and made contact.

Nothing happened. It was like there was an invisible wall along the barrier of his dreamscape.

Amara closed her eyes and focused on where her fingers met his wrist.

Still nothing.

Cold sweat poured across her body. Dart'an! What did this mean? Mother had spoken of powerful dreamscapes that were difficult to enter. Was his one of those?

Her chest tightened, and she pressed her lips together. *No! I can't fail! I* won't *fail. For Opheliana's sake.*

Amara drew upon every ounce of her power inside her and pressed against his mind. Harder. Harder.

She burst into his dreams in a flurry of feathers and flight. Finally.

She gave out a caw as she hovered high above a sandy beach, a bright blue sky above and gentle waves below. Sunlight rained down across her back and light sparkled across the sea. She spread her wings and let an air current send her forward.

She looked around her in awe. This was Lord Damien's dreamscape? It was so different than anything she had experienced before—

Focus.

She shook her head, then flexed her wings and dove down toward the sandy dunes. This was not the time for admiration. Now was the time to see what Lord Damien held in the darkest recesses of his mind.

Now was the time to complete her mission and finish off House Maris.

40

Images and feelings rushed past Selene as if she were flying from one dream to the next. Maybe she was. She hadn't dreamwalked in so long that perhaps her gift had stored up momentum, pitching her across multiple dreamscapes.

First she was playing wooden blocks with a little girl in a light blue dress on the floor of a cabin, then she was sitting at a long wooden table, reading over what looked like a very old scroll. Next, she was staring into the eyes of a pretty young woman, declaring her love before she was swept aboard a ship at sea, her hands steadying the ship's wheel.

Over and over again, moving from one mind to another, reliving the memories and feelings of so many people that her own mind was spinning. It took her a dozen dreams before she was able to pull up and hover in her raven form above what looked like Nor Esen, only it was summer and the sun was shining brightly over the rugged city and surrounding cliffs and beaches, with white-crested waves crashing against the rocks and blue water as far as the eye could see.

Home. The word reverberated within her.

Then everything went black.

When she next opened her eyes, she was

standing inside the Dark Lady's sanctuary in Rook Castle. It was exactly as she remembered it on that cold day over a year ago, the day she received the prophetic utterance from the priest about her gift. Pale, overcast light filtered in through the high windows above, and a chill hung in the air, so different compared to Nor Esen from moments ago. The dais ahead was empty, and the retable held unlit candles. The stone floor was bare between the columns, without even a speck of dust to be found.

She looked down and found herself draped in a long dark cloak, the hood pulled over her head, the way she always wore it when she visited the sanctuary the morning after a new moon. It was almost as if she were revisiting that morning, minus her mother, her sister, and the other disciples.

And the Dark Lady.

The Dark Lady never came that night, like the priest said she would. Never answered her when she prayed for help, never showed up until Selene chose to leave Rook Castle. Then the Dark Lady came, haunting her dreams.

Selene slowly turned around, half expecting the Dark Lady to be standing there, her hood covering most of her face, her black eyes peering out from beneath her cowl, painted lips pressed together, the same way she had shown up in Selene's dreamscapes.

But the hall was empty behind her as much as in front of her. Silence. Only silence. And emptiness.

Then a hand gripped her shoulder. "You've come at last," a raspy voice whispered.

Selene froze. A putrid smell wafted beneath her nostrils as the air grew even colder. She could see long white fingers along her shoulder, ending in pointed nails.

"You've come, my little raven."

She focused on her breathing as she fought the impulse to explode into her raven form and fly away. Even now her body shivered, ready to change.

No.

Selene closed her eyes, ignoring the deathly smell and the tight grip along her shoulder. No. The cycle needed to stop. No more running. No more flying away. If she transformed, the same thing would happen again and again. The Dark Lady would follow her. She would always follow her. And more people would get hurt.

If she wanted to be free of the Dark Lady, then she needed to confront her. Now.

Slowly, the Dark Lady came around her. Selene watched her move, her heart thudding inside her chest. Even this close, she could not see beneath the Dark Lady's cowl, only pinpricks of light bouncing from unending black orbs. Did the Dark Lady even have a face, save for her painted lips?

The thought sent a scream up her throat, but she kept her lips sealed shut.

"You've stayed away, little raven." The Dark Lady dropped her hand and stood in front of Selene. "Why?"

Selene remained silent.

"I only want to help you," the Dark Lady whispered in a harsh voice.

"Help?" A burst of anger sent the word flying.

Black lips turned upward. "Yes. Help you become the most powerful Raven ever."

"Why?"

"Every other house possesses gifts in the real world. You are the only one who can walk in dreams. In my world. The combination of our powers would be unstoppable."

Her mouth slowly loosened. "And what of my mother? My sisters?"

The smile slid from those black lips. "None of them are as powerful as you."

A fire began to burn inside of Selene. "My mother has served you for many years. You would discard her for me?"

"I never discard a Ravenwood. I groom the next one." The pinpricks of light seemed to stare intently out from beneath the cowl, almost as if they could see through her.

"And what if I say no?"

The air dropped in temperature, and the light in the sanctuary grew dimmer. The Dark Lady's face seemed to retreat inside her cowl, and the light in her eyes disappeared, leaving only shadows. "I will always be here in the dream world. You cannot escape from me. You cannot escape your destiny."

Selene's throat constricted as deep fears resurfaced. She would fight her destiny, but could she win against the Dark Lady, even with all of her power? What would the Dark Lady do to her if she turned away? Kill her? Suffocate her here in the dreamscape? Trap her soul?

Did the Dark Lady have that kind of power?

Then images filled her mind. Ophie standing beside the window, watching the birds flit through the trees. Amara, with her fiery looks and dark auburn hair. A little boy with hair like Damien's and her own dark eyes—

Selene's eyes went wide, and she sucked in a breath. Did that boy represent a new generation of dreamwalkers? A male dreamer?

If so, to change her family, to alter their destiny, she had to start with the Dark Lady.

"No." The word came out in a soft whisper.

The hood across the Dark Lady's head fluttered from an unseen wind. "No?"

Selene's resolve hardened, that same resolve that got her through the past year, the one that filled her with an unbending will. This was the line. She would not be moved. "I will not follow you."

"You cannot escape the shadows, little raven."

"Even still, I will not follow you." *I left my home and family behind to find a new way for us all.* Her hands tightened at her sides. *I will not be a dreamkiller. Not now, not ever. Even if it costs me my life.*

There was a pause. "So be it."

What little of the Dark Lady's face had been visible moments ago disappeared. The dark hood and cloak surged forward. Before Selene could think, her face and body were caught inside the cloak. The back of the hood pressed against her face. The fabric from the cloak wrapped around her body, pinning her arms to her sides.

She couldn't breathe. She couldn't see. She toppled over, unable to move her legs. The cloak continued to tighten its hold around her. Lights began to dance across her eyes like colorful fireflies, and her lungs were on fire. Panic became an animal set loose inside her body, clawing and fighting with an unthinking instinct.

She wanted to scream, but she couldn't. A cold, tingling chill spread across her body as her heart tried to keep up with the fear inside of her.

The colorful fireflies disappeared, leaving her vision pitch-black. The cloth across her face pressed in so tightly it was like a second skin, with no way to suck in a mouthful of air.

She was going to die.

But it's only a dream.

Everything inside of her stilled.

It's only a dream.

Which meant . . .

She could free herself.

Selene went deep inside, feeling along every nerve, every limb. Moments later, she could feel the connection of the dreamscape, like strings attached to her body. Thousands of them. A tug here, a pull there, and she could change her entire reality. She focused on the fabric taut against her body, then imagined grabbing the cloak with her hand and yanking it away.

The cloak disappeared.

Selene sat up and gulped a lungful of air as her vision returned.

"Very good. But what about memories?" the harsh voice whispered.

Before she could take another breath, Selene found herself back in Levellon's gardens at twilight, standing on a path surrounded by towering trees and scented flowers. Below her gurgled a stream, with a small wooden bridge. And on that bridge stood Damien and the Luceras siblings.

Her breath hitched at the sight, and a wave of painful loneliness swept across her body. She turned around and held her arms across her body.

"Why do you look away?"

An invisible hand yanked her face back toward the scene. Lord Elric held his sister as Damien stood beside them. Her stomach clenched. "No," Selene breathed and looked away. Again, her face was brought back.

"You're not the only one who can manipulate memories. This particular one hurts you."

"I will not be controlled by you!" Selene brought her power and force of will against the dreamscape. The scene cracked seconds later and fell away like glass, only to be replaced with the night when she walked inside Renata's dreams.

Renata lay in a pool of moonlight on her sleeping mat, her eyes distant, a speck of blood beneath her nostril.

"You did this to her," the Dark Lady whispered.

Selene stared down, horrified. "I know."

Suddenly, more people appeared inside the small cabin, all on the floor, staring up at the ceiling, their eyes like Renata's. Taegis. Karl. Cohen.

Damien and Ophie.

"You are the mind shatterer, little raven. This is your future."

"No!" Her voice tore across the dreamscape. The scene disappeared into the air like smoke from a fire.

Selene fell to her knees. Her power was a match for the Dark Lady, but only just. And already she was feeling fatigued from changing the dreamscape. She gripped the sides of her head. *I can't keep doing this. Perhaps I* will *be giving my life.* She lifted her head and dropped her hands. *But I won't follow her. I won't be a dreamkiller.*

She closed her eyes and pictured Damien's soulsphere—the first time she saw the light inside of him, and how much she wanted what he had. She still wanted it, to be filled with light, to hold it inside of her like he did. To be a reflection of *the* Light and not a vessel of darkness.

She gripped her hands tightly together as she knelt there in pitch-blackness. *Light, please hear me. Whether I live or die, do not let me go down the Dark Lady's path. Help me be strong, even to the end.*

A few seconds later, she opened her eyes. A small light appeared, no bigger than the flame on a candlewick. Just a pinprick in the darkness, but it was light, and it was something to hold on to. It was hope.

Selene held on to the image with all her being.

A great gust of wind sprang up out of the darkness. It pressed against her like a typhoon, filling her ears with its harsh whistle, tossing her hair above her head, cutting her skin with a thousand tiny blades. A voice spoke within the wind. "You can never outrun the shadows, little raven. A shadow exists even in the greatest light. I will find you again. And you will be mine." Then the voice and the wind disappeared.

When she looked back, there was nothing around her. Only a landscape of grey, from the bare ground to the empty sky above. Like an empty canvas.

The Dark Lady was gone.

Selene hunched over, gasping for air, feeling like she was going to retch. Her hands trembled across the floor. Moments later, she leaned down and touched her forehead to the ground. "Thank you," she whispered.

She knelt there, taking in the silence and solitude. She was still alive and still on her own path, one in contrast to her family. She had faced the Dark Lady and stood her ground.

There would be another confrontation, the Dark Lady hinted of it. But for now, this was enough.

Then a sense of unease swept across her spirit.

Selene lifted her head, spreading out with her senses. Danger. But not toward her. Toward someone else. In another dreamscape.

Her eyes went wide, and her whole body went rigid.

Damien.

41

Selene struggled to her feet. She stumbled forward, still exhausted from her confrontation with the Dark Lady. Then she began to run across the empty dreamscape, her thoughts on Damien. The dream barrier appeared overhead. With her eyes on the thin line that divided her dreamscape from the real world and other dreams, she burst into her raven form. Up she went in a flurry of feathers and hurled herself forward, her mind completely on Damien so she would reach his dream world.

Seconds later, she broke through the barrier and dove into the next dreamscape.

White sand, gentle waves, and a bright blue sky appeared. Sweet cool wind caught her wings and lifted her up. She knew this place. She'd crossed over into Damien's dreams.

Selene soared across the sandy beach of his dreamscape, pumping her wings as hard as she could. The sense of danger was even stronger, hitting her like a gale with its intensity. She should have known Mother would send someone after Damien once he left the protection of his water barriers. She should have been watching for an infiltrator. She should never have left him.

I just need to get to his soulsphere and wake him up.

As she crested over the last sand dune, a figure came into view, slowly making its way to Damien's radiant soul. Fear gripped Selene like never before, threatening to paralyze her wings and send her plummeting to the sandy dunes.

Mother.

I will not let her take him. She clicked her beak and pushed harder.

Wait. The figure wasn't Mother. And why was the walker in human form, and not in raven form? Details came into focus as she drew closer. The dreamwalker was smaller, with short, curly hair. Almost like . . .

Amara.

Selene dove for the space between Amara and Damien's soul. Just when she reached the gap, she swept her wings back and touched down in her human form. She drew in a deep breath and brought her arms out in front of her, her dual swords appearing in her hands. "Amara."

Amara stopped a couple of feet away from her, mouth agape. "Selene."

"What are you doing here?"

Her nostrils flared. "What do you think? I'm finishing the job." Her eyes narrowed. "But how are you here? There is no one in this room but Lord Maris. I made sure of that."

"There are a great many things I can do now in the dreamscape."

Amara studied Selene's swords, then swung her own arm out in front of her. A single blade appeared in her hand. "Impressive. Mother never taught me this."

Selene thought the same thing. She had no idea she could bring her swords here. But then again, if she could transform into a raven or change a dreamscape, it made sense she could change her own presence, including creating a replica of her swords from the real world. "Probably because there has never been a need for weapons before in the dreamscape."

Amara looked up from her blade. "So you are here to fight me."

"I will if I must to stop you."

"A Ravenwood has never killed another Ravenwood."

Mother's words rang out from Amara's mouth and hit Selene like an arrow in the gut. Was that what it was going to take to protect Damien? The death of her own sister? Before she could think on it further, Amara lunged.

Selene brought her swords together and knocked Amara's blade away. Amara lunged again, forcing her to take a step back. She could feel the warmth of Damien's soul behind her. She couldn't let Amara come close to the soulsphere—

Amara's blade came down. Selene met it with her left blade, then brought her right one around, but was forced to take another step back.

No more. She couldn't lose any more ground.

Just as Amara began another swing, Selene felt her power draw on the dreamscape. In an instant, she transformed into a raven, dove around Amara, then twisted around back into her human form with her blades in hand and went for her sister's blind spot.

Amara spun around and caught Selene's blade, but barely, knocking Selene's swords to the side. She swung her sword up into a ready stance and stared. "How did you do that?"

Selene shook her head, almost as dazed as her sister looked. It was as if she and the dreamscape were one. Whatever she thought, whatever she felt, she could do. "I've changed. I've discovered there is so much more to our gift than we've been taught." Although this was new even to her.

"Let's see if you can do it again."

Amara had grown in her sword skills. Every time Selene thought she had the upper hand, Amara proved her wrong. Sand shifted beneath their boots, and their cloaks flew around them as they fought along the dreamscape coast of Damien's mind.

Selene changed into her raven form for a second time, coming up on Amara's left side and going for the opening with her swords.

Amara twisted a moment later, caught her, and charged.

Selene switched back to her raven form, flew past the sword, then transformed into her human form between Amara and Damien's soulsphere.

Both women were panting now as they stared at each other. Then Amara's eye shifted beyond Selene to the glowing orb behind her. Selene could see the light reflected in Amara's eyes.

"Is that what made you defect?" Amara motioned toward Damien's soul with her sword.

An aching hunger emerged inside Selene. She wanted to look back at the revolving orb, but she held herself in place. "It's one reason out of many."

"It's . . . beautiful. I've never seen a soul like it."

"I know. And it's not only him. I've seen so much beauty, so much light since I left."

Amara shook her head as if clearing her thoughts and raised her sword. "It's a pity I must end him. Something you were unable to do."

Selene raised her swords again. "And I will not let you."

"I'm curious, what happens to a soul if it is pierced within the dreamscape?"

Selene paused. Mother never said. The only thing Mother had said about soulspheres was to never touch them. That it would awaken the sleeper. Would severing the soulsphere kill the sleeper?

Amara charged.

No time to ponder. She needed to get Amara away from here, away from Damien's soulsphere. Damien said she could pull people into her own dreamscape. Could she do that with Amara?

It was worth trying.

Selene concentrated on Amara. She focused until all she saw was Amara running and nothing else. The beach faded away.

Amara halted, her eyes wide. "What in the—"

Her sister's words were lost in the sudden rush of wind. It took all of Selene's strength and concentration to stay focused on both her sister and their surroundings. Whatever method she had used to bring people into her dreamscape before, it was nothing like pulling her sister from one dream to another.

Moments later, they both fell across a stone floor. The area was dimly lit and surrounded by stone. Above them clouds covered the sky. Selene blinked as she brought her mind to bear, then stood to her feet, her swords still clenched within her hands. She had no idea why, but her subconscious had brought both of them to the highest tower of Rook Castle.

Amara stumbled to her feet as well, and the dazed look from earlier vanished, replaced by a hard look with which Selene was all too familiar. "What did you do to me? Change the dreamscape?"

"No. I took you away from Damien's mind. You are in my dreamscape now."

"Th-that's not possible. No dreamer can do that." But from the way Amara's voice quavered, Selene could tell her sister was starting to realize the truth.

"It is. Use your power to feel this dream. You will find you are no longer in Damien's mind."

Selene watched her sister's eyes grow distant, then come back into focus. Amara's lips grew tight, and she let her breath out through her nostrils. "So you really are as powerful as Mother always said you were."

Whether it was because they were facing each other in the dreamscape or something more, Selene could almost feel the burn of Amara's hurt and jealousy in her words, but also a tinge of fear.

"This power hasn't come without consequence." Selene lifted up one of her swords and stared at her knuckles. "I never wanted it. It has cost a great deal." She said those words as she thought of Damien and how he gave up his choice of marriage to save her, how her gift was affecting his people, how much she missed Ophie and Father, and her recent—and last—encounter with the Dark Lady.

Amara snorted, her confidence returning. "Who cares about the cost if you possess power like that? I would give *anything* to acquire the power you have. The power to control not just a dream, but every dream. Imagine what you could do and who you could influence—wait." She opened her mouth, then closed it, then opened it again. Selene could almost see thoughts flitting across her sister's mind. "It can't be." She shook her head, her eyes bulging. "But it is. This whole time." Then she threw her head back and laughed.

Selene held her swords out in front of her. Had her sister gone mad?

Amara looked at Selene with a gleeful glare. "Mother believed the prophecy of the Dark Lady—the threat to our house—was House Maris. But it would seem she was wrong. Never would Mother have thought it was right there, right in front of her." She waved her sword. "That threat from the north was never Lord Damien. It wasn't even House Vivek." She lifted her blade and pointed it at Selene. "It's you."

Selene took a step back, her swords ready. "What are you saying?"

"You're the one the Dark Lady spoke of. The one who would come from the north and be the downfall of our house. It was you all along. Not House Vivek. Not House Maris. You. Mother's prized daughter." Her sister laughed again. "The strongest Ravenwood. The one Mother pinned all her hopes on. The traitorous offspring."

Selene stared at her sister, her vision going in

and out of focus while her lungs struggled to draw in breath. How could that be?

Then, like the pages of a book turning under the rush of the wind, dozens of thoughts clicked into place. The moment she married Damien she became part of the north. She was now the keeper of Ravenwood's secrets. She was head of House Ravenwood and yet belonged to House Maris.

And in order to protect her husband and the people of all of the nations, she would be forced to fight her own house. Every last member if she had to. And if she won . . .

House Ravenwood would be no more.

She was the threat.

That one thought rang in her ears until her mind was filled with those words. She was the threat from the north. And now even more so since she had turned her back on the Dark Lady.

But . . . did it matter?

Did it matter if House Ravenwood fell?

Selene looked around at the familiar castle where her dreamscape had brought her. Under the cloudy sky, the purple banners of Ravenwood fluttered in an unseen wind. Down below, she could see the courtyard, gardens, and open alcoves of her home. Could she really destroy her own house and watch another rise in its place? Would a lesser house move into Rook Castle and claim the mountain nation?

And yet what had House Ravenwood done for

their people? She was convinced now that yes, her predecessors had helped their people, but very little. Most of what they earned went back to the women of Ravenwood. And now Ravenwood was set on destroying every other house and people in a wave of hatred.

No, it didn't matter if her house fell.

Selene looked up. "Amara, join me. House Ravenwood is not worth saving."

Amara lowered her sword and laughed. "What failures we are for daughters. Mother would be so displeased." Then her face grew sober. "I can't."

"Why not? I'm sure you know by now that our mother has aligned our house with the Dominia Empire. Why support the empire? Once you were loyal to Mother, but I can tell something has changed. Why give your allegiance to House Ravenwood?"

"Yes, something has changed. If I leave—if I never become the grand lady of Ravenwood—then Opheliana will be in danger. I need to fulfill this mission. I need to do all that Mother commands of me so that I become the heir of our house." She lifted her face, and there was fire in her eyes. "I will do everything I can to keep Opheliana safe."

Selene's heart sped up. "Ophie is in danger?"

A cold rage settled across Amara's features. "You left in such a hurry that you never discovered Opheliana's secret."

Her hands began to shake. "What secret?"

"She is not of House Ravenwood."

Selene's mind tried to keep up with Amara's words. "What do you mean? I know she is mute, but that doesn't mean—"

"I saw the mark on her ankle. She is of House Friere."

All the air left her lungs in one swift whoosh. "House Friere?" she whispered.

Amara's lips curled. "Yes. She is the illegitimate daughter of our mother and Lord Ivulf. I'm surprised Mother even let her live. If her true heritage was ever found out, she would be put out from Rook Castle. And I doubt Lord Ivulf would welcome our mute sister into his house with open arms. And even if he did, would you want House Friere raising Opheliana? Lord Ivulf is not known for his understanding or compassion. That's why I need to stay." She lifted her blade. "Why I need to become the head of our house. To protect our sister. A responsibility you discarded when you left."

Selene flushed. "That's not true! I left to help our family, to find out the real reason we were given the gift of dreamwalking!"

"You left because you were weak! You might have had the more powerful gift, but your spirit was weak. You couldn't handle all that came with dreamwalking!"

Selene slashed her blades in front of her.

"We were never meant to use our gift in such a perverted way! We were given the gift of dreamwalking to inspire not only our people, but all people. To give them hope, to give them peace. To show them the light."

"And how's that going to help our sister?" Amara yelled and dashed forward to strike.

Selene jumped back as she brought her blades before her, catching Amara's sword between them, then thrusting the weapon aside. In this confined area, it would be hard to dodge Amara's attacks. And she wasn't sure what would happen if Amara actually managed to slash her. Or if she caught her sister with one of her own blades.

Amara controlled the middle of the tower, moving in with her sword every chance she got while Selene danced along the perimeter near the wall. She glanced briefly at the surrounding ramparts. Should she fly away? If her sister's mark was any indication, Amara was not as powerful as she or even Mother, but she still had tremendous power over the dreamscape. Already she had learned how to bring her sword here.

"I only came here to kill Lord Maris," Amara said, panting as she paused for a moment. "Give him to me, and I will let you go. I will even let you come back to Rook Castle once I am the grand lady."

"I can't. I am bonded to him, and he to me." Selene brought her swords in front of her.

"Amara, you will never be head of House Ravenwood."

Amara's neck corded beneath her short hair. "Why not?" she yelled across the tower.

"Because I am already the keeper of our house's secrets."

"What?" Amara took a step back. Her face drained of color, leaving her looking like a corpse.

"I have surpassed our mother. Our ancient house gift has recognized me as head of Ravenwood."

"You?" Her arms dropped. "Your gift is that powerful that it overtook Mother's? I-I don't even have a chance?" Her blade disappeared. She shook her head, dazed. "How can that be? I've worked as hard as you have. I, too, have sacrificed. I've done everything Mother has asked of me." She fell to her knees. "Everything I've done, has it been for nothing?"

"Amara," Selene whispered, her heart twisting at the devastation across her sister's face. "You don't have to follow Mother anymore. Join me." With a snap of her wrists, her blades disappeared, and she crossed the tower. "We were not created to be dreamkillers. That's not why we were given the gift of dreamwalking. Together, we can change the legacy of Ravenwood, save Ophie, and—"

Amara let out a startled cry and gripped her front.

"Amara?" Selene closed the distance between them and fell to her knees beside her sister. "Amara!"

Amara's eyes went out of focus, then back. She gave Selene a cynical smile accompanied by a guttural laugh. "I wasn't watching my surroundings. Just another one of my failings." Then she pulled her hand away from her chest, exposing a gushing wound above her heart.

42

N o . . ." Selene whispered, her eyes pinned to the wound. "This can't be." But the evidence was there before her. Someone had found Amara's physical body and stabbed her. And now she was manifesting in the dream world what her real body was going through. "Please, no. Amara."

Amara crumpled to the ground and stared up at the sky. "I guess you won, Selene."

Selene knelt down and placed her sister's head on her knees. Since she was not in the same room as Amara, she couldn't see who had delivered the blow. But if Amara was indeed next to Damien's bed, most likely it was Taegis.

No, I can't think about that now. She stared at the spreading stain around the hole in Amara's tunic. *There's no time.*

Using her power of will, Selene blocked out the panic and grief threatening to overwhelm her. Instead, she brushed the short curls around Amara's face, wondering for a moment when her sister had cut her hair. Was that one of the sacrifices she had mentioned? "I never wanted this." Selene caressed her sister's head. "I never wanted to fight you. I'd hoped that one day we would serve our people together, with our gift."

"I don't think it would have worked." Amara coughed and blood spluttered out of her mouth.

Selene bit back a sob. "I think it would have, if we used our gift to inspire our people. Let me show you what I've discovered so far." She placed her hand on her sister's forehead, then closed her eyes.

Images flashed from her mind to Amara's: visions of the first time she saw Damien's soul, and the overwhelming desire to carry such a light. The times she visited Damien's dreams and soothed his mind. The day of the Festival of Light when he showed her how he used his power to worship the Light.

Then she shared her own dreams and desires: to use their gift to help people, all people. To bring peace through their link to the dreamscape. To inspire the weary and the broken.

As the images sped between the sisters, Selene realized something. Every image, every memory pointed back toward the Light. Her desires, her dreams, her gift. Like Damien's worship, she began with her gift, and it ended with the Light.

Even now, she was using her gift to point her sister to the Light, without even meaning to.

Amara coughed again, and Selene opened her eyes, disconnecting their thoughts.

"I don't know . . . what to say," Amara said, her gaze growing duller by the moment. "It reminds me of some of the things Breven said."

Breven?

Before she could ask, Amara struggled beneath Selene's hand. "Don't—Don't let Opheliana die. Or be taken by House Friere. She's all I've ever cared about."

Selene cupped her sister's face while she screamed inside. She was losing her sister, and there wasn't anything she could do about it other than comfort her. "I won't. Be assured I will rescue Ophie. I will show her what I've shown you: the real reason we were given these gifts. I will make sure she grows up surrounded by love and light."

Amara's eyes went dim again as she focused on Selene. "Thank you. I-I think I cared about you too, a little. I was just too jealous to see how much we needed each other."

Selene pulled her sister close to her chest and brushed her cheek against her sister's head. Tears fell amongst the silky curls. Amara's breath was ragged and labored. Spittle mixed with blood coated the front of Selene's tunic, but she didn't care.

"Those images you showed me," Amara whispered. "Are they real?"

"Yes."

"The Light . . . he's real?"

"Yes." The moment she said that, she felt the undeniable certainty in her heart. Yes, the Light was real. And she wanted to follow him the rest of her life.

"Then I acknowledge . . . the Light."

Selene pulled Amara even tighter to her chest. A moment later, Amara went still.

At first, Selene couldn't breathe. She could still feel her sister in her arms. But inside her mind, she knew Amara was gone. This was only her dream body. Her physical one was simply a shell now, an empty one.

Her power began to build inside her chest. Selene worked her mouth. The scream was coming, she could feel it. And there was nothing she could do to stop it. It was an avalanche inside her, building until she looked up at the sky and screamed.

In answer, an invisible tidal wave swept across the dreamscape, leaving in its wake a raging storm. Selene clutched Amara's body to her chest as the wind thrashed around her, whipping her hair and her cloak. Dark clouds churned overhead.

She screamed again, her voice carrying across the dreamscape, echoing across the tempest. The world around her shuddered and heaved under the barrage of her emotions. Lightning flashed, followed by the boom of thunder, and rain came pelting down.

Selene dropped her head and rocked back and forth, sobbing as she held Amara.

A crack rang out across the sky, like the sound of a whip. It was the same sound as her heart breaking. Fissures formed along the edges of the dreamscape, spreading like ice cracking along a frozen river. The cracks grew longer and longer until pieces of the dreamscape dropped away. The clouds disappeared, and so did the rain. The tower, then finally, Amara's body.

There was no sound, no wind, nothing. Selene knelt, her head bowed, her face stained with tears. For a split second, she wondered if she had broken her own dreamscape with her power, but then she sank back into numb apathy.

Then a flicker of light appeared.

She lifted her head and stared at the tiny spark, no bigger than the head of a pin. No matter which way she turned her head, her gaze still came back to it. The same flicker of light from earlier, during her confrontation with the Dark Lady.

The monks' chant as they entered Nor Esen during the Festival of Light filled her mind.

A song about the darkness, and the light that came when all was lost.

As if sensing the words within her, the light grew, expanding the flame.

A light that spread across the lands.

Now the flame was as big as a bonfire, and still it grew, devouring the darkness around her.

A light that darkness could not extinguish.

The light grew brighter and brighter until Selene ducked her head and brought her arm up to her face to shield her eyes. Even then, bright light seeped between her lids, more blazing than the whitest light.

Dreamer.

The light tenor voice was similar to Damien's, and yet it seemed to hold so much more.

The light was so brilliant she couldn't open her eyes. "Who are you?" she said, her head bowed and her arm still across her face.

You already know. I've been waiting for you.

The Light. She was as certain of it as she was the moment she declared she would follow him the rest of her life.

Dreamer, let me show you who I made you to be.

The light disappeared.

Selene found herself in her raven form, soaring above Rook Castle on a bright summer day. The Magyr Mountains were a deep green around the towering grey castle, and the sky above her was a clear, pale blue with rolling white clouds. Rook Castle looked magnificent from this high up, the architecture ancient and open.

Cool, soft wind glided past her black wings, allowing her to soar along the slipstreams. The sun's bright rays warmed her back and head. There was a peace here, high above everything, a peace that soothed her heart.

She hovered for a moment, then dove for the towers below. Just as she reached the ramparts, she turned hard to the left, then pumped her wings as she sped back upward.

The wind caught her and lifted her higher. Selene let the air carry her and sighed. Her wings were spread wide as if embracing the wind itself. Her heart gave a wistful twinge. If only Amara could have experienced this.

As she reached the pinnacle of her ascent, she caught sight of a lush green forest to the south.

Wait.

That couldn't be right. There was no forest there, not for miles beyond the Magyr Mountains. Unless . . .

She glanced toward the west. Beyond the Omega Wastelands she could see Ironmond, the capital of House Friere. Even though she had never seen it, she knew it was Ironmond by the descriptions she had heard from her mother. And north of Ironmond lay the city of Shanalona.

Selene turned every direction. Nor Esen stood to the north, Lux Casta to the west, Rafel's capital city of Surao within the great forest to the south, and even the stronghold of House Merek, Burkhard.

She could see all the lands of all the nations from up here. And high above her was an unending sky.

Selene spread out her wings and slowly circled back down to the highest tower of Rook Castle, the same place she had been earlier with Amara.

I am everywhere. The wind seemed to spread the invisible words. *Every domain is mine. Both dreams and reality. To you I gave the gift of the dreamscape.*

"Why?"

Dreams are where the deepest part of a person dwells. It is there that fears, hopes, and desires exist.

Selene knew that only too well.

This is the gift of the dreamwalker: to remind the people of peace, hope, and joy. To comfort those who are sick and dying. To inspire those who are fighting. To bring light to those in the darkness.

"But how?" She continued to glide along the wind in her raven form above the tower.

What you receive, you pass on to others. Through their dreams.

Selene looked around, then stared at the spot in the middle of the tower, the place where she had held her dying sister. A sunbeam shone across the stone floor. It was there she had shared her own visions of the Light.

She flew to the spot, then transformed into her human form, knelt down, and brushed her hand along the warmed stone. This was how she could help people. This was what her gift—what the Ravenwood gift of dreamwalking—was meant to be.

To remind people of the Light.

"I understand." No, it was more than that. The feeling grew inside of her until it filled every part of her being. "This is what I want to do. For the rest of my life. But—" She looked up. She couldn't see the Light, only the sky above her. "What of my sister?" She swallowed. Her sister would never experience this.

All things are in my hands. Even your sister. Let them remain there. I will take care of them.

In his hands.

Selene looked down and stared at her own palm.

In the hands of the Light. Brilliant and beautiful.

A small smile spread across her lips. Her heart was still heavy with emotion, but a sudden image of Amara spreading her raven's wings and soaring beneath the light brought a measure of tranquility.

"Thank you," she whispered.

Now it is time for you to go, dreamer. And remember this: I am with you.

The scene around her began to fade into a dim grey, growing darker and darker. . . .

Selene opened her eyes. A night sky greeted her above gnarled branches. The ground beneath her was cold and soft. She slowly sat up and placed a hand along her face. She felt battered and bruised, her face blotchy.

Where am I?

"Lady Selene!" Karl came crashing through the bushes. "I've been looking everywhere for you!"

"Karl." Selene stood up on shaky legs, her hand still to her face. "I fell asleep and—" Her eyes went wide.

Damien.

She dropped her hand and looked at Karl. "We need to get back to the palace—now."

43

Damien woke up with a start, cold sweat covering his body. He drew in raspy breaths and grabbed the front of his tunic. Death. An overwhelming sense of death clung to his mind, clouding his vision and clutching at his throat. There had been a woman with short hair—and Selene—and yelling—and blades—

Selene!

His head snapped up. The bedchamber was dark, save for the bit of light coming in through the windows. A cool breeze swept in through the open casement, sending a shiver across his soaked body. Damien reached for the left side of the bed, hoping he was wrong and Selene had returned.

Empty.

His heartbeat jumped tenfold. "Taegis!" Damien yelled as he shoved the covers back and swung his legs around.

"I'm here, my lord." His guardian's voice sounded near the bed.

"Taegis, what are you doing here?"

"Careful where you step, Dart'an," Taegis muttered softly.

"What's going on? Where's Selene—?" Damien's breath caught in his throat as he spotted Taegis kneeling beside a body near the bed. He grabbed a small knife from the table and stood. His body began to shake, but he clenched his hands and gritted his teeth. "Who is that? What's going on?"

Taegis let out a long sigh and bowed his head. "I found her beside your bed, clutching your arm. When I tried to pull her away, she held on with a viselike grip. Then you began to cry out . . ." He shook his head. "I had no choice once I realized who she was."

"Who is she?"

Taegis stood and stepped away from the body. He passed Damien and reached for the candle. A moment later, dim light filled the room.

Damien stared. Her hood was back, revealing short, curly auburn hair and small feminine features.

His heart stopped.

Taegis held the candle above the woman. But Damien had already guessed who it was. The other Ravenwood daughter.

"The short hair threw me off, but there's no mistaking her. Lady Amara Ravenwood."

"Selene's sister," Damien murmured. Then he noticed the pool of blood spreading across the stone floor.

"She was sent here to kill you, of that I'm sure. And when I couldn't dislodge her hand from your arm, I had no choice." His voice was heavy with grief.

Damien looked up. He didn't know what to say. If it were any other person, he would have felt anger toward his would-be assassin. But this was Selene's sister, and although Selene was not close to her family, a member of her family had just died. "There's nothing you could've done."

Taegis rose slowly and drew in another breath. "I know. I've been guarding you and House Maris for many years. And I would still make the same choice. But it doesn't mean I like it." He pulled a cloth from his belt and wiped his blade. "We will need to inform the captain of the guard for House Luceras and make sure there are no more assassins in the palace."

If Lady Amara had been here for him, was it possible that Lady Ragna was here for Selene? "Do we know where Lady Selene is?"

"No. She never came back. But Karl is with her."

Damien gripped the knife in his hand. If he had any idea where to go, he would rush out now and find his wife.

"My lord, I need to inform the palace. And I do not want to leave you here alone."

Damien glanced back at Lady Amara and swallowed. He didn't want Selene to return to this. "Then we go quickly and come back."

"I agree."

The two men had left the bedchamber and entered the common room when the outside door burst open and Karl rushed in, Selene behind him.

Damien stopped and stared at Selene.

At the same time, Selene spotted him. "Damien." He still didn't know why she had been gone so long or where she went, but at the moment he didn't care. He moved across the room and pulled her into a tight embrace. "You're here," he whispered as he buried his face in her hair, which smelled of dirt and roses.

Her arms went around his waist, squeezing him as though her life depended on it. "I almost lost you. Amara was there . . . and the Dark Lady . . ." She hid her face in the crook of his neck.

Tears filled his eyes as he held Selene close, his face within her hair.

"I'll leave Karl here to stand guard," Damien heard Taegis say. He nodded his head, but never brought it up. Somewhere in his mind he heard the door shut, but it was only peripheral. Right now his only thought was that Selene was here, alive, in his arms.

She never made a sound, but he felt the dampness of her tears spread across his shoulder. After a while, he finally lifted his head. "Selene," he said softly, his stomach hardening at what he had to say next. But she needed to know—the sooner, the better. "I need to tell you something."

She looked at him, tears clinging to her lashes.

He swallowed. "I had a visitor tonight."

Her head dipped down. "I know."

"You know?"

"It was my sister."

He blinked. "How . . . ?"

"She came for you. I entered your dreamscape and stopped her."

"You entered . . . my dreamscape?" But she hadn't even been in the room. First she pulled him into her own dreams, and now she was entering his dreams without even touching him. . . .

"Yes. And now Amara's dead." Her fingers clutched his tunic and a moment later, she began to sob.

Damien ran his hand up and down her back, his own throat tight, dashing away his thoughts from earlier. Time enough to think about that later. There was so much to her words, so much feeling. What had she seen? What had she experienced? And yet, he felt strength within her even as she cried.

His own emotions were like a wild storm inside of him. Another assassination, another attack within his room. Selene said she had stopped her sister, but this power was more than he had ever thought possible—than any of the houses had thought possible. Should anyone have this much power?

No. I can't think about that right now. I need to comfort my wife.

Time ticked by, and slowly the sobs grew

quiet. "I almost lost you tonight," she whispered, breaking the silence.

She was right. There was no way he could have defended himself in his dreams. No one could. All lives were vulnerable in the dream world.

Selene lifted her head. Her dark eyes glistened in the candlelight, and her hair hung around her face in disarray. "Damien?"

"Yes?"

"I don't ever want to lose you." Her gaze lingered on his face a moment longer before she moved forward and brushed her lips across his.

Despite his recent thoughts and misgivings about her power, he loved this complex woman. Damien responded to her touch, pouring into his kiss all his fears and emotions. A fierce desire overtook him, filling him with a fire that roared inside his chest. He would do everything he could to keep Selene safe.

"I love you," he whispered as he pulled back. "I don't want to lose you either." He finally said the words that had been dwelling inside his soul for months now. He loved Selene Ravenwood.

A strange look came over her face, but before he could ask about it, there was a knock at the door. Both of them turned, still in each other's arms.

Taegis walked in with two of House Luceras's guards. "Captain Hamon sent these men to retrieve the body while he and the rest of his guards search the palace."

Selene stepped away from Damien. "Please, let me have a moment with my sister."

The guards looked at Taegis and he nodded.

Selene took a deep breath and turned toward the bedchambers. Damien grabbed the candle and followed, but stopped in the doorway to allow Selene privacy.

She walked over to the prone body on the floor and knelt down. With her fingertips, she brushed Lady Amara's eyes shut. Then she bent down and whispered something. Lastly, she reached for the discarded face scarf and carefully placed it over her sister's face.

"She is gone now," Selene said, looking down at her sister. "But I was able to show her who we were made to be—who the *Light* created us to be."

The Light? It was the first time he'd heard Selene talk with such confidence about the Light. Apparently more had happened tonight than he was aware of. He wanted to know more. But this was not the time. This was the time to let his wife grieve.

"Now I understand the feelings you have over the death of your family." She stood and placed a fist over her heart. "I feel them too."

Taegis and the guards came to the doorway. Selene turned her attention toward the guards. "What do you plan on doing with my sister?"

They looked at each other, then at her. "We're not sure, my lady. Our orders were to take her to the chapel."

She nodded. "If possible, may my sister be cremated and her ashes given to me? Yes, she was an assassin, but she was also a member of House Ravenwood, and as such, I would like to scatter her ashes across the Magyr Mountains in the tradition of our family."

"That will be up to House Luceras," the other guard said. "But we will ask on your behalf."

Selene bowed. "Thank you."

Damien marveled at the control Selene had. If he hadn't seen her grief firsthand, he would have almost wondered if she mourned the departing of her sister.

Selene passed the guards as they walked into the bedroom to take Lady Amara's body away. Damien stepped back, the candle still in his hand. Selene came and stood beside him. Minutes later, the two guards carried Lady Amara's body out between them. Selene watched them until they left.

He caught the eye of Taegis and Karl. Taegis seemed to understand his unspoken request and nodded. He whispered to Karl, then both men stepped out, closing the main door behind them. Damien doubted Selene would want to sleep in their room tonight, or any night. Neither did he. He would see about transferring their belongings to one of the other rooms in the suite.

Damien placed the candle down on a side table, then turned back toward her. He noted the dirt on her cheeks and the streaks of mud where her tears had fallen and wondered where Selene had been tonight. But his questions would have to wait.

Without a word, he pulled her in again and held her. There they stood, in the candlelight, her head on his shoulder, his arms wrapped around her body.

Tomorrow would bring answers, along with a renewed push to sign the treaty and prepare for war. The assassination attempt tonight was only the tip of what was to come. It was the first arrow shot, and more would be coming—and soon.

But for tonight, he would take care of his wife.

When the war came, they would face it then.

Together.

44

Harsh sunlight radiated down on Lady Ragna as she stood before the wall that for hundreds of years had kept the Dominia Empire out of their lands. But no longer.

Tents were set up behind her along the sandy hills, filled with House Friere's military. She had left her own forces behind at Rook Castle and the strongholds around the mountain area, ready to move upon a word from her. Over the last few months, she had carefully dropped hints and woven the idea of aligning with the empire for the good of the mountain people into her military. Her commander and captains were primed for when she announced the real deal. And for those who balked at the idea, they could either obey or be replaced. Permanently.

A hot wind pulled at her silk gown and headscarf. It would be a while before she was back at Rook Castle and the cooler air. This heat was abominable, and it was only spring.

Far off, near the wall, Lord Ivulf spoke with his own commanders. His scarlet cloak rippled in the wind. Not for the first time she wondered if she should have made a more permanent alliance with Lord Ivulf all those years ago, instead of with Caiaphas. But her mother had ruthlessly crushed the idea. Ravenwood women never married the heads of other Great Houses, and so she had obeyed.

Unlike her traitorous daughter.

Her nostrils flared, and Lady Ragna smoothed her gown in an effort to bring her emotions back under control. It wouldn't matter soon. At this moment, Amara was taking care of the plague that was House Maris. She might not be the strongest Ravenwood woman to ever live, but Amara was tenacious and driven. She would get the job done. Once Lord Damien was dead, Selene would be next.

With the Dark Lady at Lady Ragna's side, and her increased nightly walks, which had been steadily strengthening her own gift, she would be ready to confront her daughter. And in the end, she would win.

Lady Ragna smiled to herself as Lord Ivulf broke away from his commanders and approached the wall. The sand-colored wall towered over the area, several hundred feet high, with jagged teeth at the top, making it difficult to climb over. The few who made it between their lands and the empire had done so by boat, circumventing either the maelstrom to the south or the watchful eyes of House Vivek and House Maris to the north.

But soon the great divide between the nations would be gone.

Lord Ivulf came to a stop, a small figure next

to the massive barrier. Her smile widened as she watched him spread out his arms and prepare to use his gift. It had taken both the lords of House Maris and House Friere to erect the wall, combining water and molten earth together to form the boundary.

Today, it would take only one man to bring it down.

At first, nothing happened. Then a resounding crack filled the air. A split appeared at the top of the wall, right above where Lord Ivulf stood. The crack widened as it tore down the middle of the wall. A moment later, Lord Ivulf brought his hands together, then pulled them apart as if opening a door.

Both sides of the wall moved.

Like a set of double doors opening, the split widened until she could see blue sky and desert landscape on the other side. And not just landscape, but also an army. Tens of thousands dressed in burnt orange and olive green, with hundreds of Dominia Empire standards fluttering in the wind.

When the crack became as wide as to let in five men, shoulder to shoulder, Lord Ivulf fell to one knee, and the wall stopped moving.

Lady Ragna held up her gown and ran across the sand. Had he overexerted himself? Neither had been sure how great his gift was, or if he would even be able to do it.

Now they knew.

Just as she reached Lord Ivulf, a man came walking through the gap, flanked by four other men. He was tall and broad, with dark hair that curled around his head. There was no facial hair along his chin. Instead, a scar ran across the left side of his face, from the tip of his mouth up to the end of his eyebrow, giving him a fierce appearance. He was dressed in an elaborate uniform of the same burnt orange and olive green. A matching cloak fluttered behind him as he approached.

Lady Ragna bent down and reached for Lord Ivulf's arm, but he brushed her away forcefully and stood on his own. From the corner of her eye, he appeared very pale, sweat coating his face and dripping from his chin.

The man stopped a couple of feet away and looked them over. Lady Ragna came to her full height and looked back with as much haughtiness and chill as she could. There was no doubt who stood before them, and she would remind him of who she was, and the power she brought with her.

A few seconds later, Lord Ivulf bowed, but Lady Ragna remained where she was.

"Welcome, Commander Orion of the Dominia Empire."

Morgan L. Busse is a writer by day and a mother by night. She is the author of the FOLLOWER OF THE WORD series and the steampunk series THE SOUL CHRONICLES. She is a Christy and INSPY Award finalist and won the Carol Award in 2018 for best in Christian speculative fiction. During her spare time she enjoys playing games, taking long walks, and dreaming about her next novel. Visit her online at www.morganlbusse.com.

Books are produced in the United States using U.S.-based materials

Books are printed using a revolutionary new process called THINKtech™ that lowers energy usage by 70% and increases overall quality

Books are durable and flexible because of Smyth-sewing

Paper is sourced using environmentally responsible foresting methods and the paper is acid-free

Center Point Large Print
600 Brooks Road / PO Box 1
Thorndike, ME 04986-0001 USA

(207) 568-3717

US & Canada:
1 800 929-9108
www.centerpointlargeprint.com